# THE SAINT-FLORENTIN MURDERS

**Jean-François Parot** is a diplomat and historian. His Nicolas Le Floch mysteries have been published to much acclaim in French. The first four novels in the series, *The Châtelet Apprentice*, *The Man with the Lead Stomach*, *The Phantom of Rue Royale* and *The Nicolas Le Floch Affair* were enthusiastically reviewed on publication in English.

**Howard Curtis**'s many translations from French and Italian include five novels by Jean-Claude Izzo, four by Marek Halter and three by Gianrico Carofiglio, as well as works by Balzac, Flaubert and Pirandello.

D1004431

'. . . Le Floch is an engaging conduit for the reader through the teeming, phantasmagoric capital that is eighteenth-century Paris.' *Independent*

'The atmosphere is marvellous, the historical detail precise, and Le Floch and his colleagues are an engaging bunch . . .' *Guardian*

'An interesting evocation of place and period.' *The Literary Review*

# THE
# SAINT-FLORENTIN
# MURDERS

Also by Jean-François Parot

*The Châtelet Apprentice*
*The Man with the Lead Stomach*
*The Phantom of Rue Royale*
*The Nicolas Le Floch Affair*

THE
# SAINT-FLORENTIN
# MURDERS

JEAN-FRANÇOIS PAROT

Translated from the French by Howard Curtis

GALLIC BOOKS
London

Ouvrage publié avec le concours du Ministère français chargé de la Culture – Centre National du Livre.
This work is published with support from the French Ministry of Culture/Centre National du Livre.

A Gallic Book

First published in France as *Le crime de l'hôtel Saint-Florentin* by éditions Jean-Claude Lattès

First published in Great Britain in 2010 by Gallic Books, 134 Lots Road, London SW10 0RJ

A CIP record for this book is available from the British Library

ISBN 978-1-906040-24-6

Typeset in Fournier by SX Composing DTP, Rayleigh, Essex

Printed in the UK by CPI Bookmarque, Croydon, CR0 4TD

2 4 6 8 10 9 7 5 3 1

*For Arlette and Richard Benais*

# CONTENTS

# Background to *The Saint-Florentin Murders*

For those readers coming to the adventures of Nicolas Le Floch for the first time, it is useful to know that in the first book in the series, *The Châtelet Apprentice*, the hero, a foundling raised by Canon Le Floch in Guérande, is sent away from his native Brittany by his godfather, the Marquis de Ranreuil, who is concerned about his daughter Isabelle's growing fondness for the young man.

On arrival in Paris he is taken in by Père Grégoire at the Monastery of the Decalced Carmelites and on the recommendation of the marquis soon finds himself in the service of Monsieur de Sartine, Lieutenant General of Police in Paris. Under his tutelage, Nicolas is quick to learn and is soon familiar with the mysterious working methods of the highest ranks of the police service. At the end of his year's apprenticeship, he is entrusted with a confidential mission, one that will result in him rendering a signal service to Louis XV and the Marquise de Pompadour.

Aided by his deputy and mentor, Inspector Bourdeau, and putting his own life at risk on several occasions, he successfully unravels a complicated plot. Received at court by the King, he is rewarded with the post of commissioner of police at the Châtelet and, under the direct authority of Monsieur de Sartine, continues to be assigned to special investigations.

# DRAMATIS PERSONAE

NICOLAS LE FLOCH: a police commissioner at the Châtelet

LOUIS LE FLOCH: his son, a schoolboy

MONSIEUR DE SARTINE: Secretary of State for the Navy

MONSIEUR LENOIR: Lieutenant General of Police in Paris

MONSIEUR DE SAINT-FLORENTIN, DUC DE LA VRILLIÈRE: Minister of the King's Household

DUCHESSE DE LA VRILLIÈRE: his wife

PIERRE BOURDEAU: a police inspector

OLD MARIE: an usher at the Châtelet

TIREPOT: a police spy

RABOUINE: a police spy

AIMÉ DE NOBLECOURT: a former procurator

MARION: his cook

POITEVIN: his servant

CATHERINE GAUSS: a former canteen-keeper, Nicolas Le Floch's maid

GUILLAUME SEMACGUS: a navy surgeon

THIERRY DE VILLE D'AVRAY: First Groom of the King's Bedchamber

MONSIEUR DE LA BORDE: his predecessor

CHARLES HENRI SANSON: the public executioner

LA SATIN: Louis Le Floch's mother

LA PAULET: a former brothel-keeper

MONSIEUR DE GÉVIGLAND: a doctor

MADAME DE CUSACQUE: the Duc de La Vrillière's mistress

MONSIEUR DE CHAMBONAS: her son-in-law

MONSIEUR BOURDIER: an engineer

MONSIEUR D'ARRANET: Lieutenant General of the Naval Forces

AIMÉE D'ARRANET: his daughter

MONSIEUR TESTARD DU LYS: Criminal Lieutenant of Police

ANSELME VITRY: a gardener

MARGUERITE PINDRON: the Duchesse de La Vrillière's chambermaid

JEAN MISSERY: major-domo to the Duc de La Vrillière

EUGÉNIE GOUET: first chambermaid to the Duchesse de La Vrillière

JEANNE LE BAS, known as Jeannette: second chambermaid to the Duchesse de La Vrillière

CHARLES BIBARD, known as Provence: a valet

PIERRE MIQUETE: a Swiss Guard at the La Vrillière mansion

JACQUES BLAIN: a caretaker

JACQUES DESPIARD: a kitchen boy

GILLES DUCHAMPLAN: the late Madame Missery's elder brother

NICOLE DUCHAMPLAN: his wife

HÉLÈNE DUCHAMPLAN: the late Madame Missery's elder sister, a nun with the Daughters of Saint Michel

EUDES DUCHAMPLAN: the late Madame Missery's younger brother

RESTIF DE LA BRETONNE: a writer and pamphleteer

OLD LONGÈRES: a cattle farmer

LORD ASHBURY: an English spy

RICHARD: a gardener at Trianon

# I

# PROLOGUE

The dark night drained things of all their colour.
MAURICE SCÈVE

*Sunday 2 October 1774*

What was the meaning of this unusual rendezvous? She should have been able to wean him off such whims by now. The idea of it! The servants' floor offered sufficient opportunities, so there was no real need for him to force her into these pointless nocturnal escapades. It was a good thing her chores in Madame's apartments kept her away from her fine suitor for much of the day. He often took advantage of her slightest foray into the common parts of the La Vrillière mansion to . . . He was insatiable. But how could she refuse him? She owed him her position, and a kind of security. Still she waited, and the piece of candle, which cast a parsimonious light on the roasting room, would not last much longer. It was a large, dark room, with chimneys of blackened stone looming over the spits, trammels and dripping-pans.

She laughed at her own cleverness: every day she filched pieces of candle from the apartments on the upper floors to replenish her stock. Several times, she had come close to being caught. She had to beware, not only of her mistress's constant vigilance, but also that of the other servants, her competitors in this pilfering: they, too, were always on the lookout for anything to feed this lucrative trade in candle wax.

A metallic clinking broke the silence. Her heart pounded so hard it hurt. She held her breath, waiting for what was to follow, but nothing came. Another of those rats, she thought – impossible to get rid of them. One of those fat grey moth-eaten rats that fed on scraps from the kitchen, and from what had been left in the big adjacent larder. The best pieces from the larder were also regularly resold to a few taverns, and as for the scraps, they ended up in a soup which, sold for a few coins from a steaming carriage in the streets, provided momentary sustenance to the poorest of the poor. She had tried it herself, not so long ago, after fleeing her father's house, and still had the bitter rotten taste of it, which no seasoning could ever mask, in her mouth. Just the thought of it made her retch.

She was still listening hard, hoping to hear her lover's heavy steps. But all she heard was a distant miaow. She laughed: cats were no use here – they were too well fed on the leftovers from a rich table. Only their eyes, gleaming in the darkness whenever a ray of light struck them, scared off the most faint-hearted. Sometimes, you would see a big rat, in the peak of condition, rise up and bare its yellow teeth, defying a cat, which would slink off without a fight. As for her, she was not afraid of cats. She had seen some really formidable cats in the cowsheds belonging to her father, who raised cattle for milk in Faubourg Saint-Antoine, where they were attracted by the mice hiding in the straw and grain.

She preferred not to think about that. Better to wipe out the past. But she couldn't help remembering those last days spent with her family. Her father had been adamant that she marry a neighbour's son, a gardener in the *faubourg*. The boy was well enough built, but he had bulging eyes and did not appeal to her. His method of courtship involved listing the different kinds of lettuce, as well as the rules for cultivating plants under cold frames, the whole lecture embellished with observations on the best way to line paths with quickset hedges, trellises or picket fences. The preliminary visit she had made to the Vitry household had confirmed her in her rejection.

Their house had one room on the ground floor, looking out on the marsh. It was here that the family lived and ate. The floor was of beaten earth, a long way from the waxed tiles of her own house. Straw chairs, a large, worn wooden table, a porcelain stove, a copper fountain and an ugly dresser were the only decoration. On the first floor, two bedrooms, with straw mattresses and bunks, one of which was the son's and would be the young couple's when they married. Old Madame Vitry, a tall, thin, dark woman with soiled, worn-down nails, listed for her, in a severe tone, the duties of a gardener's wife. She would have to get up at five in the morning, in all weathers and all seasons, and work until eight in the evening, pausing only briefly for a little soup or a crust of bread. She would have to obey her in-laws as if they were her own family.

Her revulsion increased when they started discussing the marriage contract and the contributions of the bride and groom. Hers consisted, apart from a silver dowry large enough to bring a gleam to the old woman's eyes, of a supply of fresh manure for the Vitry family's gardens, to be provided in instalments spread out over several months. When the day came for the engagement to be certified before a notary, appalled by the prospect of a life with this oaf, she had yielded to a sudden impulse and decamped, leaving behind calves, cows, oxen, manure and lettuces, a stunned fiancé and two disappointed families. Fearing that they would search for her, she plunged into the great city, hoping to lose herself in an ocean of people. Appalled at his daughter's actions, old Pindron made no attempt to search for her. She had dishonoured the family, she was no longer of any account, and he immediately disowned her. He took to his bed and died four days later, leaving a widow who retired to her native Burgundy after selling off the farm for a good price to an important family who raised cattle in the *faubourg*, and who committed themselves before a notary to pay her an annuity until she died.

For months, Marguerite Pindron roamed the streets of Paris, sleeping on the *quais*, finding hiding places in the pyramids of the Port au Bois on Quai Saint-Paul or amid the casks on Quai de la Rapée. It was here that the wood carried on the river accumulated in piles as high as houses. Some were well organised into pyramids, but most were heaped up haphazardly, creating a kind of mysterious city made of detours and alleys, underground passages and inner rooms from which, early in the morning, there emerged, wild-eyed, a strange and varied collection of human beings. The few *louis* she had stolen from her father did not last long, but, being able to read and write, she used this skill among the poorest of the poor, and managed to hold out until winter. It was then, one desperate evening when she could no longer bear the hunger and cold, that she met a well-dressed young man who took her to his dwelling, washed her, and made her an object of his pleasure. He dressed her and fed her, then introduced her to his brother-in-law, who was the major-domo in the mansion of the Duc de La Vrillière. Her joy at finding a position was short-lived. She was only the latest in an army of servant girls who emptied the pots and buckets, doomed to the most repulsive chores and the harshest reprimands.

It did not take her long to realise that the brother-in-law also expected to have his way with her. The man had been a widower for two years, could not bear the solitude, and chased anything wearing skirts in the Saint-Florentin mansion. At first, she resisted his advances, but she was desperately afraid of finding herself back on the streets. She opened her heart to her original benefactor, who laughed in her face and urged her to yield: he had started making her small loans, to be repaid when she was able. Her new lover immediately conceived a genuine passion for her beauty and youth. She found it increasingly difficult to escape a bond that was proving burdensome and the constant attentions of a greybeard to whom she had been forced to yield out of necessity alone. She tried every stratagem she could think of, including brief dalliances with other, younger servants, in the hope of putting him off. The only result was to strengthen his desire for her. He was obsessively jealous, and some terrible scenes ensued.

Tears welled in her eyes. All that was nothing compared with what had happened three days earlier, which she could not get out of her mind. Her young benefactor had come looking for her in the evening after she came off duty, and had made her leave the building through a concealed door and join him in a cab. After a long journey, he had led her into an unknown house and made her put on a highly indecent costume. Why had she agreed to it?

She tried to dismiss the images of what had followed. How had she come to this? She had not protested, as if the frenzy and outrageousness of all that was happening had left her too stunned to react. Her 'friend' had appeared to her in such an ambiguous light that she found it impossible to regard him again as part of the natural order of things.

The candle flame suddenly flickered in a draught of air, sputtered a moment, then went out, giving off an acrid odour. That was all she needed! She had nothing with which to relight it. She felt suddenly anxious at being alone in this deserted place. She imagined presences around her. It was early autumn, a time when animals and insects often sought warmth in the kitchens of houses. Something creaked behind her, and she was aware of a furtive movement. She forced herself to turn round, but could see nothing. She was finding it hard to breathe: it seemed to her that there was not enough air in here. She was starting to panic. She was just about to rush madly to the staircase leading to the upper floors when she felt herself seized firmly by an unseen arm and pressed against someone's body. A terrible pain went through the base of her neck, and she collapsed without even realising that she was dying, in a stream of blood.

Early the next morning, a kitchen boy discovered two bodies. One was Marguerite Pindron, whose throat had been cut, and the other Jean Missery, the major-domo, lying unconscious and wounded. A knife lay on the tiled floor beside him, in the middle of a scarlet pool.

# I

# THE PASSING OF THE DAYS

Time uncovers secrets; time creates opportunities;
time confirms good counsel.

BOSSUET

*Sunday 2 October 1774*

Nicolas was surreptitiously looking at his son's face. He was the spitting image of how he himself had been when he was young, with that dashing air his grandfather, the Marquis de Ranreuil, had had whenever he rose to his full height and looked his interlocutor in the eye. As for La Satin, her presence was felt in the gentleness diffused through his fine, if not entirely formed features. The boy's noble but casual bearing showed none of the awkwardness common to his age. He was talking to Monsieur de Noblecourt, and his conversation was full of Greek and Latin quotations: from time to time, with a smile, the former procurator would correct his mistakes and solecisms. The presentation dinner for Louis Le Floch at Noblecourt's house in Rue Montmartre was at its height. Nicolas was happy and relieved to feel the warmth emanating from his friends, Semacgus, Bourdeau and La Borde. He himself did not take part in the discussion, wanting Louis, who in fact seemed quite at ease, to find his place here naturally. The role of father, which filled him with both joy and anguish, was still new to him, and he had to learn it step by step.

The year was ending better than it had begun. The rumours circulating about the plots and criminal investigations that had followed the death of his mistress, Madame de Lastérieux, were gradually dying down. He still carried his grief for the late King in his heart, muted but painful. This troubled period of his life had had one fortunate consequence: he had discovered the existence of a child born of his liaison with La Satin fifteen years earlier. La Paulet, alerted by a first encounter and the impression of a conspicuous resemblance, had decided to intervene. Leaving her house in Auteuil, where she led a comfortably devout life, she had come running to see Monsieur de Noblecourt to plead La Satin's case and the importance of giving Louis a father he had never known. The former procurator had taken the matter very seriously and had agreed to intercede and advise both parents.

There had been misgivings, however, on both sides. La Satin feared Nicolas's reaction, recalling that he had once questioned her as to the father of her child and had declared himself ready, if need be, to assume responsibility. Being a sensible woman, well aware of the demeaning nature of her situation, she dreaded the consequences that might ensue, for both father and son, of recognising Nicolas's paternity and thus bringing this dubious lineage out into the open. At the same time, Nicolas, who still felt a great deal of tenderness for a woman he had known when he first arrived in Paris, was fearful of hurting the new mistress of the Dauphin Couronné by taking steps to remove their child from a pernicious, corrupting environment. Nor had he any desire to loosen the natural ties binding a son to his mother.

It was left to Monsieur de Noblecourt to resolve this thorny issue. He took up his pen and, as if setting out the points for a closing statement in court, undertook to bring the interests and feelings in question, delicate as they were, into alignment. La Satin was to readopt her birth name of Antoinette Godelet and abandon her present occupation. With Nicolas's help, she would buy a shop selling fashion and toilet articles in Rue du Bac from a couple who wished to retire. The hardest part was to convince La Paulet, who, seeing her carefully laid plans for the succession of the brothel collapse, raged and cursed like a fishwife in a manner with which Nicolas had been familiar in the past. Monsieur de Noblecourt waited for the storm to pass and, making full use of his mollifying influence on the good lady, dispensed so many compliments and displayed such a benevolent ear that his intervention worked wonders, and she gradually calmed down. The unexpected arrival of La Présidente, whose English adventure had ended in disaster,[1] made it possible to overcome the last objections. La Satin's friend jumped for joy at the idea of resuming her duties at the Dauphin Couronné, but this time as mistress and manager. Grudgingly, La Paulet agreed to everything. Indeed, she went even further. Her establishment had prospered, acquiring an elegant tone that belied its reputation. In order to show her gratitude to La Satin, she decided to complement her move to Rue du Bac by buying for her the little mezzanine apartment attached to it.

For his part, Nicolas recognised his son before a notary – the boy immediately took his name – and used his influence to make sure that anything relating to La Satin's former activities went missing from the police archives. All that remained was to inform

Louis of these events which would have such consequences for his future: a delicate operation which might well distress the young man. Monsieur de Noblecourt offered to take care of it, but Nicolas wanted to begin his career as a father by being completely open and telling the whole truth. In any case, he had nothing with which to reproach himself, having been unaware of his son's existence until quite recently. But the question remained as to what the young man would think of these decisions about which he had not been consulted.

Nicolas thought about how he himself had been at that age. Whenever he talked to Louis, it was indeed that distant image of himself that he strove to convince. Their first encounter reassured him. Under the trees in the garden of La Paulet's house in Auteuil, he told the boy his life story, omitting nothing, and taking care not to offend the love the child bore his mother. Louis listened seriously and naturally, and immediately launched into a long series of questions. Their encounters continued through the summer, mostly at Dr Semacgus's house in Vaugirard, and before long their relationship blossomed into affection. Having gained some idea of his son's knowledge, Nicolas decided to have him admitted to the College of the Oratorians at Juilly: he regretted that his Jesuit masters had been expelled from the kingdom, but the education, both classical and modern, provided at the college corresponded to the ideas the Marquis de Ranreuil had drummed into Nicolas throughout his adolescence at Guérande, with modern literature and foreign languages being particularly prominent. Louis would come back and spend his holidays in Paris, sharing them equally between Rue Montmartre and Rue du Bac.

'When will I see the King, Father?'

Nicolas gave a start, and again became conscious of his surroundings. The meal was starting. Marion and Catherine had just brought in a piping hot calf's-kidney omelette.

'I'll take you to Versailles one Sunday,' he replied. 'We'll attend Mass and you'll be able to observe His Majesty at your leisure, and then at even closer quarters in the great gallery.'

Louis smiled. His expression brought a pang to Nicolas's heart: for a moment, he had been reminded of his half-sister Isabelle.

'How is Monsieur Lenoir?' La Borde asked.

'From what I see, the Lieutenant General is doing well.'

Those present noticed the bitterness of his reply.

'If truth be told,' La Borde resumed, 'he's a man extremely well disposed to everything concerning opera.'

'I fear,' Semacgus said ironically, 'that our friend's desire to be noticed has influenced his support for the successor of the late lamented Sartine.'

Nicolas shook his head.

'It's one of those phrases,' Noblecourt said, 'that suggests too much or too little. I find it a somewhat laconic remark to make about someone in such an important position. Sartine actually increased the powers of the office. What will this man do with them?'

'Oh,' said Bourdeau, 'he's become as important as a minister, even though he doesn't have the title of minister. You know how much influence he has behind the scenes. He strikes down or he saves. He spreads darkness or light. His authority is as tactful as it is extensive. He elevates and humiliates as he pleases.'

Nicolas shook his head. 'The last one liked wigs, this one richly bound books.'

'Which suggests,' said Louis timidly, 'that neither one of them can entirely cover up his own emptiness!'

They all applauded. Nicolas smiled.

'As our late King used to say,' observed La Borde, 'like father like son.'

'He gets it from his grandfather,' said Nicolas. 'The marquis was never at a loss for a witty remark.'

'Gentlemen,' resumed La Borde, 'allow me to abandon you to the aromas of this delicious omelette. I salute in passing the tenderness of these kidneys. In honour of young Louis, I lent a hand myself, as I used to at Trianon. Catherine and I are about to put the finishing touches to my surprise. Semacgus, prepare our host to resist temptation! Louis, come with me, I need a kitchen boy.'

The boy stood up, already tall for his age. How many things there were to teach him! thought Nicolas. Riding, hunting, fencing . . . He was a Ranreuil, after all. He resumed his reflections. Naturally, the new Lieutenant General of Police had received him quite promptly. Following Sartine's counsel, he had asked for an audience as early as possible. He had found Lenoir standing behind the desk where, so often, his predecessor had played with his wigs. The man was tall, with a full figure and a distinct paunch. He had a strong nose above a mouth with a fleshy lower lip which, when it moved to express dismissal or disdain, drew the eye to his double chin. His own eyes were lively and penetrating, with a hint of arrogance, a marked scepticism, and an undisguised self-satisfaction. A powdered wig with ringlets added to the magnificence of cambric bands falling in a dazzling stream over an unadorned silk gown. The interview, cut short by the arrival of a visitor, could hardly have been classed as a genuine meeting of minds.

'Commissioner,' Lenoir had said, 'my predecessor recommended you. I myself, Monsieur, had the opportunity to assess the skill and expertise with which you handled a delicate case. On the other hand, experience has taught me that personal methods, however useful and effective they may be, tend to get out of control and become a burden to those in authority. You cannot play with me the same role you played with Monsieur de Sartine. I intend to revise the rules and bring a new order to our methods, one more in keeping with my own conceptions.'

'I am at the King's service, Monseigneur.'

'He appreciates you, Monsieur,' retorted Lenoir, somewhat ill-temperedly. 'We know he appreciates you. But the rules must be the same for everyone. Some older commissioners might be offended . . .'

They probably hadn't held back, thought Nicolas.

'. . . that one of their younger colleagues should get all the attention and be allowed such independence. Can we entrust you with a district? That would hardly be appropriate. You have treated your colleagues very badly—'

'Monseigneur!'

'I know what I'm saying, don't interrupt me. Many complaints and grievances have reached my ear. The sensible thing, Monsieur, would be to take things easy, relax, go hunting, and wait for more auspicious times to return. A position as police commissioner at the Châtelet can be sold at a good price and with excellent interest. There is no shortage of candidates, as you can imagine. I have the honour to bid you good day, Commissioner.'

Nicolas made no effort to counter this fall from favour. His upright nature balked at doing so, and he was unable to feign submission. Absorbed as he was by his discovery of Louis, he was more worried about what would happen to his deputy, Bourdeau, who had been dragged into the same storm and who, with children still young enough to require support, now found himself reduced to his basic allowance without the profitable extras to which his position usually gave rise. Nicolas took steps to have substantial sums passed on to his friend, justifying them, in order not to offend the man, as payments of long-forgotten debts, expenses incurred during past missions. As far as his own condition was concerned, he approached it with an almost religious fatalism: his future would be what it would be. The only people in whom he confided unreservedly were Monsieur de Noblecourt and La Borde.

The former approved of his determination to rise above the temporary vicissitudes that marked any career devoted to the King's service. Time was a great master which arranged things well, and, in these circumstances, the only obligation that imposed itself upon an honest man was to keep up appearances. In this way, he would show that he regarded as of little account what most men would have taken for a catastrophe. Monsieur de Noblecourt, with his experience of the century and of the ways of men, was convinced that Lenoir would overcome his initial prejudices. His first reaction had been perfectly understandable, the action of someone who wished to impress others and himself. Nicolas should not forget that Lenoir was the protégé and friend of Monsieur de Sartine, who had intrigued to have him appointed in his place, hoping thereby to keep some control over this important cog in the machinery of State, this privileged instrument of influence with the monarch. The talk that had reached Monsieur de Noblecourt's ears about the new Lieutenant General of Police painted quite a different picture. He was said to be clear-headed, a good conversationalist, a man of lively perception and exquisite judgement. He had studied long and hard, but this had not, it was said, in any way blunted the graces and ornaments of an amiable wit. He was, in addition, a discriminating lover of the arts and letters. In short, the most sensible thing, for the moment, was to wait, for it sometimes happens that our salvation comes from the very same sources from which we expect our ruin.

Monsieur de La Borde's argument, although different, pointed in the same direction. He had, immediately after the King's death, decided to forget a past that had been happy but was now over and done with. They had to accept it: they were both 'old Court', and would stay that way for a long time, if not for ever. He himself had resumed a number of activities which his duties to the monarch had caused him to neglect. Swearing Nicolas to secrecy, he confessed that the late King had promised to compensate him for a financial sacrifice to which he had once consented in order to enter his service. He also revealed, much to Nicolas's surprise, that he had decided to turn over a new leaf after a life of superficiality and dissipation. He had recently married Adélaïde-Suzanne de Vismes, nineteen years his junior. The ceremony had originally been set for 1 July, but, because of the public mourning, had been postponed to September and celebrated discreetly. His wife, sorely tried by these events and the dashing of their expectations, had fallen into a terrible state of languor, inflammation and weeping. Still in the mood for confession, and no doubt inspired by Nicolas's recent fatherhood, La Borde revealed to him that he himself had legitimised, four years earlier, a daughter born of his liaison with La Guimard, the famous actress. Saying all this seemed to relieve him of a burden and, putting his own troubles aside for the moment, he returned to those of his friend.[2]

He tried fervently to make Nicolas forget his gloom. After all, he had been granted leisure. By God, he should make use of it and devote himself to his son! A man who had studied the world knew when to wait and when to take advantage of opportunities. He had to adapt his means and make his thoughts serve his loyalties. His counsel could be summed up in the Italian phrase *Volto sciolto e pensieri stretti*: Open face and secret thoughts. Dissimulation and secrecy were to be cultivated: the commissioner should stand aside for a while in favour of the Marquis de Ranreuil. He should use the disadvantages of an apparent fall from favour, don them like a suit of armour in a society where the slightest weakness was noticed and provided ammunition to those who wished to mock or crush you. He should be seen in all the right places and make sure that the King, who already knew him, noted his regular attendance and expertise on hunts and at shooting parties, to which he had free access thanks to the favour of Louis XV. That would give others nothing to seize on as evidence that Monsieur Lenoir was keeping him on the sidelines. Nothing would be gained by arguing. La Borde noted sadly that times had indeed changed: a witty remark by Monsieur de Maurepas was considered of greater import in royal circles than protecting a good servant.

Nicolas was inspired by his friends' good counsel. He judged that salvation lay in the deliberate ambiguity of his conduct, which would lead commentary in different directions and, in the long run, drain it of all meaning. Despite the rumours, the cold hearts and false minds of the city and the Court would struggle in vain to spread gossip about him. Everyone might well have his own opinion about the case of 'young Ranneuil', but it wouldn't matter. All that remained to complete the picture were a few touches intended for the chroniclers, who were always on the lookout for things that might convince the less credulous: a gratifying flirtation with an indiscreet lady, a touch of condescension in his courtesy, and, most important of all, being noticed by the King. He had the opportunity to note, with some amusement, how he excelled in the career of courtier. In August, when the Court was at Compiègne, he had several times found himself in at the kill just after the King, and had benefited from his master's simple good humour. Subsequently, they had conversed merrily about the qualities of the animal or the episodes of the hunt. At shooting, he deliberately missed, much to the satisfaction of Louis XVI, who, as a mark of his esteem, resolved to present him with the rifles which the late King had lent to Nicolas on one of his last excursions, just before his illness.

All this caused much comment at Court, his supposedly fallen star suddenly shone again as brightly as ever, and the very people who, a few days earlier, had looked at him without seeing him now came running to compliment him. He had no doubt that news of his renewed success would reach the ears of Monsieur

Lenoir, who was informed by his spies of the smallest details of life at Court. When all was said and done, he realised, the last few months had passed quickly, with a great deal of agitation and a flood of impressions and feelings. A great cry drew him from his reflections.

'*Gigot farci à la royale* accompanied by mushroom rissoles!' roared La Borde, who was carrying a silver tray from which fragrant wreaths of steam were rising.

'Doesn't he look like the herald of arms?' exclaimed Noblecourt, his eyes already gleaming greedily. 'All he needs is the tabard.'[3]

'What do you think this is, then?' asked La Borde, indicating the white apron with which he was draped.

Now it was Louis's turn to appear, his face red from the heat of the ovens, carrying a porcelain dish filled with a pyramid of rissoles arranged on a cloth.

Nicolas decided to join in the mounting gaiety. 'And what are we going to drink with all that?'

Bourdeau produced two bottles from under the table. 'A plum-coloured Saint Nicolas de Bourgueil!'

'Gentlemen, gentlemen,' said Noblecourt, 'while Poitevin carves, I propose that Monsieur de La Borde gives us the usual descriptive and appetite-whetting speech.'

'May I enquire, Monsieur,' said Louis, 'as to the reason for this custom?'

'Young man, ever since your father brought joy back to this house, a joy made all the greater today by your presence among us, it has been a tradition which I would not dream of not respecting on this feast day. The delicious dishes concocted under this roof should be tasted not only by the palate but also by the ear.'

'And the eyes!' exclaimed Semacgus. 'In any case, that is the one sense I allow myself to indulge.'

'Well,' retorted Noblecourt, 'I'm going to disobey my doctor this evening. I shall satisfy those three senses to the full!'

'Gentlemen,' said La Borde, 'may I first point out to you that I had the honour to make this dish for the late King, and that Madame de Pompadour was very fond of it in spite of a weak stomach?'

'The good lady was quite lenient,' said Semacgus.

'On the contrary, she asked for more.'

'Gentlemen, stop this foolery,' begged Noblecourt. 'It's going to get cold.'

'Imagine a fine leg of lamb,' continued La Borde emphatically, 'kept cool for several days until it's nicely tender. First you must break the knuckle to get inside and take out the meat while keeping the outside intact. To do this, I called on the skills of a master!'

'A meat roaster from Rue Saint-Honoré?' Nicolas asked.

'Not at all. A naval surgeon, adept at cutting and digging.'

'It's true,' said Semacgus, closing his eyes with a show of solemnity. 'My knives proved very useful.'

'Good heavens!' cried Nicolas. 'Do you mean to say you used the instruments that are normally for—'

'I'd like to have you believe it, just to take away your appetite!'

'I'll never finish if you keep interrupting me,' moaned La Borde. 'The meat that's been taken out has to be chopped up very small with a little bacon, marrow, fine calf's-kidney fat, mushrooms, eggs, salt, pepper and spices. Keep kneading it all, making sure that each part absorbs the taste and seasoning of the others. Then fill the skin with it so that the leg reappears in its natural form and tie it all the way round with string, in order to maintain its consistency. Let it get nicely golden, then cook it in a pot with a good thick stock and a thin piece of beef, half roasted, which will fill it with its juices and give it more taste. Add onions stuck with cloves and herbs. A good hour later, turn it in the pot until it's baked. Check it with your fingertips, to make sure the flesh is soft. As the sauce is now reduced, add some sweetbread, and, once you've carved the leg, pour this succulence over it.'

Cheers punctuated Monsieur de La Borde's recitation. Everyone proceeded to savour a dish that required a spoon rather than a knife and fork. Nicolas watched his son out of the corner of his eye, happy to see that he was eating with that nimble elegance which, once again, recalled not only the bearing of the Marquis de Ranreuil, but also his mother's innate grace.

'Now there's a dish,' said Noblecourt, 'that's well suited to my old teeth.'

'The crustiness of the wrapping and the softness of the filling go together perfectly,' said Semacgus. 'And how well this purple beverage matches the lamb!'

'Doesn't it?' said Bourdeau, delighted. 'I find that the mushrooms in this fine mixture retain their softness and all the flavours of the forest.'

Noblecourt turned to Louis. 'This is a dinner you'll remember when you're at school, one with which you'll be able to enliven your dreams.'

'I shall think of it with gratitude, Monsieur,' the boy replied, 'when I'm eating hard-boiled meat and worm-eaten herring. It will strengthen my resolve.'

They all laughed. Catherine placed a dish of crystallised quince fritters sprinkled with sugar on the table. Noblecourt smiled and made a sign to Poitevin, who went out and immediately returned with two small packages.

'Young man,' said the former procurator, opening the more voluminous of the two, 'I was a schoolboy once, and had to suffer, like you, both harsh discipline and hunger. My mother took pity on me and made sure I had a supply of quince jelly, which I sucked every evening to calm my hunger pangs.'

He took from the packet a series of small round, flat deal boxes.

'These objects, which are called *friponnes*, contain quince jelly with a little added white wine. Not only will they assuage your hunger, but they are an excellent remedy for stomach aches. They will also help to combat whatever harmful effects the school food has on your health. You will just have to conceal them carefully, as theft is all too common in schools. You have enough here to last you until Christmas.'

The conversation then turned to more general matters.

'Are they still wearing mourning for our king at Versailles?' La Borde asked with that feigned indifference that ill concealed his sadness at being separated from the centre of the world.

'The recommended attire,' said Nicolas, 'is a cloth or silk coat, depending on the weather, black silk stockings, swords and silver buckles, with a single diamond ring. Last but not least, braided cuffs on the shirt. That's all until 1 November; after that everything will be simpler as Christmas approaches.'

'For someone who is out of favour at Court,' observed La Borde, 'you seem to be well informed!'

'I still have my place there, having followed my friends' counsel.'

'I am assured,' said Noblecourt, 'that the King has ordered Monsieur de Maurepas to put right certain abuses. Have we seen the first fruits yet?'

'A hundred and thirty horses and thirty-five grooms have already been removed from the royal hunt.'

'Can you imagine?' said Bourdeau, sardonically. 'Horses are done away with, while at the same time the King yields to the Queen's whims by increasing her already well-stocked household. Why did she need a grand chaplain on top of everything else, not to mention an official to heat the sealing wax?'

'Clearly, Bourdeau is equally well informed of matters at Court,' said Semacgus.

'Not at all!' the inspector replied. 'But I keep a close eye on how the people's money is dissipated.'

'It's been quite a while,' said Semacgus, 'since we last heard your caustic criticisms.'

'In my opinion,' said Bourdeau, becoming heated, 'the creation of Court positions is putting a strain on a budget that's already increased thanks to the military operations on the island of Corsica. Just imagine, the natives don't know how lucky they are to be French! Rebels and bandits are ravaging the countryside and extorting money by menaces.'

'As a matter of fact,' said La Borde, 'that's becoming a bigger problem. Our commander in the field, Monsieur de Marbeuf, has just pacified Niolo. Rebels have been put on the wheel outside churches in the presence of the populace. Six hundred rifles were found in a tomb at the monastery, and there was a terrible reprisal: two monks were hanged on the spot. It's to be expected that this business will continue. God knows when we shall see its end!'

'Enough of sad matters,' said Noblecourt. 'La Borde, I have no doubt you attended the first performance of Monsieur Gluck's *Orpheus and Eurydice*. Tell us what you thought. Such things hold no secrets for you.'

'In truth,' replied La Borde, impervious to the hint of irony in the procurator's tone, 'the audience were enraptured by that tragic opera, and its success surpassed that of *Iphigenia in Aulis* last April.'

'That indeed is what I observed for myself,' said Noblecourt, savouring the surprised reaction of his friends, who all knew that the former procurator almost never left his house. 'Oh yes! In the absence of Nicolas, away chasing both lovely ladies and the beasts of the field, I called for my horse and carriage. Poitevin donned his newest livery, and off we set!'

He looked at Nicolas out of the corner of his eye.

'On my arrival at the Opéra, Monsieur Balbastre,[4] who was all smiles, helped me to my seat. He was very friendly . . . if a trifle unctuous.'

Nicolas shrugged.

'Anyway, I attended the performance and can confirm its success. But what kind of success? And with whom? Apart from you, who are able to judge, even though in this case I do not share your taste. What did I see? An auditorium three-quarters full of old would-be gallants and young fops, the kind who spend their time making paper cut-outs in fashionable salons. This pack goes wild every time something new appears, provided it stands out more or less from the ruck. As for what I heard, it was nothing but a stew of very diverse ingredients. A disastrous mixture of sounds and impressions that bombards and paralyses the understanding to cover the lack of fecundity of an author who ought to prostrate himself before Saint Greluchon.[5] Oh yes, I'd prefer to go and hear the Tenebrae sung by the nuns of Sainte Claire at Longchamp. In my opinion, gentlemen, Gluck is beyond the pale.'

Taking advantage of the astonishment into which his energetic outburst had plunged his audience, he grabbed a slice of lamb with one hand while nimbly emptying his glass with the other.

'My dear Noblecourt,' said La Borde, 'please allow me to contradict you. For my part, I consider that even the finest brush would not have been able to render the details of that unforgettable performance. Yes, Monsieur, at last we have something new. Enough of Italian-style vocalising! Enough of the traditional machinery of the genre and all that monotonous recitative!'

'To be replaced by what? Wrong notes and high-pitched twittering? That's all I heard from the *haute-contre* who sang the role of Orpheus.'

'Monsieur,' said Louis timidly, 'may I be so bold as to ask what an *haute-contre* is?'

'I commend you for asking the question. One should never conceal gaps in one's knowledge. It does you honour, and we will always be happy to instruct you, dear boy. It is knowledge rather than brilliant but empty wit that makes the honest man. Whoever is master of his subject will be attended to and esteemed everywhere. Monsieur de La Borde, who himself writes operas, will answer you: it will permit me to catch my breath.'

'Your breath, yes, but no more lamb or Saint-Nicolas,' said Semacgus. 'The Faculty is strongly opposed to such things.'

Noblecourt assumed a contrite expression, while Nicolas's cat, Mouchette, put her little head above the table and sniffed the tempting aromas.

'An *haute-contre*,' explained La Borde, 'is a French tenor, the highest of all male voices, producing high notes from the chest, a powerful, resonant sound. To get back to our discussion, I am surprised to hear you criticise this choice for the role of Orpheus. It was a bow to the French habits which you love. To be replaced by what? you asked.'

'Yes, by what? I stand my ground.'

'Even with your gout,' sighed Semacgus.

'By a natural way of singing,' resumed La Borde, 'always guided by the truest, most sensitive expression, with the most gratifying melodies, an unparalleled variety in the turns and the greatest effects of harmony, employed equally for drama, pathos and grace. In a word, true tragedy in music, in the tradition of Euripides and Racine. In Gluck, I recognise a man of genius and taste, in whom nothing is weak or slapdash.'

'Listening to both of you,' remarked Semacgus, 'I seem to recognise the same kind of discussion that so often arouses our host on the subject of new habits in cooking.'

'How right you are,' said La Borde. 'Except that our friend supports the natural and the true in cooking, while defending the artificial and the shallow in music.'

'I'm not admitting defeat,' said Noblecourt. 'I don't need to justify my contradictions. I certainly maintain that meat should be meat and taste like meat, but in art I'm delighted by fantasy. A well-organised fantasy that makes us dream.'

'But the depth of the new style,' said La Borde, 'stimulates our imagination by combining the emotion of tragedy with the pleasure and delight of melody.'

'I see nothing in it but faults and pretence. A kind of deceptive mishmash of meat and fish.'

'You are talking just like the directors of our Royal Academy of Music, who ignore foreign art for fear it will bring down theirs.'

'Peace, gentlemen,' growled Semacgus. 'I'm sure you're both right, but you seem to take a perverse pleasure in forcing your arguments, with even more bad faith than the Président de Saujac.'

'Oh,' said Noblecourt, laughing, 'that's the whole pleasure of the thing. To maintain the unmaintainable, push your reasoning beyond the reasonable and put forward exaggerated arguments – all that is part of the joy of the debate.'

'You admit it, then?'

'I admit nothing. All I'm saying is that we should increase the controversy and put some bite into our presentation. The alternative would be like defending a dull thesis to the academics of the Sorbonne.'

Marion approached Louis, who was starting to doze off, and gave him a bag of fresh hazelnuts from a tree in the garden. Nicolas noticed his son's tiredness.

'My friends,' he said, consulting his repeater watch, which sounded softly, 'I think it's time to bring this memorable evening to an end. Our host needs to rest after this royal feast and his excesses.'

'So early?' said Noblecourt. 'Do you really want to interrupt this delightful interlude?'

'Tomorrow has already sounded, and Louis's mother is waiting for him. He is leaving for Juilly at dawn on the first mail coach.'

'Before he leaves us, I want to give him a gift,' said the procurator.

Monsieur de Noblecourt undid the second package, took out two small leather-bound volumes bearing his arms, and opened one with infinite care. Everyone present smiled, knowing his fanatical devotion to his books.

'Here,' he said with blissful solemnity, 'are Ovid's *Metamorphoses*, translated by Abbé Banier, of the Royal Academy of Inscriptions and Belles-lettres. These fine works are decorated with frontispieces and illustrations. My dear Louis, I offer them to you with all my heart . . .' He added in a lower voice, as if to himself, 'The only gifts that matter are those from which one parts with sorrow and regret.' Then, raising his voice again, 'May these fables, with their gods made flesh, stimulate your imagination and instil in you a love of literature.

> *All is enchantment, each thing has its place,*
> *With a body, a soul, a mind and a face.*[6]

May reading them persuade you that what is elegant in Latin is not necessarily so in French, that each language has a tone, an order and a genius peculiar to it. Whenever you need to translate, remember to be simple, clear and correct, in order to render the author's ideas precisely, omitting nothing of the delicacy and elegance of his style. Everything should hold together, in fact. Just as, in life, one becomes hard and heartless by being too attached to the letter of a principle, so in translation, the tone can become dry and arid as soon as one tries to impose one's own ideas in place of the author's.'

'Monsieur,' said Louis, now completely awake again, 'I don't know what to say. I certainly wouldn't like to deprive you of a treasure to which I know you are attached. My father has told me all about your great love of the books in your library.'

'Not at all, it is a pleasure for me to offer them to you! Don't worry, I still have Monsieur Burman's large folio edition, published by Westeins and Smith in 1732, with splendid intaglio figures . . .'

'Many thanks, Monsieur. These books will be dear to me, knowing they come from you.'

While the former procurator looked on approvingly, Louis opened one of the volumes and leafed through it carefully and respectfully.

'Monsieur, what are these handwritten pages?'

He held out a piece of almond-green paper covered in small, densely packed handwriting.

'Quite simply, translations made by yours truly of the Latin quotations in the preface. You will be able to check their accuracy.'

'Louis,' said Nicolas, 'it is a true viaticum our friend is giving you. Follow his counsel. I have always benefited from it. He was my master when I first arrived in Paris, when I was only a little older than you are now.'

They all rose from the table. The farewells took a while longer.

Semacgus, who was returning to Vaugirard, would give Louis a lift and drop him at his mother's in Rue du Bac. Nicolas made his final recommendations to his son. He was particularly insistent that the boy write him a letter, however short, every week. He opened his arms and Louis threw himself into them. Moved, Nicolas had the curious feeling that he was reliving a distant past, as if the Marquis de Ranreuil had reappeared in the person of his grandson.

The guests having dispersed, he went back to his quarters, overcome with a quiet melancholy. Life often had tricks up its sleeve, chance ruled, and fate often struck repeated blows. But this time it was different: his continuing disgrace was of little importance compared with an ambiguous destiny that offered him compensations which restored the balance. The discovery of Louis constituted the most important of these unexpected favours for which he had Providence to thank.

*Monday 3 October 1774*

Nicolas's first thought, after Mouchette had woken him as usual by breathing in his ear, was for his son, who was starting a new life that morning. He had explained to him why he would be absent when his coach left. He dreaded the emotion he would feel, which Antoinette's own emotional state would merely accentuate. He found it hard to think of La Satin as Antoinette, even though that was the name by which he had known her in the early days of their liaison. But, anxious for the past to be forgotten and to offer her son a mother worthy of the unexpected future opening up to him, she had certainly turned over a new leaf.

When he left Rue Montmartre, the pedestrians and the carriages were shrouded in autumnal fog. Where should he begin the errands he had planned? First of all, he had to purchase an oil for removing stains from clothes. He knew only too well how difficult it would be for a boarder like Louis to clean his clothes, since only underwear was washed by the establishment. This oil was designed to remove stains from any kind of material, however delicate, without in any way altering its colour or sheen. In addition, it possessed the useful ability to destroy bugs and their eggs, moths and other eaters of wool. It was in Rue de Conti in Versailles that he had discovered the inventor of this precious compound. The success of the formula had encouraged the man to start selling his product in Paris, at a haberdasher's shop in the Grande-Cour des Quinze-Vingts.[7] Nicolas knew that each bottle was wrapped in an explanatory note which would enlighten his son as to the best way to use this oil.

He also wanted to go to Madame Peloise's shop opposite the Comédie-Française, which stocked a large selection of imitation gemstones of various different colours. He would choose one, have his son's initials engraved on it, and have it mounted as a seal. The idea briefly crossed his mind of adding the Ranreuil arms, to link the grandson to the grandfather in a kind of continuation of the line. Some secret instinct made him hesitate, as if he feared that this initiative might cause inconveniences for young Le Floch. He stopped for a moment to wonder about his decision. Why had both he and his father found themselves in the situation of having illegitimate sons? A mere coincidence or a kind of fatal repetition, the reason for which escaped him? Last but not least, he thought he might take a stroll around the second-

'*Tertio*,' Monsieur de Noblecourt went on, 'there's every indication that the Queen will act in the same way towards her brothers-in-law. Monsieur – reserved, cautious, even secretive – takes a certain amount of care over his conduct, but the Comte d'Artois has none and constantly falls into a familiarity he believes is permitted because it has been tolerated so far. As for the King, despite his austere life, everyone thinks he's soft and weak. He won't do anything to control his brother's activities. Only the Queen could put him in his place, if she wanted to. This situation's going to cause a lot of trouble.'

'Well, Mercury of the latest news, what of the *quarto*?'

'You can laugh, but this is much more serious. A pamphlet! No one is sure of its author, but Monsieur de Beaumarchais is suspected. Choiseul is the principal target along with the Queen, whose entourage is denounced as being in the pay of the former minister.'

He lowered his voice so much that the cat began miaowing anxiously.

'Be quiet, Mouchette!' Noblecourt growled. 'The pamphlet goes so far as to claim that the State is doomed if the King does nothing to curb his wife's ambition and coquetry. The gist of it – listen to this – is that Louis XVI cannot have children and that the princes, his brothers, should be on their guard against some new, loathsome intrigue which the young Queen may decide to go along with.'

'Yet one more example of the prevailing infection of the century!' said Nicolas, getting carried away. 'One more slander to add to all the others that have appeared over the years, against which we endlessly raise ever-illusory barricades!'

hand bookstalls, with a view to unearthing a few books to be added to the package he would soon be sending Louis at the school in Juilly.

He noted with satisfaction that all his shopping would take him to the same district, Rue Saint-Honoré and the environs of the Louvre. After a bracing walk, he began his rounds with Madame Peloise, who cleverly succeeded in making him spend much more than he had anticipated. An antique intaglio showing a Roman profile, mounted on a silver shaft, particularly attracted him and replaced his initial choice of a seal with initials. It was both more elegant and less banal, more discreet, too, and hard to imitate. From there, he proceeded to the shop selling the stain remover, where he was assured that the desired quantity of the product could be delivered to Juilly in the name of Louis Le Floch, which greatly simplified matters.

He left the maze of old streets around the Quinze-Vingts and walked to the galleries of the Louvre. He noted with regret that the former royal palace was increasingly disfigured by all kinds of excrescences. The colonnade had recently been cleared, and already a multitude of second-hand clothes dealers were insulting it with displays of rags and tatters. Nicolas also deplored the fact that the presence of the academies entailed lodging some of their members here, to the detriment of the surroundings. Everywhere, even within the precincts of the monument, frame houses had sprung up, adorned with shapeless staircases that detracted from the majesty of the complex. He recalled a conversation between Monsieur de La Borde and the Marquis de Marigny, the brother of Madame de Pompadour and super-intendent of buildings, about the noble plan to restore the palace to its former splendour. He had quoted Voltaire's complaint at seeing the Louvre, 'a monument to the greatness of Louis XIV, the zeal of Colbert and the genius of Perrault, hidden by buildings of the Goths and the Vandals'.

A multitude of stalls had taken root in the chinks of the vast edifice. Among them were those selling paintings and engravings. Fakes were more frequent here than genuine works, and the Lieutenancy General of Police was determined to settle a number of serious cases in which rich foreigners, victims of such swindles, had involved their embassies. In 1772, Nicolas had managed to unmask a group of forgers, which had been a salutary warning to the rest of the crooks.

He was well known to the merchants – both honest and dishonest – and his arrival always provoked a shudder of fear. Taking advantage of the presence of enlightened connoisseurs, some second-hand book dealers had chosen to join the sellers of prints and paintings, and offered customers a wide range, from the less good to, occasionally, the best. Nicolas recalled a few happy discoveries, like that of an original edition of François-Pierre de la Varenne's *Le Pâtissier Français*. He had presented this small red morocco-bound duodecimo volume, published in Amsterdam in 1655 by Louys and Daniel Elzevir, as a gift to Monsieur de Noblecourt, who had almost swooned at the sight of it. The dealers would visit the houses of the recently deceased, and buy whole libraries from the grieving families. Unfortunately, there was nothing now that was not known about, and rare books had gradually become impossible to find. The few there were would be immediately spotted by scouts who, in the know, no longer offered four sous for treasures which were worth a thousand times as much. Here and there, you also came across banned or condemned books, handled conspiratorially behind the stalls, in the hope of concealing them from the inquisitive glances of the police spies who frequented the place and were on the lookout for anyone bringing illicit brochures to sell or seeking out copies of such lampoons as had escaped the bonfire.

On one of the stalls, Nicolas discovered a Plautus, a Terence, the complete works of Racine and a Lesage, all of which ought to give great pleasure to a schoolboy. He found the sight of the other book lovers amusing, spellbound as they were by the range on offer. Much to the chagrin of the bookseller, who was always afraid that some work of value might be stolen, they would spend hours looking through the books and searching in the crates, often without buying anything in the end.

Absorbed in the account of a journey to the West Indies, Nicolas suddenly felt a hand tugging at one of his coat buttons. Turning, he recognised the humble, contrite face of one of the officers who worked for the Lieutenant General of Police in Rue Neuve-Saint-Augustin. The man was not alone: a second henchman, whom Nicolas did not recall having seen before, stood watching.

'Commissioner,' said the first man, 'you must follow us.'

'What do you mean?'

'We have orders to take you to Monsieur Lenoir immediately.'

Nicolas made an effort to conceal his astonishment. 'Let me at least pay for my purchases.'

Once that was done, Nicolas found himself in a cab with the two officers. With the windows raised and the curtains drawn, the unpleasant smell of unwashed bodies was overwhelming in such a confined space. He lowered the corner of his hat, withdrawing into himself to reflect on what appeared, for all the world, like an arrest. He was only too familiar with the procedures and customs of a system of which he had long been an agent. He had taken part in so many investigations and shared so many secrets that he could not help but wonder. Everything was possible, he knew. Would he be exiled to the provinces? Surely he was too small a figure for such a great honour. It was more likely that a *lettre de cachet* had been issued, and that he would be thrown into prison. But they would still have to find a reason to justify such treatment. Although . . . He laughed, making his two companions look at him in surprise. So many people had been arrested without knowing the reason. He wouldn't be the first and he wouldn't be the last! He might as well keep his composure: he would learn his fate soon enough.

Still watched by his two guards, he was left waiting in the antechamber, before the door opened and the friendly face of an elderly valet appeared. He motioned Nicolas to enter, then leaned over and whispered in his ear, 'He doesn't know anything himself!'

The old man was clearly talking about Lenoir. What was it he didn't know? Nicolas approached the desk. His chief was still writing, and had not even looked up.

'I am grateful to you, Commissioner,' he said at last, 'for responding so promptly to my summons.'

'How could I not, Monseigneur, when I was brought here by two officers? Quite an honour!'

'I think,' said Lenoir impassively, 'that they exceeded my instructions.'

'They found me, that's the main thing. As always, our police force has shown itself to be extremely efficient.'

Lenoir folded his hands. 'I am instructed to . . .' for a moment, he searched for the correct word, '. . . invite you to present yourself immediately at the Saint-Florentin mansion. The Duc de La Vrillière, Minister of the King's Household, has asked to see you.' He seemed surprised by his own words. 'I hope,' he resumed, 'that you've done nothing to offend him. You have not been assigned to any investigation for three months now. You wouldn't by any chance have become involved in some other case? I've already had occasion to deplore your independent behaviour during our first encounter.'

'Not at all, Monseigneur,' replied Nicolas. 'I have obeyed your orders completely and scrupulously. I have done nothing, I have enjoyed my leisure, and I have hunted. With His Majesty.'

His tone was so ironic that Lenoir sighed irritably. 'Go, and make sure you report back to me on anything that might be of interest to the King's service.'

'I shall not fail to do so,' said Nicolas. 'I shall take the cab which brought me here and go directly to the minister's mansion.'

With these words, Nicolas bowed and left the room. He descended the great staircase four steps at a time, watched with astonishment by the two officers, and jumped into the cab. We're back in business, he thought. His intuition told him that the Duc de La Vrillière needed him.

# II

## THE SAINT-FLORENTIN MANSION

It was neither tumult nor calm, but a silence like that
of a great fear and a great anger.

Tacitus

Like a rider facing a hurdle, Nicolas liked to give himself a lull
before launching into the thick of the action. He considered this
pause necessary to keep a clear head. He asked to be dropped at
Place Louis XV and, anxious to contemplate the Saint-Florentin
mansion, where he might well have a date with destiny, he sat
down on a bollard. Having kept him waiting for three months,
they could certainly wait a few more minutes. He admired the
classical trappings of the building, which extended the splendour
of the Garde-Meuble. For a moment, the past paraded before
him: images of that terrible night in 1770, the cries, the smoke,
the crushed bodies, and the statue of the King looking down
on the disaster of that failed firework display.[1] The facade
overlooked a small square with a fountain from which it was
possible to reach the Tuileries gardens. It had two large noble
floors and a roof crowned by a balustrade and decorated with
carved panoplies and two monumental urns. On Rue Saint-
Florentin was a splendid gate adorned with a stone coat of arms
held aloft by two deities. The coat of arms was divided into four
quarters, combining the blue of the Phélypeaux family, strewn

with gold cinquefoils and ermines, and the three red mallets of the Mailly family.

Nicolas had known Monsieur de Saint-Florentin, who was now the Duc de La Vrillière, since he had joined the police force. He pondered that remarkable career which had begun fifty years earlier in the King's councils and which had been built on a stubborn loyalty to the person of Louis XV. The man was not exactly popular, either at Court or in the city. Many envied his influence while condemning his weakness and timidity. He was also responsible for many arbitrary decisions and *lettres de cachet*. Madame Victoire thought him stupid, whereas others emphasised his gift for conciliation, his ability to appease dissenting parties without compromising the authority of the throne. On many occasions, he had demonstrated his trust in Nicolas, but a recent case in which his cousin the Duc d'Aiguillon had been involved seemed to have contributed to his current low opinion of the commissioner.

Nicolas again looked at the house, which had all the grandeur and nobility of a small palace and gave anything but a small idea of the fortune of the man who had built it. He recalled certain pieces of gossip concerning the minister's dubious morals. He lived a dissolute life in Paris, surrounded by women of ill repute, and neglected his wife in favour of a mistress, Marie-Madeleine de Cusacque, the Marquise de Langeac, whom he called 'the Beautiful Aglaé'. It was claimed at Court that this woman made use of her lover's influence and traded *lettres de cachet*, and there was good reason to believe that this was true. The duc had set up all the lady's children, despite their dubious lineage, but since the King's death he had had to conform to the new, stricter morality and give up seeing her. She had continued to appear, however, even provoking a gentleman to a duel and insulting a tribunal. Eventually, she had been ordered to remain fifty leagues from the Court and had withdrawn to an estate near Caen. As for her lover, his health had declined since this forced separation.

Nicolas finally decided to enter the mansion. A monumentally tall Swiss Guard, covered in silver braid, received him haughtily, softening only when he gave his name and occupation. He was led across the main courtyard and then up some steps into a vestibule where a valet greeted him. He was surprised by the lack of hustle and bustle in the house at this hour of the day. Several servants passed him without looking at him, with inscrutable expressions on their faces. On the great staircase, he noted a fine painting, an allegory of Prudence and Strength. On the first floor, a succession of antechambers led him to the minister's study. The valet tapped at the door. A familiar voice responded. The valet stood aside to let him in. The Duc de La Vrillière sat slumped beside the big marble fireplace, wearing a grey coat and no wig. He glanced at Nicolas expressionlessly. The man had certainly changed since their last encounter. Thin, stooped, hollow-jowled, he looked quite unlike the chubby little man Nicolas had known.

'Hmm, here's young Ranreuil,' he grunted. 'Quite cold, isn't it?'

He sighed, as if the name alone could summon up the ghost of the late King, his other passion in life. Things could have got off to a worse start, thought Nicolas.

'Monsieur,' said the minister, 'I have always held you in great esteem. I understand that you may have thought that you – how shall I put it? – did not have my trust. But that was a complete misunderstanding on your part.'

'I did indeed think so, Monseigneur,' replied Nicolas. 'In fact, I was quite convinced of it, even though I found it hard to explain. Others took it upon themselves to reinforce the impression.'

'Now who could that have been? Lenoir? Yes, that may well be what he thought. A word from me will disabuse him. It is no longer possible to do without your services. Monsieur de Sartine long ago convinced me of that. Today, I need you again.'

Nicolas had been right: he was indeed back in business. 'Monseigneur,' he said, 'I am at your service.'

The minister raised a hand clad in a grey silk glove and brought it down hard on the armrest of his chair. He sat up, and for a moment the image of the man he had been reappeared, an image of easy-going but real authority.

'Let's get straight to the point. Yesterday I was at Versailles. I came back early this morning to find my house turned upside down. The fact is, Monsieur, my major-domo has been killed.' He shook his head irritably. 'No, I'm wrong! One of my wife's maids has been killed, and my major-domo was found wounded and unconscious with a knife beside him. It would seem that, having killed the girl, he tried to punish himself by committing suicide.'

'What measures have so far been taken?' Nicolas enquired coldly, once again the professional who did not like other people to draw hasty conclusions for him.

'What? What? . . . Measures? Oh, yes, measures . . . I forbade anyone to touch the maid's body. The major-domo was taken to his room on the mezzanine, still unconscious. He is being watched by a doctor. As for the kitchens where the crime took place, I have forbidden access to them and the doors have been bolted while waiting for you to inspect the place.'

'Did you know the victim?'

The duc gave a kind of start. 'A chambermaid! One of the last to have entered my house. How could I? I don't even know her name.'

Nicolas thought to himself that servants were often regarded as furniture. Most of the time, their names were changed and their master was unaware of their real name, knowing nothing of them but the particular function for which they were paid.

'Monseigneur,' he said, 'may I be so bold as to demand full authority in this affair, which is all the more serious for having taken place in your house? No meddling, no interference, the possibility of questioning all the occupants of the house, and I mean all, and permanent permission to move around and to search.'

'All right, all right,' grumbled the duc, 'I suppose it's necessary. Sartine did tell me how inconvenient you can be.'

'The facts are more inconvenient than I. That's not all, Monseigneur. I should like to be assisted by Bourdeau. I trust you will consent.'

'The name sounds familiar. Isn't he one of our officers?'

'One of our inspectors, Monseigneur.'

'That's right,' said La Vrillière, striking his forehead, 'he's your loyal deputy. I like loyalty. Of course I consent.'

'What about Monsieur Lenoir?'

'Leave it to me. I'll reconcile the two of you. He'll be informed that this is my affair and you answer entirely to me. It's a private matter, and requires the greatest discretion. The Lieutenant General of Police will have to accede to your demands for any help or support that you may require. I hope that you will show the same zeal and efficiency in this affair as you have in others. A study has been set aside for you on the mezzanine, and orders will be given that you must be obeyed in all matters. My valet, Provence, will be your guide in this house. You can trust him, he's been with me for twenty years. Now do your work. Monsieur, I am at your disposal.'

The minister's tone was certainly in keeping with the circumstances. Nicolas had often noted in this unloved little man, lacking in personal prestige, a kind of unexpected grandeur which occasionally appeared, its roots constantly irrigated by the will and trust of the monarch. Thus, in a few short moments, the Duc de La Vrillière had been transfigured, animated by the concerns of State and the order it was his task to impose upon it. Everything vital having been said, Nicolas bowed and left the room. The valet was waiting at the door, and asked Nicolas to follow him. They took the same route by which they had come. Back on the ground floor, they came to a large hall that led to a succession of antechambers. In the third room on the right, the valet pointed out the entrance to a large study, which Nicolas judged to be situated more or less beneath that of the minister. The valet closed the door behind him. A fire was blazing in a white marble hearth, above which stood a bust of Louis XV. He stood for a moment contemplating it, suddenly overwhelmed with memories. Then he sat down at a small desk inlaid with bronze and lacquer and equipped with paper, quill pens, ink and lead pencils. He took out his little black notebook, an indispensable tool of his investigations. He was swept by a wave of excitement. It was the habitual thrill of the hunter setting off on the trail, the same ardour that sent him galloping off into the thickets of the forest of Compiègne. Already his mind was revolving around this case with which he had been presented, and his intelligence and intuition were on the alert.

Out of curiosity, he opened a door, which revealed to him a magnificently prepared bedroom. Behind this room were a fine bathroom and water closet in the English style, such as he had not seen since his return from London. He went back into the study and rang the bell. The valet appeared. The man was about fifty, with a crumpled, colourless face and faded eyes. He wore a grey wig, and his silver-trimmed blue livery hung loose on his slender frame. The only thing striking about him was how nondescript he was.

'What's your name, my friend?'

'Provence, Commissioner,' the man said, avoiding his gaze.

'What's your real name?'

'Charles Bibard.'

'Where were you born?'

'In Paris, in 1725 or 1726.'

Nicolas had been right about his age. 'Why Provence, then?'

'It was my predecessor's name. Monseigneur's father, by whom I was subsequently engaged, didn't like change.'

'Well, Provence, can you tell me what happened here this morning?'

'To be honest, I don't know much. Just before seven, I was busy making Monseigneur's apartments ready for his return from Versailles when I heard cries and screams.'

'Where were you?'

'In the bedroom. I went downstairs to the ground floor. The kitchen boy, the one who opens up in the morning, was screaming in terror and wringing his hands.'

'Was he alone?'

Nicolas noticed a slight hesitation.

'Everything was so chaotic . . . I think the Swiss Guard was there. Yes, I can see him now, just buttoning up his livery.'

'What happened then?'

'Jacques – Jacques Despiard, the kitchen boy – was kicking up such a fuss, it was impossible to understand what he was on about. He was stamping his feet like someone possessed. The caretaker arrived and helped us restrain him, then we left the caretaker to watch over him and went down into the servants' pantry.'

'So the door was open?'

'Yes. That was where Jacques had come from. The key was still in the door at the end of the passage.'

'And what did you find?'

Nicolas waited intently for the answer. Experience had taught him that a witness's first observations often turned out to be the most enlightening.

'It was still dark and the kitchen boy had dropped his candle. We went to look for another candle and lit it. There was nothing to see in the kitchen except some bloodstained footprints, but as soon as we got to the door of the roasting room we discovered Monsieur Missery lying face down on the floor in the middle of a pool of blood. We rushed to him, and I noticed there was a kitchen knife next to him.'

'What was the position of his head?'

'His right cheek was against the floor.'

'And where was the knife?'

'Also on his right. He was still breathing and, just as we were going to help him, the Swiss Guard turned and saw, slumped to her knees against the draining board, the body of a young woman. Her head looked as if it was detached from her trunk. The wound was terrible, Monsieur, she was like a pig that's been bled.'

'What happened then?'

'We carried Jean Missery to his room on the mezzanine.'

'The floor where we are now?'

'That's right, Commissioner, but on the other side of the courtyard, where you find the service rooms, the linen room, and accommodation for the Swiss Guard and the caretaker. The caretaker went to fetch a doctor from Rue Saint-Honoré. At that moment, Monseigneur arrived and took matters in hand. He immediately went down to the servants' pantry.'

'Alone?'

'Yes. Then he came back up and asked for the key I'd taken from the door and double-locked everything. Here it is — he gave it to me to give to you.'

Nicolas recognised the minister's way: his insecure character did not exclude a certain decisiveness and the greatest concern for detail. The valet handed him a thick envelope bearing the Saint-Florentin family seal.

'What did the doctor say?'

'That he'd recover. He bandaged the wound in his side, and told us to let him rest and to keep an eye on him.'

'We'll continue this conversation later. These initial facts are enough for the moment. Please show me to the kitchens.'

As they were leaving the room, Nicolas noticed that the valet's shoes, and their heels, were immaculate. He recalled a quip by Semacgus, although he did not immediately see its relevance to his observation. His friend liked to say that the doors of gilded salons were not closed to those whose minds were full of dirt, but that those same people would be turned away if there was dirt on their shoes. It was an interesting detail, which it would be worthwhile investigating further. The man led him down a smaller staircase, no doubt used by the servants. Nicolas, who had lowered his head in order not to miss the poorly lit steps, noticed some brownish prints still visible on the wood. His first reaction was to make an ironic remark on the poor maintenance of this area, so out of keeping with the gleaming splendour visible elsewhere in the mansion. On the ground floor, they walked across a small inner conservatory, then through some pantries, and found themselves in a passage which emerged into a larger one leading on the left-hand side towards the courtyard of the mansion and on the right to the door of the kitchens. Nicolas opened the envelope and took out a large key. He would have to check if there were any duplicates. His concern for details like that, which were often the most significant, was what made him a good policeman. He unlocked the door and entered the first room, where the light came in through large high windows.

'This is the kitchen itself,' said Provence, continuing towards another room. 'And this is the roasting room, this is where—'

Nicolas did not let him finish. 'Thank you,' he said with an amiable smile. 'I'd like to be alone now. Oh, there is one thing, though. Could you get a message to the duty office of the commissioners and inspectors at the Grand Châtelet?'

He tore a page from his notebook and, leaning against the wall, quickly wrote a note to Inspector Bourdeau, asking him to join him immediately at the Saint-Florentin mansion with a wagon, some officers and all the material necessary to transport a corpse. He knew that for the past few weeks his deputy had been spending every morning at the old prison in the always disappointed hope of a mission to be expedited. He searched in his pocket, found a piece of sealing wax, and used it to close his message. He wrote his signature across it with the lead pencil, in order to discourage inquisitiveness, and handed the whole thing to the valet, who seemed upset at being excluded from his exploration of the scene of the crime. This reaction seemed to him surprising. In his experience, witnesses connected with a violent crime usually preferred to avoid as far as possible the place where it had occurred. Once again he made a mental note of the fact. Perhaps, he thought, the man had been given the task by the minister of reporting back to him on Nicolas's first observations.

The floor of the roasting room was like that of a butcher's shop after an animal has been slaughtered. It was impossible to draw any conclusions from the prints still visible in the mire of blood on the black and white tiles. What did seem clear, though, was that a body had been dragged across the floor, presumably that of the major-domo, Jean Missery. On the floor, a kitchen knife with a wooden handle and a single rivet drew his attention: it was one of those common objects known as an *eustache*. It was of medium size and its blade measured a little more than a hand in length. The mustiness in the room reminded him of other situations dominated by the sickly-sweet, metallic smell of blood. Nicolas climbed on a stool to get an overall view.

The picture Provence had painted of the scene proved exact. First of all, the body of a young woman, slumped, as if kneeling, at the foot of a draining board. Her head was at a curious angle in relation to the rest of the body, and she had lost a lot of blood, which had spread, brown and glutinous, all around her. He noted an incongruous detail: her two feet, as white as ivory, as if spared by the outpouring of blood. A few steps away, another pool of blood, this one redder. You did not have to be very knowledgeable to realise that the two pools were of different origins: one from each of the two victims. Time, perhaps a long time – he would have to determine how long – had passed between the two effusions. He tried again to seek answers in the complex pattern of footprints, but was unable to discern anything other than a wild trampling. He went back to an examination of the body.

The young woman was wearing a skirt, a loose blouse, and an apron knotted at the waist and above all – the distinguishing mark of a chambermaid – at the bib. The hair was held up in a bun, revealing a narrow neck, almost a child's. The lace cap had slipped to the floor and lay in the blood. Nicolas was struck by the sight of two slippers lying a few paces from the body. These were not objects commonly associated with a young servant girl, but luxurious, even expensive items quite out of place here. He got off the stool and walked up to the body, making an effort to control his mixed feelings: apprehension at contact with a corpse and pity for a murdered human being. It was up to him to observe the state of the body and estimate the time of death. He realised that he had left his watch in Rue Montmartre. He had always been a stickler for accurate timekeeping, but, having had little to hurry him these past few months, he had become absent-minded. In his head, he tried to calculate how much time had gone by. He had left Noblecourt's house at nine, his shopping expedition had taken two hours, after which he had strolled idly among the second-hand bookstalls and had even indulged in a little reading. It must have been about midday that the officers had intercepted him. The carriage having been delayed by traffic on the way to Rue Neuve-Saint-Augustin, he must have entered Monsieur Lenoir's office at about half past twelve. Interview, cab, a conversation with the Duc de La Vrillière, another with Provence. It must now be about two o'clock in the afternoon.

He knew that rigor mortis only set in gradually. The longer it took to appear, the longer it lasted. You had to take the conditions and temperature of the place into account. Kitchens were usually cold at night, when all the lights were out and there was adequate ventilation. It was October now, and starting to feel distinctly cold. The duration of rigor mortis was supposedly shorter in damp, warm air than in dry, cold air. In addition, it was a constant feature that rigor mortis took a long time to appear when death was sudden, as seemed to be the case here. Touching the body, he noticed that there was still some residual stiffness. He estimated that the murder must have taken place between ten and midnight.

He leaned over to examine the terrible wound at the base of the neck. If a piece of wood had been driven in just below the right ear, the flesh could not have been any more bruised and shattered than it was. It was still possible to see, deep inside the wound, a piece of lace from the blouse. Life had fled from the poor girl's body in an endless haemorrhage. Her eyes stared unseeing, the corneas already obscured by a slimy membrane. He shuddered at the sight of that face, contorted in death: the forehead was lined, the nose was pinched, the lips hung over an open jaw, and the skin, dry and livid, gave the whole face a twisted appearance, as if frozen in a cruel, dazed stupor. He searched in the pockets of the apron and the skirt, and found nothing except a handkerchief and a cross on a small, broken metal chain, which had slipped into a fold in the fabric.

There was nothing else to do while waiting for the arrival of the stretcher which would take away these remains to the operating table in the Basse-Geôle. Whatever observations were made there could well open up new paths for the investigation. He still had to undertake a delicate experiment. As there was nothing to be learnt from the bloody mire on the floor, he would have to examine the surroundings. There, doubtless, there would be fewer traces and he would be able to read them more precisely. The kitchen and the roasting room were full of footprints: that was quite normal, given the servants who had come to take the wounded major-domo to his room on the mezzanine. In the kitchen, he found a whole series of knives identical to the one he had found on the floor. Was this latter a utensil that belonged to the mansion, or had it been brought in from outside? This was a good house, and the gleaming state of the whole area showed that it was well maintained. Perhaps an inventory . . . With one thought leading to another, he realised a startling fact: the broad, deep, prodigious wound to the young woman's neck could not have been caused by the *eustache*. He would have to examine Jean Missery's wound to see if the same knife had been used on him as on the maid. The result of this examination might point in a different direction.

He came back to the problem of prints. He was still obsessed by those found on the staircase between the mezzanine and the ground floor. He walked on tiptoe, trying to avoid the soiled areas, but still managed to add a few of his own prints to those already existing. A brownish trail took him to the passage leading to the courtyard. He took off his shoes to cross a section that was apparently untouched. He saw nothing in the wash house, in the small adjoining courtyard, or on the steps down to the cellars. He decided to go back along the route he had taken with Provence as far as the staircase. Nicolas carefully cleaned the soles of his shoes with water from a watering can he found in the small conservatory, then hesitated a moment. Should he continue to the first floor, where the minister's apartments were located? But where was the risk? Nobody would blame him, and besides the lead might turn out to be pointless. Provence, who had discovered the bodies, might have taken that staircase and, noticing that his shoes were dirty, immediately changed them. While he was thinking this through, a small inner voice whispered in his ear that he was right to persevere and to listen to his intuition, which, in all these years as a police officer, had stood him in good stead, on an equal level with his reason.

The trail continued, becoming increasingly indistinct. But Nicolas knew that blood, being thick and viscous, took a long time to vanish completely. He reached an empty room furnished with two old red velvet benches, with a stock of logs piled up against the panelling. He immediately realised that this was not the way to the Duc de La Vrillière's apartments, but rather a kind of halfway stage before you got to the upper parts of the mansion, given over, in this kind of dwelling, to the servants' rooms or to storerooms. He immediately began examining the state of the staircase, this time with a piece of candle he found lying in a corner. He lit it, and the flame illumined the steps. He looked as hard as he could, bent down, even lay down, his nose almost against the oak, but could not find any traces of blood. On the other hand, he did find some on the floor of the room, a trail leading to the French window at the corner of the building. As he approached, a cold draught made him shiver.

Why was it open? He saw that the catch was up. He opened the window, and immediately a keen wind lashed his face. The window led out onto a balcony with a balustrade, facing Rue Saint-Florentin. His heart beat faster: there were clear traces of blood on the stone. Bloody footprints led to the corner of the building, in the direction of the gate in the main courtyard. He followed them and leant over. Here, another surprise awaited him: he observed that there were also spots of blood on the narrow cornice of the wall, which was supported by columns. He decided to go and see at close quarters where that might lead. Luckily, unlike his friend Semacgus, he did not suffer from vertigo. During all his travels on the King's vessels, Semacgus had never been able to climb the top mast. Admittedly, he would say with a laugh, his functions as a surgeon rarely required this kind of exercise from him. Nicolas dreaded confinement and enclosed spaces, but, faced with a drop, he was as agile as a cat. Pressing his back up against the wall, he slid to the cornice above the gate. As he placed his feet on the projecting edge, he was struck by a stronger gust of wind and almost lost his balance: throwing his head back steadied him. He obtained a foothold on the cornice, holding on to the top of the upper parapet with his hands. There, the traces petered out. He sat down with his legs dangling, then lay on the edge to examine the underneath. He immediately realised that by putting his legs around the top of the column, he could easily get down as far as the spikes of the iron gate – they were only a few feet below him – and from there slide to the ground. There was one point where it could be dangerous, but the rest was child's play. He decided, however, not to go all the way with his experiment, as the flagstones, being muddy, seemed unlikely to reveal any further clues.

So someone had left the scene of the crime, gone up to the first floor of the mansion, opened the French window, and had escaped by performing a feat of acrobatics. That suggested several things: that the unknown person had a precise knowledge of the layout of the house, that his escape had taken place in the middle of the night, when there was less risk of being surprised, and, above all, that the individual was young, capable of such a difficult exercise, in which you might either fall or be impaled on the spikes of the gate. That raised some interesting questions about the sequence of events, and seemed to contradict the initial hypothesis of a murder committed by the major-domo, followed by an attempted suicide.

Nicolas put his feet back down on the balcony, but, as he was about to enter the room, he realised that, during his brief absence, the French window had been closed from inside. Whether this had been caused by a gust of wind or a human hand, he was faced with the problem of getting back inside. He thought for a moment of taking the perilous route adopted by the mysterious acrobat. He soon gave up the idea: that was all he needed, to be crushed to death in the street! He could not take the risk. He took a few steps and glanced in through the next window. There, in a kind of boudoir, was the Duc de La Vrillière, motionless and lost in thought. Unless he broke a pane in the first French window, the only thing he could do was make his presence known as naturally as possible. It took him several attempts to attract the attention of the minister, who eventually opened to him.

'Monsieur, Monsieur,' exclaimed the duc, 'I'd heard that you went out through the door and came in through the window! Well, no need to explain. That's your business.'

He appeared to reflect for a moment, then turned with a sigh to a large portrait of Louis XV, the cartouche of which indicated that it was a gift from the King, presented to Monsieur de Saint-Florentin in 1756.

'What a good master he was,' he murmured, in a tragic tone. 'He loved us, he really did. What a career you would have had, Marquis, if . . .' He left the phrase hanging. 'What he especially appreciated about you,' he resumed after a moment, 'was your handsome face, your very rare gift of being able to distract him, and an even more unusual quality: the fact that you never asked him for anything. I shan't even mention the services you rendered, performing miracles in difficult, delicate circumstances, even at the risk of your own life. Not many have been as valiant and loyal as you . . .'

Nicolas tried to take advantage of the duc's current good disposition towards him. 'Monseigneur, allow me to ask you a question. What is your opinion of your major-domo, Jean Missery?'

'To say that he keeps a firm grip on my household would be an understatement,' replied the duc. 'He's been with me for fifteen years, having succeeded his father. Everything concerning the general expenses of the mansion is his responsibility. He chooses the kitchen staff and the other servants, and he has full authority over them, including dismissing them if need be. It is also his job to buy bread, wine, meat, vegetables and fruit from the suppliers. For example, he buys wine by the cask and hands it over to the wine waiter to distribute, and the latter will report back to him on the state in which he has received it. He also has to deal with a grocer for sugar, candles, torches, oils and Lord knows what else! Wood, crockery, oats, hay, straw: all that's his province. Last but not least – by no means least! – he has to lay out the service for the lunches, dinners and midnight suppers which I give.'

'Do you think he's honest?'

'I believe he is, but, even if he were not, I would not trouble myself to constantly check up on a servant, however corrupt he might be. When we depend on others, we sometimes have to know when to close our eyes if we want to be well served. Now leave me, I still have some work to do.'

Nicolas knew there was no point in insisting. He retraced his steps to the antechambers and the great staircase. Deciding to visit the wounded man, he stopped on the mezzanine. He thought he knew his way around the house quite well by now, but realised that it was not possible to go from one wing to the other except via the ground floor. There, he had no difficulty in finding, to the left of the grand staircase, a small staircase leading up to the mezzanine. After several minutes during which he wandered through dark corridors, he at last came to a room with its door open.

It was a large room, with *bergame* hangings and three windows that looked onto an inner courtyard. A good fire was blazing in the hearth. The marble mantelpiece was adorned with a small pier glass with three mirrors set in gilded wood. On a bed with red flowered damask curtains, his legs half covered with a counterpane of quilted calico, lay a corpulent man, his torso wrapped in bloodstained sheets. On the floor, to the left of the bed, were a coat the colour of dead leaves, a matching pair of breeches, a white shirt, and a yellow cravat. The rest of the furniture consisted of a large oak wardrobe, a marquetry table, two armchairs upholstered in yellow serge, a chest of drawers, and a small writing table covered with papers. The overall impression was one of comfort, and even luxury, enhanced even more by the presence on the parquet floor of a Turkish carpet. On a chair with a dust cover sat a man in a black coat and grey wig, apparently dozing. Nicolas realised that this was not the case, and that what he was in fact doing was taking Jean Missery's pulse. The man turned. A fine pastel face, thought Nicolas, about sixty, perhaps a little more.

'Monsieur, whom do I have the honour of addressing?'

'Commissioner Nicolas Le Floch. I am in charge of the investigation. And you are Monsieur . . .?'

'Dr de Gévigland. I was sent for this morning to attend to this disaster. There was nothing I could do for the young woman. As for this man, as luck would have it, the blade of the knife missed a rib and did not harm any vital organs. In my opinion, he will recover.'

'Has he regained consciousness?'

'No – which is the only thing that worries me. The wound in itself was not the kind to put him in such a state. I fear there may be something else. He may have hit something in his fall, or it may be an inflammation of the cerebral humours. I really don't know. When it comes to this kind of symptom, our knowledge is far from complete.'

Nicolas was pleased to hear these remarks. It was comforting to know that at least one doctor was devoid of the pedantic arrogance of many of his colleagues, made no attempt to spin yarns, and approached with simple modesty and praiseworthy level-headedness the unfathomable mysteries it was his job to diagnose and treat.

'May I see the wound?'

'There is no reason why not. You will observe that the blood loss is clearly defined and that the wound is clean. If you lift the bandage a little, you can see how clean it is.'

The commissioner bent over the supine body. There was a bevelled cut across the abdomen, between the lower ribs. No comparison, he thought, with the gaping hole in the maid's neck. The kitchen knife perfectly matched the appearance of the wound. To set his mind at rest, he asked the question. The doctor's answer did not surprise him.

'The kitchen knife, which is of the sharp kind, was certainly responsible for this. That's obvious.'

'And the young woman's wound?'

'It's up to you, my dear fellow, to find the stopper that would plug up that hole!'

'I have a specific question to ask, Doctor,' said Nicolas. 'Does your observation of your patient, Monsieur Missery's, wounds point to a suicide, as some witnesses suggest?'

The doctor made a face and shook his head. 'As always, people talk without knowing what they're talking about. I have only one comment to make, but it's an important one. Would a man who intends to commit suicide strike himself on the right-hand side and risk injuring his liver and dying in terrible pain? The choice of death by a knife implies that you strike the heart, in other words on the left. Please note that I don't have all the facts that would allow me to plump for one hypothesis over another. However, let's imagine that someone attacked him from behind and, holding his head in a vice-like grip, struck him with a weapon held in his right hand. In the heat of such an attack, he may well have missed and struck the wrong side. The wounded man, having certainly lost a lot of blood, fainted and his attacker may well have thought he had killed him. Even if he didn't, the desired aim might have been to stop him escaping, thus ensuring that suspicion would fall on him.'

'Monsieur, you have clearly thought this through carefully, and what you say is very enlightening.'

Dr de Gévigland had articulated what Nicolas had already been thinking. As he had spoken, the commissioner had seen in his mind's eye, like the images in a magic lantern on the boulevards, Marguerite Pindron on her knees at the foot of the draining board in the roasting room. Were she and the major-domo both victims of a single attacker, whose steps he had detected and followed as far as the monumental gate of the Saint-Florentin mansion? Could it be that the same person had struck twice in succession in the same place? But in that case, why were the two wounds so different and apparently caused by such dissimilar objects? And why had one of those weapons been found on the floor while the other, still of an unknown nature, appeared to be missing? Was someone trying to convince them of a different theory? Nicolas's mind was racing. Someone had worked hard to create a situation so clear-cut that it would be accepted completely: a man kills a woman and then commits suicide. The two pools of blood in the roasting room, so different in appearance, flashed through his mind. He pulled himself together. An autopsy on the chambermaid's body was essential, and he expected a great deal from its conclusions. Then the refining fire of reason would clarify the various hypotheses.

'I would be grateful, Monsieur,' said Nicolas, 'if you could inform me as soon as your patient has regained consciousness. An officer will soon be here to keep an eye on him and make sure that he has no contact with anyone. For the moment, he remains our only suspect.'

'I only hope, Commissioner, that this won't take too much time. I'm needed back at my practice. If he regains consciousness, the wound itself will be a mere detail. A little rest, a good dressing, and everything will heal up nicely.'


Nicolas was back in the great vestibule on the ground floor when several carriages entered the courtyard. From one of them, Bourdeau emerged, rubbing his hands with glee. He was followed by a number of officers with a stretcher. Nicolas walked down some steps to greet his deputy.

'Good Lord,' said the inspector, 'this really is the high life! The Saint-Florentin mansion! Our minister's house! It seems we haven't been dismissed after all.'

'What you say is right, my dear Pierre,' replied Nicolas with a laugh. 'They can't do without our services, and I assure you that the case we are dealing with is not a trivial matter.'

'And our friend Lenoir in all of this?'

'I fear he has been overtaken by events. But we'll be good chaps and keep him informed. We must never insult the future.'

'You're very indulgent today!'

'It's the joy of having something to get my teeth into.'

He ordered the officers to wait, and led Bourdeau towards the stables. There, surrounded by the odour of horses, he related the facts of the case in detail. The inspector's first reaction was that the drama would turn out to be a trivial one, in which case recourse to such experienced authorities as themselves was like using a ton of gunpowder to open the door. Nicolas pointed out the ambiguous clues, the prints and other incongruous and suspicious details which had caught his attention. The inspector agreed that there was plenty to think about and added that it could turn out to be a distinctly tricky affair, given the place where the tragedy had occurred. He concluded with a laugh that, devil take the difficulties, here was a way to re-establish themselves in favour as long as luck was with them as they made their way through the thickets of this new investigation. Nicolas was delighted to see him looking so cheerful again and told him, embroidering the truth somewhat, that it was the Duc de La Vrillière himself who had wanted him to assist in the case. Bourdeau made no response to this, but the air of pride he immediately assumed spoke for itself. The commissioner loved him all the more for being so forthright and simple in his emotions.

With the officers, they proceeded to the kitchens. Before the body was taken away, Nicolas asked Bourdeau to examine the scene of the crime, in the hope that a fresh pair of eyes might spot some details that had escaped him. Like him, the inspector was struck by the very unusual nature of the wound to the young woman's neck. He also observed that she was wearing two small garnet earrings. Their presence might be of some significance, for a chambermaid on duty would never wear such ostentatious jewellery. This suggested that Marguerite Pindron had been more conscious of her appearance that evening than usual. Which in turn suggested that she might have had a rendezvous with a suitor . . . The quality of the slippers also intrigued Bourdeau. They would have to find out the provenance of these luxury items. As for the rest, his observations tallied with those of the commissioner. He searched the place meticulously, anxious to find the object that could have caused such a terrible wound. But to no avail. As he was coming to the end of his search, he stopped and looked at the corner of one of the draining boards. He bent down and delicately picked up between two fingers a small piece of metallic thread, which he held out to Nicolas.

'Looks like silver thread to me,' said Nicolas. 'What do you think?'

'I agree. Someone knocked against this wooden corner. Look at it, it's a nest of splinters. The embroidered garment they were wearing got caught and this came off. It must have been a sudden knock, and in his haste the person who was wearing the coat didn't notice.'

Who, could Nicolas remember often wearing a coat with silver embroidery? The late King, of course! But who else? He racked his brains. The figure of the Duc de La Vrillière emerged. He often copied his master's manner of dress. The commissioner had talked to the minister twice since arriving. The man had indeed been wearing a grey coat, but Nicolas could not recall the nature of the embroidery. Even if it had been silver, that would prove nothing: the duc had visited his kitchens, and in all the excitement of discovering the crime his coat might have caught on the draining board. But he would have to make sure. One thing was certain: the thread had not come from the major-domo's coat, for that was a quite different colour. He carefully slipped the little piece of silver between the pages of his black notebook, then gave the signal to take the maid's body away. Nicolas decided to go back up to the mezzanine and install himself with Bourdeau in the study that had been set aside there for him. They would carry out their interrogations there. In the antechambers, they came across Provence, who was pacing up and down in the shadow of the walls.

'Monsieur Bibard,' said Nicolas 'what was your master wearing when he got back from Versailles this morning?'

The man assumed an indefinable expression which might have escaped someone less accustomed than the commissioner to examining faces. 'A black cloak over a black silk coat, Monsieur. We are observing Court mourning to the letter.'

'But this morning? It seems to me . . .'

'This morning, as soon as he returned, Monseigneur changed into a grey coat.'

'Was this coat embroidered?'

'Yes, with silver flowers.'

'Of course! You see, Bourdeau, I wasn't wrong. The late King had one exactly the same. The minister's loyalty is really touching. Thank you, Provence.'

The man bowed, apparently relieved.

'One more thing,' said Nicolas. 'Would you please have the Swiss Guard, the caretaker and Monseigneur's coachman come to my study, to start with. I should like to question them in the company of Inspector Bourdeau.'

They reached the study, whose splendours Bourdeau examined half admiringly, half sardonically. The commissioner waited for one of those acerbic remarks Bourdeau was in the habit of making, but none came: the pleasure of being plunged back into action, he thought, had certainly had a most beneficial effect on his deputy's character.

'By the way, Nicolas . . .' Bourdeau said, reverting to the commissioner's first name as soon as they were alone. 'Did you notice our chambermaid's curious underwear? Please don't see anything licentious in the question.'

'God forbid, I know you too well!' said Nicolas, somewhat surprised. 'But what exactly do you mean?'

'Well, look. We live in strange times, and you know better than I that the honesty of women takes on some quite curious aspects these days. If an elegant woman, getting out of her carriage to enter a theatre or go for a stroll, lets curious idlers see the whole of her legs, she is in no way considered indecent. Showing one's calves is regarded as something so natural that, far from precautions being taken to prevent the sight, it is made all the easier. So, when she dresses, any woman of quality would fix a long ribbon to her belt to hold up her chemise from behind so that the legs are uncovered all the way up to the back of the knee.'

'I follow you,' said Nicolas with a smile, 'but I'm not sure how far you will climb.'

'Oh, I'm stopping there! I'm simply trying to say that our

chambermaid wears drawers, a sure sign of dubious or dissolute morals. Add to that the presence of those unusual slippers, and I think you'll see where these observations are leading me.'

'I suspect our investigation will reveal a great deal about the poor girl. This house is a closed world. I already know what's going to happen. They'll all be on their guard, resisting the temptation to gossip. Silence and mistrust will be our lot. But in the end, the hurdles will fall and everyone will have something to say, for good or ill, about everyone else. You know how servants are. The world of service is, like others, filled with hatreds, jealousies, resentments and love affairs. We're entering a fertile field, and we just have to harvest it. Everything will come together, all we have to do is wait and not frighten anyone off.'

'I'm sure of that,' said Bourdeau.

'In the meantime, Pierre, get a message to our friends Semacgus and Sanson. I hope the victim's body can be opened up as soon as possible: I need to have their opinion on that strange wound. I'd also like you to send an officer to keep an eye on the room where the suspect is.'

The inspector was away for a short time. No sooner was he back than the door leading to the suite of apartments burst open, and a fairly elderly woman entered at an angle, hampered by the wide pannier of her old-fashioned dress. She was in Court mourning. She wore a jade necklace round her already emaciated neck, her face was blotchy, without rouge or ceruse, and her expression was one of barely contained indignation. A black silk fan, which she was shaking violently, accentuated the impression produced by this dramatic entrance.

'Madame,' said Nicolas with a little bow.

'Monsieur, I am told that you are a commissioner at the Châtelet, and that you have been given the task of investigating the horrible death of that unfortunate creature. My God, how is it possible? What was I saying? Oh, yes, you are investigating, Monsieur. Your name is not unknown to me. Were you presented to the late Queen? Or to Mesdames?'

'I had the good fortune to serve Madame Adélaïde, who often honoured me by inviting me to her hunts.'

'That's it! You're young Ranreuil, who was so appreciated by the King. How fortunate we are, Monsieur, to be dealing with someone so well born, even though . . . Monsieur, you must hear me.' She threw a fierce glance at Bourdeau. 'Who is this gentleman?'

'My deputy, Inspector Bourdeau. Fully the equal of myself.'

'If you say so! Monsieur, this is all so terrible, but it was bound to happen. I had been dreading it for a long time. One cannot live like this without running the risk of such a tragedy one day.'

'Madame, may I ask you to tell me whom I have the honour of addressing?'

'What, Monsieur? I am the Duchesse de La Vrillière and this is my house.'

# III

## KNOT OF VIPERS

There is no true friendship among those
who serve in the same house
LOPE DE VEGA

This majestic announcement only half surprised Nicolas, who had already realised who the lady was. He had glimpsed her on several occasions at Versailles. She was reputed to be sanctimonious and sour-tempered, but he knew how unreliable Court rumours were, how often unjust and biased. Reacting to her with studied indifference had seemed to him the best way to take the sting out of this excessive display of wounded pride. It was, he thought with a smile, a kind of moral purging.

'Madame,' he said, 'I am your obedient servant . . .' Without letting her catch her breath, he continued, 'I've been given to understand that Marguerite Pindron was part of your entourage, as a chambermaid.'

'That's going a little far, Monsieur. Entourage is a big and noble word. We're talking about my domestic servants, that's all — indeed, one of the most subordinate. I don't know how she came to be working here, it happened quite recently, and, I should add, without my consent.'

Nicolas knew that with this kind of witness, it was necessary to adopt one of two strategies: either attempt to restrain and channel their natural outpourings, or let them have their say and hope that within the flood of their words there would be some interesting flotsam.

'It's true,' resumed the duchesse, 'that I have never had a word to say in this house, and that most of those who serve me were chosen for reasons which have nothing to do with me and which I prefer not to know. Oh, Monsieur, the misfortune of having to be served . . .'

On this point, Nicolas observed, the duchesse's sentiment hardly differed from her husband's.

'Servants, Monsieur,' she continued, 'are detestable. Even their zeal is offensive and they're always so clumsy. They complain, but have no idea of the trouble they cause you. After all, they are only in such a position because God has seen fit to reduce them to a situation of servitude in this world in order to aid our infirmity while we remedy their poverty. To be honest, we earn a place in heaven for them by heaping humiliation on their heads, just as we earn it for ourselves by the care we take of them.'

'In a way, Madame,' said Bourdeau, 'they are privileged people who owe their salvation to you.'

She looked at him as if seeing him for the first time. 'This gentleman is right, it is one of the most favoured states. Here are wretches who find themselves living in opulent houses, where they benefit greatly from all that is essential to life. They get good meat and good wine every day, wear nice clothes, are well washed, well bedded, well heated, are given easy jobs to perform, and have too much leisure time. Why should they not be satisfied? I ask you. And when they fail us or make mistakes, should we speak to them with a gracious air, neither too quickly nor too loudly, as my father confessor suggests?'

She collapsed onto a *bergère* – her dress made a great sighing noise as it was squeezed into the chair – and again began beating the air irritably with her fan.

Nicolas took advantage of the pause to get a word in. 'May I ask, Madame, how the events of last night in your house were brought to your notice?'

'Why, by all the noise and commotion my people were making below my windows just before six o'clock. I should point out that I am a light sleeper. Alas, who, in my situation, would be able to rest peacefully?' She raised her eyes to heaven and her hands shook around the ebony handle of her fan. 'On the advice of my doctor, I'm accustomed to taking some drops of Hoffman's solution with syrup of marshmallow and orange flower. If they prove to be ineffective, I use something more efficient, a mixture of ether and alcohol. I often fall into a deep sleep in the early hours of the morning. So there would have to be a lot of noise to wake me, as was the case this morning.'

'Are you quite sure of the time, Madame?'

'Monsieur, I am able to tell the time by the clock in my room.'

'Was it dark?'

'Completely.'

'What happened then?'

'My head chambermaid came into the room in great agitation and told me that something terrible had happened in the servants' pantry.'

'Do you remember the exact words she used?'

'Monsieur, my memory is as good as my sight. When I questioned her about the noise, she said breathlessly that it was bound to happen, and that the Pindron girl had been found murdered in the roasting room.'

'Was that all she said?'

'Monsieur!'

'Forgive my insistence, Madame. I need to know exactly what happened. Did she mention the major-domo?'

'What do you mean? Why would she have done that?'

'Because, Madame, the major-domo was found lying, wounded and unconscious, beside Marguerite Pindron's body, and he is suspected of having murdered her then turned his weapon on himself.'

The Duchesse de La Vrillière seemed so astonished by this that, unless she was an exceptional actress, it was impossible to doubt her good faith.

Nicolas looked at the clock on the mantelpiece. 'Have you seen your chambermaid again since then?'

'She's been no good for anything all day,' replied the duchesse, 'and I told her to go and rest. These people have no self-control! Another of my maids has the little room next to my bedroom. I went back to bed and heard the duc coming back from Versailles. His coach and horses are so noisy! I woke up at midday and this other girl dressed me.'

'What's her name?'

'Jeannette.'

'And her surname?'

'Are you mocking me, Monsieur? Do you imagine I clutter my mind with the surnames of servants?'

'It seems to me, Madame, that you knew Marguerite Pindron's surname.'

'That's possible, Monsieur. My chief maid called her by that name.'

'And what is the name of your chief maid?'

'Eugénie.'

'Did Jeannette talk to you about what happened last night?'

'How could she, she didn't know anything! She hadn't left my apartments and hadn't seen anybody.'

'Madame, may I ask what you meant when you said, at the beginning of our interview, that "it was bound to happen"?'

The duchesse rose and with an abrupt gesture snapped her fan shut. Her face seemed suddenly to have hardened. 'Of course, Monsieur. I was simply repeating what Eugénie said. I didn't mean any harm by it.'

'I'm sorry, Madame,' insisted Nicolas, 'but you added that you'd been dreading the news for a long time.'

'Monsieur, please do not persist. The hand of God always strikes houses where his commandments are ignored.'

'That is a very general statement, and may apply in many cases. Do you think, Madame, that such an assertion would be enough to convince a magistrate, by which I mean a judge or procurator dealing with a murder case?'

'Are you threatening me? Under my own roof? Do you know to whom you are talking, Monsieur?'

'I was merely advising caution.'

'That's enough. I know what I still have to do.' With both hands, she gathered her pannier and strode out of the room in a great silky shiver of fabric.

Nicolas sighed. The higher one climbed the ladder of society, the less natural respect was shown for law and order.

'What a tough nut to crack!' muttered Bourdeau.

'Let's be lenient,' countered Nicolas. 'Think of the life she has to lead. The duc is no paragon and she has had a lot to bear. But by her very reticence, the good lady implies many things. Is she suggesting, for example, that the underlying cause of this tragedy lies in the state of her household?'

'We still have to establish,' said Bourdeau, 'if it has something to do with her husband's dissolute life or some kind of intrigue or rivalry among the many servants. I'm not convinced that this grand lady takes too much notice of what her people do. At most, she lends a distracted ear to her maids' gossip when they're dressing her in the morning.'

'We shall see. Go and fetch the two chambermaids. Provence will help you to find them. He can't be far away, he's always roaming the antechambers. At my disposal, admittedly!'

Nicolas walked to the hearth, which was blazing away. He felt cold. These big fires made your throat dry without warming you, except to roast your thighs when you got close to them. What a strange business! Despite the horror of what had happened, it appeared at first sight mundane and unremarkable. Everything seemed to point to an affair of the heart between a man of a certain age and a young girl. Yet there were many details that did not tally with the generally convergent observations and testimonies so far gathered. The picture which presented itself to Nicolas, the one everybody seemed to be trying to make him accept, made him rather suspect that, beneath its plain varnish, there had been a certain amount of retouching. And what of the mysterious fugitive prowling in the shadows of the Saint-Florentin mansion and disappearing after a last bloody embrace with one of the columns of the gate?

He was drawn from his reverie by Bourdeau's return, accompanied by a woman in an apron and cap. His first reaction was to wonder why she was trying to appear older and uglier than she was. No doubt it was to avoid any comparison with the duchesse. Her hair was drawn back under her cap, making her face more angular, but her features were regular and her complexion splendidly milky. She seemed to be deliberately sucking in her lips, which made her cheeks taut and gave the impression of a strong will. He asked her to sit down, but she shook her head and remained standing, leaning on the back of an armchair. It was late afternoon by now, and the light was gradually fading. The reflection of the flames played over her face, alternately lighting it and plunging it into wavering shadow. Nicolas waited, saying nothing, aware of the effect this silence usually had on witnesses. But no emotion showed on this woman's face, if indeed she felt any. Only the whiteness of her fingers on the upholstery of the armchair attested to the tension in her hands.

'Are you Eugénie, head chambermaid of the Duchesse de La Vrillière?'

'Yes, Commissioner. Eugénie Gouet.'

'How old are you? Are you married?'

'I was thirty last Saint Michel's day. I'm single.'

'How long have you worked here?'

'In the service of Madame, since 1762. The mansion hadn't even been built then. I was still a child . . .'

'Are you one of the oldest servants?'

'Of course. With Provence, Monseigneur's valet.'

'Tell me what happened this morning.'

'I was getting ready in my room on the second floor, when I heard cries. I rushed out to find the kitchen boy, Provence, the caretaker and the Swiss Guard. They all went to the servants' pantry. Jacques, the boy, had discovered two bodies, that of Marguerite, who was apparently dead, and that of Monsieur Missery, who was still breathing. Thinking that all this noise had woken Madame, I went up to inform her.'

'Where are your mistress's apartments?'

'On the first floor, in the left wing of the mansion. Monseigneur lodges in the right wing.'

'Good. Let's take everything in order. What time was it when you went down?'

'About seven,' she said, without any hesitation.

'Was it dark?'

'Completely.'

That was a point on which everyone agreed, thought Nicolas.

'Of course,' he said, 'Provence had a dark lantern with him.'

It was a crude trap, and he wasn't sure she would fall into it. It was obvious the blow had struck home, but she recovered immediately.

'I don't know . . . I think . . . The sight of blood bothered me. It was all lit up. How? I couldn't say.'

Nicolas did not insist: that would have revealed that he was trying to trick her. The mention of the blood intrigued him. Did she mean the blood at the scene of the crime or the blood on Missery's body?

'Was your mistress asleep?'

'No, she was standing in the space between her bed and the wall, very angry, waiting to find out the reason for all the chaos — that was her word.'

'Hadn't she taken her sleeping draught the previous evening?'

She stared at him again with her grey eyes. There was something beautiful in her mixture of sadness and severity.

'Sometimes she takes it, sometimes she doesn't,' she said, slightly too curtly. 'Sometimes she remembers, sometimes she forgets, sometimes she takes more than she should.'

'But if she did take the medication, as she herself states, the noise should not have awoken her. And besides, you're the one who prepares it for her. Did you give it to her last night?'

He had thrown out this assertion at random, and had no evidence to back it up, but he had clearly hit the target, to judge by her agitation.

'No . . . Yes . . . At least what there was of it.'

'What does that mean?'

'The bottles had got broken and I was only able to collect a few drops. I was planning to get some more today from the apothecary.'

'A few drops of the potion?'

'No, of the ether and alcohol.'

'Can you show me what's left of those bottles?'

The question was a specific one, and there was no way of evading it. Nicolas was pressing home his advantage, convinced that he had put his finger on something — something that might be unconnected to the case but certainly seemed to be disturbing the duchesse's head chambermaid.

'I threw them into the cesspool, for fear that someone might get hurt,' she replied. 'If Madame had found them, it would have disturbed her peace of mind, for which I am responsible.'

These skilful excuses did not need any further commentary. She was a strong sparring partner, thought Nicolas, used to living by her wits and even able to use her own unease as a strength, presenting herself as an honest person who has been thrown into a state of shock.

He changed the subject. 'What can you tell us about Jean Missery?' he asked.

Eugénie's face turned slightly red. 'I am a chambermaid,' she replied, 'and he is a major-domo. Our tasks are different and keep us apart. It's Madame who deals with the women. However, he does sometimes reprimand us . . .'

'What about?'

'I don't know. Something about candles. It's one thing for our masters to exert their authority over us, but to obey those to whom they delegate part of their power, to be the servant of a servant, now that's something I can't stand!'

It was such a vehement assertion that Bourdeau, who was standing behind Eugénie, underlined it with an eloquent wink.

'I see,' said Nicolas. 'I suppose that kind of acrimony is perfectly common in large houses. What about the victim? What was your opinion of her? Like you, she worked for Madame, you knew her well. She must have been a friend of yours, with similar interests.'

This time, Eugénie made a contemptuous grimace. 'You can think that if you like! How could I have anything in common with that creature from the gutter, whose work consisted of emptying the buckets and cleaning the floors? She was introduced here by poor Missery. God knows where he'd met her! Everything about her suggested a dissolute origin. She led him by the nose, believe me. Her engagement here was a trap, and our major-domo fell into it. He lost his head and took advantage of Monseigneur's trust to impose a girl like that on Madame. If she'd at least been honest with him! But just think, Commissioner, she used to receive a suitor – a young one this time – here, in this very house. She would go out at night, even though Madame demands that we lead a good, regular life. She didn't suspect a thing! Just think, she'd got her claws into a widower, such a fine man, a major-domo to boot! She didn't respect him, even though he was so good, and so trusting.'

'In a word, you're saying that Marguerite Pindron was Jean Missery's mistress?'

'That's very definitely what I'm saying. Ask anyone. He'd become the laughing stock of the household. He didn't deserve it, he could have . . .'

She had been on the point of blurting something out.

'Could have what?'

'I know what I mean.'

'Do you think him capable of punishing himself?'

'He has a fiery temper. He gets angry quickly, and sometimes can't control himself. Everything about him is excessive.'

'One last thing,' said Nicolas. 'What did you mean when you told your mistress that it was bound to happen?'

She looked up, and there was a hint of provocation in her expression. 'That loose morals have fatal consequences. God teaches us that.'

'I see that we are in a very religious house,' said Nicolas with a smile. 'Thank you.'

She withdrew, bumping into Bourdeau as she did so, without a word of excuse. The two police officers looked at each other, each one sifting through his impressions for himself.

'She certainly has character!' said Nicolas. 'A somewhat enigmatic charm and a superb complexion. A bit thin, though.'

'You're not exactly sticking your neck out in saying that,' replied Bourdeau. 'As for myself, I'm less compassionate. She's trying to make us believe that butter wouldn't melt in her mouth, but I'd sum her up in this way: self-control, hatred and admiration. Self-control in the skilful way she makes innuendos, hatred towards the victim, even now, and admiration for Missery. But watch out! From admiration to love is but a step . . . And that step may have been taken.'

'I noticed that, too, as well as other contradictions,' Nicolas agreed. 'Here is a man whose authority is resented, but whose kindness, trust and good nature are praised. All these remarks are important, and I would wager that others will enlighten us on the relationship between the chambermaid and the major-domo. I don't exclude the possibility that there's something there. Bring in Jeannette. I assume she's in the antechamber. I hope Eugénie hasn't instructed her in what to say.'

As soon as the girl came in, he realised that someone had upset her. Her careworn expression, her tear-stained face, the way she was twisting a handkerchief in her hands: all these things revealed a terror that was in no way justified by the prospect of an interrogation. He felt sorry for her: she was little more than a child.

'My dear,' he began, in a fatherly tone, 'we need your help. What's your name and how old are you?'

'Jeannette,' she murmured in a faint voice, 'Jeannette Le Bas. I was born in Yvetot, in Normandy, and I'm seventeen.'

'How long have you been in service?'

'Two years, Monsieur. Since Saint Jean's day.'

'Sit down. Don't be afraid. Tell me what happened.'

She looked about her like an animal caught in a trap. 'I have nothing to say . . . Have pity, Monsieur . . . They can hear us.'

'Come now,' said Bourdeau, 'enough of this childishness!' He strode in turn to each of the doors and opened them. 'As you see,' he resumed, 'there's no one eavesdropping. What are you afraid of?'

She looked up and, as if taking a plunge into deep water, began speaking. 'Nobody. It's just that I'm not used to it. This morning, I heard a noise in Madame's bedroom, and so—'

'Wait, slow down. Where do you sleep?'

'On a bunk in the garderobe.'

'Does the room have an opening?'

'Yes, Monsieur, a window looking out on the main courtyard.'

'And you say it was your mistress who woke you?'

She blushed with embarrassment. 'Because she was using her commode.'

'Roughly what time was that?'

'I don't know, it was still dark. Then Eugénie arrived, yelling so much it was hard to understand what she was saying.'

'But you understood some of it?'

'Just that something terrible had happened. She mentioned blood, and a knife. I was so scared I put my fingers in my ears.'

'What happened then?'

'Madame went back to bed. I stayed where I was, waiting for her to call me. Which she did at midday.'

'I'd like to be clear about one thing,' said Nicolas, gravely. 'Was your mistress awake when Eugénie arrived?'

'Wide awake, I'd just seen her in the garderobe. What have I said? Is there something wrong? Oh God, protect me! I don't want to lose my job.'

'You won't lose anything at all if you tell us the truth. I promise you that. Did you know Marguerite?'

'Of course,' she replied, sniffling. 'She was very sweet and kind to me. She even wanted to teach me to read and write. I really liked her, though I shouldn't say it.'

'Why not?'

'Madame and Eugénie thought she was a bad girl.'

'And what was your opinion?'

'I think she'd had a lot of bad things happen to her, but despite all that, she had a good heart. For the rest, I don't judge.'

'Did she confide in you?'

'She told me she was very tired.'

'Tired of her work?'

'That, too. But especially the things her suitor made her do.'

'Jean Missery?'

The girl opened her eyes wide in surprise and began trembling. 'No, not him! The young man who called on her some nights.'

'Do you know his name?'

'No, she called him Aide.'

'Aide? That's unusual. Are you sure that was his name?'

'Yes.'

'What about the major-domo?'

'Oh, him! . . . He was always after her, and even . . .' Suddenly, she began shaking uncontrollably, she threw her head back, and her limbs tensed. Nicolas's first thought was that he was again confronted with a phenomenon he had once before observed in a young servant girl. Helped by Bourdeau, he laid her out on a bench. Gradually, the attack receded, and she regained consciousness, surprised to see the two men bending over her.

'My dear,' said Nicolas, 'you must calm down, nothing is going to happen to you. I've promised to look after you and I'm going to keep my word. Pierre, be so kind as to walk back with her.'

Once alone, Nicolas reflected. Of course, he was making progress with his investigation, but he had a growing feeling that the case was proving to be more complex than he had thought at first. The paths that might lead to the truth kept dividing, meeting again, merging, with so many abrupt and unexpected turns that you ended up losing your way in frustration. Why had the young servant girl had a sudden seizure just as she was talking about the major-domo? He vowed to mention it to Dr Semacgus. He recalled past conversations about strange cases of girls prone to that kind of attack. Clearly, none of the women or girls in the Saint-Florentin mansion were indifferent to Jean Missery. Bourdeau reappeared, followed by a young man with a waddling gait. Tow-coloured hair framed a regular, pimply face. His forehead was covered in sweat, and he was pulling on the lapels of his linen jacket as if trying to draw it tighter around himself.

Nicolas launched into the interrogation without further ado. 'Are you Jacques Despiard, the kitchen boy? How old are you?'

'That's me, Monsieur. I'm twenty-five.'

'How did you come to discover the bodies?'

'Every morning, I open the kitchens and light the stoves and the hearths in the roasting room. It takes a while to get things heated up properly, especially to get rid of the smoke. I always begin with the roasting room, because that's where the fire takes longest to get going. This morning, no sooner had I entered than I saw all that blood and the two bodies.'

He had started stammering, and passed his hand over his face as if to dismiss the vision. Nicolas took advantage of this pause.

'So it was light in the roasting room?'

The young man grew agitated, looking wildly from one of the two impassive police officers to the other, as if searching for help or inspiration.

'Do you understand my question?' asked Nicolas. 'At what time did you open the kitchen?'

'At six, I think.'

'I see. So it was dark?'

'If you say so.'

'The commissioner isn't saying anything,' Bourdeau cut in, irritably. 'This is about you, and we'd be grateful to you if you could remember what happened.'

'The inspector's right,' said Nicolas gently. 'How could you see the bodies in a dark basement room at six in the morning, at this time of year?'

'Did you have a candle?' asked Bourdeau.

'I can't remember . . . I don't know. You're confusing me. All that blood . . . Leave me alone!'

'Calm down. We'll come back to that when you've recovered. In the meantime, tell me about the victim.'

The young man's eyes shone through his tears. 'She was so beautiful! She always had a kind word. What a monster!'

'Who are you talking about?'

'The major-domo, Missery, of course. He killed her, he wanted all of them. But they said . . .'

'They said what?'

'Nothing.'

'You need to understand that, if you withhold the truth, you could well end up in a dungeon in the Châtelet prison, where other means will be used to make you talk. What can you tell us about Missery?'

The young man hesitated. 'A nasty piece of work,' he said at last. 'He takes it out on everyone. He sets traps for us to fall into, so he can throw us out on the street. To replace us with his pets, I suppose. He even threatened Monsieur Charles.'

'The valet?'

'Yes, Commissioner. Charles Bibard. Missery was planning to report him to Monseigneur for reselling pieces of candle from the house.'

'Perhaps Missery is just an honest man who can't tolerate certain excesses?'

The witness's face was red with indignation. 'Him, honest! He's trading illicitly with all the suppliers, taking a commission on every delivery and building up a nice little nest egg for himself. As if his wife's fortune wasn't enough for him. And he may have wept for her, but he's certainly had plenty of consolation since.'

'What do you know about that inheritance?'

'Only what everyone said. In her will, his wife left him all her fortune, but it would revert to her family if he died – unless, of course, he'd remarried and had children.'

'Thank you for your information. Try to clarify your whereabouts at the time of the murder, and we'll speak again.'


The young man fled as if he had a hundred devils at his heels. Provence appeared and announced formally, 'Commissioner, the doctor says that Monsieur Missery has regained consciousness.'

Nicolas and Bourdeau followed him to the other wing of the Saint-Florentin mansion. The inspector noted with curiosity the route they were taking through the maze-like building. On their arrival, and having dismissed the valet, they saw the major-domo sitting up in bed, propped up by pillows, his chest bandaged with pieces of his torn shirt. His eyes were closed and his head drooped over his chest. Monsieur de Gévigland was taking his pulse and passing a bottle of salts under his nose with the other hand.

'I thought,' said Nicolas, 'that your patient had regained consciousness?'

'So did I,' replied the doctor. 'But no sooner was he conscious than he fell into a swoon. It's only a slight relapse. He's finding it hard to extricate himself from the mists of sleep.'

At that moment, the man sneezed and his eyes opened then closed again, dazzled by the light. He was shaken by a coughing fit. Moaning, he put his hand on his side, where his wound was. Gradually, his breathing became easier and more sonorous. Meanwhile, Bourdeau was examining every nook and cranny of the room. While the doctor had his back to him, he took, with a wink to the commissioner, several objects from a drawer in the chest. Truly, his deputy was incomparable and never missed an opportunity. He continued his investigations discreetly. Now Missery was staring in surprise at the faces peering down at him.

'I don't feel well,' he said in a thick voice.

Nicolas noticed a strange smell emanating from his mouth.

'What are you doing in my room?' asked the major-domo. 'What's happened?'

Although his features were drawn, his face was still virile. His sparse grey hair, however, made him look older, forming a kind of crown around the baldness that had already pushed his hairline back off his forehead. His eyes went from one face to another like those of a frightened animal. He was biting his lip, giving the impression that his mind, still wandering in the mists of unconsciousness, was engaged in intense reflection.

'My dear fellow,' said the doctor, 'it is for you to enlighten us. We found you—'

Nicolas seized him by the arm to stop him saying any more. 'Asleep and wounded,' he said. 'I am a police commissioner at the Châtelet. Could you tell us what happened to you?'

'I have no idea what's going on,' replied the major-domo. 'I went to bed very late, and now I wake up and find you here! Did someone attack me while I was asleep?'

'Come on,' said Nicolas. 'Make an effort to collect your thoughts. We need to know your exact whereabouts last night.'

'Monseigneur was away. He was at Versailles with the King. Madame, indisposed as she so often is, did not dine. At about eleven o'clock, I had a last look around the house and then came up to bed.'

'Did you go down to the kitchens?'

The man showed no particular emotion. 'I had no reason to do so, the fires had been out since Saturday. So I came back to my room.'

'Did you have a candle?'

'Yes, you can see the candlestick there, on the desk.'

'And then?'

'I undressed, blew out the candle, and fell asleep.'

'The candle in that candlestick?'

'Of course.'

'Where was it?'

'Here.' And he pointed to a small marquetry bedside table on his left, half hidden by the bed curtains.

'Why is it on the desk now?' asked Nicolas. 'Was it you who moved it?'

Missery shook his head.

'You, then, Doctor?'

'Certainly not.'

'Go on,' said Nicolas.

'I fell asleep.'

'Did you have any visitors?'

He sensed a kind of imperceptible hesitation in the way the major-domo replied, 'No, nobody.'

'Doctor,' said Nicolas, 'may I have a word with you for a moment in private?'

He drew him into the corridor, leaving Bourdeau to watch over the wounded man.

'In your opinion, could that wound, which you described as benign, have led to a significant loss of blood?'

'It's strange that you should ask me that question,' replied the doctor. 'Just now, when I was replacing the bandage, I had another look at the cut. No vein or major vessel was damaged. There was no haemorrhage. And there are hardly any bloodstains on the man's breeches!'

'That tallies with my own observation. So what do you make of his loss of consciousness?'

'Oh, you shouldn't let that go to your head: some sensitive people faint at the slightest nick. There's no accounting for it! Anyway, our man doesn't appear to be aware of the gravity of the situation, and certainly isn't reacting like someone who has just tried to kill himself.'

They went back into the room.

'How is it, Monsieur,' Nicolas resumed, 'that you are not in your nightshirt?'

The man touched himself, and seemed only now to become aware of what he was wearing. 'I have no idea. I put on a freshly ironed nightshirt last night.'

'It's nowhere to be found,' said Bourdeau.

Missery seemed both appalled and frightened by this observation.

'Monsieur,' said Nicolas, 'what was your relationship with the Duchesse de La Vrillière's chambermaid, Marguerite Pindron?'

For the first time since the beginning of the interrogation, Missery looked up with a kind of contained fury. 'She's my mistress. Everyone will tell you that and it's true, and I defy anyone to . . .' He broke off.

'To what?' asked Nicolas.

'I don't know.'

'Jean Missery, you have to face certain facts. You are accused and suspected of having murdered your mistress, Marguerite Pindron, and of having tried to kill yourself in order to escape the just punishment for such a crime. As of now, you are in the hands of the law. On my orders, your condition permitting, you will be taken to the royal prison of the Châtelet to await the decision of the Criminal Lieutenant and an investigation of the case. This arrest does not imply a final judgement on your actions, but forms part of the necessary precautionary measures when there has been a murder. I can assure you that everything will be done to either invalidate or confirm the facts and presumptions for which you may well feel the full weight of the law.'

As he listened to Nicolas's solemn words, the major-domo collapsed on his bed, weeping, gasping and wringing his hands. He was soon nothing but a shapeless heap.

'Bourdeau,' said Nicolas, 'call the officers and have this man conducted to his destination. Make sure he's bound and guarded.'

Nicolas was still haunted by the memory of a sad case in which a suspect had killed himself in his cell. He felt that a surfeit of precautions and the observation of simple rules was necessary to avoid any recurrence of such a tragedy. Monsieur de Gévigland and Bourdeau helped Missery to his feet. He was made to put on his coat, which the commissioner took hold of for a moment and examined attentively. Bourdeau picked up the shoes and had a good look at them before helping the major-domo to put them on. The officer at the door of the room called his colleagues, and the suspect was taken away, closely guarded by the men from the Châtelet.

Nicolas turned to the doctor. 'Monsieur,' he said, 'I thank you for your valuable assistance and your very helpful comments. We will doubtless have need of your testimony.'

'I am at your disposal, Commissioner. Rest assured of my continued assistance. In addition, I would be honoured and delighted if one day, at your convenience, you would come to lunch or dinner. I live in Rue Saint-Honoré, opposite the Capuchin monastery. My wife and I would be happy to count you among the regular visitors to our dwelling.'

He wrapped himself in his cloak, adjusted his cocked hat, bowed to the two police officers and went out. Nicolas had been struck by the benevolence emanating from the doctor, and the elegant simplicity of his attire, embellished with a ribbon tying up his natural, unpowdered salt-and-pepper hair. Once the doctor had gone out, Bourdeau gave a slight bow.

'Everyone kowtows to the marquis,' he said. 'No sooner do they know him than they guess his rank, even if he calls himself Le Floch. Monsieur de Gévigland made no mistake! He fell into your snare.'

Nicolas did not reply to this gibe, which his friend had not been able to refrain from coming out with. To him, Bourdeau was all of a piece, with his faults and his qualities, the latter far outweighing the former in his judgement. The inspector was truly devoted to him, had twice saved his life, and had not hesitated to risk his career for his sake. Having fallen from favour together, they were now coming back into the light of day, more united than ever. What accumulated resentment, what brooded-over bitterness nourished these attacks of acrimony which Bourdeau seemed unable to control? The merest trifle could revive an unknown wound. The tragic death of his father, torn to pieces by a boar during a royal hunt, did not explain everything. The cruel game of respect and contempt which underlay a society based on the privileges of birth was something he found hard to accept. There was also a touch of possessive jealousy towards those who yielded to the commissioner's innate seductive charms. Their attentions disgusted the inspector, who always dreamed of an exclusive friendship. Fortunately, Noblecourt, La Borde and Semacgus escaped this devouring jealousy. They did not in any way threaten long-established habits, and their own feelings for the inspector were a bastion and an anchor in his life. Yes, the sensible thing was not to respond to his remarks. Nicolas dreaded that the regular recurrence of these ideas might one day lead his friend to take up extreme positions, the consequences of which he would be unable to control. It was an abscess that needed to be lanced, and perhaps he would make up his mind to speak to him about it. But the hour had not yet come for that discussion.

'Did you see the shoes?' Bourdeau went on. 'Not a trace of blood. Nothing. Clean and polished.'

'Perhaps he cleaned them, we'll have to ask him.'

Nicolas wrote something in his little black notebook, then asked Bourdeau what time it was.

'That's what I thought, it's getting late. But it's vital that we hear all the testimonies today. Let's divide up the task. I'll question the Swiss Guard and you have a word with the caretaker. Then we'll meet again and see what we've come up with.'

They again found the valet waiting for them in the shadows of the corridor. Once more, the thought crossed Nicolas's mind that the valet had not left them for a single second. Was he simply being diligent, to the point of obsequiousness, or had someone told him to keep an eye on everything they did? He led them into a new maze of corridors. They went past the linen room and came to some adjoining quarters. Provence pointed out to Bourdeau the entrance to the caretaker's lodge, then, taking another staircase, he led the commissioner to the Swiss Guard's sentry box on the ground floor below, at the corner of the left facade, near the gate. The man, who was tall and stooped, had taken off his wig, and his cranium gleamed in the candlelight. He immediately put his wig back on. He was truly monumental. Nicolas recalled that the largest houses in the city specifically sought out such giants to fill this kind of office. This one was so tall that the commissioner had to look up at him.

'You know who I am, you welcomed me earlier. What is your name and how old are you?'

'Pierre Miquete, about forty.' He did not wait for the questions. 'This is what I can tell you. There was a loud cry from the courtyard. I should tell you that the window of my bedroom looks out on the gate. I was eating my morning soup. I should tell you that I put in leftover dry bread, which the kitchen boy passes to me. It's better in soup. So, yes, the cry . . . I went running. There was Jacques, doing the same. Yes, I should tell you his name is Jacques, like the caretaker. Everyone was crying, "Murder! Murder!"'

'Everyone?'

'Provence, Eugénie, the caretaker and Jacques.'

'Was it light?'

'I don't remember. The emotion, you know. Seems to me . . .'

'Did you see the bodies?'

'Certainly not! The slightest drop of blood makes me faint.'

Nicolas risked something that sometimes worked. 'Were you in love with her?'

The response was rapid, but not what he had expected. 'With that girl? Of course not. I should tell you, Commissioner, that I've accumulated a certain amount since I've been in Monseigneur's service. I need something a bit more substantial than a little streetwalker. But the other one doesn't want me. And they all warmed his bed, her like all the rest. I could weep, I'm that besotted, but she doesn't want to know anything about me.'

'Who are you talking about?'

'I'm talking about Eugénie burning the midnight oil with Missery, but now that he's abandoned her, she still won't look at me.'

*Good Lord!* thought Nicolas. But he asked only, 'And where were you last night?'

'In my room.'

Nicolas went back to his study on the mezzanine. He wondered if he should respond immediately to the minister's wish to be informed of the initial results of the investigation. Nothing that he could tell him seemed likely to arouse his interest. Should he bother him with a host of bizarre details and vague, contradictory testimonies? Unlike Monsieur de Sartine, the Duc de La Vrillière had little taste for the nitty-gritty of police work: he needed something to get his teeth into. It would be better to hold off for the moment.

Nicolas sat staring at the fire. His mind flew back to the limbo of his childhood, and he saw himself at Guérande, watching rapt as the logs collapsed in a cloud of sparks. Night was falling by the time he returned to reality. This mansion oozed dissimulation and hatred: it was an impression that gripped him like a feeling of suffocation. All the elements had been in place for a tragedy. All the witnesses might have had reasons to hate the victim, but all of them were equally falling over each other to disparage the major-domo. It still remained to be established that the solution did indeed lie within the walls of the Saint-Florentin mansion. What was the role of that mysterious stranger whose bloody footprints had guided him as far as the balcony? Of course, that could have been an attempt to divert suspicion from the inhabitants of the house and to lead the investigators along a false path. He reflected for a long time. When Bourdeau entered the room, now dimly lit by the last gleams of the dying fire, he found him with his chin in his hand and his eyes staring into space.

'Good hunting, Pierre?'

'The caretaker, Jacques Blain, twenty-eight years old, well built, a bit of a lady killer, was mad about the chambermaid,' declared Bourdeau. 'Didn't see a thing. Just went to fetch the doctor from Rue Saint-Honoré. He hates Missery, in fact he hates the whole household. This mansion is a real cesspool of wickedness!'

'What else?'

'What else? A stew made with three rabbits, for one man. I saw the skins hanging in his window. He did me the honour of letting me try it.'

'Did you like the seasoning?'

'The sauce was a little thin. It didn't even cover the meat.'

'And what conclusion do you draw from that?'

'Where I come from, we mix the blood with vinegar to thicken the stew at the last moment and give the sauce more taste. The fact remains, three rabbits are a lot for one man. He even wanted to give me a second helping.'

'Does the mansion have a rabbit hutch?'

'Yes, in the inner courtyard.'

'We'll have a look. Any other discoveries?'

'You saw me taking some objects from the major-domo's chest of drawers. Here they are.'

The inspector had placed two boxes on a pedestal table. Nicolas leaned over them.

'Well, well! Some Sultana's Aphrodisiac and some pastilles of cantharides. Does Monsieur Missery have a few problems performing?'

'And that's not all,' said Bourdeau. 'In Marguerite's room, I found, hidden at the back of a cupboard, whole sacks full of pieces of candle. There has indeed been trafficking, but she was the culprit!'

'Three rabbits for a single man, a Don Juan who needs chemical help, and as much wax as you could wish! The plot thickens, and so does our investigation.'

# IV

## CONFUSION

*Ab hoc cadavere quidquam mihi opis expetebam?*

From this corpse left without burial, what resources could I draw?

CICERO

Sitting at a small pedestal table in Monsieur de Noblecourt's bedroom, Nicolas was just making a start on his third slice of Mainz ham. He poured himself another glass of light red wine. On his return, late in the evening, Catherine had put together this robust midnight supper and brought everything up to the bedroom. The master of the house, who had been about to go to bed and was alerted by his dog, Cyrus, of Nicolas's arrival, had rung down to make sure the commissioner was informed that he wished to speak to him. At his age you didn't need much sleep, either because your aches and pains kept you awake or because your happy or bitter memories of a long life led you into a half-dozing state of reverie. He took particular pleasure in these evening meetings in the course of which Nicolas would confide in him, taking careful note of his ever-sensible remarks. The magistrate's existence was now confined to his house, apart from a few ceremonial visits, his daily walk as prescribed by Tronchin, his doctor from Geneva, and the few special evenings when the splendours of his table were lavished on those close to him. Having devoured the ham, Nicolas next tackled a dish of orange and almond pastries all shiny with icing sugar. Two lustful pairs of eyes converged on this marvel: one belonged to the host, his mouth greedily half open, and the other to Mouchette, the cat sitting on his lap. From her difficult early days, the poor animal had retained an insatiable appetite which nothing could discourage and which extended to dishes not usually much appreciated by the feline species. Cyrus, ever the teacher, would watch over his young friend, always ready to instruct her, firmly but gently, in good manners. The old dog was indebted to her: his new responsibilities as the elder partner, wise in the ways of the house, had rejuvenated him. Monsieur de Noblecourt shook himself and adjusted his nightcap, as if wanting to break the spell the food and wine had cast on him. He delicately served himself a drop of amber-coloured herb tea from a small but thick Chinese porcelain teapot filled with hot water and maintained at the ideal temperature.

'Alas,' he sighed, tasting the beverage, 'here I am, reduced to the great King's diet! A compote of prunes and a sage tea. Fagon himself would not object.'[1]

'I assume your lunch and dinner are more abundant,' remarked Nicolas.

'Of course, but farewell the wonderful excesses I once enjoyed! One day, you'll see what it costs to restrain oneself.'

'Go on, complain! The world passes over you, leaving few traces. If you don't yield to temptations, you'll remain a young man.'

'That's enough, you flatterer. You'd do better to tell me about your day. But before that, let me tell you the latest news. A friend of mine, who came to lunch . . .'

'So you lunched in style?'

'I nibbled,' said Noblecourt with a laugh, 'and so did he. This friend of mine, as I was saying, who is well informed about the gossip at Versailles, not to mention what is said in the ministries of foreign courts, thinks — and this will interest you — that the Queen was not very happy that Monsieur de Sartine was chosen as Minister for the Navy. She's protecting him out of consideration for Choiseul, whose friend he was. She would have preferred him to succeed the Duc de La Vrillière as Minister of the King's Household. She was sorry to see that they had placed the former Lieutenant General of Police in a department so unsuited to his talents.'

'The Duc de La Vrillière does not appear to have fallen out of favour,' observed Nicolas. 'They say that the King is not on speaking terms with him because of his very existence, but Maurepas is his brother-in-law. And as for Sartine, his talents suit him for any kind of position, however distant from those fields he particularly favours.'

'Of course!' Monsieur de Noblecourt agreed. '*Secundo*, the mood of Mesdames, and especially of Madame Adélaïde, has become increasingly bitter as their influence has lessened. The Queen is said to have developed a certain bias against them, from which she will not depart. If they behave themselves, fine, but she won't tolerate any excessive pretensions, and the kind of conceit they're occasionally prone to will be repressed.'

'Mesdames have aged badly,' remarked Nicolas.

He remembered with nostalgia the radiant horsewoman in her hunting costume . . . Fourteen years had gone by since his first encounter with Madame Adélaïde in the course of a lively jaunt.

'I fear that the deplorable aberrations attributed to the late King opened the way to all kinds of knaves and rascals,' observed Noblecourt. 'We saw a succession of disturbances, scandals, injustices and upheavals. Morals and principles went by the board, and everything was left to chance. Now only the wicked remain on the scene to face a spineless government, and among them there is a spirit of intrigue and conspiracy of an intensity without precedent in this kingdom. The most sacred duties are forgotten and nothing is respected, nothing is safe from the blackest horrors.'

'Your friend seems to me quite well informed,' said Nicolas, choking on a pastry. 'And quite bitter, too.'

There was a silence. 'I won't conceal it from you any longer,' Monsieur de Noblecourt said at last. 'It was the Maréchal de Richelieu who honoured me with his visit. He stayed nearly two hours.'

It seemed to Nicolas that the maréchal, 'old Court' if anyone was, played almost no part in affairs of State now, even though, as First Gentleman of the Bedchamber, he still appeared at Versailles. Rebuffs and disdain had no effect on him: he continued to impose his presence on the new King, who looked at him without seeing him and paid him no heed. In these conditions, it was not surprising that he remembered his old friends, and Monsieur de Noblecourt, always susceptible to the attentions of the great lord, offered him the opportunity to harbour still the illusion of his own importance.

'Now I understand,' said Nicolas. 'The maréchal is champing at the bit, ever hoping for what will never come again. As I'm sure you know, his trial is dragging on in the *parlement* and is causing a scandal.'

'Not surprisingly,' said Noblecourt, again lowering his voice. 'He's accused by the opposing party, Madame de Saint-Ginest, of forgery and of bribing witnesses. They say the proceedings are alarming and the depositions unimaginably long!'

The candle in one of the candlesticks sputtered and went out, plunging the room into semi-darkness.

'That's all too true. Does he at least still seem all right?'

'The bile of the whole thing has affected his mind and he, who was always so carefree, has become embittered and endlessly repeats the same wicked barbs with which you are familiar. The things he comes out with!' Noblecourt raised a sententious finger. 'A bad word sometimes tells us more than ten beautiful sentences. He has dreamed all his life of joining the council. *Aut causa, aut nihil.*'

'No doubt,' said Nicolas. 'But what infirmity of mind makes him think he still has a future at his age? Why doesn't he prefer history, to which he contributed so much? Why doesn't he talk about his victories and the glory that went with them?'

'Alas, he lacks two essential qualities! Virtue and perspective. Concerned as he is with the impression he makes, he ought to stop complaining about the faults of the time. Serenity resides only in the soul of an honest man, and the maréchal is anything but that. But what about you? Tell me about your day.'

The former procurator sank into his armchair, his eyes half closed. Mouchette, having found nothing substantial to satisfy her appetite, began cleaning herself meticulously. Nicolas launched into a precise account, taking care not to omit any detail. He had sometimes noted Monsieur de Noblecourt's curious ability to absorb the facts of a case. His reflections often led to observations that seemed strange at first, but frequently proved to be wise and far-sighted. Nicolas's account was punctuated with exclamations of satisfaction and surprise, and when he had finished Noblecourt was silent for some time, while Nicolas, made thirsty by his speech and the salt in the ham, finished off the bottle of red wine from Champagne, more tawny-coloured than red in fact, and invigoratingly light.

'First, I must congratulate you,' Noblecourt said at last. 'Out of favour in the spring, back in favour by autumn! That's a disgrace to be envied! Here you are, back in the saddle, and I'm sure Monsieur Lenoir, in whose good faith I continue to believe, will reconsider his prejudices. I pray to heaven that the affair into which you have been drawn is not a trap intended to destroy the greatest expectations! You shake your head? Think about it. The Duc de La Vrillière has gone over the head of his Lieutenant General of Police. He's not doing you a good deed. He's involving you in an affair that concerns his own house and his own domestic staff. He himself is not so well thought of at Court, every week his exile is announced as being imminent, and only his kinship with the First Minister protects him. On the one hand, he places you in a situation in which you might annoy your own chief, and on the other, he drags you down with him in his fall, if such is the outcome. So follow my advice: tell Monsieur Lenoir everything. He will be grateful to you, and your combined interests will withstand the storms. Continue to appear at Court and try to keep the King informed. What happens privately in great kingdoms cannot leave him indifferent. In this way, you will protect your rear and be prepared for any eventuality.'

'That sounds like sensible advice to me,' said Nicolas, 'and I shall certainly follow it.'

'As for the case itself, it couldn't be more delicate. Cases involving domestics always are. It is a world in which treachery reigns. Take your chambermaids: a woman who serves another needs much more skill and flexibility than a man in the same situation. There is no middle way: a chambermaid is either in a position of the most gratifying intimacy or in one of the most humiliating dependence. A servant, if he wants to maintain his position, must always have a ready answer, anticipate his master's whim, remedy his bad mood, flatter his self-esteem, and, last but not least, feign sincerity. All this implies falsehood and deception. A noble house is a state in miniature, with its plots, its alliances, its dissimulation and, sometimes, its humble devotion.'

Noblecourt reflected for a moment before continuing.

'Add to all that one vital question. Why did the Duc de La Vrillière send for you? You are not, I wager, fooled by the compliments and vain protestations of goodwill he has lavished on you. He knows you're on the sidelines at the moment and sends for you. All right. But why? Is it because he thinks that anyone can be bought, and that a man on the sidelines, investigating a crime committed in a minister's mansion, might turn a blind eye to certain things?'

'Do you think him capable of that?'

Monsieur de Noblecourt sat up in his chair and struck the armrests with his hands. 'I am surprised, Monsieur,' he exclaimed, 'that, after so many years at the highest level of the police force, you still have that bedrock of innocence which is a tribute to your good heart but reduces your perceptiveness. But what can I do? Your old friend owes it to himself to be the devil's advocate, the worst is always a possibility and certainly shouldn't be ruled out *a priori*. I remember how hurt you were when, being yourself personally implicated in a crime, I was forced to investigate you. It was not that I believed you guilty, but the possibility had to be considered before it could be ruled out.[2] To tell the true from the false with full knowledge of the facts, one must first abandon the idea that one possesses the truth.'

Monsieur de Noblecourt always surprised Nicolas. This affable man had a strength and an authority which rarely manifested themselves but which, for that very reason, were all the more striking.

'To return to your victim,' Noblecourt went on, 'look into her origins. That's a procurator speaking. As you know, there are rules governing the servant classes, rules it's not advisable to contravene. A domestic cannot enter into service without declaring his or her name or nickname, his place of birth and where he has served. He must present a notice from his previous master, without concealing anything. He cannot leave him without his consent and a certificate. Unmarried servants of both sexes cannot have private rented rooms without the written permission of their masters. They are forbidden to give or lend their lodgings to tramps or other suspicious characters. A good police force should also be concerned with routine laws. When regulations and conventions are circumvented, we enter a shifting, uncertain terrain, which often conceals strange phenomena. The rule itself is seldom meaningful, but its lack sometimes is.'

A long silence ensued. Monsieur de Noblecourt sighed, pleased with his turn of phrase. His eyes wandered over the shadowy areas of the room, as if making an inventory of its details.

'Oh, what merit your profession possesses!' he resumed. 'The first is that of diversion. Monsieur Tronchin, my doctor, told me one day that, unable to purge certain catarrhs, he diverted them to another less dangerous part of the body . . . Dying should appear to us a natural, impartial accident. I am a happy man, in spite of everything. As a magistrate, I may have been cast aside, but I live through your investigations by proxy. Dying is a small thing, the most difficult part is to detach oneself from the affections and objects that surround one. My father often told me about the last days of Cardinal Mazarin, when he summoned up the strength to bid farewell to his collections. Alas, my books, my study, who will cast on you the loving gaze to which I have accustomed you?'

'Oh,' said Nicolas, 'I don't like you when you're in one of these strange moods. They're usually a sign that a bad attack's on the way.'

Noblecourt smiled. 'It's nothing but the melancholy of autumn.

> *But how could I confound*
> *That destiny whose round*
> *Gives each man his due . . .*
> *For I say goodbye to myself*
> *When I say farewell to you*[3]

My friends, my books, my cabinet of curiosities . . .'

'What a memory you have, like a young man's!' cried Nicolas, applauding.

'Insolent boy!' said Noblecourt, choking with laughter. 'In making that comment, you make things worse for yourself, since the second part of your sentence goes without saying.'

Reassured about his friend's condition, Nicolas took his leave and went up to his apartments. Mouchette followed him. The old tiled floor served her as a sleeping place next to the commissioner's bed.

*Tuesday 4 October 1774*

Nicolas awoke well before the daylight began turning the wallpaper in his room white. Every morning, Mouchette, sated with sleep but hungry and playful, would jump on her master's bed and tread all over it. Her purring would finally draw the sleeper from his slumbers, and he would go and open the door for her. She would run, her tail lifted in the air, to the delights left for her by Catherine, the first person up, who would be noisily lighting the stoves.

The commissioner had not given up washing in the courtyard. It was a reminder of his youth, a quick shock that restored vigour. He would then come back upstairs to shave and do his hair. Mostly he wore his natural hair, tied with a ribbon, except on solemn occasions or when he had to go to Versailles.

That morning, drawn by the hustle and bustle, the variety of sights offered to the pedestrian, he decided to go for a long walk on the banks of the river. Mentally, he ran through his schedule. Bourdeau was to inform him of the time set for the autopsy. Before that, he intended to report to Monsieur Lenoir: he would both meet the wish his chief had expressed and protect himself from the reprimand that might come from the man's irritation at a mission whose only instigator was the minister. He would have to find the most neutral, but also the most skilful way to present his report, and he always found walking a good way to clear his mind.

A bright autumn sun made everything look beautiful, bathing the scene in an already brilliant golden light. As he walked, Nicolas looked at faces. The animated crowd paraded around him, in rhythm with his steps, a plethora of brief encounters. This game fascinated him: the glances exchanged and missed, offered, retained or rejected, hinting at all kinds of possibilities. He tried – not always successfully – to bring a conclusive moral judgement to bear on each face, based on his experience as a collector of souls. He would arrange them in a corner of his mind, like the insects in the collections of the Jardin du Roi. He knew, however, how futile this approach was. If it always held true, how easy it would be to track down criminals! His own past experience had taught him that an angelic appearance could well conceal other appetites. The pace of the world and society was such that appearances often proved to be nothing but deception and illusion.

At the entrance to Pont-Neuf, he turned for a moment to look at the familiar peremptory figure of the bronze horseman, a helmsman steering the city towards the open sea.[4] He walked along Quai du Louvre, then Quai des Tuileries. He was heading towards the garden and the Terrasse des Feuillants when a crowd attracted his attention. This small chattering throng was bustling around a form lying on the edge of the embankment. He approached. An individual whom he recognised as a spy who patrolled the gardens eavesdropping on conversations immediately came up to him and informed him what was happening. A boatman had spotted a strange shape floating just below the surface as he was crossing the river on his boat. With his boat hook, he had retrieved what turned out to be a dead body. A porter turned the inert mass over with his foot, and the disfigured face of an old man was revealed. The crowd recoiled in horror. The drowned man's right eye had been gouged out, and the arch of the eyebrows was broken and gaping. Nicolas shook his head. He was accustomed to sights like this. Boatmen, for the most part, could not swim and they were sure to drown if they fell in the water. Whenever they had to rescue a drowning man, they would haul the body out of the water with a hook, latching on to an eye or wherever else the implement landed – which might well kill the person they were trying to save. In this way, even when the victim had survived the cold, the fear, the backwash from the boats, or hitting the pillars of the bridges, his rescuer's hook might well finish him off.

The watch took things in hand. Nicolas crossed the Tuileries Gardens and came to Place Louis-le-Grand[5] and Rue Neuve-Saint-Augustin, the location of police headquarters. He was greeted there by the footman as an old acquaintance and immediately led into the Lieutenant General's study. The fact that he was received so quickly and with such good manners was a favourable sign. Indeed, the reception was more courteous than usual. But there was also a hint of anxiety in it. Monsieur Lenoir could not have been expecting Nicolas to perform this requested duty so early in the case.

'I came as soon as I could,' said the commissioner with a bow, his tricorn in his hand, 'to answer your wishes, Monseigneur, and report to you, as is only proper, such news as is likely to retain your attention.'

'Rest assured, my dear Commissioner, that your zeal and promptness are much appreciated. I assume they are connected to the affair for which the minister summoned you, thanks to my intervention.'

He emphasised the word 'intervention', like an actor in the old Hôtel de Bourgogne. It seemed unnecessary to Nicolas, but his chief needed something to cling to if he wished to recover a prestige somewhat tarnished by the Duc de La Vrillière's lack of consideration towards his Lieutenant General of Police. The commissioner then embarked on an exercise at which he excelled, one which had once earned him the favour of Louis XV: telling a story without tiring, making suggestive or enlightening observations while bringing out the crucial elements. He kept strictly to the facts, careful not to mention the various hypotheses which he and Bourdeau had already formed. Lenoir listened with a forced little smile, constantly stroking his left cheek with the tip of the quill pen which he had been using when Nicolas had arrived. At the end, he did not ask any questions, and for a long while rummaged through the heap of papers on his desk. Nicolas thought nostalgically of the desk as it was in Sartine's day: never more than one paper, along with the current edition of the *Almanach royal*, or else wigs lined up as if on parade. The Lieutenant General seemed to be absorbed in his reading. At last, he looked up.

'Monsieur Le Floch, apart from the events in Rue Saint-Florentin, I would appreciate it if you could apply your usual discernment to a number of urgent matters which, given their importance, not only put me in an awkward position, but compel me not to entrust them to just anybody.'

'I await your orders, Monseigneur,' replied Nicolas soberly.

Lenoir cleared his throat. 'For example,' he resumed, 'Monsieur de Vergennes has just passed me a dispatch from our minister in Brussels. He draws our attention to the disappearance of two young girls of good family. They fled their mother's house a few days ago. One is twenty and the other seventeen. The first bears a few marks of smallpox . . .'

He plunged back into the document while Nicolas opened his notebook and began writing.

'That's a good idea, note down these details . . . What were we saying? Yes, smallpox, with a neat waist, blue eyes and black eyebrows. The younger girl also has blue eyes and black eyebrows: she is pretty and a little taller than her sister. They speak French, and also Flemish quite badly. The elder girl speaks English, better than the younger one who only knows a few words. They have a lot of good-quality clothes with them. I have a list here: two linen undershirts, camisoles embroidered in muslin, two yellow silk undershirts, one blue and grey striped satin undershirt, a blue-green dress on a white background with red flowers, a dress with a brown and yellow check pattern, a yellow damask dress, a taffeta dress with gauze embroidery, two white cotton dresses, two cotton undershirts with blue stripes, black and white English-style hats and some pink and blue satin muffs. But it's possible they've disguised themselves as men. They were seen taking the mail coach for France, and there is every reason to suppose they were planning to come to Paris. Since then, there's been no trace of them. I hardly dare imagine the dangers such innocent young girls may run in our capital . . . Look into it, and report back to me.'

'If I find them,' observed Nicolas, 'they'll have to be arrested.'

'Of course. They'll be put out of harm's way in a convent while their family makes arrangements to have them brought back home. If that happens, we'll immediately inform our people in Brussels.'

Nicolas was about to take his leave. His chief made a gesture to detain him.

'One more thing. If I am to believe what Sartine has told me about you, for a long time you were responsible for the safety of the King and the royal family.'

'Damiens's attempt on the late King's life revealed some glaring shortcomings,' replied Nicolas evasively.

'It so happens that the Queen has complained to His Majesty about the presence of mysterious strangers in her gardens at Trianon . . .' He consulted a paper. 'On 10 August, Claude Richard, the head gardener, and his son Antoine came across two women wearing dresses and hats they thought rather strange. The women looked them up and down. A relative of the Queen's had a similar encounter. The King told me about it yesterday after Mass.'

Nicolas gave a grimace of discontent. 'Why have we been informed of this so late in the day? In this kind of affair, speed is a guarantee of success.'

'I have no idea!' said Lenoir, shaking the quill he was still holding. 'The first time the Queen mentioned it to the King, he shrugged it off. She tried again after her servants started getting worried. Look into it and set her mind at rest. Last but not least . . .'

Nicolas could not believe his ears. Was there a shortage of police officers, that everything should be placed on his shoulders at the same time? He did, however, note that the instructions he had just been given implied that he should address the Queen directly.

'Last but not least,' said Lenoir solemnly, 'I am sending you on a mission of State to the cattle farmers in Faubourg Saint-Antoine. I want you to go outside the walls immediately, see the principal representatives and make sure each man takes the appropriate measures. Mutual interest calls for discreet and immediate action. The worst thing would be for the rumour to spread. The panic that would ensue if such disturbing news became known would ruin their business. I repeat, do your best and do it quickly. The King has been informed of the situation and is following the matter personally.'

He punctuated this exhortation with a blow with the flat of his hand. Nicolas, who understood nothing of this final affair, thought it all quite exaggerated. If only he had been able to grasp the nature of this new mission his chief wished to entrust to him!

'Monseigneur, I am your obedient servant, and at the King's command. But may I ask you to clarify—'

'Ah,' said Lenoir, bursting into laughter and making a small gracious bow, 'how absent-minded I am! I was talking to you as if to myself. The thing of it is, our southern provinces are infected by a putrid, pestilent disease which attacks cattle, one that has been making sporadic appearances since 1714.'

'The disease known as anthrax?'

Lenoir looked at him with a touch of surprise. 'Apparently. Not only does this plague affect animals, but the Faculty has established that it could also infect the human population. Where does it come from? you will ask. How has it reached our southern provinces? It actually began ten leagues from Bayonne, in the village of Villefranque, which only survives, it must be said, thanks to its tanneries.'

'So the problem originates with the hides?'

For the second time, Lenoir looked at Nicolas with interest. 'You think quickly, and you think well. These hides are usually unloaded at the port of Bayonne, some of them coming from Holland, but most from Guadeloupe. Be that as it may, the contagion has been rife for years among the Batavians and has destroyed most of the horned animals on our island. Whenever it has shown itself, they have tried burying the carcasses, but we have to take into account the fact that some may be tempted to disinter them in order to get at the leather. And what of the carnivores, like wolves, which try to eat them? These contaminated hides are a danger to those who work with them. For example, a letter from the priest at Salces, in the diocese of Mende in Gévaudan, notifies us that two skinners died within a few days of anthrax on the face, with monstrous swellings on the head, neck and chest.'

'Is there any known cure?' asked Nicolas.

'They keep trying to find one, they keep experimenting. The directors of the Royal Veterinary Schools have set out a presentation of the symptoms which has striking similarities to the description given by the ancients, so striking it's as if it were drawn directly from it. From which these learned men have concluded that we are no more advanced on this matter now than we were in the time of Lucretius, Virgil and Ovid, and that it is vital to bring the spirit of research and enlightenment of our present-day physicians to bear on this important subject. The doctors claim to have cured a patient with a potion composed of red wine from Bordeaux, *Theriaca Andromachi*, extract of cinchona, *contra-herva*, serpentine from Virginia, oil of amber, sweetened spirit of nitre, volatile spirit of eau-de-Luce ammonia, and God knows what else. A real alchemists' stew.'

'But surely, Monseigneur, there is no need to hurry, if the disease is confined to the south?'

'On the contrary! It has been reported that at Ploërmel in Brittany, several peasants have recently died of similar symptoms, after skinning animals who had died of putrid disease.'

'Is there no way to prevent the spread of the contagion?'

The Lieutenant General of Police smoothed his fine lace cravat with an ecclesiastical hand. 'We've certainly tried, as you can well imagine. The only weapons against this contagion are killing and separation. It is necessary to exterminate everything which is infected. That is the only way to save the entire State from this destructive scourge. The government will grant an indemnity to the owners whose cattle are sacrificed. This painful but necessary sacrifice should become easier to swallow if there is a benefit to be had from it! Failing to take such precautions would be fatal, and would make us complicit in the blindness of a rabble who threaten both their own future and the public good.'

'That implies that we must act on a large scale,' objected Nicolas.

'Indeed,' said Lenoir, 'we must not only stop animals moving from one province to another, using cordons of troops, but in villages where the scourge has struck, the cattle must be impounded and isolated. The experience of neighbouring countries proves that the slaughter of sick animals makes it possible to save the healthy ones. We need to convince the peasants of that, or their masters. The problem is when the promised indemnity is late. These delays lead some not to report the plague, in the hope, always a vain one, that their livestock might escape it. Severe measures are and will be taken by the intendants, aided by troops and by brigades of mounted constables. Everything will depend once again on good administration, on the vigilance, exactitude and efficiency of those who are given the task of applying these measures. It is also essential to permit neither the transport nor the sale of animals with the disease. Secret transactions and nocturnal transfers of animals must be suppressed ruthlessly. The worst kind of smuggling in the kingdom would be that of a single sick animal evading the cordons, bringing about the ruin of a whole province and threatening general prosperity!'

'What do you expect of me?' asked Nicolas.

'I want you to make contact with the leading lights of the guild. The regulation of supplies to Paris falls within my jurisdiction. It is absolutely vital to make them realise, although as discreetly as possible, that their salvation and the common interest require them to observe, as if they were gospel, the instructions His Majesty has issued in the southern provinces. They need to be made aware of these instructions and persuaded of their rightness. If they don't understand the reasoning behind these precepts, don't hesitate to raise your voice and remind them in no uncertain manner of their responsibilities. Paint for them a vision of their dead animals, their empty stalls, their reversed fortunes. Paint a picture of Paris hungry or, worse still, decimated by this plague which they themselves will not escape. Make it clear to them how much resentment, indeed anger, there would be towards them on the part of the common people. And if all that is not enough, threaten them with *lettres de cachet* and the Bastille, where I shan't hesitate to throw them if they disobey. But I know you are tactful and persuasive, skilful at brandishing the axe without bringing it down.'

Having no way of defending himself, Nicolas sighed inwardly. Where would he find the time to pursue his investigation at the Saint-Florentin mansion if he had to accede immediately to the Lieutenant General's three requests? Although he had no proof, he suspected Lenoir of deliberately wishing him to answer back, perhaps even to react impatiently or rebelliously, which, in the circumstances, would amount to a refusal to obey. He said nothing, bowed and withdrew without a word. With his hand on the doorknob, he heard Lenoir murmur a last request.

'I almost forgot, Monsieur. While you are conveying my orders to the cattle farmers, make sure you question them about your Marguerite Pindron. You'll find she's quite well known in those circles in Faubourg Saint-Antoine. Oh, one more thing! I have to entertain a person of quality. I am told that you have incomparable taste when it comes to food and drink. May I have your opinion? I have had brought from Strasbourg at great expense a *pâté de foie gras* prepared according to the recipe of the Maréchal de Contades. What should I serve with it?'

'A Hungarian Tokay would be ideal, Monseigneur, but if you want to stay French, I would recommend some quarter-bottles of Chaume, a wine found in Anjou which was a favourite of Madame Catherine, the widow of Henri II.'

'Thank you, Monsieur Le Floch. I am much obliged.'

\*

Nicolas did not bat an eyelid, but clenched his teeth. Was he being mocked? As a connoisseur, he had to appreciate his chief's final remarks. Had he hoped to impress a subordinate with a piece of information that was easy enough to gather for someone who had at his disposal the immense army of informers of a police force admired by all the courts of Europe? Nevertheless the conversation had been devoid of aggressiveness or arrogance, and the last question had perhaps been meant as a kind of teasing from a powerful man rather than a gratuitously unpleasant gesture. Lenoir might have been trying to demonstrate that, like his predecessor, he was maintaining standards with authority and perspicacity.

As he was crossing the courtyard of the Gramont mansion, Nicolas felt himself being pulled by the skirts of his coat. Surprised, he turned to discover the jovial face of the young boy from the Grand Châtelet who, over the past few years, had so often taken the reins of his horses as he passed or delivered his letters for him. He had grown, but his cheap brown jacket had not followed suit, leaving his forearms largely uncovered.

'Monsieur Nicolas,' he said, 'the Lieutenant General wishes to see you.'

'I've just come from there!' replied Nicolas with a laugh.

'I meant Monsieur de Sartine,' said the boy contritely.

Nicolas strove to follow the boy, who was bounding along like a goat. He led him through a door in the orchard wall into the grounds of the adjacent mansion. It was here that Sartine had moved as soon as he had been appointed. He loved this new, spacious quarter, which was both well preserved and close to the vibrant centre of the city. Nicolas glimpsed an elegant building beyond the trees. On its steps, he was placed into the hands of an elderly valet who made no attempt to conceal his jubilation at seeing him again. He led him up the stairs to the first floor and admitted him to a sumptuous study of light oak with a barrel-vault ceiling bearing a painting of the Judgement of Paris. Sartine, standing behind a marquetry desk, noticed the visitor's admiring gaze.

'What do you think, Nicolas? The Judgement of Paris for the former Lieutenant General of the Paris police, isn't that appropriate? They must have been trying to flatter me . . .' He smiled. 'Don't worry, it was already here when I arrived.'

Nicolas recognised the jovial Sartine of old: entrance into the King's councils seemed to have done him good. He had given up his black coat, and now he, too, wore, whether by chance or out of loyalty, a silky pearl-grey coat.

'I owe my latest pleasure to you,' Sartine continued. 'What do you think of this wonder?'

He lifted from beneath his desk a sumptuous mass of white curls that tumbled softly over his arms like a cascade of white horsehair.

'Did I have something to do with that?' asked Nicolas.

'Have you forgotten? Not so long ago you told me about that incomparable English shop. Our ambassador went there and found this example. Apparently, it's identical to the one worn by the Lord Mayor of the City of London during ceremonies.'

He put down the wig, whirled round, and gave a little leap which brought him directly face to face with a stunned Nicolas. He took him by the shoulders and led him towards one of the walls of the study. Against it stood a cabinet of richly veined wood with bronze adornments. The most surprising feature was the dozens of ebony buttons, each marked with a number in ivory. The cabinet seemed to be some kind of extraordinary mechanism. Nicolas was immediately reminded of an organ case. With a childlike air of triumph that made him seem younger, Sartine pressed one of the buttons. There was a kind of hiss, as if air were escaping. Nicolas saw himself as a child beside a rock at Le Croisic that siphoned the great equinoctial tides. A series of clicks followed, a slow rattling noise, then jolly music. Again there was a hiss. A panel came sliding out softly, revealing, as if on a tray, a dummy's head wearing a russet wig.

'It's the Würtemberger,' said Sartine radiantly. 'What do you say to my new library of wigs? I can't find any other word for it. I shall have to question the academicians. Can you conceive of such a wonder? They're arranged in an unchanging order, like police files, protected from dust and light, and always ready to spring up on demand.'

'But who, Monseigneur, had the skill to imagine and build such a marvel?'

'And music! Music! I'm sure you recognised the tune of the pagodas from Rameau's *Paladins*. And that's not all. The man who made this has other strings to his bow. This master of the arts, who is attached to Monseigneur the Comte d'Artois and honoured with his protection, is also the inventor of various methods for writing codes. The main one, entitled *Unum toti uni totum*, was shown, in 1769, to the Duc de Choiseul, who granted its maker a bonus of six hundred *livres*. As the father of four children, he now finds it difficult to make ends meet and, despite the commission he received from me for my dear wigs, is looking for employment.'

'What kind of employment?'

'The kind that particularly interests us. He wishes to build a steganographical arcanum. It would be a desk six feet high and three feet wide, with a decagonal cylinder inside it, worked by a stirrup of ten pedals. On different frames, and without using his hands, he claims to be able to write coded messages as rapidly and simply as on a single board, with more than sixty thousand variations – all without any other frames than the ones attached to the cylinder. You see what I'm getting at.'

Nicolas did not see anything at all, but had no desire to disrupt Sartine's good mood. 'Of course, Monseigneur.'

'We know through the Abbé Georgel, secretary to Cardinal de Rohan, our ambassador in Vienna, that our encoding methods have been discovered. He learnt from an informer that Maria Theresa has been intercepting our messages for many months, uncovering our schemes and reading them like an open book. We can hardly be surprised, then, at her ostentatious hostility towards our ambassador – who, incidentally, hasn't made things any easier with his escapades! In short, I am interested in this machine, and I need several things from you. Make enquiries about this inventor, whose name is Bourdier. The last thing we need is to be dealing with someone who is in the pay of a foreign power, someone who makes us a machine and then hands its secrets over to our enemies. I understand your misgivings, but this is a service I require of you. And that's not the most delicate thing I expect of you. You know both the Court and the city, and you know what the situation is. I am opening my heart to you . . .'

Nicolas shuddered at these words.

'His Majesty, alas, has ideas and judgement, but he is limited by an apathy of mind and body. He seems still unformed. Of course, there is no lack of common sense, although hampered by his paralysing laziness of conception and his awkward behaviour. The smallest trifle disconcerts him, as if he were revolted by objections and difficulties. Above all, he is completely lacking in firmness of character and will, the cardinal virtues of a monarch. Anyone who approaches him is soon convinced of that. Of course he knows a certain amount about particular fields . . .'

'He speaks of many things intelligently and with wide knowledge, as I myself can testify,' said Nicolas.

'That's true, but where is the determination to put things into practice? His brother Provence puts it well: "Berry is like those oiled ivory balls which cannot be kept together." He is crucially lacking in egoism and toughness. He is a prince of idylls and moral tales. That is not what the French expect . . .'

Completely horrified by Sartine's words, Nicolas realised that the death of Louis XV had changed many things. This implacable judgement certainly bore the mark of Sartine's cynicism, and such remarks, coming from his former chief, would not have surprised him on any other subject, but they were about their young monarch. That was something to raise alarm bells.

Sartine continued to hold forth as if he were alone. He was now walking up and down the room. 'Since his accession,' he went on, 'the King has proclaimed that he was taught nothing but that he has read a little history and believes that the misfortune of this State was the King's wives and mistresses. Let us pray that he applies this precept to himself! I like the Queen, who protects me.

Nevertheless, I fear the consequences of her inexperience, both for her and for us. The future is getting darker, and I do not believe she has any of the qualities necessary to see the dynasty through possible unrest or to restore it amid all these troubles.'

'And what lessons do you draw from all this, Monseigneur?' asked Nicolas softly.

'My dear Nicolas, two names are currently in the spotlight. One is that of d'Aiguillon whose dubious intrigues you yourself have suffered.[6] The other is Choiseul, my protector, to whom I have, since his fall from favour, remained secretly loyal. He has superior talent and intelligence and the dazzling memory of a long and glorious ministry.'

Nicolas sighed, thinking of his Micmac friend, Naganda, and all those orphaned by the abandonment of New France. What was so glorious about the loss of Canada and the Indies?

'In addition,' Sartine went on, 'he has the support of the *parlements*, whom we always have to go along with, the better to control them. The philosophers' party constantly praises him to the skies. Only the King is against him, having been led to believe that he poisoned his father. Gossip picked up along the way by his nurse, Madame de Marsan, and taken up by his aunts. That's all Mesdames ever talk about, the birdbrains!'

'What about Maurepas?' said Nicolas.

'He carries no weight in this matter, and it will blow up in his face in the end. Maurepas is a puppet, an automaton from the past. Ingratiating and fickle, a subject for amusing anecdotes. He's just for show! He'll fizzle out, he has the same faults as the King. We will have to choose. The Queen will make all the difference, she hates d'Aiguillon.'

He sank gracefully into his armchair and immediately plunged his hands into the wig spread out in front of him, as if trying frantically to untangle its curls.

'Many ministers of the late King are still in place,' he went on. 'They are obstacles that will have to be put aside.' He struck the flat of his desk with his hand. 'The Duc de La Vrillière first of all. I gather he's given you the task of investigating a death that took place in his mansion? Your fall from favour has been brief, you have bounced back even higher than before.'

'Yes, Monseigneur.'

'Yes for the investigation, or for the bouncing back?'

The tone was inquisitorial: this, Nicolas thought, was the Lieutenant General of old.

'You should know,' said Sartine, 'that, contrary to what you think, the master was not at Versailles last night, but in Paris for a romantic assignation – if my information is correct, and it usually is, as you know better than anyone.'

'I will take note of it, Monseigneur,' answered Nicolas prudently.

'It is not enough to take note of it, Monsieur Le Floch. You must also get down to work and, if you believe me, put me in a position to help you.'

'I am your humble servant.'

'This affair is bound up with our interests. Anything that helps to bring down La Vrillière will hasten Choiseul's return. The salvation of the State is at stake. And should you feel any misgivings, think of the unworthy manner in which that depraved individual treated you at the time of the King's death.'

Nicolas, who had not lost his independence of judgement,

recalled that Louis XV had shamelessly chosen him as the instrument of a final intrigue. All that La Vrillière had been doing was following his master's example. But, although long initiated into the ins and outs of the secret world, he was left speechless by Sartine's proposition. Sartine himself walked towards the hearth, seized the poker and again began stirring nonexistent embers. Nicolas saw in this gesture a sense of unease perhaps equal to his own. The minister knew his loyalty and rectitude. He could therefore imagine the revulsion his suggestion must have provoked, and might well be regretting having exposed himself to such a degree.

Nicolas was torn between a number of feelings. Of course, he could take all this quite simply as a mark of the renewed confidence placed in him by Monsieur de Sartine. However, he recalled some unfortunate previous examples of the man's love and inclination for manipulating things behind the scenes. Beneath the veneer of the courtier, beneath the punctilious courtesy of the gentleman, there sometimes reappeared the coldness and inflexibility of someone dealing in hidden things that crouched in the darkness like nocturnal animals. Nicolas, despite his affection and gratitude, suspected him of finding a strange pleasure in such things, a pleasure nourished by a deeply felt contempt for human beings that was born of long years of familiarity with crime and human baseness. In so doing, was he not trying to exert an obsessive control over Nicolas, like the trainer of an animal that has finally been tamed tugging the end of its lead to make sure it is truly submissive? Or perhaps he just wanted to feel that his trust was still considered a favour and thus convince himself that all was not lost in this sad world. As for Nicolas, whatever answer he gave would place him in an ambiguous position. Whether he agreed or refused to yield to Sartine's injunctions, the reasons ascribed to him would not be the correct ones, and the most plausible would appear the least convincing. Bowing to his former chief's request would certainly make him lose his own self-esteem. He was a police officer, not an informer. He decided to be himself and to trust in fate, which had got him out of difficult situations so many times before.

The silence which had fallen was broken by Sartine. 'I asked you a question.'

'There is no doubt, Monseigneur, that you are best placed to make allowances.'

'What do you mean?'

'You have just demonstrated once again that you are the first to be informed of all things. However quick I am, reporting to you would be pointless. In addition, I cannot suppose that the Lieutenant General of Police, who knows everything, will not hasten to respond in detail to any demand you see fit to make of him. Why should I, a poor subordinate, interfere between two such powers?'

Sartine's face turned pale and tense. He began muttering, and Nicolas thought he made out the words 'disciple of Loyala' and 'emulator of the Jesuits of Vannes'. But then he calmed down, and looked at the commissioner with a kind of indulgent commiseration.

'You will never change! Fourteen years in the highest echelons of the police, and here you are, just as you were before, filled with honour and scruples and . . . mental limitations. But not devoid of skill, oh no! Yes, the marquis would be proud of you. The head of a Ranreuil and the skull of a Breton. Stubborn, but still a little innocent – apparently . . .'

'That's the second time in two days.'

'What do you mean?'

'That I've been called innocent. Last night, Monsieur de Noblecourt . . .'

'He's absolutely right. Well, be that as it may. At least promise me you'll let me know if anything in this case is likely to tarnish the throne. You certainly can't refuse that request.'

'I'll do my best, Monseigneur.'

'Now go on, get out of here, you rascal. I suppose you're rushing off to meet up with your usual accomplices and cut up some bloody body or other in order to stimulate that famous intuition of yours.'

Nicolas laughed. 'It's impossible to hide anything from you. Even the future.'

Sartine, half smiling, half angry, wagged a threatening finger at him and sighed.

Nicolas was walking towards the river, his face aflame. Although the interview had ended pleasantly enough, it had left him with a bitter taste in his mouth. He was torn between his joy at having seen his former chief again and a sense of anguish. How difficult life was! In a flash, he saw his father, the Marquis de Ranreuil, striding about the lower hall in the family chateau. While Nicolas, then a little boy, crouched beneath the chimney hood and looked on, the marquis, usually so ready to embrace change, cursed the mediocrity of the times. He missed the heroic days when history was made with great sweeps of the sword and the only skill lay in knowing how to die. He condemned that degenerate nobility 'of parquet floors and wood panelling, cut off from its roots, whose only world is one of ridicule and disputes over etiquette in the drawing rooms of Versailles'. Once again, Nicolas had the feeling of emptiness that had come over him so often since the death of Louis XV. Everyone was acting as if his successor was of no significance. Even Sartine gave the impression that he had broken the sacred bond connecting him with the new monarch. He was no longer the same man, and he seemed interested in nobody but Choiseul, dazzled by a star which Nicolas, colder or less committed, had long judged to be on a declining orbit. He would not have wagered a farthing on the possibility of the hermit of Chanteloup returning to affairs. Everyone knew the distaste, even the revulsion, which the former minister inspired in the monarch. In this situation, who was the real innocent? Sartine no doubt had ambitions to occupy the position of Minister of the King's Household, which had previously escaped his grasp. He still hoped to achieve it with the help of the Queen and Choiseul. The gods always blinded those they sought to bring down. As for himself, if he could prevent yet another disappointment for his protector, he would do so without hesitation.

The foamy ochre Seine was carrying all kinds of doubtful flotsam on its autumn tides. He spotted the carcass of an animal swirling round and round in an eddy, and recalled his conversation with Lenoir. Could that pestilential disease really spread to the whole of the kingdom and infect both animals and people? He continued thinking about this until he reached the gates of the old Châtelet. He sighed, feeling a kind of weariness at the thought of what was about to take place in the secrecy of the cellars of the Basse-Geôle. As he passed, he glanced mechanically at the grim slab where the latest bodies lay, washed and salted. He noted that the watch had been diligent and that the poor wretch fished out of the waters near the Quai des Tuileries was already resting beside his companions in misfortune. He heard the sounds of conversation, and was delighted to recognise the voices of his friends.

'Here is our Nicolas!' exclaimed Dr Semacgus in his bass voice.

He was carefully removing his doublet. Ever since he had abandoned himself to the tender tyranny of a relationship with his maid, the surgeon was always extremely well dressed and took as much care of his appearance as a young man. Beside him, Bourdeau sat on a stool, calmly smoking an old pipe. Nicolas took his snuff box from his pocket. The sight of it brought a pang to his heart: it was a present from Madame du Barry, and the lid bore the face of a young, smiling Louis XV. He shook Sanson's hand and offered him a pinch of snuff. There followed a pleasant session of sneezing.

'In this damp, cold weather,' said Sanson sententiously, 'tobacco protects against congestion and catarrh. Nicolas, Madame Sanson has asked me to tell you that our doors are always open to you and that she would deem it a great honour if you came at your convenience for lunch or dinner.' He blushed and hesitated. 'I should add that the children would be pleased to see their father's friend again.'

'A thousand thanks to your wife,' replied Nicolas. 'I would be glad to come, once this case has been cleared up.'

'Come, gentlemen,' said Semacgus solemnly, 'this is not a drawing room. Let's raise the curtain on the autopsy.'

With a grand gesture, he pulled the jute cloth off the victim's body. Bourdeau had risen, and they all leaned over the table where Marguerite Pindron lay. The torchlight cast their elongated, dancing shadows on the dark walls. Nicolas explained the circumstances under which the crime had been discovered, and also indicated his own estimate of the approximate time of death.

'A fine-looking girl,' said Semacgus. 'What's the temperature in the kitchens of the Saint-Florentin mansion?'

'It was as cold as outside,' said Bourdeau. 'No food had been served the previous night, Sunday, and the furnaces, chimneys and stoves had all been out since Saturday night.'

The two practitioners kneaded the body. Semacgus looked at his watch, said a few words in a low voice to Sanson, and seemed to be thinking hard.

Sanson cleared his throat. 'We believe death occurred sometime between ten and twelve o'clock.'

Nicolas could not conceal his surprise. 'I'm pleased to see that your expertise confirms my own impressions so closely. However, to truly enlighten me, would it not be possible for you to be more precise? Please understand that the peace of mind of the innocent depends on your observations.'

'The young rascal's trying to teach us our job,' grumbled Semacgus, 'even after we let him witness the birth of criminal surgery.'

They all started laughing. An overjoyed Bourdeau took several enthusiastic puffs at his pipe and Nicolas let out a long and very satisfying series of sneezes. He was not mistaken: proximity with the most tangible and terrifying forms of violent death often brought about these bursts of artificial and somewhat forced relaxation. Each man took advantage of them to conceal his emotions – sometimes, his horror.

'Alas,' said Sanson, 'your question contains its own answer. The coldness of the place no doubt slowed down certain natural phenomena. This context complicates our ability to judge and makes it difficult for us to deliver a more exact verdict.'

'As for the rest . . .' resumed Semacgus, who had just taken several shiny instruments from a small varnished wooden case and had noticed Nicolas's curious glance at this fine object. 'You're admiring my casket. You've never seen this one. I acquired it in the Dutch Indies. It's the only one of its kind. Cut to measure from a single stump of rot-proof ironwood.'

'Perfect, I imagine,' continued Nicolas, completing his friend's description, 'for avoiding erosion by dampness and salt while crossing the seas and oceans.'

'Precisely, the essential thing being to preserve my instruments from rust. As for the rest, as I was saying, in other words, the cause of death, it's perfectly obvious. What do you think, my dear colleague?'

Sanson smiled contentedly at this appellation. They leaned over the body. As always at an autopsy, Nicolas could not help comparing them to two crows he had seen as a child on a path on the edge of Vilaine, busy with the carcass of a dead animal. For a while, the usual ceremonial went through its obligatory phases. Constantly coming back to the neck wound, they proceeded with all the necessary examinations.

'Come closer, Nicolas,' said Semacgus, 'and you, too, Pierre. What do we observe? The wound in the hollow beneath the shoulder is deep, funnel-shaped and, by its very nature, fatal. Look how lacerated the inner walls of the wound are and how crushed and compressed the skin is. What do you deduce from that?'

'That we can rule out the use of a sharp instrument,' said Nicolas.

'That the object used was such a strange shape,' said Bourdeau, 'that it created a kind of pear-shaped hole!'

'That's a perfect description.'

Sanson whispered something in the doctor's ear. 'I agree,' he said, 'though I doubt that our friends will savour the experience!'

'As the good apprentices and scholars that we are,' proclaimed Nicolas, 'we accept anything that leads to the truth.'

'Of course, Bourdeau's tobacco and the cooking salt which I suspect is in the commissioner's pocket will help the two of you to bear it.'

Semacgus was alluding to something Fine, Nicolas's nurse in Guérande, always used to ward off the evil spells of the devil. This remark once again set them laughing. Once that was over, Semacgus clenched his fist and resolutely plunged his hand into the neck wound. It fitted almost exactly. The two police officers watched with shock and astonishment.

Bourdeau was the first to break the silence. 'Do you mean to say that someone killed this poor creature with their bare hands?'

Sanson shook his head. 'It isn't our intention to put that forward as a theory. A hand, even one of exceptional strength, would not be able to go through flesh and produce the cuts and compressions we've observed.'

Nicolas was thinking. 'So, if I understand correctly, the murder appears to have been perpetrated using an object shaped like a hand and sufficiently solid to penetrate flesh?'

'Penetration is not essential,' said Semacgus. 'Let's not forget the lacerations and compressions. Note, gentlemen, that the wound is in the right shoulder. From that I conclude either that the victim was attacked from the front, which does not tally with the description of the scene of the crime, or that she was attacked from behind, which would imply . . .'

He placed himself behind Sanson, pressed him against his chest with his left arm, and mimed striking a blow with his right hand.

'. . . that the attacker was armed with an unknown object. But if, unusually, that was the case, a hand would not have been able to twist and still keep its shape and strength.'

'Couldn't the wound,' said Bourdeau doubtfully, 'have been caused by repeated blows with a knife?'

'The cuts would have looked quite different.'

'I'm reminded of the wooden pegs they use for sealing barrels where I come from.'

'There speaks the man from Touraine!'

Semacgus let go of Sanson, who readjusted his plum-coloured coat where it had been displaced by the surgeon's extremely firm grip.

'I think our two practitioners should come to a conclusion,' said Nicolas, who was becoming impatient.

'The young woman died of a fatal blow to the base of her neck. This fatal wound opened the subclavian vessels of the large branches of the axillary artery. This was likely to cause immediate death through loss of blood.'

'As we observed,' said Nicolas.

'But most of it would have been internal,' said Sanson. 'The loss of blood compressed the lungs and suffocation followed.'

'In other words,' concluded Semacgus, 'it was quite unlikely that the victim could have survived.'

'Anything else?' asked Nicolas.

'Ah, yes! The girl had been leading a life of pleasure, and quite recently, too. Some of our observations indicate that clearly.'

'On the evening of the murder?'

'No, the previous day or days. I shan't go into the detail of our observations. They are similar to those noted in prostitutes of the lower class who sell themselves to one man after another.'

'So she indulged in debauchery?'

'Of the most dissolute kind, there's no doubt of it. We found significant erosion, as well as traces of an astringent lotion, the kind that makes it possible to remove all traces of excessive and repeated male penetration.'

'It's an unguent taken from the root of a rosaceous plant, the *pied-de-lion*,' Sanson remarked learnedly. 'The whores use it to repair all kinds of damage.'

'Last but not least,' said Semacgus, handing the two police officers something small and brown at the end of a small pair of pincers, 'this is what we discovered in the "window in the middle". It's an intimate preventive sponge, which proves at least one thing – that the girl was expecting to meet a suitor!'

A long silence fell over the gathering, soon broken by Nicolas's resolute voice. 'Pierre,' he said, 'when we've found the murder weapon, we'll be close to finding the murderer.'

# V

## BETWEEN CITY AND *FAUBOURGS*

His tongue is as a devouring fire.
Isaiah XXX, 27

Bourdeau and Nicolas were both back in the duty office, the former filling his pipe, the latter preparing his battle plan. Nobody, Nicolas thought, was going to force him to do anything that he had not decided to do himself. Overwhelmed with requests from both the minister and the Lieutenant General of Police, he would take the path dictated by his own free will, certain that whichever he decided upon would be more innocent than any of the others, because it would be in pursuit of the truth. In the order of priorities, one choice appeared to be the imperative one. He would have to keep to it and discard anything superfluous in order to devote himself to what mattered most. He talked about this with the inspector after briefly relating his conversation with Lenoir. As for Sartine's strange request, he preferred to keep silent about it, at least for the moment. However, he did not conceal the question mark hanging over the Duc de La Vrillière's presence at Versailles on the night of the murder.

'Whatever the tasks imposed upon us, my dear Pierre, you know how important it is to solve a crime quickly. We must at all costs find the murder weapon, although I do not harbour any illusions on the subject. The sewer and the river were both quite close. I also need to question the family of the wounded major-domo. There may well be something to be gleaned there.'

'I have the names and addresses of his in-laws, the family of his late wife,' said Bourdeau, taking a paper from his pocket. 'It consists of three people: first of all, his sister-in-law, a nun at the convent of the Daughters of Saint Michel at Notre-Dame de la Charité, in Rue des Postes—'

'Of what order? There are so many in Paris.'

'The establishment was opened by the founder of the Eudists, with female boarders who wish to repent their past sins.'

'The nuns?'

'No, the boarders!'

'What is this person's name?'

'Hélène Duchamplan. Her religious name is Louise of the Annunciation. Then we have the first brother-in-law, Gilles Duchamplan, and his wife, Nicole. Finally, Eudes, the second brother-in-law, the younger of the two, who lives with them in Rue Christine.'

'Try to find out more about these people, and don't slacken with the servants in the Saint-Florentin mansion. One of them is bound to end up saying more than they intended. Let's meet in Rue Montmartre at dinner time. I'd be most surprised if Catherine and Marion couldn't find something for us to eat.'

'Aren't you afraid of disturbing Monsieur de Noblecourt?'

'Of course not. He doesn't have anything in the evenings except a few prunes and a herbal tea. I'm sure he'll be delighted to drink in our company. In fact, it will be an opportunity for him to come out with a few of those finely polished maxims which always seem to be miraculously applicable to the matter in hand.'

As he was leaving Bourdeau, Nicolas consulted his watch: it was midday. Walking out through the main entrance, he stepped aside to let a prisoner's funeral procession pass. He thought with a shudder of that coffin of chipped black wood which, it was said, had been used at the Châtelet for a century for the funerals of dead prisoners, and to which the gaolers gave the humorous nickname 'the pork pie': it had a panel in it which opened to let the body slide out into the common grave. The corpses of drowned people benefited from a different procedure: after being displayed on the stone in the Basse-Geôle, they were transported on a stretcher to the Hospitallers of Sainte Catherine, nuns whose constitutions committed them to washing these mortal remains, wrapping them in shrouds, and burying them in the cemetery of Saints-Innocents.

Amid the hustle and bustle of the street stalls, he hailed a cab. He wanted to get back to Rue Neuve-Saint-Augustin as soon as possible. Confined in the worn velvet of the narrow interior, he sank into a kind of dreamy somnolence which could have been more comfortable. His head half raised, he made out the tops of houses, the balconies, the barred windows, the corbels, and the pompous or grimacing figures decorating the facades of the buildings. When he walked, he mainly observed faces, but, ever since his arrival in Paris, he had realised the danger of admiring the tops of houses: anyone who indulged in this perilous distraction might find himself in trouble when, in a thunderous din, a carriage, cab or wagon suddenly loomed up, leaving him no chance of salvation other than to flatten himself against the wall, his face turned sideways, or to leap through the doorway of a shop.

When he got to police headquarters, he went straight to the offices. Through pursed lips, the first clerk he approached explained that it was necessary to distinguish between living animals and slaughtered meat and that, in consequence, the trade and control of livestock should not be confused with the business of butchery. In short, the person he was looking for did not work with Monsieur Lenoir, due to shortage of space, and he would have to ask for him elsewhere. After much equivocation, he was informed that he would have to go and see Monsieur Poisson in Rue Saint-Marc. Nicolas decided that he would get a horse from the stables of the Lieutenant General of Police, as he had been doing regularly for fourteen years. A groom who was new to the place arrogantly refused him one, and Nicolas, patient as he was and as little inclined to play the marquis, had to restrain himself from shaking the fellow. Champing at the bit, he was forced to go to another employee and request a signed paper. This man detained him for a long time, asking him a thousand trifling questions before agreeing to his demand. Once in the saddle, he regretted that he had not kept the cab. The horse, which was not of his choice, turned out to be restive and rattled several times, either by abruptly pulling up short and then kicking in all directions, or by going as close to the wall as possible at the risk of crushing its rider's leg.

In Rue Saint-Marc, a new discovery awaited him: Monsieur Poisson dealt with wine, fruit and vegetables, while butchery and livestock were the province of Monsieur Imbert, who could be found in Rue Richelieu. That was not far, and he proceeded there immediately. Unfortunately, it appeared that this Monsieur Imbert was indeed involved with meat, and also cattle, but only those that had passed through the city gates and were already the property of the butchers. Therefore he would have to glean the information he sought by addressing himself to Monsieur Collart du Tilleul in Rue de la Soudière, near the market of Saints-Innocents. Nicolas sped to his new destination, tempting his mount with a heap of cabbage.

He had to force open the door of his new interlocutor, who had claimed not to be available. Nicolas entered angrily, regretting that he did not have a riding crop with which to lash his boots. The panic-stricken clerk took shelter behind an unstable pile of official paperwork over the top of which only his trembling black skullcap appeared. His master assured Nicolas that Monsieur Longères, on Place Popincourt, both because of his age and the esteem and trust of his colleagues, appeared to be the primary authority among the cattle farmers in the viscounty and generality of Paris, and the man best able to answer questions from the authorities. Nicolas thanked Monsieur Collart du Tilleul curtly and ordered him to have the restive horse taken back to police headquarters. Exasperated by his mount's capriciousness, he had decided to continue his journey outside Paris by other means. He had to go all the way back to Rue Saint-Honoré before he found a cab cruising for fares. The interior was so dirty and the upholstery so repulsive, with dubious-looking stains, that he had to sit sideways on the very edge of the seat. His policeman's eye spotted a large number of bloodstains, which someone had tried to remove without success. What on earth had this vehicle been carrying? Some wounded person, no doubt, picked up from the gutter and carried home after a drinking session. He lowered the window to get a little air.

The cab advanced by fits and starts, steering a path through the hurrying, distracted crowd. It had to stop in front of a small gathering of laughing girls and boys dancing hand in hand in the middle of Rue du Faubourg-Saint-Antoine to the harsh, merry music of a hurdy-gurdy. The musician wore the costume of his remote province, and was turning the handle with one hand and playing the melody with the other, all the while tapping his clogs in time to the music. Nicolas contemplated this sight with a somewhat nostalgic benevolence. What remained to him of his youth? He remembered running off to the marshes with boys of his age. Then came his interminable studies, gloomy and stifling. He recalled the anguish of school, where, despite his successes, he was despised as a poor orphan by companions who came from the best families in Brittany, and his ambiguous position at the notary's office in Rennes, where his aristocratic connections had made him both envied and despised by the other pupils. Solitude had been his companion throughout these years, illumined however by the tutelary figures of Canon Le Floch and the Marquis of Ranreuil, his father, and by the even more moving figure, now distant and almost faded, of his sister Isabelle. He prayed that his son, Louis, would be spared such vicissitudes.

As they drove through Faubourg Saint-Antoine, in the shadow of the Bastille, he was struck once again by the diversity of the sights on offer. The various strata of the population all came together here: tranquil bourgeois strolling with their families, factory workers out for a good time, rich peasants from the *faubourg* whose costumes looked out of place, brazen women of the streets, and last but not least the armies of beggars and cripples, real or simulated, who poured into the capital of the kingdom from the provinces. Every day, poor wretches arrived by road, attracted by the prestige and illusion of Paris, and hoping to find a solution to their misfortunes and an end to their poverty. Statute labourers, pushed to the point of despair by the unimaginable drudgery of their work and the meagreness of their subsistence wages, would decide to take refuge in the cities, where they swelled the ranks of the destitute. As Nicolas had been observing for years, many of these people became petty thieves, pickpockets, and even murderers, and would end up in gaol, or in chains in the King's galleys, or worse still as pitiful figures on the gallows.

He ordered the driver to turn off towards Popincourt. As soon as they left the main road, the hustle and bustle gave way to a more provincial atmosphere, like that of a large country village. The main open space was shared by workshops, the shops of cabinet makers and artisans, and furniture factories, separated from one another by gardens and farms. The warm, heavy odour of manure imbued the air, chasing away the foul smells of the city. Nicolas noticed a sad troop of cows, their sides covered in mud and slurry, being led towards the city gates, from where they would proceed to the slaughterhouse.

By the side of the road, furniture had been laid out to attract customers. Nicolas remembered with some bitterness having one day bought a small writing desk from one of these workshops.

Monsieur de Noblecourt had been curious enough to climb the stairs to see it. His reaction had disappointed Nicolas: what was the meaning of that stifled laugh? He had been so happy with what he had thought was a genuine bargain that he had been really surprised when, a few weeks later, the desk had simply fallen to pieces. There were many crooks and fakers operating here, and they harmed the reputation of the genuine craftsmen, who were a credit to their guild and true artists in furniture. The dregs of the trade would continue to fabricate phantom constructions which, after a mere couple of weeks, would turn out to be rickety, obsolete and worm-eaten.

In a small dead-end street planted with lime trees, he finally came to a collection of rustic buildings surrounded by cowsheds, gardens and orchards. A woman sitting on a milestone looked at him curiously and confirmed that he was indeed outside the house of old Longères. He got out of the cab and paid the driver, who obstinately kept his hat pulled down over his face. Nicolas observed that the carriage had the number 34, followed by an N and the regulation two capital Ps on a white background. He laughed at the coincidence: the initial of his Christian name, and his own age. He was unsure whether or not to notify the transport office about the filthy state of the cab. In the end, he decided to drop it, given that favourable registration number. It was a weakness of his to believe in signs: although he claimed to be a good Parisian, his Celtic soul often came to the surface.

Cautiously, he entered the farm, anxious not to provoke a nasty-looking yellow dog which was barking and pulling on a rope. A stooped elderly man emerged from a lean-to. His face was lined and weather-beaten, and a crown of sparse white hair framed a skull covered in brown blotches. He was wearing a brown jacket with horn buttons, grey breeches, rough woollen stockings and sturdy hobnailed clogs. Leaning with both hands on a gnarled stick, he looked at the intruder without saying a word.

'Monsieur,' Nicolas said, feigning a detached, casual air, 'would you be able to tell me where I could find Monsieur Longères?'

The man turned aside and spat. 'Do you want the young one or the old one? If it's the old one, here I am.' He angrily kicked the beaten earth. 'Not the same bloody story again, damn it! We've already told you everything's been settled. I'd have thought the commissioner was satisfied. It's not going to look good for us. To tell you the truth, I'm the one who has to see to all that, and it doesn't make me popular in spite of my white hair . . .' He threw a stone at the dog, which was howling. 'Shut up, Sartine!' He gave Nicolas a sideways glance. 'No offence. He's a good guard dog.' He laughed and slapped his thigh with his hand.

Nicolas was smiling to himself. He had previously come across a parrot bearing the name of the former Lieutenant General of Police. He pretended to understand the meaning of the farmer's speech, convinced that the truth sometimes emerged from the most incoherent statements.

'I can well imagine,' he said solemnly, 'that your task has not been easy in these circumstances. And how did you first become aware of them?'

'No one told me anything. But everyone was talking about it, and then the police arrived. Otherwise, we keep our own house in order, if you know what I mean. Anyone who doesn't play fair, we obviously try to find out what's happening, confound the culprit and drive him away without any kind of trial, even if he doesn't want to go.'

'Let's be clear about this, Monsieur. If I understand correctly, when you discover a criminal in your ranks, your first reaction is to dispense justice, whatever his resistance?'

'That's right! My God, you're quick on the uptake!'

'Why, what did you imagine?'

'That you were from the police, and that you were investigating the traffic in spent grain.'

'Spent grain?'

'That's right, spent grain! You get it from the breweries, which are only too happy to get rid of it. Take the ripe crushed barley they've put to ferment. Well, some of us, the crooks among us, grab the residue at a low price and feed the cattle with that rubbish. And when I say some . . .'

'Well?'

'Well? Don't try and mollycoddle me. The animal swells up, the meat is spoiled, and the buyer has been had. Even the weight is faked: everyone's a loser, except the crook!' He stamped his foot in indignation. 'Me, I love my animals, Monsieur. I feed them like they're my own children. Well, that's all in the past. Why are you here? What do you want?'

'Don't worry, Monsieur Longères, my presence has nothing to do with the fraudulent use of spent grain. The Lieutenant General of Police, Monsieur Lenoir, has given me the task of informing your honourable guild of the dangers of an epidemic of anthrax which is spreading to several provinces of the kingdom.'

Nicolas was trying desperately to find a way to introduce the case of Marguerite Pindron. He explained, with a wealth of details, the reason for his coming to Popincourt, the scale of the epidemic, its consequences, and the risks incurred, while insisting on the government's desire to take precautionary measures. He sprinkled his words with so many veiled threats and admonishments that old Longères, horrified by what he heard, hunched over his stick, abandoning his own propensity to chatter.

'So,' continued Nicolas, 'what you need to do, immediately – but at the same time without raising the alarm because, as I'm sure you realise, any panic would be seen as your fault – is inform your colleagues of the present danger and the risks they are running, and insist on the importance of taking the necessary precautions.'

At this point, he respectfully touched on the King's kindly concern for his people, as well as that of his ministers and the Lieutenant General of Police, not to mention the *parlement*, in an affair so heavy with consequences for the life and smooth running of the kingdom. He punctuated his words with sweeping gestures, deliberately looking insistently at different parts of the cowsheds, as if trying to make an inventory of the contents and detect some anomaly. He strode towards one of the buildings and then immediately changed direction before again veering off, followed by the farmer, who had become extremely alarmed by this inquisition and the flood of words that accompanied it.

'Gather your colleagues, explain the situation,' Nicolas resumed, forcefully. 'The information needs to be passed to everyone in your guild, from Popincourt to Ivry, where there are so many dairies, and from Vincennnes to Chaillot. By the way . . .' he had decided to try a direct shot, '. . . how is old Pindron?'

The man stopped, as if taken aback by something incongruous. 'Old Pindron? The poor man died last year. A sad story, Monsieur, a really sad story. A good man. Yes. Not much of a laugh. No, certainly not much of a laugh, always stubbornly refused a drink. But a fine man, an honest man, who knew his job. Alas, his daughter killed him, or as good as. I assume you know the story?'

'Not all the details.' Nicolas was pleased with his ruse. He had hit the target at the first shot.

'A little madam who brought misfortune to two families. I have no hesitation in saying that. Yes, she killed the old man and launched a poor boy on a career of misfortune.'

'I'd like to hear all about it – if you have time, that is.'

'Certainly, Monsieur. Monsieur . . .?'

'Nicolas Le Floch, commissioner of police at the Châtelet.'

'By God, I knew it! Accept my hospitality and have a drink. Talking makes you thirsty, and so does listening. To tell you the truth, with age, my legs grow heavy. If I stand too long, I'm likely to take root.'

Old Longères led him to the elongated one-storey main building. They walked down a few steps into a vast room with a floor of beaten earth and whitewashed walls. A dresser, a long, worn oak table with two parallel benches, a resplendent copper drinking fountain and a fireplace with a trammel were the only furnishings. Old Longères clapped his hands. Immediately, an elderly maidservant limped in to take her master's orders. She went back out through a door in the corner of the room and down to the cellar, and came up again with a pitcher and two thick glasses. They sat down at the table, and the host poured a little raspberry-coloured wine.

'It's Suresnes, fresh from the cask.'

He pushed a bowl of walnuts towards Nicolas, and himself grabbed two and cracked them in his fist. The crumbs fell on his brown jacket.

'You can imagine the kind of things people said in the *faubourg*,' he began. 'That a beautiful girl from a good home should refuse the hand of a worthy suitor, a gardener like his father before him, was a real scandal. How could she reject the union of the garden and the farm? The fortunes of the Pindrons and the Vitrys would have been linked and everyone would have been satisfied. Why did she have to give it all up? It's as if, begging your pardon, she had a fire between her legs! Oh, I know what they said, that her suitor was a bit of a simpleton, that he wasn't able to charm her and drive out her crazy ideas. But isn't that what happens when people get married? They have to realise that self-interest is more important than excitement. That's what it's like in the *faubourg*: the only things that matter are the animals and the plants! What girls really want doesn't count. But believe me, marriages are no worse for that.'

'So it had a tragic end?'

'More than tragic! It killed old Pindron. We have a sense of honour round here. Madame Pindron sold everything to buy an annuity, and disowned her only daughter. She retired to her native province, far away from the scandal.'

'What happened to the daughter?'

'She vanished! No one's had any news of her. Oh, there've been rumours, every now and again. Some say she's in La Force prison, others say they saw her dancing with a bear at a fair on the boulevards, and some claim she's walking the streets around

Quai Pelletier and even that she's trawling for men in the wooden pyramids on the banks of the river, where you get all kinds of dissolute characters. Lord knows if there's any truth in these tales.'

'And what about the suitor?'

'Young Vitry? Anselme? He abandoned the garden and the vegetables he loved so much, not to mention his parents. They say he was seen in the Faubourg Saint-Marceau, rolling in the gutter. I heard that he caught a foul disease and did so many mad things that he was locked up in Bicêtre, either with the patients suffering from venereal disease or with the lunatics. That's quite some misfortune! The Vitrys don't want to have anything more to do with him.'

Nicolas had heard enough. To allay suspicion, he made another pointless speech about the epidemic, drank a few glasses of wine, ate some walnuts, then took leave of his host. Longères, delighted by his visit, made him promise firmly to return. He vowed that everyone – God bless the young King – would do their duty and strive to preserve the city from the anticipated calamity. If anyone grumbled, he himself would plunge his pitchfork into their backside. All the same, he had to point out, without wishing anyone any harm, that the butchers shouldn't be forgotten, and that the police should check that they really had certificates and receipts from those who sold them their animals. Not to mention their obligation to slaughter within twenty-four hours after purchase.

Nicolas promised everything that was asked for.

Once in the street, he regretted having paid his fare and dismissed the cab. He found himself forced to go back to Rue du

Faubourg-Saint-Antoine to find transport. Paris awaited him, and a projected visit to the major-domo's family. But before that, he planned to question Jean Missery's sister-in-law. Once past the Bastille, he would take Rue Saint-Antoine, then Rue Saint-Honoré as far as the junction with Rue Saint-Jacques, then turn right into Rue Planche Mitray, a true source of pestilence where you had to hold your nose, cross Pont Notre-Dame and the Petit Pont, carry on as far as Rue de l'Estrapade until, behind the Sainte-Geneviève Abbey, and not far from Place de la Vieille Estrapade, he reached Rue des Postes, where the house of the Daughters of Saint Michel was located.

He hailed a spruce-looking, freshly polished two-wheel carriage. He called out his destination to the coachman, then lost himself in his reflections, his eyes half closed. His little trip to Popincourt had proved highly instructive. Not only had he fulfilled to the letter his mission regarding the preservation of the cattle of Paris – or had that been only a pretext to send him in search of information about Marguerite Pindron? – but he had also learnt a great deal. When you thought about it, it was obvious that, as far as the anthrax was concerned, anyone else could have done the job as well as he had. Did that mean that Lenoir knew more than he had revealed? Was there, in spite of appearances, some kind of collusion between the minister and the head of police? Was the Duc de La Vrillière trying to control the progress of the commissioner's investigation? And yet, if Sartine was to be believed . . . But was he telling the truth or did he have some cards up his sleeve which changed the whole game? He shouldn't get carried away, thought Nicolas, shouldn't let his imagination run away with him. Take the bare facts as they came, sift through them, compare them, follow the new leads that were opened up. The Pindron girl had left her family home to escape an arranged marriage. Everything suggested that, having fallen into debauchery, she had wandered the streets of Paris before becoming, after who knew what encounters and what rebuffs, a chambermaid to the Duchesse de La Vrillière. The contradictions, heightened by the fog of hatred among this group of servants, a veritable battlefield of rivalries and jealousies, were endlessly intriguing. Nicolas vowed to take a closer look at the tangle of relationships among the occupants of the Saint-Florentin mansion. He even envisaged drawing up, in the form of a written document, a detailed picture of the testimonies they had so far gathered. He would also have to dispatch an officer to question the Vitry family, apparently market gardeners in Faubourg Saint-Antoine. The smallest piece of information would help to reconstruct the whole mosaic. He himself would go to Bicêtre, which he did not yet know, despite Monsieur de Sartine's recommendations to him to visit it. He recalled the grave air he had adopted whenever he happened to mention this establishment, which, he said, was comparable in horror to the hell described by Dante.

The coachman's cries of encouragement to his horse drew Nicolas from his meditations. The slope leading up to Place de la Vieille Estrapade, the highest point in the city, was steep. The services of the Lieutenancy of Police had recently examined a project for a hydraulic system to bring river water from the Port à l'Anglais with a view to building a public drinking fountain. Owing to the problems of transportation, the price of water was constantly increasing, and was a burden on the poorest inhabitants. Admittedly, in the past few decades, especially under the late King, this type of construction had proliferated in the city. The carriage set off again with difficulty, just in front of the sparkling sign of the monumental mason Caignard, who, it was said, could supply all kinds of tombs and epitaphs. At the entrance to Rue des Postes, he spotted the office where those Parisians who ventured out at night could hire children to carry lanterns for them. These lanterns were duly numbered, and their carriers registered by the police, who issued them with a stamped licence. Naturally, these young people also served as spies, and their daily reports were part of the gigantic spider's web whose threads all led back to the Lieutenant General of Police. Nicolas saw a group of austere buildings in the middle of which there rose a grim openwork steeple. His cab stopped, and the coachman pointed out the house of the Daughters of Saint Michel.

This time, Nicolas made sure he asked the driver to wait. Knowing what these men were like, he promised him a princely tip if he found him waiting faithfully at his post. In the corner of a massive door, he saw a handle which he supposed set off a distant bell, and was surprised, when he pulled the mechanism, to hear a metallic clanging from somewhere nearby. Some time passed before the wicket was opened. He introduced himself and stated that he wished to see Sister Louise of the Annunciation. The wicket closed again with a snap and his wait began. The door opened at last. The figure of a tall nun appeared, silhouetted against the light. She admitted him, then carefully closed the door behind him with a suspicious glance at the outside world. She glided rather than walked along the waxed tile floor of a long dark corridor, lit only at its end by a high stained-glass window depicting Saint Michel slaying the dragon. He was introduced into a kind of parlour on the left, where the only furniture consisted of two armchairs with old-fashioned upholstery.

'I am listening, Commissioner. I am Sister Louise of the Annunciation.'

The high-pitched voice took him by surprise. Behind him, a little slip of a woman had entered without a sound, so short that he had to lower his eyes to see her. She was as tall as she was wide, almost a dwarf, like one he had seen dancing with a macaque in aristocratic dress at the Saint-Germain fair. She had a puffy, blotchy oval face, and her half-closed eyes were deep-set, as if sunk into the skin. She had full lips, and was smiling vaguely. In her hands, she was twisting a rosary with black beads. With a movement of her head, she motioned him to sit down.

'Sister,' said Nicolas, 'I think that you know of the events which justify my presence and oblige me to disturb your holy work?'

'The world, Monsieur, is beyond these walls. Nothing can disturb the peace of this place. Are we to suppose that your arrival has some connection with one of our boarders? These sinners sometimes feel the tug of the devil long after they have come here.'

'Don't worry, that's not what this is about. Have you had any news of your brother-in-law, Jean Missery, major-domo to the Duc de La Vrillière?'

The nun's slit-like eyes narrowed even more, like those of a cat pretending to sleep. 'I have hardly seen him since the death of my sister, except at masses marking the anniversary. And even before that . . .'

She left the sentence unfinished. Nicolas said nothing: he was good at waiting.

'I always deplored that marriage,' she resumed. 'My sister wouldn't listen to me. Alas, it killed her.'

He could not let such a statement pass unchallenged. 'What do you mean by that?'

'That the Lord did not bless it and that its still-born fruit killed my sister.'

She opened her hands and the rosary fell, but she did not take any notice. Nicolas picked it up and handed it to her. She resumed speaking.

'But do you think he was stricken with remorse and contrition? Of course not. I doubt that he deserved such grace. At first, he feigned grief, and those who did not know him may have believed he was sincere. However, in the heat of charity, apparent zeal is only a passing mood, and not a movement of that same grace. It is only too true that the Lord knows our powerlessness . . . Perdition to him through whom scandal arrives! And as for us, we complain in secret that we are not permitted to condemn out loud, for one does not work for one's own salvation by neglecting that of one's brothers . . .'

What on earth, thought Nicolas, did this obscure speech mean? What was the point of such a pompous declaration? What dark resentment led her to these words full of bitterness and innuendo? He would have to bring her down to earth.

'Sister, Jean Missery was stabbed last night.'

'He's dead, then,' she said immediately.

He did not reply. The sentence was ambiguous. Was it a question, a statement, a kind of challenge, or was she trying to confirm something she already knew, something she had long wished for?

'I shall accuse myself in public confession of the joy that I feel,' she resumed. 'May God have mercy on him: "He puts no trust in His holy ones, and the heavens are not pure in His sight."'

He still could not determine whether or not she knew anything about what had happened. He would not have sworn to it.

'Don't you find your resentment quite surprising, Sister, you who wear that robe of pity and compassion?'

Her little eyes glittered with a cold light, and her voice turned very shrill. 'Pity? Compassion? Did he ever have any towards my sister? Did he ever show the least respect for her memory? He preferred to wallow in the mud, and let the beast immediately awaken in him . . .' She was wringing her hands. 'I say this quite bluntly: even if he had asked God to free him from the evil passions that possessed him, do you think that deep down he wished that prayer to be granted? What he wanted, he only half wanted. And to only half want something, means, as far as the result is concerned, not to want it at all.'

'I understand your emotion, Sister, but what exactly are you referring to?'

'I'm referring to the various criminal attachments in which my brother-in-law indulged after my sister's death. His heart was constantly occupied by the perverse concerns of his base being. He put all his senses at the service of his animal desires, adding the scandal of his dissolute conduct in public. Even the walls of this house were shaken by it.'

'And for these very human sins, did he deserve to lose his life? Could he not have made amends?'

She was looking at him suspiciously. 'There are a great many minds, my brother, with which there is no other stand to take but that of silence and disapproval. Whatever you say or do, you will never change them: "If your eye offends you, pluck it out, if your hand offends you, cut it off."'

'What I don't understand,' said Nicolas, 'is this hatred for a man who no longer had any connection with you.'

'My sister's marriage verged on misalliance. Consider that. To marry a man who was nothing but a servant!' The little woman rose to her full height.

'Would it not have shown humility to consent to a union sanctified by a sincere mutual affection?' asked Nicolas.

'You speak of it very lightly. Not content with getting his hands on a large dowry, he inherited from my sister a substantial fortune which would return to its legitimate source if he died.'

'Its legitimate source?'

'Us, the Duchamplans.'

Nicolas paused, then said, 'Sister, at this juncture I must ask you to clarify a certain number of points.'

She sat down, put her rosary back inside her sleeve, and her face reflected a kind of benign placidity.

'The words of the Gospel,' Nicolas went on, 'edifying as they may be, are not enough to illuminate more material facts. How were you kept informed of the dissolute life your brother-in-law had been leading since he became a widower?'

She shook her head in disgust, as if to say that these debauches had started even before her sister's death, perhaps when they were first married. 'My family kept me informed, as was only right: I am the eldest . . .'

'I must insist. You appear very familiar with everyday life at the Saint-Florentin mansion.'

She looked at him in silence, with a contemptuous expression on her face, as if he were talking nonsense.

'Madame,' Nicolas went on, 'I remind you that you must answer the questions of a magistrate engaged in a criminal investigation. I have the power to arrest you if I consider that you are not being as honest as I would have hoped. Do you understand that?'

'Do not threaten me, Monsieur. Do I, a poor Daughter of Saint Michel, need to remind you that your authority ceases where that of the Church begins?'

'What does that mean?'

'That, as a nun of this house, I am dependent on the abbot of Sainte-Geneviève, who has rights of lower, medium and high justice in the jurisdiction of his bailiwick. And please don't tell me that these rights were suppressed by Louis the Great in 1674. Later edicts have restored them to their legitimate holder.'

'I see, Sister, that you are very clever, argumentative, and a stickler for the rules, with a degree of knowledge hardly in keeping with the habit that you wear!'

'My late father, Commissioner, was a sealer of verdicts at the Châtelet.'

'That's as may be, but why argue in such an acerbic tone? You are not incriminated, as far as I know. I haven't forgotten my lessons, and I know that the monarchy prevails over all other authorities, although there is little danger that we will reach that point. There remain, nevertheless, some flaws in your reasoning. You're forgetting a vital detail, for example: the restoration of the rights of justice of which you speak is clearly defined in the texts as referring only to enclosures, courtyards and cloisters. Now, as far as I know, your house is located in Rue des Postes and not within the limits of the abbey. Therefore you are within my legitimate power.'

She immediately bristled, purple with rage. 'I shall appeal to the ecclesiastical authorities, I shall appeal to the Archbishop.'

'I know Monseigneur de Beaumont very well. In his position, he can hardly be expected to listen to an insignificant nun who rejects the justice of her King.'

She grew even more purple with outrage. 'I shall not yield.'

'Well, persist in this obstruction and I shall go to a magistrate and request a monitory, compelling you to reveal to your superiors everything you know about this case. After three monitories without response, you will be excommunicated.'

'All right, what do you want to know?'

'Who kept you informed of Jean Missery's conduct in the Saint-Florentin mansion?'

'It is painful for me to have to mention a highly placed lady, the Duchesse de La Vrillière, who, as you seem to be unaware . . .' here, her voice became ingratiating, even mocking, '. . . is a benefactress of this house. Without her charitable support, how could we hope to care for our unfortunate boarders?'

'So it was she who kept you informed?'

'She told me that for months he had been completely besotted with a little hussy, a girl of the streets who had entered her service. The duchesse had rejected her at first, but her husband had insisted. It made her weep with humiliation, and in her pain she came to our altar to pray for the duc's soul. I would pray with her.'

'So the duc, too . . .'

Sister Louise of the Annunciation closed her eyes with a sorrowful air.

'Didn't your brothers try to persuade the widower to behave in a more decent fashion?' Nicolas asked.

'The older one is spineless and the younger one lives a carefree life. As for my sister-in-law, she just keeps complaining instead of giving me nephews.'

'One last thing,' said the commissioner. 'What were you doing on the night of Sunday to Monday, let's say from seven o'clock in the evening to seven o'clock in the morning?'

'I was sleeping in my cell, until prime. Everyone here will confirm that.'

'I shall leave you now, Sister, but I would ask you to think carefully and see if you can recall anything that might be of interest to me.'

He took his leave of her. At the door, he turned and saw her standing a few paces behind him, on the alert. He could not resist a parting shot. 'I almost forgot. Your brother-in-law is not dead. His wound was only superficial. His mistress, on the other hand, was indeed murdered.'

She swivelled round like a top and disappeared through another exit, while the extern sister who had accompanied him came running to open the door.

'Why should Sister Louise run away like that?' he asked. 'I thought she was more concerned with decorum.' He thought he heard a little laugh in response. 'Sister,' he continued, 'when was the last time the Duchesse de La Vrillière visited your establishment?'

'Madame de Saint-Florentin? It's strange you should mention her. She was here just this morning and had a long talk with Sister Louise . . .' She burst out laughing. 'She's going to get up on her high horse again because of that, and . . . we'll be the ones to pay.'

'At what hour does the community retire?'

'At eight o'clock.'

'Sister Louise, too?'

'Oh, no, *she* has privileges. Her family has given so much money to this house that she sometimes dines in town.'

'On what days?'

'On Sunday evenings. With her brother, they say.'

'What about last Sunday?'

'Yes, she was out that night.'

He thanked her and left. In Rue des Postes, he found his coachman waiting impatiently. Night was already falling: he had to join Bourdeau. He was still reeling from what he had just learnt. So Louise of the Annunciation knew everything! She had tried to deceive him. What a dissembler! With that air of hers that would have made the most resolute slink away, she had hidden behind legal technicalities and taken him where she had wanted him to go. She had led him up the garden path, making him look a fool, much to her own amusement.

That mixture of anger, genuine confidences and clever omissions made him confused and uneasy. It was not easy to tell the difference between a truthful presentation of facts and a subtle attempt to divert suspicion. After all, she herself had revealed to him the interest the Duchamplans might have in Jean Missery's death. That reinforced the idea that they had been alarmed at the widower's passionate attachment to a young girl like Marguerite Pindron, especially if, since her escape from the *faubourgs*, she had acquired a certain experience. Whether that man, grief-stricken and tormented by desire, had managed to win her heart or she herself had discovered where her interest lay, a marriage could only be harmful to the expectations of the Duchamplan family. Marguerite had become a threat and an obstacle.

But her death did not resolve the matter. If the widower became infatuated with someone else, then the fortune he had inherited from his wife would melt like snow in the sun. Examples abounded, both at Court and in the city, of men of his age so ruled by their senses that they yielded to the most extravagant demands of greedy young girls, who in their turn hastened to transfer the goldmine to some good-looking and hot-blooded secret lover. In this way, a fortune could vanish in the blink of an eye. It would therefore seem much more sensible to get rid of the widower rather than his mistress, the latter being merely a stopgap solution. Admittedly, thought Nicolas, the Duchamplans were one lead among many others. He recalled Sister Louise's reaction to his announcement that her brother-in-law had been wounded. What had she known at that point? What had the Duchesse de La Vrillière told her during their long interview that morning? Nicolas recalled having told the duchesse at the Saint-Florentin mansion the previous evening that the major-domo was wounded and that it seemed likely he had turned on himself the weapon with which he was believed to have cut his mistress's throat.

The nun's reaction seemed false if that was what she had been told. Had she assumed that the facts were known, or did she have some hidden reason not to believe in the suicide theory?

It was already dark when Nicolas's carriage dropped him in Rue Montmartre. His sudden appearance interrupted the baker's boys from the shop on the ground floor as they were mercilessly teasing the bell ringer of the dead. This old man, dressed in a dalmatic adorned with an embroidered silver skull and crossbones, was shaking his bell with one hand and holding a lantern in the other, and calling out in a pitiful tone his lugubrious refrain:

> *'Wake up, wake up, all you who sleep,*
> *Pray for the dead who lie so deep!'*

He thanked Nicolas, who slipped him an *écu* before reprimanding the baker's boys with a smile. As soon as he entered the servants' pantry, he sensed that something dramatic had occurred. Marion sat slumped on a bench, her head in her hands, while Poitevin was polishing with fanatical care a pewter ewer which did not require so much attention. Only the sight of Bourdeau in an apron and of Catherine beside him, the two of them bent over the bread oven, reassured him somewhat. They did not seem to be part of the atmosphere of anxiety that weighed on the house.

'What's going on?' asked Nicolas.

'Oh, Monsieur Nicolas,' moaned Marion, 'our master was taken ill when he came back from Saint-Eustache. As you know, he's a churchwarden of his parish. This evening there was a meeting of the council. He came back completely red in the face, with the veins sticking out on his forehead! He collapsed in the doorway.'

'I went to fetch the doctor,' said Poitevin, 'the same one who tended Monsieur when he was attacked.[1] God be praised, Dr Dienert was at home in Rue Montorgueil, and came running immediately. At first, he suspected an apoplexy. We laid Monsieur down – he had already regained consciousness. We made him take some drops of *alcali fluor* diluted in water, as well as a decoction of tamarind, and we also made him tighten his garters to slow down the rush of blood to his head. He's much better now. He asked us not to bother you with his condition, he says he'll receive you with Monsieur Bourdeau as soon as you've finished eating. That's bound to cheer him up.'

Despite this advice, Nicolas was already rushing upstairs. Catherine stopped him with an emphatic look.

'Don't move, he'd only think he's worse than he is. He's quite all right. I should know. He's just too edgy. Something got on his nerves. Bourdeau was there, he'll tell you.'

Nicolas sighed, telling himself that Catherine, a former canteen-keeper in the King's armies and something of a witch, possessed the skill and the means to treat many illnesses, and that he himself had often benefited from her care.

'I gave him some liquid to counter it, the kind that you know,' she whispered in his ear.

He went upstairs to change after this day of constant errands, following Mouchette up the concealed staircase that led to his quarters. As usual, she kept putting her head between the bars and giving provocative little cries as she slouched up the steps. Every time he made a move to grab hold of her, she leapt out of his reach. Feeling fresher, he went back to the servants' pantry and discovered an unusual spectacle.

Bourdeau was hopping on the spot and moaning as he placed some steaming puffed-up rolls, which gave off an appetising odour, on the large table in the pantry. Once he had divested himself of his burden, he blew on his burning fingers and rubbed them on the vast apron that enveloped his paunch. Meanwhile, Catherine was bustling at the stove. Nicolas's nose quivered: the aroma of roast poultry reminded him how hungry he was.

'Oh, oh!' moaned the inspector. 'It's hotter than hot.'

'Your little creatures seem done,' said Catherine. 'I'll take out the pot.'

'Please don't lift the lid – the taste would escape with the steam. You should leave them to cool in their own juice.'

'Jesus, Mary and Joseph!' cried Nicolas. 'What feast is being prepared here? Is this some gluttonous annexe of Ramponneau's?[2] Have we been transported to Gargantua's pantry or to his "painted cellar" of Chinon?'

'He doesn't know how right he is!' cried Bourdeau, delighted.

Marion put a finger to her lips. 'My God, how noisy you all are. You're going to wake Monsieur.'

'A cousin of mine from Chinon is visiting my house,' explained the inspector. 'As a feast was expected and I didn't want to take Marion and Catherine by surprise, I plundered Madame Bourdeau's preparations and brought what we needed. Catherine lent me a hand baking the *pâtons*.'

'The *pâtons*?'

'Yes, here they are, all hot. Where I come from, they're called *fouées*.'

Bourdeau brought out a vast wicker basket from under the table. From it, he extracted an earthenware pot covered with an oiled paper tied with straw, and three bottles of wine.

'A *fouée*,' he went on, 'is like bread but much better. Ground flour, leaven, salt and water. Knead it well then let it rest. After that, you just have to shape the *pâtons* by hand, then into the oven with them. They pretend to ignore the heat, they move, shake, rise, swell, form bubbles, climb, collapse, rise again, relax, and finally turn golden brown, and you take them out and burn your fingers. That's the whole story!'

He grabbed one of these little treats, cut it with a knife, and opened the earthenware pot to reveal an immaculately white layer of fat. This he removed, then took out some crushed *rillettes* with which he stuffed the roll. Nicolas's mouth was watering at the mere sight of this operation. He only took a mouthful: it melted in the mouth, so well did the whole thing combine the crusty and the soft. The heat loosened the meat, which in turn moistened the bread with its juices.

'The secret of good *rillettes*,' said Bourdeau with his eyes lowered, 'lies in matching the pieces of pork used. These are of my own invention. I put in shoulder, loin, tenderloin, and belly, and add plenty of salt, pepper, herbs and spices. Plus my secret, which I shall reveal to you: a spoonful of honey and a splash of white wine! Add water until everything is covered and leave for six hours. When the whole thing has cooled down, I knead it and mix the meat and the fat.'

'You're a saint, my dear Pierre . . .'

Bourdeau continued stuffing the *pâtons*.

'And still the *fouées* keep coming!'

'Indeed,' a sepulchral voice suddenly proclaimed, 'it's not a fairy tale but a *fouée* tale!'

Monsieur de Noblecourt had appeared, draped in an indoor robe of wine-coloured calico, his head wrapped in a knotted madras.

Everyone laughed and cried out. A chair was brought forward and the newcomer dropped majestically onto it. Marion began complaining loudly about his foolhardiness, but Catherine, delighted by the turn that the evening had taken, calmed the old nurse.

'I'm starving,' said Noblecourt. 'My bedroom was gradually filling with sweet aromas that tickled my nose. Cyrus's nose, too, I think!'

The dog, who was lying under the armchair, barked happily at his master's voice. Bourdeau and Nicolas sat down in their turn. More *fouées* were prepared, which the magistrate gobbled up. He demanded wine.

'Where is this nectar from?'

'From a small, well-exposed vineyard, covered with flint gravel. Small peach trees grow between the vines. Their fruit with its pink and white flesh bursts with a thick, delicious juice . . .'

'Talking about fruit,' continued Noblecourt, 'no prunes and sage tea for me tonight. I'm eating and drinking. Does that good Dr Dienert think I don't know he suspected apoplexy? Why should I be living on light and not very nourishing food, and depriving myself of strong liquor, spicy and tasty food? From now on, I am going to stuff my face, and seek out violent passions, excessive heat and excessive cold!'

He looked around provocatively at his audience.

Catherine clapped her hands. 'Where there is appetite, there is no danger!'

'In truth,' said the procurator, 'the joy of finding myself surrounded by my friends tempers my irritation.'

'Tell us what happened,' said Nicolas. 'Nothing is likelier to calm the temperament and dispel an anxiety than to talk about it freely.'

'How right you are. You all know that I am a churchwarden of my parish, Saint-Eustache, and that I'm the oldest on the council. At six o'clock, I was there, dealing with council matters, when a man named Bouin suddenly appeared and demanded to be heard immediately. He was kicking up such a fuss that in the end we agreed to see him. All puffed up with arrogance, he introduced himself as a former timpanist of the company of the King's gendarmes.'

'There's that one,' said Nicolas, 'plus four companies of bodyguards: Charost, Noailles, Villeroi and d'Harcourt.'

'He continued in a shrill tone and told us quite bluntly that the King having granted, through the edict of 1756, the right of commensality to the timpanist of his gendarmes, after twenty years of service, of which this Bouin fellow felt justly proud, he should therefore enjoy the honours, prerogatives, privileges, franchises, freedoms, pledges, rights, fruits, profits, revenues and emoluments befitting his status. He peppered his speech with words which aroused the ire of the assembly, words so brazen I prefer to pass over them in silence.'

'Today's a day for petty quibbling,' sighed Nicolas.

'And toads who want to inflate themselves,' replied Noblecourt, his hearing as sharp as ever. 'Without getting off his high horse, and without drawing breath, he commanded us, the company of wardens of Saint-Eustache church, to make sure that he enjoyed full honours, was given precedence in assemblies immediately after the King's magistrates, and had the privilege of being brought in by the above-mentioned churchwardens . . . by us, would you believe it . . .'

He was choking with anger, and beating his chest with his clenched fists, startling Mouchette, who called him to order with a determined blow of her paw, her final warning before she retaliated by scratching him.

'Calm down, my darling, I'm not angry with you! Being brought in, as I was saying, by the churchwardens and presented with the consecrated bread immediately after the choir and the nobility, and before everyone else. Not content with this demand, he added the obligations of his rank in parish assemblies and processions, citing in support of this claim a royal decree of 1686. In short, I thought I was hearing again the bitter recriminations of my friend the Duc de Saint-Simon, fulminating against the disputes over precedence at the Court of the great King. But he was an eagle!'

He emptied his glass in large gulps and peered into the pot, which was still emitting little hissing noises.

'How could such an insignificant individual ever imagine that all this was possible? Did he really intend to appear with the characteristic insignia of his former state? Why not with his timpani? Does the scoundrel not know that the consecrated bread is always distributed indiscriminately, without any fuss, depending simply on the place occupied by each person in the church? Did

Our Lord, when he distributed the bread, establish a list of privileged people? Did he not say, "The first shall be last"? What nonsense to maintain, as this Bouin does, that in such an assembly, such a great throng of people, one should oblige each person to state his name and status, and assign him a chair to sit on, somehow describing oblique and circumflex lines, offering each parishioner a particular oblation according to his claims, while trying not to humiliate some nor arouse the jealousy of others.'[3]

'Who on earth put such an idea in his head?' asked Bourdeau.

'Do you need to ask? An outstanding casuist in the *parlement*: Président de Saujac, to name but one. Just when we needed it, his proverbial bad faith has blossomed into a cause without rhyme or reason. Although he versifies pleasantly enough, so I've been told. But he's taking poor Bouin for a ride, because for him the prose verdicts of that herald are gospel truth!'

'And, just like a young man, you're falling into the trap of this provocation! Your blood has been stirred and there's sweat on your brow!'

'That's how I've managed to stay so young,' said Noblecourt with majestic pomposity. 'Everyone thinks so, and you yourself just confirmed it.'

A new burst of laughter punctuated his words.

'But,' he continued, stirring in his armchair, 'isn't there something else to get my teeth into? This moaning, steaming pot is afraid, I think, of being neglected.'

'Oh,' said Bourdeau, 'that's my masterpiece. You will consider it as such after you've tasted it. Here are a couple of hens from my province. My cousins raised them lovingly. Last night, Madame Bourdeau poached them in a thick, well-conditioned poultry stock. Today, I braised them in the oven in a good-sized pot with the lid firmly closed. This method has the double advantage of not drying out the meat while at the same time giving it a crispy skin.'

'And I,' said Catherine, 'in order not to leave these poor beasts alone, have made some noodles from *my* province, some *spaetzle* gently fried in butter, with a touch of Muscat.'

Bourdeau took out the fowl with a delicacy unusual in this big, fiery man. He carved them with a silver knife handed to him by Poitevin. With each incision of the blade, little jets of juice and grease spurted out, like so many fragrant fountains. The three guests threw themselves on their plates. A great appreciative silence fell over the room, broken only by the snapping of bones, Cyrus's moans and Mouchette's imploring cries: both animals were trembling with envy and demanding their share of the feast.

'See how reasonable I am,' said Noblecourt, who had contented himself with a wing. 'I shall be the first to speak. Let us give thanks to Bourdeau for this delight. Assure your wife of our ravenous gratitude. I am your humble servant. That said, my children, where are we with our investigation?'

Bourdeau smote his head. 'I should have told you, Nicolas . . .'

'Is there some news? You're forgiven in advance. The hens plead in your favour.'

But Bourdeau's expression was sufficient indication that the joking was over.

'This morning in Rue Glatigny, at the bottom of the steps leading to the river, at the corner of the priory of Saint-Denis-de-la-Chartre, the watch discovered the body of a young girl.'

'Alas,' said Nicolas. 'Every day . . .'

'Except that this one had had her throat cut. I saw her in the Basse-Geôle. Exactly the same wound as the Pindron girl! A curious funnel shape and a great loss of blood . . .'

# VI

# DIVERSIONS OF THE HEART

If the grass had borne her, a flower would not
have received the imprint of her steps.
LA FONTAINE

Everything had frozen in the room, where, a moment earlier, the greatest merriment had reigned. It was Nicolas who broke the silence.

'Many crimes are committed in this city,' he said in an unsteady voice. 'It could always be a coincidence.'

'Highly unlikely. I went to the Basse-Geôle, where the body had, of course, been taken. I was able to proceed with the usual observations and Sanson, back from a session using the boot, was quite happy to help me. After much reflection, he went out and came back soon afterwards with a quarter-pound of plaster. He quickly prepared a paste and turned his attention to the body from the Saint-Florentin mansion.'

Marion gave a cry of horror.

'Catherine,' said Noblecourt, 'I think it's time for Marion to rest. She's been exerting herself far too much today . . . These evenings aren't good for her at her age; they're only for young men like me. Go, and may the night be kind to you.'

'The things I've seen on the field of battle without whining,' muttered Catherine, who was dying to hear the rest of Bourdeau's story.

But she obeyed and led Marion to her quarters. She was soon back.

'Why was Sanson so interested in the body of Marguerite Pindron?' asked Nicolas. 'What did he want with it?'

'With his plaster, he took a cast of the wound to the neck. The way they do with death masks.'

'Aren't they usually cast in yellow wax?'

'You're both right,' Noblecourt said, smiling wickedly. 'Before they bought themselves into the nobility of the robe, my ancestors were master wax moulders . . .'

There was a general cry of surprise.

'Now I understand why you're so interested in those theatres of corruption in your cabinet of curiosities,'[1] said Nicolas.

'An ancestor of mine helped to take the death mask of King Henry II in 1559, after he was mortally wounded by Montgomery's spear. It made a big impression on him, as the mask, cast only a few moments after death, cruelly revealed all the suffering that had preceded it. To go back to what I was saying, to make this kind of mask, you need to use thick strips of cloth, which surround and pull together the oval of the face, from the skull to the chin. You pour in the plaster paste, which, once solidified, gives a cast of the features, from which you can make a copy in wax.'

'What do they do with these masks?'

'Are you unaware, gentlemen, that the bodies of our kings are put on display except for the last one because of the risk of contagion from smallpox? Actually, they're just models wearing wax masks and the royal insignia, and the people troop past them to pay tribute. The impressions are preserved at Saint-Denis, where you can admire the collection.[2] But we're getting off the point.'

'There's always something to learn, Monsieur, from your wide experience.'

Noblecourt nodded, at the same time grabbing from the plate which Catherine had placed on the table a few quince pastries freshly removed from their moulds and put onto small lozenges of unleavened bread.

'It's a good thing Marion isn't here!' muttered Catherine.

'Let's get back to our corpses,' said Bourdeau. 'Sanson took the impression he'd made from Marguerite's body, and placed it on the wound of the unknown girl from Rue Glatigny. There was no room for doubt. Remember, Nicolas, that horrible funnel? The impression matched it almost exactly, with identical tears and compressions of the skin, looking for all the world like a shapeless hand.'

'Anything else?' asked Nicolas.

'Yes. The victim bears a strong resemblance to Marguerite Pindron. I mean, she's the same type of young woman, even though the two may differ in certain details.'

'An interesting comment. Do we have any idea of the time of death? It's vital to determine that. We already have many suspects for the murder in the Saint-Florentin mansion. Now we have another murder using the same method, with the added curiosity that the victims resemble one another. We need to find out if any of the possible suspects for the first crime could also have been the perpetrator of the second. If we know when death occurred, we can then check each of the suspects' whereabouts at the time.'

'It'll be no easy matter, Nicolas,' replied Bourdeau. 'The body is in very poor condition. It's not so much that it's been submerged in water at times, but rather that dogs, rats and crows have been at work on it. All things considered, Sanson estimates that death could not have occurred more than twenty-four hours earlier. We examined the corpse at one o'clock this afternoon.'

'Could it have been thrown in the river and then washed up?' asked Noblecourt.

'I don't think so. I went to the place. There are traces in the mud, tracks rather, suggesting that the body had been brought from the Cité, and before that from town. That bank of the island, opposite Quai Pelletier, is almost deserted at night.'

'All right,' said Nicolas. 'But nothing that would tell us more? Footprints, the marks of shoes?'

'Yes, lots, because people had started to gather before the watch arrived. I had a good look around. The mud is thick, and the backwash from passing boats and barges doesn't help. However . . .' He searched in his coat skirts. 'I did find this on the steps leading down to the river.'

He handed Nicolas a small stone that shimmered in the candlelight. The commissioner lifted it to his face.

'The button from a garment. It could be a gemstone, or—'

'An imitation gemstone,' Bourdeau hastened to say. 'I had it checked by a jeweller. Nothing but coloured glass.'

'It may have nothing to do with our case.'

'That's possible. We'll see.'

Nicolas slipped the button into his pocket.

'In the meantime,' resumed Bourdeau, 'I investigated a little more. There wasn't a body on the steps by the river between eleven o'clock on Monday night and about six o'clock this

Tuesday morning, when it was discovered. As the murder was not committed on the spot—'

'How do you know that?'

'By the fact that there's hardly any blood around. That gives us, let's see . . . one in the afternoon, take away twenty-four hours . . . Yes, a period on Monday between two in the afternoon and eleven o'clock in the evening, when there was still nothing on the bank.'

'Who told you that?'

'A man who lives in the area and walks his dog there every evening. Someone above suspicion, I checked.'

'And the victim?'

'Not many clues. A handkerchief, a key, a comb made of bone. A girl of lower class. However, I did find twenty-five *livres* and six sous in her pocket.'

'Good Lord, that's quite a lot for a girl of lower class. Was she wearing shoes?'

'No, we looked. Of course, so many people had been hanging around the corpse that they may well have been stolen.'

'Who found the body?'

'The old gardener from the priory of Saint-Denis-de-la-Chartre. He'd gone there to fetch water.'

'Doesn't the garden have a well?'

'It recently caved in.'

'Was the victim pretty?'

'Judging by what remained of her face, probably.'

'A prostitute?'

'The victim was dressed modestly but smartly.'

'Put your spies on the case,' ordered Nicolas. 'Speak to

Tirepot. He's getting older, and doesn't get around as much as he used to, but his network of informers is still unequalled. I need everything on this girl, and fast. For the rest, my dear Pierre, I rely on your discernment. I'll leave you the chore of checking our suspects' alibis for the time period you've mentioned. For my part, I have to go to Versailles tomorrow.'

'Are you seeing His Majesty?' asked Noblecourt.

'The King if I can, the Queen if I must, and two gardeners. I'll also pay my respects to Monsieur de Maurepas.'

'All the powers of the day united,' Bourdeau said, gently sardonic. 'You're young Court now!'

'Don't mock,' said Noblecourt. 'It's wise to conduct oneself well. Remember me to Monsieur de Maurepas. I knew him when I was young. In the thirties, he and I, along with the Chevalier d'Orléans, the legitimate son of the Regent and the Comtesse d'Argentan, d'Argenson, the minister of war and Caylus, would go, disguised in frock coats and round hats, to watch the parades at the Saint-Germain fair . . .'

He poured himself a full glass of wine and swallowed it in one go. 'Especially,' he went on, dreamily, 'when the strolling players took scenes from plays and parodied them. They were hilarious, with their bawdy ways and their strange pronunciation. God, how we laughed. With our mouths wide open and our breeches unbuttoned . . .'

But Nicolas was in a hurry to get back to the new case. 'Anything else, Pierre?'

'I thought I'd draw up a detailed chart of the activities of the various suspects on the night of the murder.' He moved his apron away from his coat skirts and took out a bulky document, the sheets of which were tied together by pieces of sealing wax. Seeing this, Nicolas stood up and, taking Bourdeau in his arms, kissed him on both cheeks, much to the amazement of the company. The inspector blushed with pleasure at this rare and unexpected demonstration of esteem from his chief.

'I tell you this,' proclaimed Nicolas, 'when it comes to *rillettes*, hens and investigations, he's irreplaceable. Now he even anticipates what I'm about to ask him to do!'

'Fourteen years of working together will do that,' said Noblecourt, clearly moved.

'Here in the first column,' resumed Bourdeau, 'you will find the names of the victim and the witnesses, including' – he lowered his voice – 'the Duc and Duchesse de La Vrillière.'

'Good for you,' remarked Nicolas. 'I have it on good authority that the duc was not at Versailles on Sunday evening as he claimed. And that he spent the night in Paris.'

'With the Beautiful Aglaé?'

'That would be surprising, given that she's in exile.'

Bourdeau nodded with a knowing air. 'The second column indicates the whereabouts of each person from ten o'clock to midnight on Sunday evening. The third shows their various activities the following morning. The fourth has each person's observations, the fifth my own observations, the sixth the clues found at the scene of the crime, the seventh the various opinions of the victim, and the eighth and last column the doctor's diagnosis of Jean Missery and his wound.'

Nicolas spent a while looking through the document. 'This is a very striking picture you paint. What are the first conclusions you draw from it?'

'Nothing really fits, neither the times, nor the testimonies. How to distinguish in all this what is the truth and what is a careful concealment of the truth? It all seems to me like one big conjuring trick.'

'I'd say the same,' said Nicolas, 'about the major-domo's sister-in-law, the nun. It's impossible to believe a word she says. She appears to tell the truth the better to lie, spends the night away from her convent but conceals the fact, and, note this, had a long conversation this very morning with the Duchesse de La Vrillière. What does it all add up to?'

'Is she a Carmelite?' asked Noblecourt.

'No, a Daughter of Saint Michel, a Eudist. Why do you ask?'

'The great King said one day to Monsieur, his brother, that he was well aware that the Carmelites might be deceivers, intriguers and weavers of yarns, but that he did not think they were poisoners. Admittedly, they had almost killed his niece with one of their medicines!'

Nicolas then recounted his day and his discoveries at Popincourt.

'Heaven,' said Noblecourt, 'has chosen you to untangle the most complex but also the most dangerous cases. Listen to a man who, although a recluse, lives with men ...'

'And may on occasion be imbued with their prejudices, as Rousseau says,' Bourdeau cut in.

For the second time that evening, the inspector went red in the face as his two friends turned their appreciative gaze to him.

'So you read and esteem Jean-Jacques?' exclaimed Noblecourt.

'I admit I am quite infatuated with his work. Believe me, his ideas will change our world. There is a fervour in him, the fervour of the citizen. "The great man becomes small, the rich man becomes poor, and the monarch becomes a subject. We are approaching a state of crisis and a century of revolutions."[3]

'That may be so,' said Noblecourt. 'Our philosopher Bourdeau should, however, beware for, if the passionate man reasons badly and contrary to the laws of logic, the fool finds reason in the same source, for his passion is cold. My children, I am grateful to you for this evening, but I am feeling sleepy now.'

He stood up and walked to the staircase, escorted by Cyrus and Mouchette. On the top step, he turned.

'In this case of yours, remember that you have to look for the least likely solution, even if it seems to you highly unusual. Goodnight, gentlemen, goodnight . . .'

As soon as the familiar figure had disappeared, Bourdeau turned to Nicolas with a touch of anxiety in his voice. 'Didn't he strike you as strange this evening? That parting shot . . . the things he was saying . . .'

'Don't look so worried,' replied Nicolas with a laugh. 'You don't know him as well as I do. He has a surprising ability, of which I have often been the fortunate beneficiary, of seeing through to the kernel of a case even before we have all the facts. He cannot even explain it himself. It manifests itself, as it did a moment ago, in sententious phrases whose primary meaning escapes us, but which always conceal a truth that has somehow been revealed to him. In addition, thanks to your Chinon wine, he drank more than usual this evening. That's why he was so cheerful and so talkative.'

They conversed a little more, constructing hypotheses each of which fell short because of some detail they had neglected. No sooner were they formulated than they collapsed like so many houses of cards. Beside the stove, on a straw chair that looked more like a prie-dieu than any other piece of furniture, Catherine sat darning, her head drooping from time to time with tiredness. Old pains were reawakened, memories of long bivouacs in the icy rain on the battlefields of Europe. Her hearing, however, was still sharp, and, without appearing to, she was listening out to make sure that the stock she had prepared for next day's meals from three meats and some roots was boiling away nicely. Bourdeau took his leave, and Nicolas walked with him along Rue Montmartre. He was laden not only with the basket containing the pot and the bottles, but also with a lantern. The commissioner had insisted in spite of Bourdeau's refusals: at this hour, the spaces between the street lamps were wide enough to attract prowlers who were only held at bay by the watch and by a light, however feeble.

Nicolas went back up to his room, which had been deserted by Mouchette: the strumpet shared her favours, and sometimes preferred to nestle in Cyrus's fur, where she soon began to purr with the regularity of an automaton. That reminded Nicolas of the promise he had made Monsieur de Sartine to investigate Bourdier, the eminent creator of the library of wigs and the inventor of a new encoding machine. With this thought, he undressed and went to bed.

*Wednesday 5 October 1774*

Monsieur de Sartine grimaced as he manipulated the ivory and ebony keys of his library. The mechanism was no longer playing the joyful music of Rameau, but a grim chant, a kind of *Dies Irae*.

The drawer sprang out with a snap. Sartine clutched Nicolas, who was horrified to see, instead of the expected wig, the bloodstained body of a young woman. He turned. The minister had disappeared, and cut flowers were strewn on the ground. In a panic, he saw a man striking the trunk of a great oak with an axe. He seemed to be moved by strings, like the puppets sold on Pont-Neuf. Nicolas recognised Bourdeau's impassive face. He saw the flash of the blade as it struck his chest, but felt nothing except a light tap. He opened his eyes. Mouchette was treading on him, and affectionately pressing her nose to his chin.

As he dressed, he felt weighed down by this nightmare, whose meaning eluded him. He prepared his trunk, checked the rifles Louis XV had given him, then brushed his spare coats, his ceremonial dress, and his hunting costumes. Since Monsieur de La Borde no longer had an apartment in the palace, Nicolas was putting up at the Hôtel de la Belle Image in Versailles. His arms and his clothes now had to follow him wherever he went, an inconvenience which was a source of silent irritation. He did not wake the household, where even Catherine was still sleeping. A baker's boy from the shop on the ground floor ran to find him a carriage. Day had not yet risen, and it looked as if rain was on the way. It began to fall as soon as he had passed the Porte de la Conférence and did not stop, accompanied by a squally wind.

Nicolas, haunted by dark thoughts and sombre presentiments, remembered Monsieur de Noblecourt's fainting fit. He thought of how much he owed the former procurator and how fond of him he was. He felt a sense of anguish at the fleeting nature of life. Of all those who had mattered to him, many had already gone. His guardian, Canon Le Floch, to whose affection and kindness he owed his moral conscience. His father, the Marquis de Ranreuil, a model of intelligence and courage. Sartine, who had taught him so much. Even Commissioner Lardin,[4] whose death he had avenged without underestimating his faults, and whose cold, grim face often came back to him. Without showing Nicolas any real friendship, he had been an efficient, demanding and conscientious master.

The carriage drove along the Champs-Élysées, which looked wild and sinister in the pale light of this early morning storm. The late King, with his benevolence, had reinforced the innate devotion Nicolas had felt as a child seeing his finely chiselled face on the *louis d'or*. In their different ways, Sartine, Bourdeau and Semacgus had also made him the man he had become, and of course Noblecourt had had a very special place in those years when his character had been moulded. He realised with a kind of almost sacred terror that, in their concern for him and their generosity, they had been like a succession of fathers to him. All of them had prepared him for life and its threats, had armed him from head to foot. Yes, he really did owe them a lot. This thought chased away his feelings of gloom, and encouraged him to face his destiny with renewed strength, in the service of the King – God and Saint Anne willing.


Just before Versailles, as the carriage was crawling through the Fausses Reposes woods, the storm increased in intensity. It was one of those heavy, blustery autumn downpours that lashed the ground and laid waste to everything. Nicolas was gazing out, spellbound, at this upheaval when something strange attracted his attention. At first, it was a blur, like something seen through the lens of a badly focused telescope. An indistinct shape had collapsed on the ground not far from him. He knocked on the partition to stop the carriage. The vehicle swerved and slid, and finally came to a halt in a chorus of cries and neighing. He rushed outside. A woman was lying unconscious on the ground. He bent down and took her in his arms to raise her. She was so light that he quickly got her into the carriage. She had a thin, pale face framed by unruly brown curls that tumbled down over her bodice. There rose from her warm, wet body an imperceptible scent of verbena, along with wilder autumn aromas, the smell of wet earth and dead leaves. He took his handkerchief and wiped her hands, which were covered in scratches from the gravel. She stirred, moaned, and stretched her body against his. Her mouth brushed his chin. He thought of Mouchette, so fragile . . . She regained consciousness completely, and colour came back into her face. Her eyes opened inquisitively; grey, he noted, with dark-blue flecks. She folded her spotted lace fichu over her chest and sat up.

'Monsieur, I am quite confused. What happened to me?'

Nicolas loosened his embrace and gently sat her on the seat. Having had a chance to get a closer look at her, he judged that she might be just over twenty.

'I saw you fall, Madame, and stopped my carriage to come to your aid.'

She smiled. He noticed that she had perfect dazzlingly white teeth.

'You have saved me, Monsieur. Whom shall I thank?'

'Nicolas Le Floch, commissioner at the Châtelet.'

There was no reason for him to keep silent about an honourable position. Experience had taught him that doing so inevitably led to further complications.

'Ah,' she remarked, looking interested. 'Young Ranreuil.'

Nicolas's eyes immediately clouded over. This was encroaching on personal territory, and he felt it as an intrusion. It was his precious link with the royal family. The late King, the current King, Mesdames and, in the old days, the royal mistresses had all used the name to do him honour. She glanced at him out of the corner of her eye. Had she sensed his irritation? She rolled one of her curls and, with the other hand, squeezed the water from it before wiping it on her bodice.

'We have a mutual friend, Monsieur de La Borde,' she explained. 'His wife is a close friend of mine. He never stops singing your praises. I think he'd like to set them to music!'

She half raised herself as if trying to curtsey. 'Aimée d'Arranet, your humble servant.'

He relaxed. His irritation suddenly gave way to an astonishing sense of well-being. The young woman huddled into a corner of the carriage. The silence between them lengthened. Filled with wonder, he was becoming aware of the grace and sweetness she exuded. He felt like a young man again.

'And what were you looking for in this storm?'

'You're being indiscreet, Monsieur. Nevertheless, it would be bad taste of me not to satisfy your curiosity . . .' She opened a cloth pouch hanging from her belt. 'I was gathering chestnuts, if you must know, when I was caught in the rain.'

'So early in the morning?'

She gave an irritable little pout. 'He persists! I was walking at dawn, and to answer your question, Commissioner, the original aim of my stroll was to gather mushrooms. Did you not know that the best mushrooms open at dawn, when there is dew on the ground?'

The conversation risked coming to an abrupt end if it kept along that track, and he hastened to abandon the subject. Commentaries on autumn fruits were leading nowhere. Was she younger than he had supposed? Her self-assurance was misleading, her self-control, her charm, her lack of affected gestures, her casualness . . . He rebuked himself: where was this sudden elation leading him? He had not felt anything like this in a very long time, since a certain concert at Balbastre's house.[5] The memory of Julie de Lastérieux came back to him, bitter and sweet at the same time.

'Monsieur, you are suddenly very silent,' said the young woman. 'Oh, look, because of me, you're completely soaked!'

Before he could stop her, she had taken a lace handkerchief from her sleeve and was wiping his forehead. It was like a caress. He had to restrain himself from taking her hand.

'Mademoiselle, you're too kind . . . Where can I take you? The rain is getting heavier.'

She smiled again. 'My company is a burden to you, I think, and I have made you late. Come now, don't blush. That's how I am, impertinent by nature, always teasing. The house of my father, the Comte d'Arranet, is not far from here, in Avenue de Paris. But before that, could I ask you to fetch my shoes? The poor things must be floating, unless they've already sunk!'

He hurried outside and ran to collect the shoes, which looked quite pathetic. They were filled with water, and he emptied them before bringing them back.

'Oh, well, never mind,' she said. 'Perhaps you could drop me at the foot of the front steps. I'll jump up them in my stockings.'

She giggled. Nicolas ordered the coachman to drive on. The carriage swayed from side to side under the impact of the wind. A silence fell, while the young woman strove to rearrange her clothes. On the great avenue leading to the palace, Mademoiselle d'Arranet shouted some instructions to the coachman. The carriage turned right into a drive lined with old lime trees, towards an elegant two-storey dressed-stone house. Nicolas saw a swarm of footmen emerge to open the door and help his companion to descend. The house seemed as if it were raised up on a great foot.

'Monsieur, many thanks,' Aimée d'Arranet said, turning to him. 'But that doesn't mean you are free. I'll run and get changed. Tribord will show you to the library. My father absolutely must make the acquaintance of my saviour.'

'Oh, it was nothing, 'said Nicolas. 'I wouldn't like to exaggerate.'

'Come now, Monsieur, be quiet and obey with good grace.'

She put a finger on his mouth, and he fell silent. He got out of the carriage and meekly followed the footman in his red and grey livery who answered to this strange name. The man's face was covered in scars. Noticing Nicolas's curious gaze, he smiled although the smile was more like a grimace.

'Monsieur should not be surprised: I served with Mademoiselle's father.'

Once they had climbed the steps, they went in through the carved bronze double door and found themselves in a bright vestibule with black and white marble flagstones. From here, Nicolas was led into a library with grey and gold moulding on the ceiling, and walls completely covered in bookshelves apart from the fireplace and two windows. Above the mantelpiece, where a pier glass would normally have been, was a full-length portrait of a general officer. At first sight, he looked like a sailor, and Nicolas noticed a naval scene in the background of the painting. The room clearly functioned as a drawing room. Armchairs, pedestal tables and gaming tables were arranged harmoniously. His attention was drawn to an unusual piece of furniture occupying the centre of the room – a low table bearing a coloured plaster reconstruction of a battle at sea. He bent over it to take a closer look at the details of this curious assemblage. Six vessels with English colours seemed to be laying siege to two others, almost completely wrecked, flying a white flag. Everything was rendered meticulously. Each ship, a fragile construction the size of a hand, had its sails, tufts of oakum represented the smoke of cannon-fire, and little balls of lead the cannonballs strewn over the decks. Nicolas even noticed piles of corpses and an officer standing on a poop deck with a telescope under one arm and a raised sword in the other.

'Ah, Monsieur, there you are, leaning over the ship's rail. I can see you're intrigued by the spectacle.'

The voice, which was somewhat coarse, came from behind Nicolas. He turned and saw a tall, well-built man looking at him affably with merry grey eyes. He recognised the original of the painting above the mantelpiece. The man was wearing a dark blue coat of military cut with brass buttons and a sash of Saint Louis. His powdered wig did not in any way detract from the virile energy of a deeply lined, weather-beaten face. He was leaning on a walking stick. He held out his hand to the commissioner, in the English style.

'Thank you for having rescued my scatterbrained daughter who, ignoring my advice that the wind was getting stronger, took it into her head to go wandering in the woods at the crack of dawn.'

Nicolas bowed. 'Anyone would have done the same.'

'My daughter seemed pleased that it was you . . . I am extremely grateful to you. So you're a friend of La Borde's? A charming couple. His wife was at convent school with my daughter. I knew your father well, both at Court and in the field . . . You look like him. A brave man, and what a wit!'

Beneath his rough exterior, the man was not lacking in the social graces. Everything was said in such a way that it could not wound.

'I am the Comte d'Arranet, Lieutenant General of the Naval Forces. Unemployed. For the moment only, I hope.'

'Might I ask you, Monsieur, to be so kind as to enlighten me about this tableau, which has, I admit, aroused my interest and my curiosity? I hope I'm not being indiscreet . . .'

His request seemed to delight his host. 'Please take a seat, Monsieur. Your request pleases and honours me.'

He himself pulled up a *bergère* and sat down, making the chair groan under his weight. Nicolas noticed a slight limp, presumably the result of an old wound.

'This relief map depicts the battle of Cape Finisterre. In 1747, my then chief, François des Herbiers, the Marquis de l'Étenduère, had to escort a convoy of boats laden with provisions for the West Indies. What a sight! Imagine a long procession of two hundred and sixty merchant ships escorted by eight vessels, each with seventy or seventy-four cannon . . . My God, it gives me the shivers even now! Once we had left the harbour at Brest, Rear Admiral Hawke's English fleet, which was waiting off the cape, tried to cut us off.'

'Did they outnumber you?'

'By almost two to one, alas! They had fourteen large vessels lined up. The marquis, who was an excellent sailor, quickly formed his eight vessels into a line to resist the English attack. We managed to hold our own long enough to allow the convoy to get away, with the wind behind them.'

'And the enemy let you do so?'

'Oh, hardly! Hawke realised that he was risking the failure of his mission, and he dispatched the *Lion* and the *Princess Louisa* to chase the convoy. It was a risky move, given the progress of the battle and the state of the sea. Despite all that, they tried to pass in front of our line. As if we were ready to let them make headway! We fired linked cannonballs at them, making it difficult for them to continue their pursuit. Damn, this account is making me thirsty! While the filly's still rubbing herself down, let's take advantage. God has my late wife in His holy safekeeping, but looking after her daughter is easily the worst calamity that could befall a man of my character. The strumpet is in charge here!'

They walked towards a row of books. Inside a false binding were a crystal carafe and two glasses. He poured a fine amber liquid into them and held one out to Nicolas.

'An old rum from Île Bourbon. Do you like rum?'

'Indeed I do. A friend of mine, a naval surgeon, introduced me to it.'

'What's his name?'

'Guillaume Semacgus.'

Monsieur d'Arranet slapped his thigh. 'Guillaume! Good Lord, I owe him a leg! It was he who pulled out a piece of a sharp spar that had gone through my calf and broken a bone. I would be most happy, Monsieur, to see him again. Please be my ambassador.'

They drank. The rum had a strong but delicious taste.

'Getting back to my story, Hawke, who was furious, set out to destroy us. He threw his whole squadron at us. The defence was worthy of the attack. He overtook the rear of our line. Several of our vessels were forced to strike their flags after a terrible fight lasting eight hours. By the time the *Tonnant* surrendered, there was nothing left of it but a burning wreck filled with the dead and the dying. A guard named Monsieur de Suffren, who was twenty years old, wept with rage and absolutely forbade anyone to touch the halyard of the flag on the poop deck.'

He offered Nicolas another glass of rum, but the commissioner refused. He poured one for himself.

'As you wish! By the time the sun went down, the French squadron was not entirely reduced. There remained the *Tonnant*, where the admiral had his quarters, and the *Intrépide*, commanded by Vaudreuil, although, without its masts, the *Tonnant* was nothing but a piece of flotsam.'

'And where were you, Monsieur?'

'I was Vaudreuil's first mate. He attempted a desperate manoeuvre. He tacked under enemy fire, even though his shrouds and stays had been cut to shreds by the grapeshot, and lowered a small boat to carry two cables to the *Tonnant*. All within pistol range of the English. The *Intrépide* towed the *Tonnant* behind it, each vessel having its flag pinned to the small mast in its stern. Six days later, the commander of the squadron returned to Brest, but, more importantly, the convoy reached the West Indies and relieved the food shortage there.'

A merry voice rang out. 'Father, you'll never change! There you are holding forth, drinking your infernal liquor, and tiring our guest with your exploits!'

The comte assumed a contrite air. His daughter flung her arms round his neck and kissed him.

'What you haven't heard,' she went on, turning to Nicolas, 'is that the boat that saved the day was under his command. I see you have become acquainted.'

The comte winked at Nicolas. 'Look at how a girl brought up in a convent treats her old father! Did you know, Aimée, that our friend knows Guillaume Semacgus, whom I've told you so much about, you know, the man to whom I owe the fact that I'm still on my two legs? What a coincidence, eh? For that, I forgive you your foolishness.'

'He's a very dear friend, who means a lot to me,' said Nicolas.

'And where does the old pirate live now?'

'In Vaugirard, near the Croix-Nivert.'

'Monsieur, I've just remembered. I'm giving a dinner tomorrow in honour of Monsieur de Sartine, Secretary of State for the Navy. Would you like to come?' With a knowing air, he went on, 'I'm hoping for a command. Perhaps the evening will help me get one. He was, they say, your protector with the late King. Your name was enough . . . and the exploits people attribute to you . . . No doubt the former Lieutenant General of Police will be pleased to see you again.'

'Monsieur, I don't know if I can—'

'Come now, I shan't accept any refusal. It's an order. At best, a plea.'

'With which I associate myself,' said Aimée d'Arranet.

Her smile made his mind up for him.

'In that case,' said Nicolas, 'I accept.'

When he found himself back in his carriage after taking his leave, all he could think about was the young woman's face as she made a slightly mocking half-curtsey. Back on the avenue, he observed that destiny had sent him to the same place twice – for very near the d'Arranet mansion was the house where the solution to the mystery of the man with the lead stomach had gradually been revealed.

The wind was reaching its maximum intensity as the sun rose. As soon as the carriage turned in front of the large stables to reach the square, recently renamed Dauphine, Nicolas was gripped by the spectacle of nature in a state of crisis. The proud buildings were lit up as if by invisible barrages of gunfire. Like a tall, dark stem, the chapel stood out against a slate-grey sky that matched the colour of the palace roofs. The lightning accentuated the red hue of the bricks on the facade of the marble courtyard, while the ministers' wing emerged from the clouds haloed in liquid gold. Gradually, the rays of the sun shifted, striking each of the great windows in turn, causing the frames and panes to gleam. The light rippled, creating a semblance of life in the heart of the palace. Thick, high clouds pushed small purple and pink clouds before them; some escaped and ran towards the nearby forests, while others, tumbling, joined the darkest mass as if drawn to it by a magnet and soon melted into its blackness. There was a resplendent rainbow, which immediately faded. Everything was extinguished in an instant. There was a kind of lull, a moment of silence and calm, before the sky once again caught fire in a cascade of lightning flashes followed soon afterwards by the muted bass notes of thunder. The rain came down even harder, covering the glorious vision of the palace with a hazy curtain of liquid, blotting out the decorations and reliefs, reducing the whole thing to an unstable mass that seemed on the verge of dissolving. The smell of earth and saltpetre filled Nicolas's chest. His frightened team of horses gave a few kicks and set off again at a full gallop.

He reached the Hôtel de la Belle Image. Nicolas was familiar with this type of accommodation. The rooms, although cramped, were always clean and well maintained, and there were far fewer cockroaches in the bed linen than elsewhere. Nicolas's first concern was to find an emissary who could convey the Comte d'Arranet's invitation to Semacgus. He scribbled a few words of explanation on a page of his black notebook and sealed it with sealing wax. It did not take him long to discover a wine merchant who was returning to Paris, having completed his business, and who was due to pass through Vaugirard, where he had customers. He was very pleased to take on the errand. Nicolas, whose insides had been warmed by the morning's rum, offered him a light meal of eggs and bacon, which made the man his friend for life. He then went up to his room to sort out the contents of his trunks. He had plenty of time since there was no chance that he could participate in that morning's hunt. True, if he hurried up, he would be in time to join the royal cortege, but, in this domain, hurrying was contrary to good manners. The most important thing was to be well informed. You did not venture into the treacherous swamps of the Court without knowing what kind of game was being hunted. Although, for simple shooting parties, elaborate costumes had been tolerated by the late King, this was not the case when it came to hunting roe deer, stags or boar. The new monarch was reputed to be more punctilious than his grandfather in this regard. The usual hunting costume – rich blue with gold braid – was de rigueur and the arrangement of the braid indicated the kind of animal one was going to hunt. How strange it all was! thought Nicolas. Nevertheless, these apparently insignificant details were meaningful: what they meant, above all, was that one had a name and the right to enter the King's coaches, which was the equivalent, for a man, of being presented at Court for a woman. This privilege was something of which Nicolas could not help feeling proud. Of course, he owed it to his birth, even though it was illegitimate, but, more importantly, it was because of the word of Louis XV that it had been granted to him for ever. He saw himself again on that fateful day when he had found a father, acquired what others took centuries to obtain, and gained the right to serve his King.

He was annoyed to see some stains on the patina of one of his rifles. Nothing ought to tarnish the splendour of the royal gift. He did his best to wipe them off. His mind flew from object to object. When would such trifles be regarded with indifference? Once, coming back from a choral concert with his friend Pigneau de Behaine, now bishop of the mission in Cochinchina, he had heard him describe the religion of the Buddhist monks, which taught its followers to renounce all things, to become detached from all ties, in order to attain supreme indifference and the peace of the soul. He had rebelled against that idea, considering it an inaccessible dream, a kind of moral suicide in a universe in which nothing any longer had a price or a meaning. Pigneau had gently observed that this renunciation was not so different from the communion of the mystics and the saints with the power of the Lord, and that Christ, too, had called for asceticism in old age . . . I'm becoming quite a philosopher, he thought. In a corner of his mind, the laughing eyes of Aimée d'Arranet were staring at him with a touch of mockery. In the end he decided to go to the ceremony of the removal of the King's boots. He would glean the latest news, would enquire about the kind of hunting due to take place the next day, and would also have a chance to investigate the strange story of the Trianon garden. However well-organised and far-sighted he was, he was not unaware that at Court any plan was subject to whims and chance.

Nicolas dressed in half-mourning, intending to get to the palace on foot. At the sight of the potholes in the roadway, he immediately realised that he had made a mistake and that his costume would not withstand the mud. He resigned himself to hiring a sedan chair, a means of transport he hated above all others, its swaying making him nauseous and the use of his fellow men seeming to him an insult not only to their dignity but also to his.

He passed through all the cordons like a peer of the realm and came to the foot of the ambassadors' staircase. He proceeded to the room where the removal of the boots took place, where, on questioning the guards, he realised that he had a little time to spare before everyone got back from the hunt. This would be an opportunity to stroll through the palace. He went down to the ground floor, where large stone galleries filled with a buzzing crowd welcomed those whom the rain had chased from the gardens. Idle courtiers were conversing in small groups, peering at the bourgeois ladies and their maids who had come to gawp at the surroundings. Nicolas remembered how surprised foreign visitors always were to discover that the place was a kind of permanent fair. The setting up of shops and stalls had long been tolerated. They had gradually spread, and now filled the vestibules, corridors and even the landings of the great staircase, and, although they were eyesores, everyone was so used to them, they had stopped seeing them. The Queen, while still the Dauphine, had often lingered over these stalls, much to the horror of Madame Victoire and Madame Adélaïde. The two aunts did manage to get a perfume seller who had colonised the vestibule of the marble staircase to leave – with the support of the royal princes and the maréchals of France, who were the only people who had the right to bring their coaches up to the steps of the palace.

Nicolas suddenly sensed that someone was staring at him. He turned and saw a potbellied little man wearing a curious white wig. The individual, realising that he was being observed, immediately lowered his tinted glasses over his eyes, did an about-turn, and vanished into the crowd. Nicolas was about to set off after him to find out the reason for such strange behaviour when an arm held him back. By the time he had turned again, the man was out of sight and out of reach. Angrily, Nicolas was about to rebuke the busybody who had stopped him when he recognised the gentle face of La Satin looking at him with an expression of sweet adoration.

'Antoinette? You here, in Versailles? You made me . . . No, it doesn't matter.'

'The thing is,' she said, 'an opportunity presented itself to increase my little business.' She was talking very quickly as if out of breath. 'I've done a deal with Marie Mercier, a widow who owns a perfume shop with her sister in Rue de Satory in Versailles.'

'How did you meet them?' he said, immediately regretting his inquisitorial tone.

'They often go to Paris to replenish their stocks. They liked what I sell. We talked and the idea of forming a partnership gradually grew. After each season, it's the custom for well-dressed ladies and the Queen's entourage to sell off their dresses and lace finery once they've been worn. We've obtained the exclusive right to buy and sell them.'

'Of course,' he said, 'that must make everybody happy.'

She lowered her head like a child caught doing something wrong.

'And what about your shop in Rue du Bac?'

'I'm only at Versailles for two days. I've hired an assistant. The rest of the week, she looks after the house and does the shopping.'

He found it hard to disentangle his confused feelings. Of course, he was pleased to see La Satin so committed to her new life, but, on the other hand, her presence at Versailles could not help but disturb him. It was pointless trying to hide it: seeing his worlds come together like this disturbed him greatly. His annoyance increased the guiltier La Satin looked. They talked about Louis and the start of his school career. Both were waiting impatiently for his first letters. But even that did not bring them closer together. A wall had gradually risen between them. He blamed himself, but was unable to dismiss his unease. They bade each other farewell like strangers. He suddenly remembered the unknown man in the wig. What was Lord Ashbury, a member of the British secret service,[6] doing in Versailles, and why had he fled at his approach?

# VII

## THIS COUNTRY

Maurepas has returned in glory
No power, but that's another story
The King gives him a hug and says
You and I are birds of a feather
It's better that we stay together
ANON., 1774

Nicolas was striding through the gallery, having not even noticed the desolate look in Antoinette's eyes. Feeling faint, as if suffocating, but unwilling to look into the reasons why, he tried to distract himself by observing the curious manners of the Court. Husbands would meet their wives and greet them with an indifference appropriate to strangers. It was true, he thought, that these days men were busy increasing the number of their conquests and women publicly displaying their lovers. Couples living together hardly met, and never took the same carriage, nor did they ever find themselves in the same house, except in the palace. Possession for men, seduction for women: they were the only motives for attack or surrender. Loving without pleasure, surrendering without a fight, leaving one another without regrets, calling duty weakness, honour prejudice, delicacy dullness, such were the manners which Nicolas attentively observed: seduction had its code and immorality its principles.

The time had come for the removal of the King's boots. As he entered the room where the small company was beginning to gather, buzzing with the murmur of courtiers, guards, grooms and those who were only there because their position required it, an acrid, sickly-sweet smell, a mixture of musk, scent and powder seized him by the nostrils, and a claw-like hand gripped his shoulder. From the aroma, he recognised the Maréchal de Richelieu. Thirteen years earlier, he had been in this same room when Monsieur de Sartine had brought him to see Louis XV for the first time.

'Young Ranreuil, returning like a ghost!' exclaimed the old man. 'How nice to see you again. How is Noblecourt?'

The question did not require an answer, but Nicolas made the mistake of forgetting that. 'Very well, Monseigneur, like his contemporaries.'

'I thank you, Monsieur,' squealed the maréchal, with a horrible grimace. 'I am younger than him, by a long way! What work brings you to this country?'

'Hunting. I hope the First Gentleman of His Majesty's Bedchamber will permit me to question him about tomorrow's hunt.'

This respect for the proprieties seemed to delight the maréchal, who proudly lifted a face coated with ceruse and rouge. His grinning mouth revealed teeth that were well on the road to ruin.

'Well, Marquis, today they were tracking a monstrous boar, a creature of the devil usually confined to the great park. Damnation, the beast ran all the way to the gardens, frightening our people with his bloodthirsty eyes. The King, who is not a

Bourbon for nothing, gave orders for the animal to be hunted down. The big footprint it left this morning did the rest. By this time, they should be paying it their last respects.'

'And what about tomorrow?'

'Tomorrow, for His Majesty's pleasure, they'll be hunting both animals and birds in the plain of Grenelle.'

He rose up on tiptoe and clutched Nicolas's arm to whisper something in his ear, but his voice was still so high-pitched that Nicolas doubted his words escaped anyone.

'I'm going to tell you the latest piece of bad taste. The Prince-Abbé de Salms was crossing the bull's-eye antechamber yesterday with a few friends. Some young dandies who were warming themselves there started, if you can believe it, to mock him so loudly that he heard them. "There's Aesop and his court!" You know how deformed the man is! Well, he was not in the least disconcerted, and paid them back for their effrontery. "Gentlemen," he replied, "the comparison is quite flattering to me, for Aesop made the animals speak."'

'Alas,' said Nicolas, 'it seems there are countries where ridicule and flattery are so closely intertwined that it is impossible to practise one without producing more of the other!'

'You are very censorious today,' observed the maréchal. 'An unhappy love affair, perhaps? In this world, it is not enough to know that in order to succeed one must be ridiculous, one must also study carefully the circle in which our rank has placed us, the ridiculous ways which most concern our state, those, in a word, which are in credit, and this demands more delicacy and care than one may imagine.'[1]

Nicolas was surprised by the maréchal's tone. It was true that the wind had changed and that he was still determinedly trying to assert himself in a Court where everyone was turning away from him, including the young royal couple. This glorious relic had known the great King as a page, Madame de Maintenon, the young Duchesse de Bourgogne . . . He had seen the whole century. Nicolas could not help feeling a touch of compassion for this old man determined to perpetuate an immutable order.

'Tell me, tell me,' the maréchal continued, 'does your presence at Court have anything to do with the tragedy everyone is talking about?'

Surprised by these words, Nicolas remained silent.

'Madame de Maurepas's angora cat has been murdered! Since then, there has been nothing but wailing and gnashing of teeth, and the culprit's head demanded on a platter. No, I see it's something else.'

He breathed in. He had underestimated the Duc de Richelieu, as people so often did.

'Yes, I sense rather that you are here because of a somewhat unfortunate affair concerning Monsieur de La Vrillière. Are you going to tell me . . .?'

Nicolas did not bat an eyelid.

'Oh, don't worry, I can read you like a book. You say nothing, but your sealed lips are all the more eloquent. Could you at least—'

The cries of the ushers and the dull thud of the halberds striking the floor, announcing the return of the King's procession from the hunt, saved Nicolas, who ignored Richelieu's insistence and bowed deferentially. The room was a sea of bent backs. The King, his face flushed and his coat dripping water, looked around the gathering. He was so tall that he dominated it, and his hunting boots made him even taller, but, as he did not rise to his full height, the effect was not as majestic as it might have been. He seemed to look at everyone surreptitiously, screwing up his eyes without, however, appearing to recognise anyone. He made a few hesitant advances and retreats, his arms dangling. Nicolas noticed that his profile recalled that of the late King, but was less firm. His already bloated neck sank between his shoulders. His blue eyes were inscrutable, lacking the dark velvetiness of his predecessor's. On his lips there hovered an inexpressive, almost innocent smile. He passed Nicolas, approached him, bent down and focused his gaze on him.

'Ranreuil, follow me when I go back to my private rooms.'

These few words created a stir. All eyes turned to the beneficiary of the King's attention. Everyone knew how short-sighted the monarch was and how hard he found it to recognise his servants. The Maréchal de Richelieu saw fit to intervene at this point. 'Sire,' he said, 'please allow the First Gentleman—'

The King turned his back on him, without giving any indication that he had even heard him. Nicolas knew that the royal couple had been behaving particularly badly to Richelieu lately, hoping in this way to force him to give up his position and stop bothering them with a presence that reminded the Queen all too sharply of the hated Madame du Barry. But it was no good, he just kept on, pretending not to understand the many eloquent signs of his fall from favour and ignoring the many jokes of which he was the butt.

After the King had wiped himself down with towels, some of his servants changed his clothes. Or at least, with the twenty-year-old monarch behaving more like an adolescent, they tried to. With a laugh, he dodged the shirt he was handed, lowering his neck at the crucial moment. The grooms were accustomed to these jokes and played the game with good grace. The King choked with laughter and stamped now one foot, now the other. The arrival of a newcomer brought the joking to an end. Nicolas recognised Monsieur de Maurepas. He ceremoniously greeted Louis XVI, gave Richelieu a knowing smile, and looked at Nicolas inquisitively.

Tall and thin, with a noble bearing, lean legs, a high forehead, wide blue eyes and a pale face, Maurepas smiled without opening his small mouth. His image, nonchalant, self-assured, reassuring, was that of an old, still handsome man with a good-natured, easy-going air. Richelieu pulled Nicolas back and, again clinging to his arm to raise himself a little, whispered in his ear, 'Did you know that his reputation for impotence is extremely well founded? He has all the faults of a eunuch, loving and tormenting women without satisfying them . . .' He laughed. 'He hates nothing more than to have his back against the wall. Or should I say, against the bed?'

Nicolas was sweating blood for fear that the maréchal's shrill voice would be overheard. But the King was talking about the hunt and the solitary old boar, which he himself had dispatched with a well-aimed blow of his dagger. A murmur of approval followed this announcement. The minister began talking to the monarch in a low voice. The commissioner looked at this curious combination of the past and future. He knew what people said: that on the vessel of State, Monsieur de Maurepas was more of a passenger than a pilot, that there were two men inside him, the one who saw and the one who navigated. Alas, continued the rumour, the former was perceptive and enlightened, the latter fickle and irresolute. The King liked him, because his own qualities and flaws were similar to the old man's. It was as if he were seeing himself in a mirror.

With the ease of half a century's expertise, the minister, having begun speaking, would not stop. He talked interminably, for in him everything began and ended with words. He had the reputation of rarely listening to anyone else, and of always speaking before thinking. Nicolas watched the scene, and the attentive gathering around it, without really seeing them. What was he, the man for special investigations, doing here? What role was he playing? Of course, he was perfectly familiar with the circumlocution, the etiquette, the true and false faces, the traps of all kinds. A traveller accustomed to the tempests of this country, he nevertheless felt like an outsider. It was as if he were watching himself playing a game, a game in which he participated without becoming involved, a game in which he knew all the required words and gestures by heart but could only hold his own by remaining cold, analytical and devoid of passion. In this society where the only things that mattered were subtle distinctions and the precise hierarchy of rank and privilege, he was dancing on shifting sands to a music whose scales he had learnt a long time ago – to tell the truth, ever since his father's salons in the chateau at Ranreuil. Skilful at avoiding the dangers, never uttering a word for which he might have been reprimanded, a courtier by obligation, a servant by necessity, a man of the King by profession, loyal by inclination, he had mastered the customs of this world and these people without embarrassment or pleasure, but was separated from them by an invisible wall, and had no wish to know who had decided to build it.

Whether this wall was a means of attack or defence, even he himself was not sure. Free within his armour, nothing could touch him; no word, however deadly in these times of ridicule, could reach him. The only words that could have an effect on him were those that might come, whether through misfortune or by some strange chance, from the mouth of the King. He felt a kind of wave of happiness and pride at being, basically, so free and so detached. Yes, he thought, fate had thrust him into a setting from which he could always escape, just as in his childhood dreams, whatever the circumstances. That was how he was able to maintain his rightful place within a rigid system where the slightest false step could break a reputation, tarnish a name and compromise a career. This thicket of traps, the home to so many false reputations, was negotiated by Commissioner Nicolas Le Floch with polite indifference and the confidence of experience.

Maurepas continued to hold forth while the King listened in open-eyed wonder and his servants attended to him. Nicolas compared the minister to Noblecourt. More or less the same age, they had once attended the festivities of Regency Paris together. One seemed to have endured without learning anything, while the other belonged to 'that small, select number of excellent men who, having been endowed with a fine and particular natural strength, have carefully honed it, through study and by skill, and have brought it to the highest point of wisdom it can reach'. Montaigne's words had come spontaneously to his mind, a vestige of his adolescent reading in the library of the chateau at Ranreuil. His basic feelings about d'Aiguillon's successor echoed the public's judgement: Maurepas, well shaven, well powdered, well rejuvenated, gave the impression of thinking deeply about nothing.

The noise of the arms carried by the guards, announcing the departure of the King, brought him back to reality. He hastened to follow, along the same route he had taken during his first visit to Versailles. Reaching his apartments, the King turned and signalled to Nicolas to come with him to another, even more private domain. From the little gallery overlooking the Cour des Cerfs, there was a dark, narrow spiral staircase. This led them to a wide door, which opened into a large attic room dominated, from the first, by a strong smell of filings, leather and rope. From there, it was possible to reach a small belvedere with a view over the roofs of the palace, the gardens and the park. At a glance, Nicolas saw model ships, navigational instruments, clocks either intact or dismantled, locks and various mechanisms. Books and maps were scattered everywhere, along with other objects which all pointed to their owner's curiosity. Clearly this was a personal hideaway, a place for the King to relax. Of course, he had known his visitor for a long time.

'Will you be with us at tomorrow's shoot?' asked Louis XVI.

'Yes, Sire. I have brought the rifles you know to Versailles with me.'

'We like the fact that these memories of our grandfather are still in the hands of his most loyal servants. What's the latest about the investigation in the house of the Duc de La Vrillière?'

So he already knew. How could it have been otherwise?

'The elements are falling into place.'

'You're clever, you'll get there.'

He seemed embarrassed suddenly, like a child caught doing something wrong. He motioned to Nicolas to sit down. The commissioner bowed but did not move. He felt that he ought to help the King to express himself.

'Your Majesty knows my loyalty. What can I do to serve you?'

His interlocutor appeared to take the plunge. 'Monsieur, you must get me out of trouble . . . From time to time, from the belvedere, I fire at the cats that swarm on the roofs. They disturb us at night . . .'

A strange pastime, thought Nicolas, remembering dear Mouchette.

'Alas,' continued the King, 'I shot one that must have been Madame de Maurepas's angora cat. What do you advise me to do?'

'Sire, I fear that the only acceptable thing to do is to tell the truth. Your ancestor once dismissed a page who had tormented his cat. However . . .'

'However?' said the King.

'However,' said Nicolas, 'if Your Majesty will allow me to speak on his behalf, I will be his ambassador to Madame de Maurepas. I will go to the trenches to withstand the first attack. Of course, she will have to listen to reason and realise that what happened was an accident. The King was simply shooting at pigeons, and a cat got in the way . . .'

'That's it,' said Louis XVI approvingly, 'that's it exactly.'

He pushed the hand of a clock, and listened with delight as it rang. He rubbed his hands, filled with a satisfaction that he could not conceal. He changed the subject and began speaking with surprising fluency.

'Are you aware, Ranreuil, of the disputes over the northern passage? I am turning to my advantage the works that scholars send me. One of my correspondents, a native of the Swiss cantons, has called me "a delight of the human race".' He laughed. 'He stresses my principles of fairness, justice and humanity. Which Roman emperor was called that?'

'Titus, Sire.'

'That's it. I'd really like to send these newspapers and extracts from this friend's letters to Monsieur La Harpe,[2] who denounced the work of my predecessors in *Le Mercure*.'

The King was becoming increasingly heated, and his face turning redder and redder.

'The man has no respect for anything. Anyway, attacking the government of kings is small beer for him, it's religion this philosopher really attacks! If the people are constantly subjected to a flood of writings and ungodly lampoons, he'll end up destroying their ancient beliefs and their loyalty to both divine and royal majesty.'

Calmer now, he tapped a little morocco-bound book.

'My Swiss friend assures me that Monsieur de Bougainville, with whom he is in correspondence, is trying to find the best way to get to the pole and that this work partly deals with it.'

The King approached a window. He again appeared ill at ease and embarrassed. He walked towards a small forge, which had gone out, and worked the bellows.

'Have you asked to see the Queen?'

'Not yet, Sire. I was about to. My presence at Versailles . . .' He did not finish the sentence.

'Settle this Trianon business as quickly as you can, it's been going on for far too long. I don't want anything to trouble my wife's peace of mind. We have to put paid to these rumours.'

Nicolas found the tone too bourgeois by far. The King continued walking up and down, looking at various objects without lingering over any of them.

'I've not had any news from our Micmac,'[3] he resumed, again changing the subject. 'He's been going around the tribes, and I hope . . . But what I have had is a report from one of our naval officers which includes some information about your friend Pigneau.'

Nicolas gave a start. How did the King know that he was acquainted with the missionary? Sartine had to be somewhere behind it.

'His consecration,' Louis XVI went on, 'was deferred for a long time because of the bishop's absence in Pondicherry. You'll be pleased to hear that it finally took place in São Tomé, near Madras, last February. My God, how long news takes to reach us, and always by unusual routes!'

'Unusual routes? Well, that's better than usual routine, which is an inevitable evil!'

The King laughed, suddenly a young man again. 'That's a play on words I'll repeat. I was merely talking about unusual and roundabout ways.'

'May Your Majesty forgive me,' said Nicolas, also laughing.

'Not at all, I am grateful to you for this distraction. I understand it was one of the reasons my grandfather appreciated you. Your friend was preparing to go back to Cochinchina, after trying to assert his authority over the Franciscans. We wish him good luck with those people, they want it all for themselves. Is he a man of character at least?'

'Of very sturdy character, Sire, with a sharp, well-stocked mind.'

'Monsieur,' said the King, slightly hesitantly, 'I appreciate your judgement and your knowledge of men. Promise me you will always tell us the truth. I need honest men about me. You must help me . . .'

With his frank, sensitive nature, Nicolas was touched by this simply expressed appeal. He threw himself at the King's feet. Moved, the King raised him and led him, with disarming naturalness, back to the small staircase. In his embarrassment, Nicolas tried without success to withdraw backwards as etiquette demanded. He descended the stairs as if in a dream and walked through a maze of corridors until he found himself outside in the gardens. Moving as it was, the monarch's simplicity did raise a few questions. It elevated the private man in Nicolas's estimation, but what of the supreme symbol of the State? Could one feel as much respect for a person one knew too well? The love of royalty demanded a boundless respect for the conventions. But there was nothing servile about total obedience and humble submission when they were given to one who, as the representative of God on earth, would very soon be crowned at Reims.

He was now walking towards Trianon, dreading to return to a place where, a few months earlier, the late King, leaning on his arm, had climbed into his carriage for his last journey back to the palace. The park was suffused with the melancholy of autumn, and the pervasive smell of boxwood rose from the ordered clumps of trees. Coming to the vast steps of the chateau, Nicolas stopped to get his bearings. On his left was a short avenue which ended in a staircase leading to the door of the chapel. There, a man was busy gathering fallen leaves. Nicolas asked him where his chief was, and the man pointed to the greenhouse opposite the chapel. Nicolas walked along the facade of the chateau to the greenhouse, where Louis XV had striven to grow exotic species. Struck as soon as he entered by the damp, suffocating heat of this mass of enclosed vegetation, he saw two men in brown coats leaning over a workbench. Approaching, he recognised the older of the men as Claude Richard, the head gardener, whom he had often seen in the past. The other man must be his son. One thing, though, intrigued him: their attire. He was accustomed to seeing Richard in the red, white and blue livery of the King. As the young Queen now had the Petit Trianon at her disposal, they should have been wearing her livery, which was red and silver. He realised all at once that these two veteran servants were wearing mourning for their master after their fashion. The gardener looked up, annoyed at being disturbed. His son, intent on planting some kind of cutting, ignored the newcomer. Claude Richard looked hard at Nicolas. He had faded grey eyes and a weather-beaten face.

'Monsieur,' he said, 'I think I recognise you. I have seen you several times with the King, I mean, our late master . . .'

Nicolas was moved by this simple loyalty.

'He used to call you "young Ranreuil",' Richard continued with a smile.

'You have a good memory. Forgive me for distracting you from your task. Are you in the middle of some remarkable acclimatisation?'

'I was collecting root sprouts from this plant.'

He pointed to a shrub. Nicolas gave him a questioning look.

'Root sprouts are suckers that are detached from the mother plant and then replanted.'

'And this shrub?'

'It's a kind of acacia, a locust tree, which produces bunches of highly scented white flowers and fruit in the form of pods. But to what do I owe the honour of your visit, Marquis?'

Nicolas waved his hand as if chasing away an importunate fly. 'It is not the marquis who needs your help, but the police commissioner. His Majesty has told the Lieutenant General of Police how worried he is regarding a strange incident about which the Queen informed him. Those visitors in the gardens whom you also saw and whose presence you reported. Can you tell me what happened, in as much detail as possible?'

Richard seized a long stick to support himself and led his guest towards a wooden bench, onto which he collapsed heavily.

'Autumn revives my aches and pains, especially when I keep still,' he began. 'Now let's see. Last 10 August, my son and I were crossing the gardens, towards the avenue, when we came across two women. Even if they had not hailed us, we would have been surprised to see them.'

'Why is that?'

'Their dress, Marquis, their dress! We may not be up to date with the latest fashions here, but by God, we do see the Queen and her women, and we don't keep our eyes in our pockets. I had never seen such a costume. Shapeless dresses, quite plain, without bodices, blouses with sleeves swollen like goat's skins, square hats covered with muslin . . . Spectacles . . . And that accent . . .'

'So they spoke to you?'

'Yes, in an accent that reminded me of the English visitors who've been coming here in such numbers since the peace treaty.'

'Can you draw, Monsieur Richard?'

'In my job, you have to.'

'Could you make a sketch of these strange women?'

'Of course.'

The gardener took a folded sheet of paper and a piece of charcoal from his pocket, and struggled away with them for a few minutes. Nicolas looked in puzzlement at the drawn shapes, which were extremely vivid but resembled nothing in human knowledge. He had certainly not seen anyone dressed like that during his recent stay in London.

'What did they ask you?'

'The way to the palace.'

'Was that all?'

'Yes, and then they disappeared.'

'Disappeared? You mean they withdrew, walked away . . .'

'Oh no, I mean disappeared. The common people, as you know, have access to the gardens. I am worried sometimes for my flowers and the Queen's peace of mind. So I wanted to know where the visitors were really going. But when I turned into the avenue . . . Well, my son can confirm this. Right, Antoine?'

The young man nodded firmly. 'My father's right, Marquis. They just weren't where they'd been before.'

'In addition,' the father continued, 'one of my assistants who was coming in the opposite direction didn't pass them.'

'Was it hot?'

Nicolas was thinking of some stories that Semacgus had told

him about the phenomenon of mirages in hot dry weather in deserts. But mirages did not speak, and certainly did not ask the way.

'It happened at four o'clock in the afternoon. The sun was still high in the sky.'

'Have you ever seen them again?' Nicolas asked, after further reflection.

'No, not so far.'

'If anything should happen, please send for me immediately. Thank you for your help. I'll take your sketch with me.'[4]

Nicolas was puzzled. He considered Richard a man of experience and common sense. His testimony was unimpeachable, even if reason could not account for it. Deep down, Nicolas could not help linking this business to the presence of Lord Ashbury in Versailles. Why? He did not know. Of course, there had been peace between the two nations for years, but it was an armed peace, beset with mutual caution and suspicion. The English suspected the French of harbouring thoughts of revenge. This obsession was exacerbated by every new episode in the rebellion of the American colonies. He, of all people, was in a position to know that there was some foundation for this and that Naganda was not constantly travelling the length and breadth of the Indian Territories just to find new places to hunt caribou and beaver.

The questions were piling up. If these two women had harboured evil intentions towards the Queen, why would they have made themselves so conspicuous by their dress and way of speaking? And how to account for something which made the whole thing even more puzzling, that sudden disappearance, which brought back some very bad memories? He felt again the terror he had once before experienced in the face of the inexplicable and the nagging irritation of having failed to find a rational explanation for such phenomena.

It was well into the afternoon by now. Nicolas was wandering in the hall of mirrors, undecided whether to visit the Queen or to do what he had to do with Madame de Maurepas. Lost in thought, he bumped into someone, who held him back in a friendly way.

'Come now, Monsieur Le Floch,' said the newcomer, with a jovial expression, 'where are you going with such a puzzled air?'

He recognised Monsieur de Ville d'Avray, the First Groom of the King's Bedchamber. He had had the good fortune to meet him when he had taken up his post in succession to Monsieur de La Borde.[5]

'Walk with me,' he said, taking Nicolas's arm, 'and you can tell me your troubles. I'm just off to deliver a note to Monsieur de Maurepas.'

'Gladly. Your kind offer resolves my indecision. I was torn between the Queen and the minister, and now you've made up my mind for me!'

'Perfect timing! I'm going to see the Queen next. His Majesty has arranged a surprise for her and has asked me to take care of it. You can accompany me there once you've seen to your business with Monsieur de Maurepas. You see, everything works out without any effort. You just have to meet the right person.'

'Monsieur, I am your humble servant.'

'And I yours. I found the King very calm after he had seen you. Since yesterday, I had been finding him quite dejected. Something about a cat . . .'

Nicolas nodded. 'That's my business, as it happens. I have to convince Madame de Maurepas that he was shooting at a pigeon and missed.'

'A pigeon? I understand your anxiety. It won't be easy to get the good lady to swallow that. Do you know her?'

'She hasn't been at Versailles long, and I haven't been here very often lately . . .'

'Come on, you're here now, and very much in favour! The important thing is not to be put off by her repulsive exterior. In fact, she's quite open-handed. She acts high and mighty and likes nothing better than to grumble about the ills of her house – all material ones, don't worry – the failings of the time and the misfortune of being at Versailles. To do so, she persists in using the old language of the Regency period, with a vulgarity that has become second nature to her.'

'I fear the worst,' said Nicolas, with a smile.

'She has a natural wit which gives her the upper hand over those devoid of it, and, although you might find that she rattles on, she'll like you. She has a sixth sense about when people are being honest with her.'

That wasn't what Nicolas needed to hear. Was his pigeon idea the right one after all? They reached the apartments which the King had given the minister and which were close to his. They were admitted to a drawing room dominated by the harsh voice of an elderly woman of rare ugliness, sitting in a *bergère*, surrounded by a number of attentive ladies. Leaning on the mantelpiece, Monsieur de Maurepas was conversing with Richelieu. It seemed, however, that the lady's words were addressed to him.

'You run away from me because I get on your nerves, so you say, and I'm always grumbling. What else do you want? I got into the habit of doing it at Pontchartrain[6] for forty years through *lettres de cachet* and kicking up as much fuss as I could, so why shouldn't I do it at Versailles? All that time spent paying off your debts, and those of Monsieur de Pontchartrain, who acts like Solomon, and those of Monsieur de La Vrillière, may God confound him! And then those of the Archbishop of Bourges, who builds castles for his stupid brother and even the Marquis of Phélypeaux, who also ended up with debts . . .'

'She'll mention the whole family,' Ville d'Avray whispered in Nicolas's ear.

'The fact is, I paid millions, while being forced to skimp and save. All the same, I had a hundred and thirteen servants.'

'My darling . . .' said Maurepas.

'I know what I'm talking about. A hundred and thirteen servants to pay, and a hundred and ten people to see every day that God creates. So don't go throwing stones at me. That's right, laugh! You have no heart, no liver, no lungs, no spleen! You drag me to Versailles, and they kill my cat! My God, I must have had a jinx on me to fall for someone like you, who's always giving me a rough time!'

She looked long and hard at the new arrivals.

'Here's the hero of the day!' said Richelieu, addressing Nicolas. 'I was recounting your adventures to Maurepas, who was kind enough to enquire about you.'

What was irritating about the maréchal, thought Nicolas, was that smugness that shone through in everything he said, however well meant. He bowed to the minister.

'Monsieur,' said Maurepas, 'what the maréchal has revealed makes me anxious to know you better. My separation from the Court has not given me a chance to . . . Tell me, do you ever seize lampoons, songs or other seditious material?'

'That is indeed a frequent occurrence.'

'Good, good! Think of me sometimes. One example will suffice for me. I've been collecting material of this kind for many years. It's a mania of mine. Clairambault, the genealogist of the King's Orders, has already offered me a copy of his song book. If you can help me to enrich it, my collection will constitute the true history of the century.'

'I'll see what I can do, Comte.'

'There he goes, claiming an exclusive right to my visitors!' cried the duchesse. 'Approach, young man.'

This appellation delighted Nicolas, less and less accustomed to being addressed in this way.

'So, Monsieur, to what do we owe your presence?'

'Madame, His Majesty . . .'

'That's enough, Monsieur. Not another word.'

Had she understood? Did she know all about it? She rose, leaned on Nicolas's arm, waved the other ladies out of her way with an imperious gesture and, walking with a stoop, drew him into a cramped boudoir, where she collapsed into a love seat with a painful sigh. She gave him a stern look and urged him to speak.

'Madame, I shan't beat about the bush. The King is so unhappy about the loss of your angora cat that he does not dare speak to you himself. He genuinely wants you to know the truth: I admit to my great shame that it was I who suggested to him the excuse that he had been shooting at pigeons.'

A long silence ensued.

'Monsieur, tell the King that I am much aggrieved at having lost an old companion who guzzled and slept in my lap. But listen to this. I would far rather lose my cat than find out the King had lied. He does not need my forgiveness, I am his servant. He's a good boy, and so are you. Keep an eye on Monsieur de Maurepas.'

She held out her hand for him to kiss. Nicolas went back to the other room, and everyone turned to look at him, intrigued. For the second time that day, 'young Ranreuil' was creating a stir.

'No outbursts, no yelling,' said Ville d'Avray. 'I think I've been quite clairvoyant in this matter. He has cast a spell on the lady.'

'I'm an expert at exorcisms,' said Nicolas wryly. 'I followed your advice and have done well by it. May I ask you to tell His Majesty that the affair has been settled, truthfully . . . And without the pigeon. And that Madame de Maurepas is his servant.'

Ville d'Avray bowed. 'Thank you for making me the herald of such good news. I hope your mission to the Queen is less delicate.'

'It's only some information I must pass on to her at the King's request.'

They reached the room of the Queen's guards.

'Don't hesitate,' said Ville d'Avray, hurrying on, 'to call on my services. Your friend La Borde used to lodge you when you stayed at Versailles. Rest assured that there will always be a bed for you. The King has divided the rooms on the mezzanine once occupied by the Comtesse du Barry. He's given some to Monsieur de Maurepas and the rest, which are above his head, to myself. I've been loyal to him since his earliest childhood and he's always very good to me.'

'I'm grateful to you for your proposal.'

Nicolas reserved the right to decide later whether this offer had been made because he was now someone to be reckoned with or out of simple kindness.

'As you will have noticed,' resumed Ville d'Avray, 'everyone is alike in Madame de Maurepas's salon. That's the true Court, the ideal place to talk about politics. All those who matter – especially the ministers – frequent that highly convenient meeting place, and the kingdom is fashioned anew every evening.'

From the first-floor landing of the marble staircase, he entered the room of the Queen's guards. A spruce little old man, dressed all in black, was sitting waiting on a window seat, his chin resting on the pommel of his cane. Next to him, two grooms were carrying shapes wrapped in crimson velvet. Nicolas recognised Monsieur de Vaucanson, of the Royal Academy of Sciences, a renowned engineer and a maker of remarkable automata. Sartine, who made it his job to know everything, and at the urging of Madame de Pompadour, had once dispatched Nicolas to see the scientist under some pretext or other to try to discover the secret of his magic dolls. A few *louis* appropriately distributed to his servants had given him a clearer view of the matter.

Ville d'Avray told him that the King had sent for this visitor in order for him to show his masterworks to the Queen. It was therefore a kind of procession that entered the Grand Couvert antechamber where the presentation was to take place. The grooms carefully arranged the prodigious mechanisms on the table set up for that purpose. A large armchair awaited the Queen who, announced by the usher, entered surrounded by her women.

Her incomparable gait aroused Nicolas's admiration. She seemed to glide across the floor, her whole body swaying gently. This impression was strengthened by the haughty way she held her head. He was reminded of a swan. Since their first encounter, four years earlier, he had only seen her from a distance. She seemed to have broadened out a little; she was no longer a child, not yet a woman. Not very tall, with a dazzling complexion, she dominated the room, turning her slightly heavy but expressive blue eyes on each of her visitors. Her high, domed forehead recalled the portraits of her father, Emperor Franz. The gentleness of her smile countered the disdainful set of her mouth. She was wearing a taffeta dress adorned with flecked gauze, with trimmings of the same fabric and an English-style bonnet. Responding to her guests' bows, she gracefully inclined her head. Monsieur de Ville d'Avray introduced Monsieur de Vaucanson. At that moment, a woman with a stiff bearing and a severe expression whispered a few words in the Queen's ear. Her Majesty looked at Nicolas.

'Madame de Noailles[7] is intrigued by you, Monsieur,' she said. 'She is unaware that we are old friends from the forest of Compiègne.[8] Marquis, welcome.'

'Madame,' resumed Ville d'Avray, 'His Majesty has deemed it a pleasant idea to have Monsieur de Vaucanson show you two of his automata, which are famous throughout Europe.'

'The King has anticipated my desires. No one was more anxious than I to meet the father of these animated creatures, of which my mother so often spoke in Vienna.'

'Madame, this is too much honour for an old man,' said

Vaucanson, bowing. 'Allow me to present my children.'

He struck the floor with his cane. The grooms uncovered the first machine.

'Your Majesty, I have called this first automaton the Flute Player. It is a wooden statue, copied from *The Faun* by Coysevox, playing the transverse flute. He can play twelve different tunes with extreme precision. The fingers make the required movements. The automaton can modify the wind entering the instrument by increasing or decreasing the speed, following the different tones, varying the disposition of the lips to do so. The lips work a valve similar to a tongue which makes it possible to imitate everything a man is obliged to do.'

He approached the automaton and pressed a little button at the base of the mechanism. The musician suddenly came to life; his eyes moved, and he lifted the flute to his lips, while his nimble fingers ran up and down the body of the instrument. The thumb was in exactly the right place to produce the octave, and the raised and slightly tilted head seemed animated by the feeling of the music that now rose.

The assembly watched and listened, spellbound, to the small living form, born of the genius of its maker, which mimed the appearance of life to such perfection. The tune came to an end, and the flautist winked and resumed his initial position. Her head tilted and resting on her hand, the Queen seemed moved. She clapped, imitated by her women, apart from Madame de Noailles, who was muttering to herself, clearly appalled by this spectacle.

'Monsieur,' said the Queen, her German accent more noticeable because of her emotion, 'I thank you for this wonderful moment and for the sensitivity which made you choose an air by

Gluck, the Kappellmeister of the Empress in Vienna.'

Nicolas had also recognised the tune; it was from *Iphigenia in Aulis*, which Gluck had put on in Paris in April, a performance strongly supported by the Queen. Monsieur de Vaucanson was an experienced courtier. He bowed and again struck the floor. The grooms covered the flautist and unveiled a second mechanism. This object was smaller, and a murmur of surprise rose at the sight of a duck sitting motionless in a porcelain basin, into which the contents of a large flask of water were poured. The animal seemed more real than nature.

'May Her Majesty consider this second example,' said Vaucanson. 'This duck, motionless for the moment, will, at my command, rise up on its legs and move about like a farmyard fowl.'

He set off the mechanism. The duck rose, shook itself, moved its neck right then left, then quacked and splashed about, as if startled at finding itself in such noble company. All the poses of nature were exactly reproduced. Vaucanson took a small packet of grain from his pocket and approached the Queen.

'Would Her Majesty like to feed the bird?'

The Queen rose with all the enthusiasm of a child delighted with a new toy. Madame de Noailles tried to stop her, and was dismissed with a gesture.

'How should I proceed, Monsieur?'

'I'm going to empty the grain into Your Majesty's hand, and she will present it to the bird's beak. I assure you, there is no danger.'

She approached and held out her hand to the duck, which stretched its neck, seized the offered grain with a little shake and gobbled it up. Delighted, the Queen burst out laughing like a mischievous child. She went back to her seat. Vaucanson waited a few moments, then picked up the duck and placed it on a silver platter. The fowl froze and gave up its perfectly digested meal through the natural channels. Madame de Noailles appeared to be about to faint, but the rest of the gathering was swept by gales of laughter.

'Monsieur,' said the Queen, trying hard to keep a straight face, 'I shall never forget this session, and I will tell the King how much it interested and amused me. I am completely astonished by this latest expression of your genius. What is the secret of that perfect digestion?'

'May Your Majesty forgive me, but it's the secret of life!'

'I see. So you're a bit of a sorcerer, Monsieur!' She held out her hand to him, and he kissed it with devotion then withdrew. Ville d'Avray and Nicolas, who was uncertain what to do next, were about to follow him when the Queen made a sign.

'I wish to speak with the Marquis de Ranreuil. Leave us.'

Madame de Noailles took a step forward, apparently outraged by this decision. With an imperious look, Marie Antoinette silenced her.

'The Queen wishes it, the Queen demands it.'

The duenna withdrew, subdued. Nicolas approached.

'I believe you have some things to tell me, Monsieur.'

Nicolas informed her that, at the request of Monsieur Lenoir, he had made enquiries at Trianon and seen the Richards. That such incidents would not recur. That it might perhaps be a good idea to limit the common people's access to the gardens, and that in any case he would post informers to keep an eye on the area and report to him any suspicious intrusion or disturbing episode occurring on the Queen's estate.

'Thank you for dealing with this matter,' the Queen said. 'I don't wish access to the gardens to be forbidden. The people have a right to approach their monarchs, and I don't want to be confined, hiding my amusements behind bars like an animal in a menagerie. Continue, and keep me informed. I don't want the King to be upset with all this.' She smiled at him. 'You know everything. How does that duck of Monsieur de Vaucanson's digest the grain it is served? It's beyond me, and I shan't rest until I know the secret.'

'The Queen may hear a confession,' said Nicolas with a laugh, 'but she also knows that she cannot divulge its contents.'

'That may be so, Monsieur. Your conditions are quite tough . . .'

'Monsieur de Sartine, once questioned about this famous duck by Madame de Pompadour, gave me the task of investigating it and finding an answer. How indeed to explain this reconstruction of the natural functions: swallowing, dissolving, and expelling? In fact, the grain given to the automaton falls into a box placed beneath its belly, a kind of drawer which is emptied every three or four sessions. The material to be evacuated is prepared in advance, a kind of gruel composed of breadcrumbs coloured green. This is forced out by a pump to look as if it has really gone through a digestive process. The rest is a matter of mechanics; of cogs and springs and keys to be wound, a perfect piece of clockwork.'

'Then we shall share a secret . . . I understand why the King is so interested. Monsieur, have you been at Court for a long time?'

'My duties mainly keep me in Paris. However, Madame, I have often been here since 1762. As well as dealing with special investigations, I had the task of providing security for the King and the royal family.'

'As henchman to the marquise and the comtesse?'

It was a direct hit, and it seemed pointless to prevaricate. 'Madame, I was obeying the late King's orders.'

'Don't worry, I have been informed of his judgement on your loyalty. Did you know that the Duc de La Vrillière does not like me at all?'

It was rather the reverse: she could not forgive him for his support for Madame du Barry. It was clear to Nicolas that the Queen of France had not forgotten the offence caused to her as Dauphine.

'I am not in his confidence.'

'May I count on you, Monsieur?'

'I am your servant and the King's. I hope Your Majesty is convinced of that.'

Calmer now, she held out her hand. How could he refuse her anything?

Nicolas was unable to find Monsieur de Ville d'Avray, doubtless on his way to announce to the King that a peace treaty had been signed with Madame de Maurepas. Nicolas felt both pleased and anxious. Pleased that his appearance at Court had been marked by a dazzling return to favour which strengthened his position with both the Duc de La Vrillière and the Lieutenant General of Police, but anxious at the thought that the same favour might earn him many adversaries, the most dangerous not being the most visible. Everyone was turning to him to ensure his loyalty and demand his support and his services. Could he satisfy them all? The King must be served first; that was his motto and his yardstick, as always. After that, he would just have to see how things worked out.

Lost in thought, he returned to his hotel. The wind, which had continued blowing, had dried up the waters from that dawn's storm. Angry little gusts sent the dead leaves whirling madly. At the noisy table for guests, where he discouraged his neighbours with his silence, he dined on spit-roasted chicken and a blancmange soaked in cider. He went to bed early and dreamed of Mademoiselle d'Arranet.

*Thursday 6 October 1774*

Nicolas returned at the appointed time to the area between the palace and the park where the King's carriages were assembled for the day's hunt. Accustomed for years to the unchanging ceremonial of the hunt, he observed with indulgent curiosity the timidity and awkwardness of those newly presented. It had always seemed to him strange that hunting was chosen to mark this event, and that being presented, for a man, consisted simply of being able to climb into one of the King's carriages on a day marked down for hunting. It cost ten *louis* to the first groom who presented the horse and ten *louis* to the driver of the coach. He dozed as far as the plain of Grenelle, where his position was next to the King's. Radiant with happiness, the monarch gave him a little wave, which showed that he could see better at a distance than at close quarters. He was surrounded by pages from the large stable who had abandoned their blue costumes covered with crimson and white silk braid for blue twill jackets and gaiters of hide. They would stand behind the King, each with a rifle, and, once the monarch had fired, would provide him with another weapon while the first would be passed from hand to hand until it reached the arquebusier, who would reload it. Meanwhile, the first page would make sure the game was collected, keeping an exact account of it on little slates. The King, a great hunter like his forefathers, killed several hundred animals and birds at every shooting party.

Suddenly, Nicolas heard, somewhere to his left, a louder explosion than the usual shots. Cries rang out. He saw coachmen running, then returning carrying a body covered in blood. When he got back into his coach after the hunt, his neighbour explained to him what had happened. One of the newcomers being presented that day, a young gentleman from Berry, had brought an old family weapon for the occasion. Long unused, it had exploded, taking away his hand.

'All he can do now is ask for the address of the silversmith who made the silver hand.'

'The silver hand?'

'Yes, Monsieur de Saint-Florentin, or rather the Duc de La Vrillière, had the same thing happen to him a few years ago. The late King presented him with a substitute hand.'

Nicolas sat huddled and silent in a corner of the coach. So that gaping hole in the throats of the two victims, shaped like a stiff hand, could be . . . The idea seemed so monstrous, he bit his lips until they bled.

# VIII

## NAVIGATION

What is a naval battle? You fire cannon, you separate,
and the sea is just as salty as it was before!

MAUREPAS

Nicolas returned to the palace, frozen with fear. How could he have forgotten that characteristic of the Minister of the King's Household? So many years spent close to him, and yet . . . It was precisely that proximity, a matter of habit and routine, which played games with your memory and blunted your powers of reasoning. He had long wondered about the nature of the late King's fondness for that colourless little man who led a life of debauchery and was so hated within the royal family . . . Madame Adélaïde and Madame Victoire endlessly belittled him, and never lost an opportunity to humiliate him in public. Had not the Queen, as she had herself just reminded Nicolas, once told the duc that she could not forget that he had taken sides against her at the end of the former reign? For Nicolas, however, there remained the minister's loyalty to Louis XV, not to mention the vital support he had given his commissioner on a number of critical occasions.

The new King had retained him against all the odds, although he had exiled his mistress, the Beautiful Aglaé, and was keeping him somewhat at arm's length. For what reason? Did his office put him in a position to know too many State secrets? Was it too risky to even conceive of the idea of removing him? Or did the fact that he was a cousin of the First Minister demand a certain indulgence, at least for the time being? Sartine, who had long been his follower, had gradually distanced himself from him, having become aware that La Vrillière had benefited greatly from the successes of his service but had done nothing to support him when things had become unpleasant for him.

When it came down to it, Nicolas did not really care about all these intrigues, and followed their ins and outs only from a very great distance. What mattered was that he now found himself in possession of a clue, perhaps even a piece of evidence, the importance of which was still to be assessed. He could not dismiss the possibility that it was a coincidence, and it was vital that he be extremely cautious. Could somebody else have got hold of an object the Duc de La Vrillière obviously had to take off from time to time – to sleep, for example? Was it possible that someone had made a copy of the artificial hand with a view to compromising the minister? On the other hand, the initial stages of the investigation had revealed a number of contradictions in those testimonies which could have provided the master of the house with an alibi. Nor could Nicolas forget that even the duchesse had lied about Monsieur de La Vrillière being at Versailles on the night of the murder.

The minister's private life, which certainly could be called dissolute, was an open secret. So why, in this particular case, strive to conceal what he had been doing that night, unless in an attempt to cover up the unspeakable? Nicolas recalled his uncertainty about the real purpose of his mission: did they have such a low opinion of him as to imagine that, finding himself out of favour and removed from affairs, he would agree to be a malleable instrument and carry out the semblance of an investigation the conclusion of which was inevitable? He was thinking so fast that the blood was beating in his temples. There was no point tormenting himself with speculations, he just had to get a move on. Only a return to action would allow him to throw some light on an affair which was becoming increasingly obscured by new facts and in which sham and pretence were everywhere.

The most important thing was to determine if the Duc de La Vrillière still wore the silver hand given to him by the late King. How to proceed? Should he simply ask the minister, and never mind his possible reaction? As Nicolas prepared his strategy, he became aware of the enormity of the implications: whether he liked it or not, he was now considering the duc to be the prime suspect in a murder committed in his own house. His sense of embarrassment increased when a new thought occurred to him: a second victim had been discovered, bearing on her neck the same characteristic wound. The two murders seemed to have been committed using an identical weapon, which meant that the person responsible for the first could also have been responsible for the second. He would definitely have to verify the duc's whereabouts at those times. Nicolas rebuked himself for wasting too much time in hypothesising. Yes, it really was essential to get down to action and stop himself getting needlessly carried away.

The Minister of the King's Household must surely be back in Versailles, where the affairs of his office required him. He was a man of habit, and usually lunched at about one in the afternoon. Nicolas judged that this was a good time to be received. He would not change, as his hunting costume denoted his privileged rank at Court . . . He had a perfect excuse: to give an up-to-date report on his inquiry into the murder at the Saint-Florentin mansion.

In the ministers' wing, he was greeted like a regular visitor by the elderly groom, who, after tapping at the door, admitted him to the Duc de La Vrillière's study. As predicted, he was in the middle of lunch, sitting at a pedestal table near the window. A fire was blazing in the hearth.

'What, have the animals got into the palace?' he said, looking up. 'How long have you been at Versailles?'

Nicolas realised that the opening remark referred to his hunting costume. 'Since yesterday morning, Monseigneur. On the instructions of Monsieur Lenoir.'

'And you've only just deigned to come and pay me a visit!'

'His Majesty wanted to see me, then Monsieur de Maurepas, and, last but not least, the Queen. In addition, the King requested my presence at this morning's shoot.'

'Ah, that's how they poach our people . . .' The duc seemed tense, even anxious. 'I'm listening,' he said.

'Monseigneur,' began Nicolas, 'I should like to give you a brief report of my investigation. Most of your servants have been misrepresenting the truth, and sometimes openly lying. Your major-domo's attempted suicide was nothing but a minor cut. He doesn't remember a thing.'

'What?' said the duc, agitated. 'And will that be enough to exonerate him in your opinion?'

'I'm not saying that. I'm merely observing that there is nothing to support the charges against him, no significant corroborating evidence . . .'

'Come now, it must be him! Who else could it be? You need to speed things up, Monsieur.'

'Justice, Monseigneur, walks hand in hand with truth, which by definition is slow and cautious.'

The duc stiffened on his chair. 'I hope you're not trying to teach me a lesson, Commissioner.'

'God forbid,' replied Nicolas. 'It was merely an aside. There are many others who think the same way as you and are urging me to bring matters to a conclusion.'

The minister was eating *oublies*, dipping them into a cup of chocolate. A little pot contained the rest of the drink. The pedestal table was unsteady, and the pot badly balanced. The duc's gloved right hand was flat on the table, motionless. Only his left hand was moving. If he became any more irritable, thought Nicolas, the whole thing would come crashing to the floor. With a little luck . . .

'What?' yelled the duc. 'Who are these others? Why is an affair which should have remained secret being openly discussed? Who have you been talking to about it? Can't you hold your tongue after all these years? Sartine, of course! He doesn't matter any more, don't you understand? He doesn't matter at all!'

The little man was pallid with rage.

'Monseigneur is mistaken,' Nicolas replied, in his most placatory tone. 'It may well be that Monsieur de Sartine knows, he's always well informed about everything. Imagining the contrary would be an illusion. I was thinking of the Duc de Richelieu, who runs everywhere spreading news from group to group. Naturally he questioned me, and I pretended to know nothing. As for the King, he was of the opinion that I would succeed in the end.'

Purple blotches appeared on the minister's face. 'Richelieu! He's always fussing around, thinking he's indispensable. Why doesn't he just retire, after more than sixty years at Court? Damn the fellow! And as for the King . . .'

He raised his gloved hand and brought it down heavily on the pedestal table. The table swayed, the cup tinkled in its saucer, as if taking fright, and the pot overturned, covering the silk glove with dark liquid. Furious, the duc rose and took it off. Nicolas saw what he had wanted to see: the artificial hand was made, not of silver, but of wood.

The chaos which followed this incident gave Nicolas time to reflect on the measures to be taken. Monsieur de La Vrillière had rushed to take another glove from his desk drawer, while the groom repaired the damage and took away the soiled pedestal table. Now Nicolas would have to pull out all the stops, while pretending to continue with his report.

'There is still one strange fact of which I must inform you, Monseigneur . . .'

'Well, hurry up about it.'

'The examinations our people carried out at the Basse-Geôle allowed them to take a plaster cast of the weapon used to cut the throats of the two victims.'

'What two victims? As far as I know, my major-domo didn't die, you just told me he was barely scratched. Are you inventing new victims for your own pleasure?'

'Alas, no! Another young girl was discovered in Impasse

Glatigny on Tuesday morning, with her throat cut in an identical way. There can be no possible doubt: the same weapon was used on both occasions.'

He had the impression that the blow had struck home.

'So you found it and took a cast?' the minister said, in a cold, measured tone.

'We took a cast from the shape of the wound. Just as one can get back to the original seal by taking a cast from the seal on a letter.'

'And what's so strange about it?'

'Its strangeness justifies the question you will forgive me asking, Monseigneur. The cast is in the shape of a hand. Now, no living hand could produce the wounds we found. I note that you are wearing a wooden hand. Where is the silver hand given you by our late lamented King and master?'

La Vrillière did not bat an eyelid. He looked Nicolas in the eye, as if trying to grasp his precise motive in daring to ask such a question. 'Monsieur Le Floch,' he said, 'I wear what I feel comfortable with. The hand given me by our late master I reserve for special occasions.'

'Nevertheless, Monseigneur, you always wear a glove . . . I'm sure you will permit me to examine the precious original more closely. The fact that it is sometimes out of your sight gives rise, if it were necessary, to the suspicion . . . What if someone borrowed it, or worse still . . .'

The minister appeared to have lost patience. 'Of course, of course . . . I've never claimed that it was still in my possession. To tell the truth . . . to tell the truth, I've lost it. I may have left it somewhere.'

'Monseigneur must recall where this loss took place?'

'Yes, yes, of course,' he said, and appeared to hesitate. 'At Madame de Cusacque's house in Normandy.'

'Is it conceivable that this object, which is precious for more than one reason, could have been stolen?'

The minister appeared increasingly perturbed. 'How should I know? Anything's possible.'

'Monseigneur, one last detail. Who actually made that silver hand? Some details on the nature of the object would be useful to me.'

'Monsieur de Villedeuil. In 1765, he was an engineer in Place Royale. Dead now, I think. Le Floch, does the King know about this affair?'

'Yes, Monseigneur. His Majesty mentioned the matter briefly to me, as I have already said.'

The minister took up his quill, dipped it in the inkwell, and began writing. Nicolas understood that the interview was over.

The Court carriage took him back to the Hôtel de la Belle Image, where this triumphant arrival added greatly to his prestige. He immediately went up to his room, shut himself in, and, while once again cleaning his rifles with fanatical care, reflected on what he had just heard, trying to hone his impressions of the encounter with the Duc de La Vrillière. His first observation, a vital one, concerned the lack of openness and honesty in the interview. The second concerned the major element of the artificial hand.

The minister's assertion that he wore a wooden model for everyday use was plausible. Perhaps the original really had disappeared, and its owner really did not know the exact circumstances. His answers about the place where it had been stolen or lost were exceedingly vague. Had it happened in Caen, where his mistress Madame de Cusacque, the Beautiful Aglaé, lived in exile? If so, that would certainly not help them get at the truth. The minister was in a position to know that no inquiry would be carried out in the immediate future so far from Paris and that his word would suffice to put an end to the question.

The duc's anger on learning that the news of the tragedy in his Parisian mansion had spread to Versailles, as well as his acrimony towards Sartine, also gave the commissioner food for thought. Should it lead him to respond favourably to the former Lieutenant General of Police's demand to be kept informed of everything concerning the Minister of the King's Household? He did not really like such a role. But could he refuse Sartine, to whom he owed everything and whose actions had always been dictated by an overriding concern for the interests of the throne? A final thought helped him to make up his mind: if the pot of chocolate had not been overturned, would he have discovered that Monsieur de La Vrillière's silver hand had disappeared? Deep down, he thought himself quite a casuist; if Sartine had been there, he would again have called him a disciple of Loyola . . .

Nicolas knew he was becoming over-excited, and to calm down he decided to write to his son. He could not help being slightly anxious about the beginning of Louis's life as a schoolboy. How would a boy like that, his character already well formed, a boy in whom Nicolas was delighted to find traces and memories of his own father, the Marquis de Ranreuil, react to school? However extraordinary his situation might seem to him,

Louis appeared to rise above it with a praiseworthy straight-forwardness and sense of proportion. Nevertheless, Nicolas could not quite shake off the unease caused by the circumstances of his early youth. On the one hand, he was the spoilt child of a brothel, and on the other, the brilliant, refined schoolboy who had delighted everyone in the Noblecourt household. Nicolas had to give due recognition to La Satin for having, in such conditions, been able to avoid the worst. Louis was now proud of the glorious family of which he was the descendant, but was quite lacking in arrogance. Did he fully realise, though, the ambiguity of his position in the world? The steep path of truth had been chosen for him, and it might lead him down many treacherous side roads. Nicolas dreaded the suffering it might bring him, while hoping that, if such strains did indeed make themselves felt in such a young soul, he would gain from them, like a burning blade made supple and hard by being dipped in water. It was therefore a tender letter full of the most judicious advice – the very same advice he had received twenty years earlier from the Marquis de Ranreuil – which he addressed to his son. He corrected it carefully, copied it out neatly, and sealed it. Then he set about getting ready for his dinner at the Comte d'Arranet's house.

He shaved with a dexterity he had inherited from his father. When he had reached the age when he needed to start shaving, much to the consternation of Canon Le Floch, for whom all care of the body was the work of the devil, the marquis had taught him the rudiments and given him a little treatise, which contained instructions on how to shave without danger to oneself, which stones to use for sharpening blades, and how to prepare leather for a strop. He chose a dark-grey coat; the colour was known as

London chimney soot, and it was a recent model from the workshop of his tailor, Master Vachon, the discreet elegance of whose clothes were ideally suited for the end of the period of mourning. He took from his portmanteau some fine Mechlin lace cuffs and a cravat and shirt that were both dazzlingly white, the result of the combined care of Catherine and Marion: the old servant had taught her protégée the use of a charcoal iron, which had not been a feature of her life in military camps. He brushed his hair, straightened his wig, powdered it, arranged the strands of hair that peeped out with a little agate handle, and checked his flattering reflection in the mottled mirror on the dressing table. Last but not least, he fastened the old sword which, two years earlier, a messenger from Brittany had left in Rue Montmartre, wrapped in a blanket, without a word of explanation. Nicolas had recognised the Marquis de Ranreuil's ceremonial sword and had assumed that it was his half-sister Isabelle who had sent it to him, just as, not long after the death of her father, she had given him the signet ring bearing the family arms, which he would one day pass on to Louis. Nostalgia overcame him for a moment. He closed his eyes and saw again the wild shore of the ocean, almost heard the cries of the seabirds above his head . . .

Having dismissed the Court carriage, he asked for a cab to take him to the d'Arranet mansion. Night had fallen. Nature was calm again, the wind having dropped at sunset. The hotel-keeper bustled around him obsequiously, suddenly convinced that he was dealing with some important person travelling incognito. Since Peter the Great, northern princes had taken to moving about under false identities. It was true that Nicolas, with his grave, silent demeanour, looked the part.

Having reached his destination, he was greeted by the formidable footman and former sailor, who gave him a friendly wink.

'The admiral's in the library, Monsieur, with that damned butcher who's suddenly turned up again. He was the one who sewed up my throat after a bloody Biscayan had cut it. He did it in the blink of an eye, while I was biting into a piece of leather soaked with rum. The bastard was good, I'll give him that. By God, it's really good to see him again!'

'Tribord, I like you,' said Nicolas, slipping a double *louis* into his hand. 'Dr Semacgus is my friend, too.'

He was happy to discover some unknown aspects of the naval surgeon. The footman opened the door to the library. There was a mixture of odours: the warm smell of candles and the exotic scent of rum. The Comte d'Arranet was at one of the open windows, talking to Semacgus. Their words were punctuated by gales of laughter. Nicolas was struck by the majestic presence of the former general officer, who had put on his uniform for the occasion. Flame-red breeches, a matching doublet braided and embroidered in gold, a blue coat, the sash of the order of Saint Louis threaded through the epaulette on the right shoulder; everything contributed to the splendour of his appearance. The uniform gleamed in the lights, its martial elegance accentuating the energy in d'Arranet's face. Semacgus, in his black coat and powdered wig, made a distinguished foil for his former chief and companion at arms.

'Ah, here's Ranreuil,' said the admiral, turning. 'You are both on familiar territory.'

Before it could even get under way, the conversation was interrupted by the sound of a number of carriages stopping at the front steps. The host put down his glass and hurried, one hand supporting his wounded leg, to greet the newcomers. Monsieur de Sartine and La Borde appeared in a symphony of grey, which reinforced Nicolas in his choice of coat. Monsieur d'Arranet introduced Semacgus to the minister, who recalled, with some humour, that he had had the pleasure of finding the naval surgeon innocent in a criminal case during which he had been wrongly imprisoned fourteen years earlier.[1] All of this was recounted with that air of self-satisfaction that always made Nicolas angry, even though he was accustomed to the former Lieutenant General of Police taking credit for his men's successes. But he was wrong about the object of his annoyance; its target was not Monsieur de Sartine, or only by default. He had in fact just realised that this was a dinner for men only and that Mademoiselle d'Arranet would not be making an appearance. He was surprised at how displeased he felt. Drinks were served and the company grew lively. La Borde immediately drew Nicolas into the garden. He wanted to get something off his chest. His young wife's health had hardly improved, despite the rigorous treatment to which she was being subjected. Her nervous irritation persisted, accompanied by convulsions and by a melancholy that nothing appeared able to dispel. It was difficult to break through her apathy. Nicolas was upset to see his friend so concerned, and he also sensed that he was still just as affected by the loss of the King. He had not realised, a few days earlier at Noblecourt's house, how false his good mood had been and how tactfully he had striven not to cast a shadow over the party given in honour of

Louis. He assured him of his loyalty and his wish to be introduced to Madame de La Borde at a more propitious time. Tribord announced that the dinner for the minister was served, and they moved to the dining room.

Nicolas suspected Aimée's hand in the arrangement and discreet elegance of the table. There was a dazzlingly white table runner on which stood emblazoned items of silverware interspersed with pieces of white coral containing mixed flowers. Monsieur de Sartine presided at the head of the table, with his host on his left, and Monsieur de La Borde on his right. Tribord supervised the five servants who stood behind the guests and served them food and drink. The first course consisted of mussels in an egg and lemon juice sauce, turbot coated in breadcrumbs, and a huge trout frozen in jelly and accompanied by *pannequets* of prawns and carved vegetables. Wine from Champagne and Burgundy waited in silver-gilt cooling pitchers.

'Admiral,' said Sartine, 'you honour me with a most uncommon creature of the depths. I haven't come across one of this size since those which occasionally appeared at the late King's little dinners, and which were brought from Switzerland at top speed by relays of couriers. How much does it weigh? Twelve, fifteen pounds?'

'More than that!' said d'Arranet, beaming. 'It's twenty pounds at least and yesterday morning was still swimming in Lake Geneva. I love fresh fish, although some claim that you should leave it for a few days to enhance the taste. I'm not one of them.'

'It's true of skate,' said Semacgus, 'which is inedible on the first day. But you have to be careful. A little too long and the animal gets too much ammonia and starts to smell.'

'Is fishing practised on our vessels?'

'During longer crossings, it can be a pleasant diversion, and a definite improvement on the routine fare on board. I can still see Semacgus, abeam off Taranto, catching some fifteen tuna in a row! The crew thought they were eating fresh meat. That was on the frigate *Cassiopée*.'

'Otherwise, it's always beef and salted pork, I suppose?'

'Always,' said the comte, 'and it's often old and rotten. Now there's a reform you could make: supplies.'

'You never take live cattle or poultry on board?'

'Yes, of course! On departure and at every port of call. But they don't last long, and if there's a battle, it's a disaster. All it takes is one cannonball hitting a scuttle, and it's farewell to the livestock.'

'I observe,' said Sartine pensively, 'that supplying the navy is not a simple business. Well, I've come here wanting to learn. I've never sailed.'

'Nor I,' said La Borde.

'I crossed the English Channel on a steamship,' said Nicolas.

'Comte,' Sartine went on, 'you're an old sailor, I mean an experienced sailor, not one of those officers who are all show but never put to sea, you know what I mean . . . What advice would you give me?'

'God forbid that I should presume to give advice to one of my master's ministers! However, I can make a few fairly obvious suggestions. The first is that you must restore hope to the navy. Monsieur de Choiseul may have meant well, in his day, but this century has been disastrous for a force so vital to the greatness of France.'

'It is a false accusation that people make against the late King,' Sartine replied curtly. 'Not you, Admiral, but others. The truth is that it was all a matter of savings and economy. Louis XV used to complain bitterly about it, but his ministers did nothing to raise his hopes. To tell the truth, we were living with political choices conceived under the Regency and pursued by Cardinal Fleury.'

'And on what principles were these choices based?' asked La Borde.

They broke off while the second course was laid on the table: pigs' trotters with truffles, a hare pie and a salad of young rabbit. A Madeira brought back from the Indies, which they immediately sampled, met with unanimous approval.

'To answer your question,' resumed Sartine, 'it is necessary to understand that our policy consisted of not making the other maritime powers jealous, especially England. It was believed that the surest way to maintain peace was to reduce the navy in order not to offend that nation.'

'But, Monseigneur,' cried d'Arranet passionately, 'it is contrary to the honour and interests of the kingdom to have left our navy in the same state of weakness and decay for so long!'

'Alas! As I said, the incompetence of the people involved, the financial crisis, the constant problem of debt, and the permanent opposition of the *parlements*, all these factors conspired to compromise everything. For more than twenty years, when Monsieur de Maurepas was in charge of the navy, he hoped to obtain a ratio of one to three in relation to the English fleet, but couldn't manage it. Will I? I'm certainly going to try my best, especially now that events in the English colonies in America have made it vital for us to stay on the alert. Have I answered your question, Admiral?'

'Yes, indeed! But my second suggestion is a bolder one. I fear that we need to reflect on the way we fight. Let me explain. We French fight in a line and try essentially to knock down the enemy's masts and cripple him. Applied mechanically, this tactic encourages routine and makes it impossible for us to adapt to circumstances. The English method is quite different; they fire directly into the hull. You should see the damage when a well-aimed shot has sliced through a ship, the splinters of wood like so many daggers . . . And what about when a vessel is behind you and tearing your stern to pieces with general fire that goes the whole length of the ship? The loss of life is appalling. Not to mention the fact that it takes a long time to replace the most experienced men.'

'So what do you suggest?' asked Sartine.

'That we need to think about it! A career at sea requires courage, endurance, competence, but also reflection and a spirit of decisiveness in the most varied circumstances. I don't think one should become too attached to a single tactic, but that each should be applied as and when the situation calls for it, sometimes both in succession. I know the English are very well trained. They really learn how to fire, how to board an enemy ship in heavy weather, and everything's always precisely timed. While we, on the other hand, train very little and always with the thought of making savings. Faced with the enemy's formidable efficiency, we've paid a high price for our lack of training!'

'I tend to agree with you,' Semacgus cut in. 'When the time

comes for battle, the amount of time spent at sea counts more than the size of the cannon!'

'Talking of cannon, Monseigneur,' d'Arranet went on, 'I hope your offices have sent you the announcement of the invention by an English engineer of a new type of cannon: the caronade, which is already being used by the Royal Navy.'

'I've heard of it,' replied Sartine, 'though I haven't quite grasped how it works.'

'It's shorter, doesn't have wheels, and its gun carriage consists of two wooden boards that can be slid one on top of the other. Its great interest, apart from that, is that it has a line of sight and a lever with a threaded shaft that make it possible to give the weapon the desired angle of fire. With a double load or filled with grapeshot, the caronade can cause havoc . . .'

Sartine was thinking. He glanced around him. The servants had cleared away the second course, and no one could overhear.

'I have a plan, my friends, to create a service whose job will be to gather information on the English fleet and what those gentlemen in the Admiralty have in store for us. It's all still a bit vague in my mind, but the salvation of the State depends on being well informed. We'll have to do some recruiting to find suitable men for this great project.'

He threw Nicolas a long, eloquent look. The servants were coming back, and the comte created a diversion.

'The frigate is the queen of battleships,' he declared. 'Quick, and easy to handle. The seventy-four has good firing strength and can still manoeuvre. Apart from that, they're ungovernable monsters whose losses are proportionate to their mass. Just think: nearly nine hundred men on board! It's not a good idea to put all one's eggs in one basket . . . Finally, Monsieur, one last thing: I believe it's necessary to develop infantry on our vessels. At sea, our crews are not armed. They're handed out rifles and pikes. I think it would be advisable to strengthen a corps to provide heavy fire during close combat or boarding.'

'A well-aimed shot that kills the commander can change the outcome of a battle,' said Semacgus. 'That's happened before.'

The third course was ready: bacon pies, ramekins of Italian cheese, puréed partridge, duck à l'espagnole, tendrons of veal with Bengal curry, cardoons with grated cheese, and fried celery.

The minister adjusted his wig with both hands, a gesture which always indicated that he was highly satisfied. 'We haven't really looked into the question yet,' he said, 'but your observations have enlightened me in no uncertain manner. I'm planning to carry out some on-the-spot investigations. I shall start with a study journey to Brittany, concentrating on the administration of our ports and arsenals. I plan to dig new dry docks and increase the capacity for building vessels of the line. What would you say, Admiral, to helping me prepare for this visit and coming with me? I really need the opinion of a man who has sailed, fought and commanded! Later, once a plan of action has been drawn up, we'll be joined by another officer of great merit, the Chevalier de Fleurieu, who at the moment is trying to improve the navy's precision clocks to make the calculation of longitude easier. The King will like the man, he's very fond of that kind of research.'

'Monseigneur, I am at the minister's service,' said a delighted d'Arranet, half rising in his chair.

'That's settled then! Present yourself at my offices as soon as you can. My clerks will have orders to settle you in immediately.

We shall work in concert. Nicolas, tell us a little of the news of the city; I miss it. That'll cheer us up after this grim conversation.'

'Most of the rumours,' replied Nicolas, 'are about the opera and the theatre, as usual! It's said that in Vienna, the Emperor has become very fond of Chevalier Gluck and doesn't want him to leave his Court any more. In order to make sure of this, he's just granted him a pension of two thousand crowns. Out of consideration for his sister, our Queen, and in order not to deprive him of the advantages he has in France, the Emperor has given him permission to come here every year to put on some of his works.'

'Her Majesty won't appreciate the way her brother treats her favourite musician.'

'She was very grateful to Monsieur de Vaucanson for his choice of music yesterday, after the flute player played some tunes by Gluck.'

'It should be said,' remarked La Borde, 'that Ranreuil has caused quite a stir at Court. The whole of Versailles is buzzing with his return to favour. A private audience with the King, an intimate interview with Madame de Maurepas, a conversation with the First Minister, and, to crown it all, an interview with the Queen away from the prying eyes of Madame de Noailles. Last but not least, they say he amiably resolved a domestic drama . . .'

'For a newly-wed who's withdrawn from the world,' said Nicolas, 'I find you're extremely well informed. You are violating my discretion. Let us talk rather of the exploits of our actresses. The second rumour concerns the quarrel between Mademoiselle Arnoux and Mademoiselle Raucoux, which has degenerated into open war. It's said that Mademoiselle Arnoux's lover, Monsieur

Bellenger, the draughtsman of the Menus,[2] has taken up the cudgels on her behalf against the Marquis de La Villette, Mademoiselle Raucoux's knight errant. Words were exchanged – more than words, threats, and in the presence of many witnesses. Fearing the marquis's wrath, Bellenger brought a criminal complaint. However, others have mediated and the two rivals have come to the rather absurd arrangement that they will meet one another with their swords in their hands and that then they will immediately be separated. This ludicrous reconciliation has given rise to a story in the Persian manner condemning the marquis's cowardice.'

'Where is the honour in all that?' cried the Comte d'Arranet. 'It's a farce, and a fine example of the madness that affects such people over totally trivial matters!'

'May the former Lieutenant General of Police remind you, gentlemen,' said Sartine with a laugh, 'that duelling is forbidden and that the King has vowed never to pardon the slightest disobedience regarding this.'

Sweets now appeared on the table, then the host rose and led his guests into the library. Sartine drew Nicolas into a corner of the room.

'The navy is not the police,' he began, in the tone of someone talking to himself. 'I am alone there, under observation and without support. Age has increased Maurepas's egoism, and I fear that the one aim of his ministry is to avoid any upheaval, to abstain from any great measure that might disturb his peace and quiet. All he wants is to keep his position and live the rest of his life with no problems! But how are you getting on with your case?'

The question was abrupt, but it had the merit of getting straight to the point.

'Quite well, as far as the murder weapon is concerned,' replied Nicolas. 'There is no doubt that it was an artificial hand, made of silver, similar to the one once given by the late King to Monsieur de Saint-Florentin after a hunting accident. The fact remains that—'

'A silver hand . . .' murmured Sartine, pensively. 'Imagine that!'

'When I asked the Duc de La Vrillière to explain this coincidence, his answers were vague and prevaricating. Apparently he uses a wooden replica, and claims not to know the whereabouts of the original. He's not even sure if it was stolen or lost. He suggests it may have happened at Madame de Cusacque's house in Normandy.'

'Ah, the Beautiful Aglaé! Well, well! Now that's something new; I congratulate you. And you think—'

'I try not to think, Monseigneur. I merely observe that the duc is now a suspect, especially as he refuses to give an account of his whereabouts that night.'

He told the minister about the discovery of a second victim.

'Did the King talk to you about this case?' Sartine asked, with a thin-lipped smile.

'He did in fact enquire about it.'

'Please keep me informed of any new developments, Nicolas.'

He was about to rejoin the company when Nicolas detained him.

'Is there something else?'

'Yes, Monseigneur. An unexpected encounter which I'd like

to bring to your attention. Yesterday, in the lower gallery of the palace, I met a man who appeared to be wearing makeup and had spectacles with tinted lenses. He fled when he saw me approach.'

'Did you recognise him? Who was he?'

'Lord Ashbury, with whom I had dealings in London. That mission with which you are familiar . . .'

Sartine reflected for a moment. 'The head of British intelligence in Paris! That's as strange as it's disturbing. I don't like it. Inform Lenoir. Find out what foreigners entered our ports and Paris. We need to know what false name he's using. Nicolas, we've never stopped working together, and the future . . . But don't forget to check up on Bourdier. The navy is waiting for its system of codemaking.'

Nicolas was pleased that Sartine had not reiterated his obsession with the return of Choiseul. He was under no illusions about the sincerity of a man whose capacity for secrecy and devious intrigues he had often observed. Working beside him every day for many years had convinced him that Sartine tended to conceal the true reasons behind his actions. He kept his secrets close to his chest and, like all good politicians, always had several irons in the fire. In addition, one area of his activities was still a closed book to the commissioner: his membership of the Freemasons. Did his work in the lodge lead him to embrace the theories of the philosophers' party? In doing so, was he conforming to the spirit of the times, or had he compromised with this hidden influence the better to control it?

In truth, what bound Nicolas to Sartine, apart from a grateful loyalty reinforced by the vicissitudes of the investigations and tribulations they had been through together, was the certainty that this Frenchman from Barcelona, who did not belong to the high nobility – less even than the commissioner himself – constantly demonstrated at every moment a devotion, a passion, a love of the public good in the person of the King. It was not for nothing that the ermine that adorned his magistrate's gown, a symbolic part of the mantle of ceremony, represented the authority and exercise of a justice delegated to him by the monarch.

As for Nicolas, he felt himself to be above all these political choices. The religious debate which had scarred the century only preoccupied him as a cause of public unrest. What made him indignant was the mingling of opposites, the unnatural collusion between the pious, the Jansenists and the *parlements*. The constant aggressive opposition from the *parlements*, briefly brought down by the imperious will of Maupeou with the support of the late King, made him fear the future, especially as Louis XVI's youth and inexperience made it unusually hard to predict. But he would do his duty, trying to remain an honest man amid the compromises required by his position.

Midnight was approaching when the Comte d'Arranet walked the minister to his carriage. The scene was illumined by the torches of the servants, who stood in a semicircle. Semacgus offered Nicolas a lift back to the Hôtel de la Belle Image in his carriage. La Borde was returning to Paris, where his young wife was waiting for him. As he was leaving the house, Nicolas thought he caught a glimpse of a face at the top of the staircase, a face that could only be Aimée's. Sartine's proposal had filled the admiral with excitement. Clearly, the prospect of leaving this period of inactivity behind delighted a man who, like so many general officers of his age and seniority, feared he would no longer be able to serve. They all promised to see each other soon, and Nicolas was asked to regard this house as his own.

Semacgus's carriage slowly turned into the drive which led to the Avenue de Paris. As it was about to go through the gate, it suddenly came to a halt.

### Friday 7 October 1774

Distant voices echoed in his head. They faded then came back again, sounding more distinct. There was some kind of pressure on his left temple. Where was he? In what kind of dream? He could not open his eyelids, they were too heavy . . . He had an overwhelming desire to let go, to spiral slowly down into a bottomless pit. To sink, to sink for ever . . .

'Damnation! He's fainting again. Pass me the vinegar, Mademoiselle.'

'It's a good thing he has a hard head,' said d'Arranet. 'And that the shot went wide. And that you're here, my dear Semacgus.'

'It's my coachman you should thank. His reflexes were good; without him we'd be holding a wake!'

'Trying to kill my guests at my door, in Versailles! Could the real target have been the minister?'

'Anything's possible,' said Semacgus. 'This isn't the first time they've tried to kill him. It's been a bad year for him, this is the third time. Ah, now he's getting a bit of colour back.'

Nicolas opened his eyes. He was lying on a bed in a richly decorated room. Semacgus was looking at him anxiously, the Comte d'Arranet standing beside him. Aimée was sitting on the bed, holding his hand. He tried to sit up, and the pain went to his head. But it was no worse, he thought, than when he'd been hit while playing with his schoolmates in Guérande.

'Don't move,' said Semacgus. 'A bullet grazed your temple. With that kind of wound, you lose a lot of blood and you faint. But you've been through worse. I'm going to put a bandage on. Mademoiselle will now tear your beautiful shirt to shreds.'

To his embarrassment, Nicolas realised that he was bare-chested.

'And you will sleep here, Monsieur,' said d'Arranet. 'That's an order. The idea of someone trying to kill people on my property! I feel responsible for your condition . . .'

Nicolas tried to protest.

'Not a word. I'm going to check the surrounding area. Tonight, everyone will take turns on watch. Tribord will see to that. Semacgus, you will sleep here, and don't argue.'

'Why did they miss me?'

'Heavens!' said the surgeon with a laugh. 'I fear the wound has made him stupid. Instead of congratulating yourself! My coachman, caught by surprise when that long face appeared, hesitated for a moment and then struck the individual with his whip. The lash was red with blood. Watch out for people with scars from now on. That deflected the shot from its intended trajectory and saved you.'

'Didn't you catch him?'

'There's gratitude for you!' retorted Semacgus, showing him his blood-spattered grey doublet. 'You fell into my arms. For all I knew, you were dying. Was I supposed to leave you there?'

'I'm sorry, Guillaume. I'm not quite myself yet.'

Could it be that this attempt had some connection with the

progress of his investigation into the murder at the Saint-Florentin mansion? Semacgus cauterised the wound with rum, as if he were back on board ship and tending the wounded during a sea battle. He made his patient take a large swig of the liquor, lightly bandaged his head, told him he ought to get some sleep, and snuffed out the candles. He would look in on him again tomorrow. There was a certain amount of bustling about as a room was got ready for the doctor. For some time after that, Nicolas could hear the master of the house giving orders to his servants. Aimée took a last glance at the wounded man and went back to her room. The d'Arranet mansion went to sleep, protected by the comte's men, who were posted about the grounds with lanterns.

Nicolas woke with a start. The parquet floor was creaking so much that it was impossible to mistake the source of the sound: someone had entered the room. His heart began to pound. He forced himself to remain still and tried to control his breathing. Perhaps because of the emotion, the pain in his temple, he realised, had receded. Someone had very carefully turned the key in the lock and was now approaching the bed. He was surprised to find that he did not feel afraid. He breathed in a smell of verbena, and another aroma, that of a warm body. A moist finger touched his mouth and a hand slid over his chest. He sensed rather than heard a garment being impatiently removed and falling to the floor. His mind was a mixture of confusion and expectation. Suddenly, he was submerged in a stream of hair. He put out his hands, touched a naked body, and at the contact that body collapsed on him. His mouth found another mouth, lips that opened. The satiny softness of a shoulder devastated him. Slowly, he turned over. Between the kisses sighs replaced words. More tender, more complex, more ardent, they responded to the sensations, marked their stages, and the last sigh of all, which hung suspended for a time, told Nicolas that he should render thanks to love.

A deep voice was muttering something close to him. He sat up with a start.

'Well, well!' cried Semacgus. 'You've been fighting windmills! Your bed is ravaged. You must have had a fever . . . You've even lost your breeches.'

Embarrassed, Nicolas pulled up the sheet. Semacgus lifted the bandage and examined the wound. His big nose was quivering and his eyes smiling in a manner that was extremely ironic.

'It's looking good. The wound has already closed and a scab is forming. One more scar to your name. You bear your service record on your body. It enhances your innate charm.'

Nicolas was wondering about what had happened that night. Had it been a dream? But there were so many details he remembered . . . Wasn't he completely unpregnated with a light scent and the smell of another body? It was obvious that the wily Semacgus had noticed, which explained that air of smugness. He mocked himself. Was it only when someone tried to kill him that he found himself in such a flattering position? The same thing had happened with La Satin . . . He felt sufficiently recovered to get back to Paris. The naval surgeon had no objection.

After putting on one of the admiral's shirts, his own having been torn to shreds, Nicolas again donned his fine grey coat, now stained, and went down to take his leave. He was greeted warmly by the Comte d'Arranet, who again invited him to consider this house as his own. There was no sign of Aimée; admittedly, it was early. His departure went off without incident. The coast was clear: the servants had been up all night to make sure that no new danger threatened him. Tribord gave him an enthusiastic wave. Semacgus remarked that he had made a friend, a friend who could be useful.

Nicolas did not reply, still trying to catch any allusion on the part of the surgeon to the events of the previous night. From time to time, he wondered if it had all been a dream. And yet, the memories and traces of Mademoiselle d'Arranet's nocturnal visit remained so vivid, so tangible that he found that hard to believe. He strove not to think, putting off until later the task of contemplating a situation the consequences of which were hard to untangle in the heat of the moment. Too many different feelings were at work in him. Above all, he preferred for now to dismiss his qualms at having betrayed the Comte d'Arranet's trust and violated the laws of hospitality.

So it was that they rode back to the Hôtel de la Belle Image in silence. There, he changed and paid his bill. On the road to Paris, Semacgus abandoned him to his thoughts. Nicolas pretended to sleep. In the end, he shook himself like a horse confronted with a hurdle and, once past the Porte de la Conférence, asked to be taken to the Châtelet. There was no more time to lose; the investigation had to resume. It was almost midday and he was hoping to find Bourdeau.

Looking grave, the inspector greeted them at the door of the duty office with the news that a third victim of the killer with the hand had just been discovered in the early hours of the morning, on the banks of Île des Cygnes.

# IX

# APPROACHES

As Semacgus wanted to take part in the expedition, he put his carriage at their disposal. Without omitting any detail, Nicolas informed them of the events that had taken place at Versailles and the state of his investigations. What he had discovered about the Duc de La Vrillière's artificial hand astounded them. The inspector admitted that it was an extremely important clue, which could take the investigation into some very murky areas. He spontaneously posed the question that Nicolas had already been asking himself: why had he, supposedly loyal to Sartine, been chosen to conduct the investigation?

Semacgus suggested two possible answers: either the minister was hoping in this way to keep a close watch on the investigation by using a colleague who was well known to him, or he considered the case so serious that only Nicolas appeared to him capable of solving it. To this, Nicolas himself objected that, if that were so, the minister should have been perfectly open with him, which had not been the case. A long silence followed, in which the three friends continued to pursue their thoughts. The carriage had crossed the Seine and was driving along the *quais* on the left bank, through the neighbourhoods of Beau Grenelle and

Gros Caillou, to get to the *faubourg* downstream of the city.

Nicolas forced himself out of his reverie. 'How did you learn of the discovery of the third body?' he asked.

'There was a general instruction to all the commissioners and inspectors, as well as the men of the watch, to report any discovery of this nature to the duty office,' replied Bourdeau.

'Do we know anything so far?'

An unformulated thought crossed his mind like a sacrilege: he would have to include the Duc de La Vrillière among the suspects and check his whereabouts at the time of the murder.

Bourdeau appeared embarrassed. 'What we know so far is fairly gruesome. You know the nature of the place where the victim was discovered. The hundred thousand oxen brought into Paris to be slaughtered for meat leave behind four hundred thousand feet, not to mention horns and intestines. All these remains are collected together, put on wagons, taken to that infernal island and thrown into vast incinerators, which work round the clock, to be turned into oil for lamps, night lights, frying, and to grease the cogs of machines. That's Île des Cygnes!'

'A pretty name for such an unpleasant place!' said Semacgus. 'It would appear that we're getting close to it, judging by the stench. It's worse than the bilges on a three-decker!'

The carriage turned right towards the little arched bridge over the canal separating the island from the bank. A number of rudimentary smoke-shrouded buildings rose amid dismal vegetation strewn with a few poplars. They saw horses, a stretcher, an empty wagon and a group of men who seemed to be waiting for them.

Nicolas recognised Rabouine, no doubt dispatched by Bourdeau to keep an eye on things, and an officer of the watch named

Baroliot, whom he had met several times in the course of his investigations. A large red-faced man was talking to them excitedly and wiping his brow with a kind of rage.

Baroliot approached and greeted them. 'Nasty business, Commissioner.'

He led them to the far end of a small yard, where a wagon was parked, with a grey nag harnessed to it. The contents were piled high, and covered with a tarpaulin; the stench that escaped from it left no doubt as to their nature. Behind the wagon was a tall openwork door half concealing the top of a huge incinerator from which thick black smoke emerged.

'The tripe shop of Île des Cygnes,' said Rabouine.

Helped by Baroliot, he removed the tarpaulin. The smell became even more overpowering. Bourdeau took out a pipe and hastened to light it. Nicolas took out his snuff box, hurriedly took a pinch, and abandoned himself with delight to a prolonged bout of sneezing.

At first sight, the wagon contained a heap of feet, horns and guts. The last flies of the season covered it like a thick black cloak, making it difficult to get a good look at the contents. It was only when they moved closer that they were able to make out a body amid this horror, although all that could really be seen was a pale, almost yellow face with its eyes open, the young, almost childlike features frozen in an expression of terrified surprise. Nicolas ordered the corpse to be taken down. Some workers were called. Armed with huge wooden shovels, they carefully dug out the body and placed it on a stretcher. Semacgus waved a branch which he had just torn off a shrub to disperse the persistent swarm of insects. He leant over the body.

'A young girl or woman of about, hmmm . . . eighteen or twenty . . . Marks of smallpox. Eyes blue, as far as it's still possible to judge. Gaping wound on the neck. Appears to be almost naked. An undershirt, striped.'

'Time of death?' asked Nicolas.

'Hard to say. We should find out more from the autopsy.'

'Who found her?' asked Bourdeau.

The fat man hurried forward. 'The morning shift, as they emptied the wagon.' He pointed to the tall door. 'There's a slope up there. The guts are slid straight into the incinerator. The men are so used to it, they don't really think about it any more.'

'Could the body have escaped their attention?'

'Yes, of course. According to them, they carry out their work quite mechanically.'

'So something unusual alerted them?'

The man opened his hand and gave Nicolas a small round object. 'The rays of the rising sun hit this; that was how they saw the girl. Actually, apart from that, the wagon seemed less full than usual.'

'A sweet box,' said Nicolas. He turned it, making it shimmer. It was golden, and bore a garland of green stones and, on the lid, a coloured enamel miniature representing four Cupids freeing birds from a cage, with the words 'Cupid the engraver' and four lines of verse:

> *In childhood love dreams*
> *That when the birds are freed*
> *To our hearts it seems*
> *That pleasure is what we need*

He asked Semacgus for his spectacles. The doctor handed them to him, annoyed at having to put on public display a resource that had become indispensable to him. Nicolas folded them to use as a magnifying glass. He turned the sweet box, now this way, now that. At last, with a sigh of pleasure, he made out a hallmark depicting the head of a pointer. He opened the box.

'My friends,' he said, 'this is, in fact, a pill box . . .' When he saw the contents, he exclaimed in surprise, 'Cantharides! What are these stimulants doing on the body of a young girl?'

'Or a prostitute,' said Semacgus. 'The less robust of them use it as an aid. It also helps to release a reproductive frenzy in the most barren of women.'

In this field, thought Nicolas, Semacgus's experience was unequalled, although he was never sure if it was his experience as a doctor or as a former libertine. The other thing that occurred to him was that this was the second time this particular aphrodisiac had made an appearance in the investigation.

Pursuing his thoughts, Nicolas turned to Rabouine. 'Do you have any idea how these workers managed to see this object? In any case, I think we should thank them for their honesty.'

'It must have slipped out of the pocket of her undershirt . . . There's a gusset.'

Nicolas was musing over these various pieces of information, trying to pull them all together. There was one element missing.

'I need to know the exact route followed by this wagon, as well as its timetable, if that's possible. Bring me the driver.'

The fat man with the bulging eyes stepped forward. 'You need to understand, Commissioner, that this transport goes on without interruption throughout the day. The last wagon arrives here at about three in the morning, and the driver comes and picks it up, empty, at about seven. Today he never turned up . . .'

'That's an interesting point, and it limits the period of time during which the murder may have been committed. If Semacgus can narrow it down even more, we won't be far from the truth.'

'Quite right, Pierre,' said Nicolas. 'Let's draw up a plan of campaign. The body needs to be taken to the Basse-Geôle, where Monsieur Semacgus will give it a closer examination. If he agrees.'

The surgeon nodded his consent.

'Pierre and Rabouine, I have two missions for you,' the commissioner went on. 'Find me the driver of this wagon. I want to question him. As for this sweet box or pill box, try to find an expert who can determine its origin. It's an expensive item and I have no doubt we will find its maker. And when we do . . .' He consulted his watch. 'Let's meet again at the Grand Châtelet on the stroke of six to see where we've got to. Bourdeau, anything new on the second victim?' His mind was racing. 'Unfortunately, we only have the doctor's carriage at our disposal.'

'No,' said Bourdeau, 'I arranged for another one to follow us in case we needed it. As for the second victim, fate has smiled on me. My spies have been concentrating on the world of prostitutes. It's a world where everyone knows everyone else and the slightest absence, however short, or a change in habits, gets noticed.'

He tapped out his pipe, put it away, took out his glasses and a piece of paper, and started reading.

'Mademoiselle Julie Jeanne Marot, born in Suzonnecourt, Champagne, aged nineteen. Lost both her father and mother, vineyard owners of that locality, and came to Paris a year ago to enter service. Was picked up by Madame Larue, a midwife of Rue Bourg-l'Abbé, well known as a brothel-keeper. She immediately procured her to a young man of her acquaintance, an old customer, who, despite the girl's screams, deflowered her. Later, the girl, realising that the old woman was prostituting her without paying her anything, left her and went and joined La Hilaire, in Cul-de-sac Saint-Fiacre. Her new mistress thought she was the perfect addition to her stable and took better care of her. She renamed her L'Étoile and introduced her to everyone as the new star. Now completely adapted to the life, she participated in parties and dinners of extreme debauchery.'

'Congratulations! We must go further into this. Who was keeping her? Were there several men? Apart from servicing casual customers, these girls usually combine business and pleasure and latch on to some good-looking beau. What were her haunts? Make the usual enquiries. You know what to do, and you do it much better than I could.'

The corpse was placed on a wagon belonging to the watch and covered with a tarpaulin. The cortege set off towards Paris. Nicolas, looking out through the lowered window, noticed a street at right angles to the one they were on.

'Let's not forget the Invalides slaughterhouse, it's quite close to here. We mustn't forget to check if the wagon from Île des Cygnes stops there.'

He was thinking aloud, and Semacgus, who was listening, did not think he had to answer.

'It's vitally important that we determine when and where the body was dumped on the wagon. Either to be discovered, or to disappear without a trace in the incinerator on Île des Cygnes.'

'And the sweet box?' said Semacgus. 'Valuable items like that often bear the name either of the donor or of the person who receives it.'

'There's the rub! Nothing, silence. Just the hallmark. Why abandon such a treasure? Was it simply forgotten? I don't think so, the girl was half naked. I suspect that it was put there on purpose, to arouse our curiosity.'

'That answers your previous questions. In that case, the body was meant to be found.'

'It seems like it. Let's sum up. The murderer dumps the body on the wagon. For some reason, the sweet box is with it. It's assumed, even hoped, that it will be discovered.'

'Perhaps. But there's no name on the box.'

'Precisely, precisely!' He gave a disconcerted Semacgus a friendly tap on the shoulder. 'Isn't it the subtlest thing to pretend to fall into traps which are set for us?'

'I don't quite know what you mean.'

'Could we be dealing with someone really clever? This sweet box is urging us to wager on our own intelligence.'

Semacgus was starting to be worried. Was this some kind of attack, a result of last night's wound? Nicolas certainly appeared feverish.

'I'm finding it increasingly hard to follow you.'

'Just think! If this sweet box, being such an obvious clue, led us directly to its owner or to the person who received it and made him or her a suspect, we would be within our rights to doubt the genuineness of the clue and we would be led to assume that someone was trying to force our hand.'

'Instead of which . . .'

'Without direct clues, we're faced with a difficult task, which may present us with more genuine discoveries. Let me remind you that the Duc de La Vrillière remains the prime suspect, because of the very nature of the murder weapon. That this weapon has disappeared without his being able to account for that disappearance. That his whereabouts at the time of the first murder do not appear to give him an alibi. That we need to determine his whereabouts for the two other murders, once we've narrowed down the exact time of the latest one.'

'If I understand correctly, you fear there will be no alibi for any of the three crimes?'

'I do indeed fear so, for, if our hypothesis is correct, we are dealing with a tough adversary.'

A long silence fell. Semacgus did not like to see Nicolas looking so feverish. He also knew how stupid it would be to try to calm him down. Like a hunting dog, when he was on the trail he would not give up.

'Are you feeling all right?' he asked, to set his mind at rest.

Nicolas did not reply. There was a fleeting thought at the back of his mind, something he could not at the moment pin down, but something he was convinced was important. He was still searching for it when they were in the main hall of the Basse-Geôle. Pressed for time, he had given up the idea of sending for Sanson. He needed a rapid result to give the investigation a new impetus. Semacgus had had to borrow some instruments from the local doctor at the Châtelet, who had only agreed on the express orders of the commissioner. A few days earlier, thought Nicolas, there was no doubt that he would have been refused, considered by that mediocre little world as being on the sidelines, discredited, in virtual exile. The news of his return to favour had spread like wildfire, and everything had returned to normal.

Nicolas looked closely at the undershirt the surgeon had just taken off the corpse. Something was nagging at him. He cursed his own forgetfulness. It drove out any good ideas he had and, in his job, that was tantamount to a sin. He felt in the bottom of his pocket for his little black notebook, pulled it out, and looked through it with a kind of rage. Why hadn't he thought of this earlier? When Lenoir had burdened him with all those assignments to such a point that it had even occurred to him that it was a deliberate attempt to thwart his investigation, one of them had been to track down two young girls who had run away from Brussels. He looked at the page where he had noted their descriptions. 'The first . . . smallpox . . . blue eyes, black eyebrows.' And further on – and this was what had unconsciously stirred his memory – 'Undershirt . . . blue and grey striped satin.' He glanced at the soiled, bloodstained garment. It exactly matched the description he had written down.

'Guillaume,' he said, 'do you see any marks of smallpox on the face?'

'Of course,' replied Semacgus. 'I told you that back on the island. Blue eyes, black eyebrows and marks of smallpox. For the rest . . .' He poured water over his arms and hands from an earthenware jug. 'The poor girl wasn't a courtesan. She hadn't even been a woman for long . . . I mean she'd recently been deflowered, and probably raped several times, from the front and the rear. A sad business!'

'Are you sure?'

'I'd swear it before a judge, without any qualms.'

'Time of death?'

'That's harder to establish. Taking a number of factors into account – the night temperature, the heat given off by a heap of decomposing animal flesh – I estimate the probable time of death at about two in the morning. Let's say between one and two.'

'We know that the wagon arrived on Île des Cygnes at about three . . . We need to know where it was about two, or even a little earlier.'

He was thinking hard, but Semacgus, with an expression of barely suppressed jubilation on his broad, ruddy face, interrupted this exercise.

'That's not all, Nicolas. There's another observation I've made, I don't know how important it is, but I'm sure you'll find it intriguing. Before she died, the victim was immersed in a soapy solution, which dried as it evaporated. You just have to wet the skin to notice it. You can still smell the scent a bit.'

'You'll need to be a little clearer than that, Guillaume. Don't forget you're talking to someone who's had a bit of a shock and spent last night . . .'

He broke off, noticing Semacgus's mocking look. He felt his face go red.

'The girl took a bath,' said the surgeon. 'A scented bath, to boot!'

'I'll refrain from drawing any conclusion from that for the time being. I'll just remark that, at every stage in this case, water is never very far away. The Saint-Florentin mansion, close to the Seine. Rue de Glatigny, on the banks of the Cité. And, finally, Île des Cygnes. We're never far from the river!'

'Which makes it all the more interesting to find out where the wagon gained its deadly load.'

'Any other observations?'

'One last one. I found a fragment of nail with some skin attached. The attacker must have grabbed hold of the victim's garment during the struggle. Here it is, for what it's worth. I don't suppose it'll help you find the person it belongs to, but who knows? It's just possible it may be of use to you . . .'

Nicolas put the item inside a folded sheet of his black notebook. 'You haven't mentioned this,' he said, 'but I assume that the murder weapon—'

'Is indeed the artificial hand. At least, the plaster cast fits the wound. There's no doubt about it. What are you going to do now?'

'I've put off meeting the major-domo's in-laws for too long. After that, I'm going to Bicêtre to see what I can find out about the rejected suitor of the first victim, Marguerite Pindron.'

Deep in thought, they went back up to the duty office, where they were greeted by Old Marie, the usher, who, having followed Nicolas's career from the beginning, was delighted that things were getting back to normal for him. He handed him a small folded note on which he immediately recognised the three sardines of Monsieur de Sartine's coat of arms. The message was a brief one: 'Monsieur Bourdier, the man I spoke to you about, is living with his family in a furnished room in Rue Galante.'

Nicolas, who always kept spare clothes and clean linen in a cubbyhole, changed and asked Old Marie to take his fine grey coat to the cleaner.

'Marie,' he said, 'I'm a bit short of men. Could you do me a service? I know you're perfectly capable.'

'By God, I'd jump out of the window for you! Problem is, with my damned aches and pains, I'd find it hard to climb up onto the sill!'

'I'm not asking that much,' said Nicolas with a laugh. 'I'll send you a box of camphorated beaver fat that Monsieur de Noblecourt swears by. Aren't you bored in your cage?'

'Of course, Monsieur Nicolas! At least I have my pipe and my cordial. Apart from that, I'm bored stiff.'

'All right, then. What would you say to searching in the register of foreigners for a middle-aged Englishman, of medium height and with a definite paunch? He's wearing tinted folding glasses and speaks quite good French. I'd also quite like to have a list of foreigners staying in furnished hotels in Paris and Versailles.'

'It would be very careless of him to always frequent such conspicuous establishments,' said Semacgus.

'Lodging with the locals would be even more so. It's possible he's staying with the British ambassador. Lord Ashbury is a clever man. We'll see . . . So, Marie, is that all right with you?'

'I'll go and look at the registers straight away.'

Nicolas handed him a few *louis*.

'That's far too much,' said the usher, stunned.

'It's to pay the cleaner. Keep the change for tobacco and cordial.'

He set off at top speed.

'You're good, I'll give you that,' said Semacgus. 'Always a promise of scraps from the table.'

'I don't have to try too hard. He's a good man, and a Breton, to boot. *Evit ur baoninqenn, kant modigenn!* "For a little pain, a hundred pleasures," as they say where we come from. I'm going to visit the Duchamplans in Rue Christine. Will you come with me? I don't have much time, so we'll have to skip lunch. We can dine together this evening, we'll have plenty of time then . . .'

Semacgus was grimacing at the thought of this sacrifice.

'Would you dare to abandon a patient?' joked Nicolas. 'Imagine if I failed in my duty—'

'You're beating down my defences. All right then, I'll fast in your honour. This evening, you'll all be my guests.'

The surgeon's carriage was waiting for them at the entrance. Nicolas suddenly remembered to thank the coachman, who, by his presence of mind, had probably saved his life. The man in question, blushing with emotion, told them that he had taken advantage of their absence to buy, from one of those stalls which cluttered the square all the way to the Apport-Paris, a basket of little hot pies from Champagne and two bottles of simple wine. He had guessed that the gentlemen, too absorbed in their affairs, were going to have to tighten their belts. Both congratulated him on his initiative, and Nicolas again got rid of a few extra *écus*.

Assuaging their raging hunger, they crossed the Seine and soon reached Rue Christine, which was situated between Rue des Grands-Augustins and Rue Dauphine. This tranquil street was full of large bourgeois houses. The Duchamplan house was not out of place here, with its austere facade devoid of excessive decoration, apart from a mascaron depicting the face of a chubby Triton. Six floors including the attic, noted Nicolas. The three upper floors appeared, from certain aspects, to be given over to furnished rooms. They went through the carriage entrance. The caretaker was sitting on a stool with the straw removed, shelling beans. He told them that Monsieur Duchamplan the elder lived on the first and second floors, and Monsieur Duchamplan the younger on the mezzanine. But the latter was not in at the moment; in fact, he had not been in for several days. There was nothing to explain this absence, which appeared to worry his brother greatly. To the left of the courtyard was an impressive flight of stairs, the state of which indicated that it was for the exclusive use of the owner, while everyone else used a more modest staircase, as did the servants, the suppliers, the carriers of water and wood . . .

Nicolas remarked to Semacgus that chance remained the most constant element in investigations, and that you often discovered things when you were least expecting to. It would be useful to speak a bit more to such a talkative character as that caretaker. Having rung the bell-pull, they waited until a middle-aged manservant opened the door. Nicolas asked to see the master of the house. A few minutes later, the man himself appeared.

From the first, Nicolas found it hard to define his appearance. He was neither tall nor short, neither fat nor thin, and wore a black, rather old-fashioned coat. He was pale, with washed-out eyes, and resembled his sister the nun, although his face was puffier. His hands, hidden beneath wide cuffs, were clasped together, as if he were trying to overcome a degree of nervousness.

'Nicolas Le Floch, commissioner at the Châtelet. Dr Guillaume Semacgus.'

He stopped there. It was the best way to force the witness to make the next move.

'Please come in, gentlemen.'

He admitted them into a large, richly furnished drawing room. The curtains at the windows looking out on the street were half drawn, plunging the room into relative darkness. He motioned them to take their seats in large high-backed armchairs from the previous century.

'I'm listening, Monsieur,' said Nicolas.

'You've rather caught me on the hop, Commissioner. I've just learnt about the tragedy that happened at the minister's house and my brother-in-law Missery's wound.'

This was not getting them very far.

'Could you tell me who informed you of these events?'

'My sister, Hélène, who's a nun with the Daughters of Saint Michel. But you know that, since you've already met her.'

This was said with a kind of bitter irony.

'So you're aware of the serious accusations made against your brother-in-law?' said Nicolas.

'I find it hard to believe that he could be capable of something so terrible. He can be violent, yes, touchy, difficult, not always very honest, much given to debauchery, but a murderer, no, I don't really think so.'

As a connoisseur, Nicolas appreciated the man's skill at appearing to be contemptuous of the major-domo while avoiding directly accusing him. The overall picture, though, was certainly a black one.

'Has your relationship with him remained close?'

'We rarely see each other.'

'When did you see him last?'

'At the Mass for the anniversary of my sister's death.'

'Do you have any joint interests? I should point out to you, before anything else, that I know all about your family affairs. Missery is in possession of your sister's fortune – correct me if I'm wrong – and it will revert to your family if he should die.'

'Whether he has remarried or not, Monsieur. That is quite important.'

'I assume you're referring to the danger represented by his passionate relationship with a chambermaid in the Saint-Florentin household?'

'Precisely. Let's be clear about this: if you're trying to insinuate that my brother-in-law was nearly murdered on account of the coincidence of our interests, you're making a big mistake. Didn't you tell my sister that he was merely grazed?'

He was still expressing himself in a restrained, level-headed manner, staring straight ahead, never looking at the commissioner.

'That's all well and good, Monsieur,' said Nicolas. 'I've heard your answers on your joint interests with your brother-in-law, and we've talked about your sister's fortune. Are you yourself involved in some occupation?'

'I manage my money. I have a private income, and I also earn revenue from my interests in a number of companies of which I am the administrator.'

'What companies?'

'Aren't you going beyond your prerogatives? I am known and protected by the Prince de Condé.'

'Do you have a position in his household?' asked Nicolas with a touch of sarcasm.

'The prince and I,' retorted Duchamplan proudly, 'are in

partnership on a project to supply the city with water.'

'I only know of one such project: that of the Perier brothers, supported by the Duc d'Orléans.'

The man seemed surprised by Nicolas's knowledge. 'You are badly informed, there are others.'

'And are you involved in other enterprises?'

'A transport company.'

'And what else?'

'I am an administrator of the royal hospital of Bicêtre.'

'I see,' said Nicolas. 'I assume that covers everything. Where were you on the night of Sunday to Monday?'

'Here, with my wife and my sister.'

'Did you go out?'

'Not at all. We went to bed about eleven.'

Nicolas noted that the time could be approximate. The contradiction with the sister's declaration that she had gone to bed at ten was only a small one. Of course, she had 'forgotten' to mention that she had visited her family.

'When you say "we", are you including your brother, Eudes?'

'My brother is a young man who has his own amusements, and we don't interfere with them. He lives on the mezzanine, and has his own entrance.'

'And did he come home the following day?'

'I have no idea. He comes and goes. He's a will-o'-the-wisp . . . whom I support come what may.' His mouth tensed in a grimace that was meant to be a smile.

'I'd like to speak to your wife,' said Nicolas.

'She's gone out to pay a visit.'

The words had come out very quickly. It was better to

stop there for the moment. Nicolas was just standing up when Semacgus raised his hand.

'With your permission, Commissioner. Monsieur Duchamplan mentioned a transport company. What kind of company?'

'We have a fleet of cabs.'

'One company has the monopoly on cabs in Paris. Is it that one?'

Duchamplan gave Nicolas a look of commiseration. 'As I'm sure you know, that monopoly has long since been superseded. There are more than a thousand cabs and more than seven hundred hired coaches in Paris now, and joint-stock companies have proliferated. The vehicles just have to be numbered and registered.'

'I see. I would be grateful if you could inform me as soon as your brother reappears.'

'I shall certainly do so, although he is often away a long time.'


In the courtyard, the shelling of beans was still going on. Nicolas offered the caretaker a pinch of snuff, which was gratefully accepted. There followed a vigorous series of sneezes.

'You're softening up the customer,' said Semacgus in Nicolas's ear.

The commissioner winked, then asked the caretaker a straight question. 'What time did Madame Duchamplan go out?'

'Go out? That poor pale thing, who's always coughing? I'd like to see her go out! You must be joking, Monsieur. She's been confined to her room for several days now.'

'Since when?'

'Monday, I think,' said the man, sneezing.

'And what about Monsieur Duchamplan's sister?'

'Oh, that one . . . For a nun, she certainly has a lot of pride. Never a greeting, never a smile. The last time I saw her come here for dinner was Sunday.'

'What time did she leave?'

'About ten. I had to run out in the cold to hail a carriage, at my age!'

'Thank you very much.'

'At your service. This snuff is good! Not like the sawdust you sometimes find. Count on me whenever you want. The name's Taqueminet.'

As they were leaving Rue Christine, Nicolas, who was looking in the direction of Rue des Grands-Augustins, suddenly cried out and set off at a run, much to the surprise of Semacgus. He seemed to be trying to catch up with a carriage which was speeding away and which soon disappeared round the corner. Breathless and furious, the commissioner came walking back. He had to catch his breath before explaining what had just happened. He took off his tricorn and wiped his forehead, which was half covered with a bandage. Semacgus noticed blood spreading over the linen and gently reprimanded him.

'How could you think of getting in such a state? You've reopened your wound. We'll have to find an apothecary and get it seen to. Good Lord, you ran off like the fire of a fuse trying to reach Saint Barbara!'

Nicolas laughed. 'I'm sorry, I'm not twenty years old any more! Perhaps I was dreaming, and yet I'm sure the person I saw get into that carriage is the very same person who ran away the day before yesterday in the lower gallery of the palace at my approach. I told you about him. Lord Ashbury. I just saw him coming out of a house . . . The head, or one of the heads, of the British secret service. Is that fever or reality?'

Semacgus grabbed his wrist and took out his watch, then felt his forehead. 'It's not fever. Your pulse is fine now that you've caught your breath, and your forehead is cool.'

Nicolas tugged at his arm. 'Let's take a look at that house, I want to set my mind at rest. How stupid I am! We should have got in our carriage . . .'

'There's no point regretting that, it would have had to make a U turn!'

They walked back up Rue Christine as far as a fine-looking double-fronted building, which, according to the inscription on its pediment, was the Hôtel de Russie. A well-dressed lady greeted them.

'Welcome, gentlemen. No doubt you wish to take lodgings in our establishment, which is so well known that the *Almanach Parisien* draws the attention of foreigners and visitors to it . . .'

She spoke so quickly it was impossible for Nicolas to interrupt her.

'We only lodge persons of the first rank, who have carriages. We have richly furnished apartments, bedrooms, wardrobes, reception rooms with damask hangings and other appropriate adornments. There are very clean water closets on every floor. You can use the sheds and stables for your carriage. We don't provide food, but we allow you to have what you need brought in from the best caterers in the neighbourhood, and we have information on the best inns in the city. I am at your disposal.'

She gave a deep curtsey which would have made a duchess envious.

'Madame,' said Nicolas, 'you misconstrue the reasons for our visit. We simply wish to have some information about a customer of yours who left barely five minutes ago and got into a carriage.'

These words immediately cast a cloud over her welcoming face, and she assumed an inscrutable, almost duplicitous air. 'Who are you talking about? No one went out as far as I know.'

'Madame,' said Nicolas firmly, 'I would have preferred not to have to remind you of your duties. I am a commissioner of police at the Châtelet. I seem to remember that the owners of hotels and furnished rooms must inform us in good time of all foreigners staying with them. Whenever a foreigner arrives, within twenty-four hours the Lieutenant General of Police needs to know his name, where he comes from, the reason for his visit, where he is staying, with whom he is in correspondence, and whom he receives. That supposes that the said owners are devoted to His Majesty's interests. Have I made myself quite clear? Do you realise how much at fault you've been? I fear you may have to follow us to a less pleasant location to be checked and interrogated.'

This speech seemed to have hit home; the lady burst into tears, and made no further attempt to brazen it out. Nicolas confirmed his resolution by remaining sternly impassive.

'Alas, alas, Commissioner, do you want to ruin me – me, a poor widow, with a family to support, working myself to death to run this establishment? I am, it is true, guilty of having neglected my duties, but only because of my good heart. The foreign gentleman, an Englishman I think, forbade me to report his presence. The reason he's in France is because he wants to track down a child he once had with a French lady who's now married. Think how discreet he needs to be about something like that!'

'Madame, I fear that is simply a tall tale which you, in your innocence, swallowed whole. Under what name did this gentleman present himself?'

'He said his name was Francis Sefton – though he asked me in a threatening tone never to mention it – and that he bought and sold racehorses.'

'A clever story, horse racing is becoming fashionable. When did he arrive?'

'On 20 September.'

'Did he have any luggage with him?'

'Some portmanteaus. The servant girl told me that he had a lot of coats, all very different from each other, with some wigs and even some ladies' dresses. No doubt to sell them when he returned to his island.'

'Has he received anyone?'

'No, nobody.'

'Did he have a carriage?'

'A cab came to fetch him.'

'Has he been regular in his habits?'

'Definitely not! He often comes back early in the morning and sometimes stays out all night. He's been paying his weeks regularly. He left in a hurry this morning, after being away for two days, and obligingly paid for an extra week even though the week isn't yet over. He asked me again not to say anything about his being here, because his old friend's husband has been informed of his presence in Paris.'

'All right, Madame. If he comes back, tell the local commissioner immediately to inform Commissioner Le Floch at the Châtelet. For your guidance, I must tell you that you risk the closure of this hotel as well as legal action if you contravene these instructions. Now show me Monsieur Sefton's apartment.'

She led them to a cosy apartment on the first floor, comprising a bedroom, a bathroom and a small drawing room. The bed had not been slept in. Nicolas noted a bottle of port and two glasses on a pedestal table. He sniffed, then went to the fireplace: a large number of papers had been burnt. In the heap of ashes he discovered part of a sheet that had escaped the destruction. On it were only a few printed letters: '*elles ne*'. A newspaper, an official document, an advertisement? They would have to see.

'Has he had a visitor?' Nicolas asked the hostess, pointing to the two glasses.

'No.'

He sniffed the glasses. 'Last night, I'd say . . . No, he wasn't here . . .This morning, then. Are you telling me that you're behind your desk for twenty-four hours a day?'

'Of course not, but . . . To tell the truth, I really don't know what to think any more, it may have happened.'

Once again she burst into tears. Nicolas shrugged, depressed by so much thoughtlessness. Semacgus pointed out the rim of one of the two glasses. There were traces of rouge.

'Who knows?' said Nicolas. 'These days men sometimes make themselves up more heavily than women. They all smear rouge and ceruse on their faces. For the moment, let's just make a note of it.'

*

As soon as they had got back in the carriage – the hotel-keeper had followed them out, lamenting volubly – Nicolas tried to draw a few conclusions from their visit to Rue Christine.

'Using a false identity, Lord Ashbury has been in Paris for two weeks. That woman's stupidity and our own people's shortcomings – I fear that since Sartine's departure there has been some laxity – explain the fact that he has managed to evade all police supervision of foreigners. He comes and goes quite freely, meets whoever he likes, and even goes to Versailles for God knows what intrigue. There, he almost comes face to face with me, runs away, but finds the time and the means to have me followed and, I believe, orders me to be killed. An attempt is made outside the Comte d'Arranet's house, and fails. What's the reason? He assumes that I'm pursuing him. He hurries back to Paris, says he has business, receives an associate, and then escapes into the big city! But where?'

'He may simply have set off for Calais,' said Semacgus.

'I don't think so. His mission isn't over. Somehow, I've got in his way. What are his intentions? I'll tell you this: there's no such thing as coincidence . . .' Nicolas was beating the plush seat with his fist, raising small clouds of dust. 'No one's going to make me believe that Lord Ashbury, alias Francis Sefton, has been staying at a hotel a few doors from the Duchamplan house by mere chance. I don't know why he has, but I'm going to find out!'

'It is indeed vital to discover why he came to France,' said Semacgus, 'especially as it's a clandestine visit. And there are also these Duchamplans, who seem to me very much involved in all these mysteries.'

'I didn't want to take things too far by going back up to see the wife. We must give them the false impression that they're safe. It won't hurt them to wait. As for the younger brother, I get the feeling he won't be back very soon. I find it hard to believe that the motive for the murder in the Saint-Florentin mansion is financial gain. These people are very well off. What is it then?'

'You must calm down, or the fever will come back.'

'I fear I'm going to have to start all over again. Lenoir has assigned me to so many different cases they've made me lose the thread of the main one. We must question Missery again. Where did he find Marguerite Pindron? I'll also need to have a conversation with the Duchesse de La Vrillière. The rumour of her good relations with Madame de Maurepas may help me . . . Last but not least, I need to find the Pindron girl's young man. He's the real mystery. The duchesse's young Norman maid told me his name is Aide.'

'Did she have a Norman accent?' Semacgus suddenly asked, slyly.

'Indeed she did, a very strong one.'

'Then we've found the lover. Your Aide is quite simply Eudes, the first name of the younger Duchamplan. Missery, if he's telling the truth, ought to confirm that, and it would explain many things.'

'Thank you, my dear Guillaume. That's the second time today you've been a great help. And your coachman saved my life. However, even though it opens up some interesting avenues, it doesn't solve everything. There are elements in this case that are being deliberately hidden from us.'

Semacgus called to the coachman to take them to Rue de la Joaillerie, to the shop of Monsieur Nicaise, the apothecary.

# X

## BICÊTRE

I was not aware that Bicêtre had been built to
engender disease and give birth to crime.

MIRABEAU

Nicolas recognised the apothecary: Monsieur Nicaise had
bandaged him up once before, during his investigation into
the disappearance of Commissioner Lardin. Semacgus and he
conferred for a short time after examining the wound. They
rejected the use of spirits, tinctures and balms: the wound was not
serious enough to warrant it. In addition, such remedies, far from
speeding up the healing process, delayed it, often turning a simple
wound into an ulcer. They stopped the blood from flowing but
made the injured parts callous. The two men settled for a common
agglutinative plaster to close the wound. As the bullet had burnt
and ripped the skin, they cleaned it with calcined alum and placed
over it a plaster of breadcrumbs and milk mixed with olive oil, to
be changed three times a day. Listening to them, Nicolas thought
they were discussing him as if he were a chicken they were getting
ready to cook.

Night was falling by the time the carriage dropped them at the
entrance to the Grand Châtelet. Bourdeau and Rabouine were
waiting for them in the duty office. The inspector was very
concerned about the consequences of Nicolas's wound. He still

felt mortified, blaming himself for not having been with his friend at such a dangerous moment.

'Bourdeau likes people to try and kill you just so that he can save you,' said Semacgus, provoking general laughter.

'Well, now, my bloodhounds,' said Nicolas, 'any news?'

'First,' said Bourdeau, 'about the sweet box, because that's what it in fact is. We went to the Johac mansion in Rue Saint-Merri, where there's a large shop selling all kinds of precious boxes, including snuff boxes, in vast quantities, all different from one another and all in the latest fashions. I would never have thought there were so many, in gold, silver, enamel, pasteboard, shell, ivory, Irish leather, shagreen and God knows what else!'

'I see you were dazzled.'

'Shocked, rather, by this display of pointless luxury. What it all cost could have fed a great many starving mouths.'

'Ah,' said Semacgus sardonically, 'here comes Rousseau again!'

'You may mock, but the day will come ... Well, now's not the time. Anyway, we showed them the box. Although they weren't absolutely sure, they all thought it was the work of a master. One of the assistants, the oldest of them, suggested that although there was no signature, it might be from the hand of Robert-Joseph Auguste, a highly regarded maker, who lives in Rue de la Monnaie. We found him and questioned him. He's a silversmith who supplies the leading courts of Europe. He formally identified his work from his hallmark, the pointer's head.'

'But who was the buyer?'

'I'm coming to that,' said Bourdeau, amused by Nicolas's impatience. 'This is going to surprise you. The box turns out to have been ordered by the Comte de Saint-Florentin, Duc de La Vrillière, the current Minister of the King's Household.'

'Let's take things one at a time. Was he sure it was him?'

'No, because he didn't come in person. He sent a messenger. But Auguste, who appears to know the Court, recognised this messenger as a person of quality. In addition, he paid the full amount in one go.'

'Which is not always characteristic of a gentleman these days,' remarked Nicolas with a smile. 'Did he provide you with a description?'

'Medium height, a haughty expression, bulging eyes, expensive clothes. Powdered wig.'

'That won't get us very far! But good work all the same!'

'I have something even more curious, if possible,' said Rabouine, straightening his thin body. 'That particular wagon only covers the left bank of the river. It leaves from Pont des Tournelles. We found the driver. Where? At the police station in the Port aux Tuiles. He told us a really unbelievable story . . .'

'Yet another one!'

'This morning, about one or one thirty, he got down to pass water near the Fort des Tournelles. He had already begun his shift outside the walls. He exchanged a few words with a man who wanted a light for his pipe. To thank him, this individual offered to buy him a drink in a low tavern. Our driver claims to have drunk too much and can't remember anything else after that. He came to on the river bank, stripped of his clothes and money, surrounded by boys and outraged women shouting, "What a mess!" He was taken to the police station, but couldn't give any other details.'

'To cut a long story short,' said Bourdeau, 'he can't throw any light on what happened to his load. The fact remains that an unknown person, having got the driver drunk, stripped him and presumably put on his clothes to deceive the night watchman on Île des Cygnes. What about the next stops on the itinerary? you will ask. The wagon didn't stop to pick up anything between Quai Saint-Bernard and the Gros Caillou, much to everyone's surprise.'

'But how in heaven's name,' said Semacgus, 'could the guard at the incinerator on Île des Cygnes not notice anything?'

'He's half asleep by the time he opens the gate. It was pitch dark. There was a new moon.'

Nicolas consulted the calendar in the *Almanach royal* for 1774, which as usual was lying on the table. 'That's correct, new moon on 5 October, the feast day of Sainte Aure, the abbess. Well, gentlemen, I'm very pleased with your work. Let's sum up. The body was dumped on the wagon between one and one thirty, two at the latest, by an unknown person who got rid of the driver. Bearing in mind the estimate of the time given by Dr Semacgus here, I think we can state without too much fear of contradiction that the murder was committed somewhere quite close to Quai des Tournelles.'

'Unless,' said Bourdeau, 'it was taken there to put us off the scent.'

Semacgus seemed puzzled. 'I wonder about this elaborate staging. They could have just hidden the body, if they wanted to be sure it would go into the incinerator.'

'That's precisely what the criminal didn't want,' replied Nicolas. 'If he had let the wagon do its usual round, the body of the unfortunate victim would have been well hidden and would never have attracted attention and been discovered. Of course, there was still a risk it might not have been, but the gamble paid off and the body was found. It's also obvious that whoever did this knew that the round existed. All of which brings us back to the idea that the solution to this mystery can be found in the area of Pont des Tournelles.'

'Water,' Semacgus went on, 'and consequently the river, are ever present in this case. What our friends here don't know is that the body of the victim, who was raped, was covered with evaporated soapy water. What do you make of that?'

At this point, Old Marie appeared, bearing Nicolas's beautiful grey coat, now perfectly cleaned. Nicolas checked that the bloodstains had left no trace that might have condemned Master Vachon's masterpiece to the attentions of the second-hand clothes dealers. The art of the cleaners was more than a match for the dangers of a dirty city. But Marie was shaking his head sadly.

'I didn't find anything about your foreigner, Monsieur Nicolas, although I looked in all the registers. He must have slipped through the net.'

'Don't worry,' said Nicolas. 'His name is Francis Sefton, and he arrived in Paris on about 20 September. He's passing himself off as a racehorse merchant. And for good measure, let me tell you that the lover of Marguerite Pindron is very likely to have been young Duchamplan, first name Eudes.'

'Good Lord!' said Bourdeau. 'Where did you find that out?'

'It was all thanks to Dr Semacgus's knowledge of the Norman accent.'

\*

The doctor invited the company to dinner at an inn in Rue Montorgueil chosen as much for its reputation for good food as for its proximity to Noblecourt's house. He did not want to tire Nicolas out, knowing how trying his night and day had been. At first, the conversation of the four guests continued to turn around the case that had brought them together. A hamper of oysters gave Nicolas the opportunity to assert that he loved this mollusc when it was white and fat, which scandalised the rest of the table, except for Semacgus, who did not give an opinion, but merely stated that he could not imagine any other joy for the oyster than health, which pleased everyone. A macaroni pie followed. The final course was a dish of sheep's tongues in parcels, which they enjoyed so much that the host was treated to a drink and asked to conform to tradition and detail all the stages of the making of this delight. What you had to do, he said, was cut the tongues in half and fry them in a little oil with parsley, chopped shallots, diced chives and mushrooms, salt, pepper and nutmeg. When they had cooled, you had to place them, one by one, between thick slices of bacon then wrap them in paper. Once they were wrapped, you grilled them and served them when they were simmering. As a final touch, before serving you sprinkled a little veal juice over them. Wild applause greeted this poem, before a dish of late vineyard peaches appeared to refresh both mouths and heads. Semacgus accompanied Nicolas back to Rue Montmartre, where only Catherine was still up, dozing by the fireplace in the servants' pantry. He did not wake her, but was unable to escape the vigilance of Mouchette, who spat at him, doubtless angered by an absence she found unacceptable. But she was not one to bear a grudge; no sooner had Nicolas got into bed than he heard her purr and felt her weight on his chest and her little cold nose come to rest against his cheek. He fell asleep immediately.

*Saturday 8 October 1774*

Nicolas rose refreshed by a dreamless sleep. Catherine, who was shocked by nothing after the horrors of war, changed his plaster and bombarded him with questions. Given the hour, Monsieur de Noblecourt had not yet rung, so Nicolas wrote him a little note to reassure him and to give him a brief summary of the progress of his investigation. As he was planning to visit Bicêtre, he would have to appear in a manner befitting the solemnity of his office. He put on his black magistrate's gown. The width and length of the sleeves allowed him to conceal two loaded pistols. He gave up the idea of wearing a wig, which would compress his wound and stop it healing. He took his ivory rod, the symbol of his authority.

Before he left, it occurred to him that the presence of Lord Ashbury demanded a degree of caution. In spite of his cumbersome attire, he would have to leave Noblecourt's house by an unusual route. With Poitevin's help, he placed a ladder against the wall between Noblecourt's garden and that of the neighbouring house. Thanks to this ploy, he was able to leave through a carriage entrance leading to Rue du Jour, opposite the convent of the Daughters of Sainte Agnès.

From there, he got to Rue Coquillière, where he hired a cab for the day. He left Paris through Faubourg Saint-Marceau, which was just waking up. He was struck once again by the hustle and bustle of the countless taverns serving adulterated brandy, cheap wine and cider to a sinister-looking collection of characters – and sometimes even to children.

Barely a league separated Bicêtre from the centre of Paris. Nicolas, leaning out of the window, suddenly saw on the horizon a huge building on the top of a hill to the right of the road to Fontainebleau. From that distance, the hospital looked like a palace, its bright mass towering over the surrounding countryside with its vineyards, windmills, and, in the distance, the Seine. It seemed to Nicolas that this ideal location must be of great benefit to the sick. The air there must be pure, not to be compared with the miasma enveloping hospitals in the city. But he changed his mind when he began gradually to smell a stench that reminded him of the great knacker's yard at Montfaucon and the incinerator on Île des Cygnes.

His carriage arrived at the main entrance just as an elegant coupé was coming to a halt ahead of it. A man dressed all in black got out and gave him a friendly wave. As Nicolas approached, he recognised Dr de Gévigland, who had treated Jean Missery at the Saint-Florentin mansion. He took off his tricorn and returned the doctor's greeting.

'I didn't think I'd see you again so soon,' he said. 'I'm more delighted than I can say. Have you come to see a patient?'

The doctor smiled but appeared embarrassed. 'Believe it or not,' he murmured, 'I've come to buy a few corpses.'

Nicolas, hardened by his experience of the Basse-Geôle, did not bat an eyelid. 'For anatomical purposes, I assume?'

Gévigland's black eyes grew even more sombre, as if drowning in sadness. 'Alas, I wish that were the case, but it so happens that for a long time now I've been studying the bodies of those suffering from venereal diseases or, more precisely, I've been performing autopsies in order to assess the side-effects of the remedies inflicted on them, from which, most of the time, they die. Sometimes, the cure is deadlier than the disease.'

'What methods do they use here?'

'Rubbing with mercury ointment, sulphur baths and a prolonged diet. Patients are immersed four at a time for several hours in the same bathtub, because there aren't enough of them. Nor is there enough access to water. One single very deep well, inadequate channels, and thousands of inmates! Is this your first visit here?'

'My duties have never brought me here before. All I know is that Bicêtre is both a prison and a hospital.'

'A prison for the most repulsive dregs of humanity, a hospital for the most terrible of diseases, and a tomb for the incurably insane. May I suggest you visit the place in my company, unless you're here on urgent business . . .?'

'I'm here in connection with my investigation into the case with which you are familiar. I am looking for a man who's suffering from venereal disease, the victim's former fiancé. Is he still here? I have no idea. In the meantime, I'll gladly follow you.'

'Leave it to me, I know everyone here. The house is run by a mother superior who has officiating nuns and an army of assistants at her command. Admittedly, the population of this place fluctuates during the year. In winter, it can reach four thousand five hundred.'

With a pang in his heart, Nicolas followed his guide, who explained to him in measured tones the terrible scenes that appeared before them. The hospital, which they visited first, housed individuals infected with venereal disease. The wards were filled with rows of beds that seemed to stretch to infinity. He noted that each bed often contained five or six unfortunates stagnating in their own excrement. The atmosphere was so stifling that he was almost overcome with nausea. Hideously cankered creatures crawled across the floor towards the visitors and held out their hands.

'They prefer the hard floor,' said Gévigland, 'to the infection and filth of the beds.'

'Are they forced to take refuge in this hell?' asked Nicolas, appalled.

'The police pick them up in places of ill repute. Others come of their own accord. Some reserve their places a long time in advance, when they're still only suffering light symptoms. By the time they finally get here, the disease has often reached its deadliest stage.'

'Do any of them ever recover?'

'Yes, sometimes. But I should point out that it's the rule in this hospital that recovery must occur within a given time. Unfortunately, the disease itself doesn't play by the rules. The result is that the patient, after being tormented with useless remedies, leaves without being cured. You can imagine the consequences!'

They entered a series of long, echoing galleries. Through the windows, the great well in the central courtyard could be seen. They climbed some steps, descended others, and finally reached the area for the insane and the common prisoners. Gévigland gave his name, and the gate to the insane enclosure was opened.

'Here begins the final circle of hell,' he said. 'Everything you've seen so far was nothing. This isn't a hospital, it's a freak show. The worst part of it is that the sane prisoners are mixed with the mad. This means that men who are in any case despised for their conduct, have to bear, in addition to their sentence, the aggression and insults of the insane. As a result, a stay in this house of detention often becomes a slow descent into madness.'

'What do the doctors do?'

'You must be joking! They've never had any doctors. Worse still, the place has become a kind of theatre for fashionable society. From time to time, for a little money to the guards, people who like that kind of thing come to feast their eyes on these degrading visions. Being treated as objects of curiosity causes slight signs of madness to degenerate into paroxysms of frenzy. They start out mad and end up rabid. Some of these visitors treat them as if they were wild beasts in cages, teasing them and provoking their fury. You have to see it to believe it.'

'To think that I, a commissioner at the Châtelet, knew nothing of these horrors!' said Nicolas, his blood running cold with revulsion.

Their presence unleashed a pandemonium of cries and obscene gestures.

'That doesn't surprise me,' replied the doctor. 'For many Parisians, especially among those of the highest rank and the most enlightened, the cruelties committed at the very gates of the city are as foreign as those of the savage populations in the New World.'

'What about the Church?' asked Nicolas.

'The opinion of the Church is that the patients should be grateful for the charity shown them and that the prisoners must expiate their sins. You have to understand that everyone follows the logic of his own viewpoint. The philosophers obviously protest at prisoners and madmen being put together. But in their sensitive humanity, they're interested – with justification – in what happens to the prisoners, but they ignore how badly the insane are treated, with the horrors of prison added to the terrible burden of their condition. Everyone agrees they should be hidden away and prevented from harming others, but it might be more sensible to understand them and treat them.'

They proceeded to a building reserved for young children. Gévigland explained to Nicolas that only those aged under twelve were kept there.

'You mean, I suppose,' said Nicolas, 'that this is part of the hospital, and that these are orphans who've been brought here through public charity.'

'Not a bit of it. They're actually prisoners, and the parents of these wretches are still alive.'

'I'm astonished that creatures of that age can become the victims of laws of which they know nothing and which they wouldn't understand even if they'd known of them. If they've committed punishable acts, they should be sent back to their parents to be chastised by them.'

'But these children haven't broken the laws of the kingdom in any way. They're only guilty of small domestic misdemeanours. It's their parents who've placed them here.'

'And I assume this terrible treatment doesn't reform them?'

'You assume correctly. They usually leave prison worse than when they came in. A hundred times worse. Even separated into cells, they can at least hear each other, corrupt each other with their words, urge each other to vice. In this way, blind parents themselves become the instruments of their own children's depravity and inflict on them the most refined as well as the most terrible of all punishments.'

The worst still remained to be seen. The doctor led Nicolas to the centre of the hospital courtyard. The commissioner shuddered at the sight of the barred windows that overlooked it, behind which pale, hideous figures screamed insults.

Gévigland stamped his foot on the cobbled ground.

'Just imagine, Monsieur, twenty feet underground, directly below where we are now, there are different kinds of dungeons, veritable tombs. Can you see these narrow slits here and there? They're skylights, which let in a feeble semblance of light, not into the dungeons, which have to be kept in total darkness, but into the passage that leads from one to the other. But if I were ever, by some misfortune, to find myself in such a deplorable situation, I think I'd prefer the tomb-like solitude of these cells rather than the communal room in the prison.'

'Why is that?'

'The foulest excesses are committed on the prisoners' very bodies. All kinds of vices are practised as a matter of course, and even in public. Simple decency forbids me to go into detail. I'm told that many prisoners are *"simillimi faeminis moeres, stuprati e constupratores"*, lost to all modesty.'

'But who are the unfortunates who've been plunged into this hell?'

'Do you need to ask?' said the doctor, with bitter irony. 'Minor offenders, guilty of street brawls, drunkenness, indecency, debauchery, and God knows what else. None is here after being convicted of the worst crimes in a regular court. They're all here for what are called offences of disorder.' He smiled. 'Please don't think that observation is directed at you. I can see how indignant these things make you feel, and I appreciate that.'

'But it should be directed at me,' replied Nicolas. 'At the beginning of my career I recall reading a report addressed to Monsieur de Sartine, who was then Lieutenant General of Police, which said that the prisoners at Bicêtre were there because of arrests made by the military police, courts martial, the Criminal Lieutenant, and local justices, especially for poaching. You can rest assured that I shall inform Monsieur Lenoir of the situation here.'

'Nobody so far has ever taken the slightest steps to remedy such terrible conditions.'

For a long time they were silent, while their presence continued to provoke a cacophony of cries and insults.

'I think your gown has a lot to do with this welcome,' observed Gévigland. 'They recognise that you're a commissioner . . . But I've taken up too much of your time. I'll take you to the mother superior and she will point you in the direction of the gaolers who keep the registers.'


An elegant staircase led them to the first floor of the central building. A nun hurried forward, making the flagstones resonate. Nicolas asked her to announce him to the mother superior, and took his leave of Monsieur de Gévigland. He was admitted into a small cell in which the only furniture consisted of a deal table and two stools. A short woman shrouded in black veils was looking at him, her hands in her sleeves.

'Many commissioners pass through this house,' she said in a

high-pitched voice, 'but few have asked to see me. Is this another inspection, like the one in 1770? Isn't the charity dispensed by this establishment enough to justify its existence? Are you trying to pick a quarrel with us?'

She made a gesture with her hand, as if swatting flies.

'Don't worry, Reverend Mother,' replied Nicolas, 'I haven't come to Bicêtre for an inspection. In connection with a case I'm investigating, I need to find someone I believe is currently in this house.'

'A madman or a patient?' she asked curtly.

'A patient, according to our sources. Admitted in the last six or eight months. His name is Anselme Vitry, he was a gardener in Popincourt, and he's between twenty and thirty years of age.'

'Did he come here of his own free will, or was he brought here by the military police? That's an important point.'

'Without being absolutely sure, I would incline to the second hypothesis.'

She clapped her hands. The nun who had ushered Nicolas in immediately appeared and received instructions from her superior.

'Do you know the Duchamplan family, Reverend Mother?' asked Nicolas.

She seemed to relax as soon as she heard this name. 'Of course! Monsieur Duchamplan the elder is an administrator of Bicêtre, and we can always count on his benevolence. As for his sister, Louise of the Annunciation, of the Daughters of Saint Michel, we sometimes write to one another. Occasionally, she sends us unfortunate creatures to treat, and sometimes, in her great compassion, she takes in patients of ours who've been cured.'

'You must surely also have met her younger brother?'

She laughed. 'Such a charming boy! He sometimes comes to visit our patients. He talks to them and brings them treats.'

'Isn't that a somewhat unusual activity for a young man of his age?'

'Charity has no age,' she said, testily.

The nun came back into the cell. 'The commissioner must come with me to the clerk's office.'

'I shall not detain you, Monsieur,' said the mother superior.

He bowed to her and left the room.

The clerk, an unassuming man, eventually found Anselme Vitry in the registers. Some marginal annotations beside his name cast light on his situation. Arrested during a raid on a brothel in the company of an infected girl, he had been brought to Bicêtre. There, it had been found that he was not suffering from the disease. As they were not sure what to do with him, he had been freed after a short stay in the house of detention.

'I remember him well, Commissioner,' said the clerk. 'He would tell his story to anyone who'd listen. That he'd been betrayed by his fiancée, that he'd felt so desperate he'd left his house, his parents and his beloved garden. But he was lucky, the rascal.'

'In what way, my friend, did this luck manifest itself?'

'A gentleman who often visits us took an interest in his fate. And as this gentleman was looking for a coachman and Anselme knew how to handle horses, he ended up hiring him.'

'Can you tell me the name of this unexpected saviour?'

The man again consulted his register. 'His name is Monsieur Duchamplan.'

*

Nicolas rewarded the clerk and left Bicêtre. For a long time, he had the feeling that the foul stench of the place was following him about. So, as he had foreseen, a new suspect had emerged in the case of the murder of Marguerite Pindron. However, this discovery, far from simplifying his conducting of the investigation, was leading him down some disquieting paths. A definite connection had been established between the victim's former fiancé and the major-domo's family. It was now all the more vital to question Eudes Duchamplan, and also to track down young Vitry. Nicolas ordered his coachman to return to the Grand Châtelet. On his arrival, Old Marie told him in a low voice that a strange visitor was waiting for him in the duty office. There, he was greeted as soon as he entered by a man with a sickly face, wearing a beaver hat, whom he knew well, having benefited from his help on a previous case.

'Good day to you, Monsieur Restif,' he said, removing his black gown. 'Has "the owl" trapped some prey he would like to offer the police as a tribute?'

'There's no need to mock me, Monsieur Le Floch. Fate has pursued me since our last encounter. The roof of my lodging at the Presles mansion collapsed. I am now living in Rue du Fouarre. I am pursued by creditors demanding I pay off the debts of my last wife, who abandoned me, and reduce my publisher's bankruptcy. In addition, I'm suffering the consequences of a nasty bout of the clap. As you know, I'm never in a brothel without a purpose. For years, I've been seriously engaged in a rational organisation of vice in Paris: in a word, bringing order to disorder.'

Nicolas knew that, if he did not intervene, he was in for a long sermon. 'Yes,' he cut in, 'we know you're determined that order and morality should reign in our streets, and we appreciate it, believe me. But have you something particular to confide in me?'

Restif de la Bretonne lowered his head and looked down at his dog-eared shoes. His demeanour was a surprise to Nicolas, who was accustomed to the fellow being boastful.

At last, Restif made up his mind to speak. 'As you know, I'm in the habit of roaming the streets of this vast capital in the middle of the night. I try to do good, and sometimes manage to save a poor girl from perdition. A week ago, on the corner of Rue Pavée and Rue de Savoie, I saw a man running after a girl of about twenty. You can imagine the kind of thing he was saying to her. She seemed more curious than lost. I approached and introduced myself as usual. I told the man he was committing a terrible act, he'd even gone so far as to suggest . . . I spoke to the girl about honour and modesty and implored her not to yield to the corrupter. The man went off to other base acts, and the girl cursed me, told me to leave her alone, and ran away . . . Imagine my surprise, on the night of Sunday to Monday, as I was looking at the river at the end of Impasse Glatigny, to discover on the steps leading down to the water the body of that same girl, with her throat cut.'

'Why didn't you call the watch immediately?'

'Nothing could have brought her back to life, and where she was she was sure to be discovered as soon as the sun rose. But . . . you know my little ways . . . I couldn't resist . . . they were so delightful . . .'

From his brown woollen frock coat, he took a pair of dancing shoes similar to those worn by Marguerite Pindron, and of the same elegant workmanship.

'The interest of what you've brought me somewhat tempers my anger at the fact that you concealed information and clues from the King's police force,' said Nicolas. 'Are you aware how great a sin that is?'

'I dare to hope, Commissioner,' replied Restif, hypocritically, 'that the interest of my words, and what I still have to tell you, will appease your legitimate annoyance.'

'I'm listening.'

'Not only did I recognise the girl, but I have a description of the man who was talking to her.'

'As far as the girl's concerned,' replied Nicolas, impassively, 'you're not off the hook yet. You'll have to come with me to the Basse-Geôle to identify the body, and take a look at another.'

'Will I be able to see the feet?'

Nicolas shrugged in exasperation. 'That's enough, Monsieur! Just carry on, I'm listening.'

'The corrupter in Rue Pavée,' he said, rubbing his hands, 'was not unknown to me. This wasn't the first time I'd caught him at these vile activities.'

'Do you know his name?'

'Oh, no. Nor can I describe him, for he habitually wears a cloak with the collar turned up and his hat pulled right down. On the other hand, I've twice managed to follow him. He uses a cab and, would you believe, drives it himself.'

'Would you by any chance have noticed the number?'

'Indeed I did,' said Restif triumphantly. 'It's 34 NPP.'

Nicolas gave a start. Could it really be that, by some incredible coincidence, the cab he had taken to go to Popincourt, the number of which echoed his own age, had been driven by someone involved in this grim affair? Sometimes, a detective's luck depended on coincidence.

'Do you think he picks up women for himself?'

'Hardly! My instinct tells me he's part of a group. In fact, I'm convinced of it. The brothel-keepers probably know more about this than I do. They're the ones you should ask.'

There was a knock at the door of the duty office. It opened and the merry faces of Sanson and Semacgus appeared. Restif turned pale when he recognised the executioner, and had to sit down as if he were about to faint. Nicolas drew his friends into the gallery and asked Old Marie to give the visitor a shot of his herbal remedy.

'My dear friends, you both look very cheerful. And you seem in a hurry to tell me something.'

'Very definitely,' said Sanson. 'The doctor and I have continued our examination of the two victims, and we've been able to make an observation which we're sure will surprise you.'

'An observation,' said Semacgus, 'that would have been surprising in only one victim, but in two . . .'

'Gentlemen, tell me what you have to say, I'm undergoing tortures just listening to you.'

'In the stomachs of the two victims, we found traces of their last meals.'

'Is that all?' said Nicolas, stamping his feet with impatience.

'Without Monsieur Semacgus, who has been around the world, and whose knowledge of botany is considerable, I wouldn't have known what it was. But undigested fibre is not all that common.'

'To cut a long story short,' said Semacgus, 'they had both been gorging themselves on pineapples. Now in this part of the world, even cultivated in a greenhouse, this *bromelia* doesn't always ripen well, which can make it hard to digest. Whether we may conclude from this that they were both in the same place, I leave to a certain highly able commissioner at the Châtelet to determine.'

Nicolas was silent for a moment. 'What would I do without the two of you? Semacgus, where can one find greenhouse pineapples in Paris?'

'At the Jardin du Roi, certainly. In some aristocratic mansions and, outside the walls, in certain private houses.'

Now Bourdeau appeared, followed by Rabouine. Nicolas suddenly remembered that Restif was waiting. They went to fetch him, and a long procession wound through the bowels of the old feudal castle. It did not take Restif long to identify the girl from Impasse Glatigny. To be even more certain, Nicolas had the shoes tried on the corpse. They were also found to match the ones discovered in the roasting room of the Saint-Florentin mansion. Restif had recovered his spirits and was watching these experiments with an expression of ecstasy. He was unable to identify the other body. He was ceremoniously conducted to the entrance of the Grand Châtelet, where he immediately melted into the crowd. The conference resumed in the duty office. Nicolas informed those who had not been present what he had just learnt from 'the owl'.

'In order to restrict the search,' he said, 'I suggest we rule out the aristocratic mansions and the Jardin du Roi. We can always go back to them if our search proves fruitless. Given that the corpses have been discovered in Paris, the solution lies in the city or in the *faubourgs*.'

'What are your immediate intentions?' asked Bourdeau. 'Any instructions?'

'Following Restif's advice, I'm going to pay a little visit to the Dauphin Couronné. I want to find out a little more about these Parisian parties and the people who organise them. I'm sure La Présidente will be able to tell me something on the subject. As for you, Pierre, I'd like you to investigate Monsieur Bourdier, the engineer who lives at the corner of Rue des Canettes. He's needed for some top-secret work. Monsieur de Sartine wants to know if he can count on the man's loyalty.' He looked at his watch; it was two thirty. 'Let's meet here again at seven.'

Nicolas got back to his carriage. He noted that a new young messenger boy had replaced the old one, who had shot up and now served the Secretary of State for the Navy. In passing, he also observed that Rue Royale was being cleared, and that the stones and trenches which had caused the terrible disaster of 1770 had completely disappeared. The door of the Dauphin Couronné brought back memories of his early years in Paris. The little black girl who used to open the door to him was now a tall young woman who greeted him joyfully and threw her arms around his neck.

'Madame will be pleased to see Monsieur!'

Her words surprised him somewhat, for his relations with La Présidente had always been quite distant – although he was grateful to her, of course, for her indiscretion in London, without which he would never have discovered that he was a father.

He thought he had gone back ten years into the past. There, on an upholstered chaise longue, lay La Paulet, the former mistress of the place, enveloped in a satin chenille with a flowery pattern, apparently asleep. Her slack face revealed her ravaged, distended flesh, in whose folds, as always, the top layers of cream and rouge had cracked. Her dressing gown had slipped, revealing monstrously swollen legs, wrapped in bands of pink fabric. He felt as if he were in front of a flower stall in the market from which a pair of swollen feet stuck out incongruously, spilling over the sides of her soft leather slippers. He coughed, to announce himself. The mass shook itself, and all at once he saw those familiar inquisitive little eyes. An ambiguous smile lit up her face. She lifted her wig and scratched her ivory-white cranium. He remembered that in the old days she would take great care of what remained of her hair, massaging it every day with ointment of beef extract and orange flower water. The years had passed . . .

She guessed what he was thinking. 'You're peering at . . . my poor head,' she said with her customary familiarity. 'There were only a few tufts left. Now I just sponge it. No more vermin, no more scabs. Everything is clear. Damn it, don't just stand there gawping! I know you're surprised to see me. Yes, I'm back on duty and plan to make a few new appointments.'

'But what about La Présidente?'

'Oh, don't talk to me about her! No sooner was she in the saddle than she started playing the grand lady, looking down her nose at everyone as if she was born in the chapter of Notre-Dame!' She crossed herself. 'Instead of running the business as I asked her, she lorded it over everyone, got drunk, spent her money on trifles. The way it was going, everything that had taken years of hard labour on my part to build up would soon have been frittered away.'

'So what happened?'

'You know me. I don't bear a grudge, but things had gone too far, and the bailiffs would have been at the door before long. I left my retreat and my poor people to save the house. Otherwise, ruin! You can't imagine how hard it was to restore order. La Présidente had lost control, and everyone was taking advantage of her, to the detriment of the house's reputation. Once Madame Disaster had been booted out, I got down to work despite my infirmities.' She sighed. 'Oh, how I miss La Satin!'

'But you seem to be in rude health,' said Nicolas. 'You've put on a little weight perhaps, but your complexion is just as rosy.'

'That's very bold of you to make fun of me! All this is your fault. Did you have to make La Satin desert me? I was too good-hearted. And why did you thrust me into the arms of your smooth-talking master, that Monsieur de Noblecourt I didn't know from Adam? He really hoodwinked me, that one! Madame Paulet here, Madame Paulet there. I should have stuck to my path, which is to believe only what I find out for myself and not listen to yarns. He played on old Paulet, staking everything on my goodness: my affection for the boy, my concern to please an old friend like you. And to what end? Here I am, plunged back into business and putting my immortal soul at risk.'

She began to weep, but Nicolas noticed that no tears fell.

'Come now,' he said, 'you've made La Satin and my son very happy. That should weigh heavily in the eyes of the Lord.'

'Don't talk to me about La Satin!' she retorted through pursed lips. 'You've made her really unhappy. I visited her yesterday in Rue du Bac. You wanted to put her in a shop, as if white lace could wipe out the past . . . Well, why don't you let her do as she sees fit? You seem to forget that your son was born in the aristocracy of the lower depths and that, whether you like it or not, he will graze where he has crawled! Oh yes, Marquis . . .'

Nicolas bit his lips in order not to reply. Nothing good would come of quarrelling. He knew there was a kernel of truth in the old woman's criticisms. Better to avoid saying anything he could not retract; that would only make her more stubborn.

'That's a private matter,' he said. 'We can talk about it again when we've both cooled down. For the moment, my friend Paulet should not forget that her house enjoys a special leniency from the police and that if she does not want things to change . . .'

She gave a forced smile. 'I knew that was coming . . . So, if I understand correctly, you have something to ask old Paulet?'

'My dear Paulet, you always understand men who know the right way to speak to you. In the old days, you used to organise parties in certain well-equipped houses, little performances in which you couldn't tell where fantasy ended and reality began. What about now?'

'They still go on,' she said, obstinately. 'But times have changed, and the devotees handle it all themselves.'

'What do you mean?'

Her little eyes twinkled, as if hit by a strong light. 'A young man came here several times and asked me to supply him with young girls for his seraglio and some well-built stallions, as he put it, who could provide . . . La Paulet doesn't stoop to things like that.'

'Can you describe him?'

'Young, the usual buck.'

'If he shows up again let me know.'

'I don't dip my toes in those waters, my boy. I have my morality. I've already told you too much. Alas, everything's going from bad to worse, girls are flooding in from all over, driving the taste for novelty. The days when we were like a family – that's all over! This is the age of matchmakers and pimps!'

'As always, La Paulet remains true to her principles,' concluded Nicolas with a smile. 'A well-kept house, no gambling, regular girls and the best possible relationship with the police. I bid you farewell.'

'Go on, make fun of your poor friend,' she grunted. 'You've always brought me trouble.' She collapsed onto her chaise longue which creaked beneath her weight.

'This is the first time you haven't offered me any ratafia.'

As he went out, he heard a curse and the sound of a piece of porcelain smashing against a wall.


At seven o'clock, Bourdeau and Rabouine joined Nicolas at the Grand Châtelet. They had had the idea of consulting a botanist from the Jardin du Roi to try and establish who had made enquiries about purchasing pineapple seeds. In this way, they had drawn up a list of some fifteen residences, which would all have to be checked the following day. Then they had proceeded to Rue des Canettes. It was here that the man who had made Monsieur de Sartine's organ of wigs had his workshop. The family were in desperate straits. Driven into a corner, Bourdier had revealed that he was under pressure from an Englishman who was offering him a fantastic fee to go to England and use his skills in a cotton mill, where he would make technical improvements for the benefit of the East India Company. The description of his English contact matched that of Lord Ashbury, alias Francis Sefton. Nicolas reflected for a moment.

'This man is under threat, and so are our interests,' he said. 'He will end up yielding to these blandishments from across the Channel. Take the carriages you need and bring him here with his family. I'll go and see Sartine, he'll deal with it.'

Bourdeau sat down and began filling his pipe. 'It's already been done,' he said sardonically. 'The Bourdier family are waiting for you downstairs.'

# XI

## MANOEUVRES

And the liberty that follows our places
stops the mouths of all find-faults.
SHAKESPEARE

A cohort of three carriages set off, with Nicolas in the first. In the middle carriage, the panic-stricken engineer hugged his wife and four children to him. When they got to Rue Neuve-Saint-Augustin, they found that the minister had not yet returned from Versailles. But his return was imminent, as the royal family were getting ready to move to their hunting quarters in Fontainebleau. Nicolas thought of going to Monsieur Lenoir's house, which was nearby, but just as he was about to make up his mind to do so, a carriage arrived, and Sartine got out. He took him into his study and immediately began mechanically playing his organ of wigs; a magnificent specimen, full of curls and knots, appeared in all its dazzling blondness.

'It comes from Vienna, from the person who supplies Prince Kaunitz, who's a great connoisseur like me!' He was lovingly stroking the wig. 'The Abbé Georgel, Prince Louis's secretary, sent it to me. But tell me what's going on in my courtyard. *Quid novi* in your investigation? As always, corpses have been piling up, and your usual acolytes are getting ready to poke about inside them. Or am I mistaken?'

'Have you ever been mistaken, Monseigneur? First of all, your organ maker seems to me a very honest man although, reduced as he is to poverty, he has almost been persuaded with false pretexts and tempting offers to go to England.'

The minister dropped his wig, which spread over the desk like a sea creature stretching its tentacles. 'Don't tell me the British secret services have had their hands on him!'

'Indeed they have. And again it's the work of Lord Ashbury, alias Francis Sefton. To avoid such a thing happening, I've made the first move – or, rather, Bourdeau has – by immediately moving our man and his family. I've promised Bourdier that we'll make sure nothing happens to him and that he will be taken to a residence of the State where his work will be protected.'

'Excellent. So that was the screaming, moaning cohort that greeted me in my courtyard, was it? Let them stay here tonight. I'll give the necessary instructions for them to be taken somewhere safe tomorrow. And what of your investigation?'

'Everything seems to point to the Duc de La Vrillière, but I've yet to be convinced that he's guilty. There are still elements I can't explain, but I have the feeling I'm slowly getting closer to the truth. By the way, there are now three corpses, and I haven't given up hope—'

'Of finding even more?' Sartine said, his cold face lighting up in a smile. 'I wish my successor luck . . . How are you getting on with him?'

'Our last audience went well, with no acrimony.'

After reassuring the Bourdiers about their fate and receiving their thanks and blessings, he went back to Rue Montmartre, where Catherine changed his dressing and served him some soup.

He dipped croutons into it and washed it down with wine, then climbed on a stool to cut several thick slices from a ham on the mantelpiece, which he devoured greedily. Fresh nuts and apples rounded off this rustic snack. Later, as he was about to fall asleep, exhausted, three faces came into his mind, that of his son, that of La Satin, and finally that of Aimée d'Arranet.

*Sunday 9 October 1774*

Nicolas was woken by the distant trilling of a flute. Monsieur de Noblecourt was practising, which suggested that he was feeling fit and was in a good mood. Immediately Nicolas had dressed and had his breakfast, he joined him. The sight that greeted him would have delighted a painter skilled at capturing intimate domestic interiors. The morning light enveloped the old magistrate in a golden halo as, marking time with his foot, he played a countrydance tune with his usual mastery. Cyrus and Mouchette sat shoulder to shoulder, watching him attentively. Nicolas, motionless, was carried away by the tranquillity of the moment and waited for the piece to end before he showed himself.

'What a pleasure it is to see you recovered,' he said.

Noblecourt sank into his favourite armchair. 'You, on the other hand, seem to have been collecting wounds and bumps.'

'Oh,' said Nicolas, 'I'm used to being under fire. When I was ten, a guest of my father's nearly killed me after mistaking me for a hare! Bullets are in the habit of grazing me.'

'Don't try to laugh it off, your friends live on their nerves when you're far from them. But tell me about your latest adventures. It'll cheer me up and give me a rest from all this trilling. You can't imagine how difficult it is, when there are two trills in succession, to avoid playing them both in the same way!'

Nicolas launched himself into the details of his stay at Versailles and the progress of his investigation. His old friend became quite troubled and pensive.

'Have you thought carefully about the implications of this attempt on your life? If we disregard the fact that it is similar to those to which you were subjected at the beginning of this year – since those responsible have already been banished – we must conclude that your attacker, or rather your would-be assassin, is determined to prevent you from pursuing your investigations. Who are you threatening? What interests are jeopardised by your actions? Wisdom and logic would suggest that this mysterious Englishman is lurking in the shadows, as is common for people of his ilk, not showing himself in public . . .'

'All the same . . .'

'I foresee your objection: you recognised him in the great gallery despite his disguise. If he is determined to thwart you, it must be because your actions have touched on a sensitive area where your interests conflict. Since you are investigating a series of murders in which suspicion seems gradually to be pointing to one of the King's ministers, that means, if you follow my reasoning, that the Englishman in question could well be in league with the killers. Your skills as a detective are threatening his mission, which seems to me, infirm of mind and body as I am, to be targeting a great man. Consider this: Monsieur de Saint-Florentin would hardly have called you in to investigate a murder committed by himself – did I say murder? I mean murders – and then try to get rid of you! It doesn't make any sense. There is something else behind this inexplicable sequence of events.'

He sank further into a kind of trance-like meditation.

'You attract double-dealing, my dear Nicolas. In the fourteen years you've dealt with special investigations, you have been waging an endless struggle against shadows. Self-interest, revenge, ambition, lust and hatred have, like ghosts, dragged you into the forest of crime, and the dead seem to you like the two-faced god of ancient times.'

'Good heavens,' said Nicolas, 'you remind me of a certain Micmac who used to question the spirits by playing on his drum! With you, it's the flute. You are the Delphic oracle of Rue Montmartre!'

'You may mock! At my age, I have a licence to indulge certain whims, and if I choose to be erratic . . .'

'No one would ever dream of denying you that right.'

'I'd like to see him try! For now, the oracle is hungry. Let them bring me my soup and almond biscuits.'

Their attention was suddenly attracted by a song about the Duc de La Vrillière being bawled by a singer in the street, which rose to them through the open window.

> *Minister with no talent that anyone can see,*
> *Man more debased than a minister can be,*
> *We want you to go, we want you to fall,*
> *Out the window with you for the good of all.*

'The rhyme is poor but the content is poisonous,' said Noblecourt. 'The man is not liked – as if a minister could ever be liked. Will you come with me to High Mass at Saint-Eustache?'

'With pleasure, if the music and the food have dispelled the warden's annoyance with those who claim to usurp the privileges of the consecrated bread. And if you don't fear the presence beside you of a man who for some time has been a target for evildoers!'

'I would be dying in noble company, Marquis . . .'

To go the short distance from the house to the church, Nicolas would have preferred to use the cul-de-sac, which led to a side entrance, but Noblecourt wished to make a grander entrance through the front door. There, a large number of parishioners rushed forward to assure the former procurator of their friendship. He doffed his hat to the plaque bearing the epitaph of General Chevert, which had recently been placed there, and proceeded to the pews reserved for the churchwardens, surrounded by a flattering, respectful murmur. Nicolas took his seat a few paces back, near a pillar on which hung a notice from the priest of Saint-Eustache informing his flock of the parish's funeral charges. He noted the size of the sums demanded, doubtless a reflection of the fact that this was a wealthy district. Prices were listed for everything: the digging of the grave, the decoration of the master altar, the choir, the confessor, the white gloves, and the coffin which had to be bought from the parish workshop and not from an outside carpenter. There was a disparity here in the way death was dealt with that gave Nicolas food for thought.

The service was beginning, and Nicolas let himself be carried away by the litany, following it with simple devotion. He looked up into the upper reaches of the building. From where he was, he could see Colbert's black marble tomb behind the choir. The officiating priest mounted the pulpit for his sermon, which today was on the theme of charity. "'Who does not know that all property originally belonged to all men in common, that nature itself knew nothing of property or division and that it first left each of us in possession of the whole universe?'"[1] Nicolas thought of Bourdeau, who would no doubt have approved this introduction. He could not make up his mind whether the inspector's increasingly frequent outbursts were part of his very nature, a consequence of his personal history, or whether, with the passing of the years, it was developing into a more active desire to overthrow the traditions of society and of a power structure which he nevertheless continued to serve without demur.

He had just decided to abandon these reflections, which were leading nowhere, when he heard sounds of creaking and shaking. The door of the central porch suddenly opened with a strident creak, and an angry ox ran into the nave and began overturning everything it found in its path, its bellowing joining the chanting of the service. Chairs and worshippers were thrown to the ground, barricades were raised as protection from the creature's horns. For a good half-hour, Nicolas strove to organise a response. It turned out that the beast had not been properly killed and had escaped from a butcher's stall. The butcher's colleagues in the guild were sent for and eventually got the animal under control. The injured were evacuated and the service resumed.[2] It was not, however, destined to pass without further incident. A man in black clothes and boots came walking down the aisle, clearly looking for someone. Some of the worshippers cursed this noisy intrusion. The Swiss Guard raised his halberd and brought it down on the flagstones. Nicolas recognised the tall, raw-boned figure as Rabouine. Getting to his feet, he made a sign for the spy to follow him.

'What was the meaning of that catastrophic entrance?'

'I had no choice. Bourdeau sent me to fetch you from Rue Montmartre, where Poitevin told me you were here. The thing is, they've found an abandoned cab near the summer pleasure gardens. In it is the body of a young man, and all the indications are that it might be Jean Missery's brother-in-law.'

'The elder Duchamplan?'

'No, the younger one, Eudes. Everything's been taken to the Châtelet, where the inspector is waiting for you. I came in a carriage to take you there. It's waiting in the cul-de-sac.'

Nicolas went to tell Monsieur de Noblecourt. He explained the situation, and advised him not to wait for him to come back.

Outside the entrance to the Grand Châtelet, a noisy, restless crowd were trying to break through the cordon of French Guards and men of the watch surrounding the cab. The little messenger boy was trying without much success to control the horse, which was neighing in panic, startled by the movements of the crowd. Nicolas jumped down, followed by Rabouine, and approached. From the outside of the cab, nothing was visible; a dark film seemed to cover the windows, which were broken in places.

'Curious,' said Nicolas.

'Open, and you'll understand,' said Rabouine, with a fixed expression on his face.

He followed his spy's suggestion. More than most people, he had had to confront some unspeakable scenes in his time, but few as horrifying as this. The whole of the inside of the cab was covered in dried blood. On the seat, arms outstretched, was the body of a man with his face completely shot away. The floor was covered in a blackish liquid, and a large-bore cavalry pistol lay at the man's feet.

Rabouine, seeing what his chief was looking at, nodded and said, 'Suicide, at first sight.'

Nicolas slowly closed the door again. The horse was still neighing softly, stamping the ground with its forelegs, shivers rippling through its coat like waves, eyes wide with fright. He approached it and whispered in its ear, then boldly massaged its gums. The animal moved its head slowly up and down and gradually calmed down.

'You're good with horses,' said Rabouine admiringly.

Nicolas was thinking hard. 'We have to get all this out of the public gaze as soon as possible, or we'll be in trouble. I want the courtyard of the prison cleared so that we can take the cab in there. We'll unharness the horse, and the body can be taken into the Basse-Geôle. It'll have to be cleaned.'

Bourdeau had joined them. 'Today, a Sunday? We'd have to get hold of the guards, and even then . . . No, we'll have to do it ourselves.'

'Then we will. We've been through worse things in the past. Get Old Marie to find some of those leather aprons in the torture chamber, the kind Sanson's assistants sometimes use. Don't forget to retrieve the weapon and examine the bodywork of the cab. The autopsy will be done tomorrow. We'll have to inform

Sanson in Rue d'Enfer as soon as possible. A member of the watch can do that.'

What followed would remain one of Nicolas's worst memories, and he already had quite a few of those. Once the corpse had been taken away on a stretcher to the Basse-Geôle, he examined the bodywork of the cab in the minutest detail. This examination went on for so long that Bourdeau, who knew his chief, assumed he must have discovered a clue. As so often, the commissioner preferred to keep silent until he had had the chance to confirm his findings with other observations. The inspector noticed that he gave equal attention to the wheels, the insides and outsides of the doors, and the frame. Nicolas took out a small pocket knife, scraped some mud or earth from the axles, wrapped it in paper and placed it carefully in his pocket. Then they both descended into the bowels of the Châtelet. In the autopsy room, they put on leather aprons and carefully cleaned the bloodstained body. Bourdeau moved a torch closer and pointed to the coat pocket. In it was the letter which had made it possible to identify the dead man. It was unsigned, an invitation to a rendezvous in Versailles: '*Join us in the place you know*.' Nicolas noted that it had been sent on the very day he himself had arrived at Court.

'Is this why Rabouine said it was the younger Duchamplan?'

'That's the name on the address. The letter must have been delivered by hand, there's no postmark.'

They continued to wash the body, although without undressing it. The water fell from the table in a purple stream, and there was a sickening metallic odour. No conclusions could be drawn from the mangled face. For a long time, Nicolas looked at the hands. Then he took off the shoes and stockings, and gave the feet the same kind of examination. They would have to wait for Sanson's conclusions the following day before they could speculate any further. They went back up to the courtyard of the Châtelet. It was then that Nicolas, looking mechanically at the cab, was struck by the number: 34 NPP. Could it be the same vehicle that had driven him to Popincourt, where he had conveyed Lenoir's instructions to the dairy farmers, and the conversation had turned to the misadventures of Marguerite Pindron's fiancé? Closing his eyes, he tried to recall the driver's face, but found it impossible. All he remembered was a seat stained with what could well have been blood.

'Bourdeau,' he said, 'what would you say to a little visit to Boulevard Saint-Martin and then to the Duchamplan house in Rue Christine?'

'I'd say that my orphans won't see their father today, and that Madame Bourdeau . . .'

'. . . will curse Commissioner Le Floch and the Châtelet, as one might expect!'

In Boulevard Saint-Martin, the inspector showed Nicolas the place where the watch had found the cab. Nicolas sniffed about, his nose to the ground, entered the vast area of the pleasure gardens, and picked something up from the muddy ground. Again, Bourdeau preferred not to ask any questions, even though the action seemed incomprehensible at first sight. They got back into their carriage and drove across Paris. Nicolas, his chin on the door and his eyes half closed, was thinking, whistling an opera aria and beating time with his foot.

'We really mustn't procrastinate,' he said to Bourdeau as they were crossing Pont-Royal. 'This has gone on far too long.'

The inspector made no attempt to find out what he was referring to.

'Let's go straight to our target. That mezzanine apartment in Rue Christine. I need to know what it contains right now. I'd be very surprised if it didn't tell us something about its occupant. Do you have your picklocks?'

Bourdeau struck the pocket of his coat, making a metallic sound.

'Good,' said Nicolas. 'We'll open the door. Forget about due process and authorisation.'

'Do you have an idea in mind?'

'Not one, but several. Don't be offended by my silence, Pierre. It's only a reflection of the fact that I'm torn between various hypotheses. To reveal one would be to throw out the others. They need to remain together until the mind is able to take one last look at all of them and come down in favour of the most likely.'

'You haven't been talking to Monsieur de Noblecourt this morning, have you?' said Bourdeau with a smile. 'Your style bears his imprint.'

'It's impossible to conceal anything from you. As he is wont to say, the most obvious answer is often that which is the least hidden.'

'Which means, I assume,' said Bourdeau, laughing, 'that the solution is near.'

'Much more so than if you had actually thought it within reach.'

When they reached Rue Christine, they found the courtyard of the Duchamplan house deserted. A domestic quarrel could be heard from the upper floors, but there was no sign of the caretaker. They ran to the staircase. Once on the mezzanine, Bourdeau did not take long to pick the lock, and the door opened onto a small, dark antechamber. No sooner had they cautiously entered the apartment than they heard creaking, followed by hurried footsteps. They rushed forward, trying to find their way in the darkness. They pulled open a door, discovered a wardrobe, retraced their steps and chose another door, which this time led to a foul-smelling water closet. The third was the right one. They found themselves in an untidy drawing room where the remains of meals and empty bottles lay strewn over the furniture. At the far end of the room, where the light came in through windows looking out on the courtyard, there was another door. Bourdeau grabbed hold of the handle, but it resisted. He was about to step back and rush at it with his shoulder when Nicolas stopped him, moved him aside and pointed to a small chest of drawers. They slid it across the floor and slammed it into the door, which shattered. Immediately, there was a deafening explosion, and pieces of marquetry and marble were projected into the middle of the drawing room. Bourdeau's wig was blown off, and fell to the floor like a ball of wool, covered in splinters.

'I think,' he said, pale and out of breath, 'that I owe you my life.'

'It's merely a first instalment,' said Nicolas with a bow. 'I'm still in debt to you.'

'But how did you know?'

'Intuition. I had a feeling there was someone armed waiting behind the door.'

Entering the room, which was quite small, they discovered an ingenious mechanism, consisting of a rifle fixed at an angle to the wall, its trigger being connected to the door by a horsehair thread wound around a pulley. Anyone entering would have been unable to escape its effects.

'Where is he?' asked Nicolas, regaining his composure. 'There's no other door, and the window's closed. He can't just have disappeared. Look at the fireplace, it may be similar to Richelieu's.'[3]

Bourdeau took out a folding knife, opened it, and began to probe the surround of the fireplace, without finding anything. Nicolas looked under the bed, then opened a cubbyhole which led into a narrow corridor ending, after a few steps, with another door. They opened it cautiously, revealing a stone spiral staircase.

'It's like Sartine's secret exit at the Châtelet,' said Bourdeau.

The staircase took them down into a cellar, from which an openwork door led out to a little orchard. The bird had well and truly flown. They went back up to the mezzanine. Nicolas continued searching. As he walked, he trod on something. He bent down and picked up a broken pair of glasses with tinted lenses.

'No need to look any further,' he said. 'Lord Ashbury must have taken refuge here after we flushed him out of the Hôtel de Russie.' He struck his head with his fist. 'Noblecourt was right! Isn't it obvious that the safest hiding place was a stone's throw from the hotel, a place where no one would ever think of looking for him? He's played us, well and truly played us. Who took him in?' he went on feverishly. 'Clearly, his accomplice, Eudes Duchamplan, who I assume is one of his agents! The body may be his. Did he kill him, and if so, why? Did he get rid of him before he went to earth in here? What really angers me is the thought that he may already be a long way away.'

'Who brought him food?' asked Bourdeau.

'He's a master of disguise. We know now that there's a way out. It wouldn't have been difficult for him to come and go.'

Nicolas went back to the wardrobe at the entrance. It contained cloaks, hats and shoes. He picked up a pair of shoes and handed them to Bourdeau.

'Keep hold of these, they may prove useful.'

Bourdeau nodded, not quite sure he understood what his chief was alluding to. The commissioner was walking in and out with long strides, as if measuring something.

'You see,' said Nicolas, 'however thick the wall between this wardrobe and the drawing room, it can't be as thick as all that, it's impossible.'

They walked into the wardrobe and moved aside the clothes. The wooden wall at the back was panelled. The commissioner discovered that one of the panels had been cut along the edge: it must surely be movable. He carefully manipulated it until it came out at a right angle, releasing a mechanism which revealed the wall as a hidden door. Once through the door, they discovered, by the light of a candle, what looked like the lair of a second-hand clothes dealer, filled with female clothes – dresses, undershirts, camisoles, petticoats, shawls, lace, bodices, mantles – and a collection of wigs that would have turned Monsieur de Sartine green with envy. These wigs were hanging on nails; some were women's, others men's, and they were of extraordinary variety and elaboration.

'It reminds me of our own collection of disguises,' said Bourdeau, delighted.

There were also some women's shoes. Nicolas compared them with the pair he had already found; they were identical in size.

Bourdeau laughed. 'My God, you anticipated that as well!'

'Not exactly,' said Nicolas, who really had not imagined anything like this.

In a corner lay a man's shirt, rolled into a ball and covered in blood. Nicolas was pondering the fact that, ever since the beginning of this investigation, they had amassed a large number of significant but contradictory clues, but had not yet found a thread to connect them. He was reflecting on this when two people entered the apartment. They turned to see the horrified faces of the elder of the Duchamplan brothers and a woman of indeterminate age, pale and red-eyed, wearing a grey dress and matching mantilla.

'May I ask, Commissioner, what you are doing in my brother's apartment? We heard a terrible explosion.'

Nicolas stood in front of the door to the wardrobe, concealing its contents. 'Have you seen your brother again since my last visit?'

'No. What's happened here?'

He was trying to push Nicolas aside to see inside the wardrobe, but Bourdeau had blown out the candle.

'Someone has been living here,' declared Nicolas sternly. 'Did you know that?'

'Certainly not.'

Nicolas made a signal to Bourdeau, who stood aside and relit the candle.

'Well, then, what can you tell me about this bazaar? Don't you have any useful comment to make about a closet of old clothes worthy of the Temple?'

Duchamplan looked around, more aghast than surprised. The

woman, who had moved closer, was clinging to her husband's arm. She had started trembling.

'You must tell him,' she moaned. 'You can't keep quiet. You've delayed too long.'

'Tell me what?' growled Nicolas, threateningly. 'What are these women's clothes?'

'Old oddments from my wife's trousseau.'

'Indeed?' said Nicolas. 'I congratulate you, Madame, on having such elaborate wigs to wear, and on being able to get rid of such adornments when they are still almost new. I can quite understand that you cast them off! The shoes, too, I assume?'

'Certainly, Monsieur.'

'In that case, let's see, Madame. Would you please try these on?' He handed her some dancing slippers covered with white lace.

'But, Commissioner, what is the point of that?'

'I advise you, Madame, to do as I say.'

She hesitated, wrung her hands, and looked at her husband. Finally, she burst into sobs.

'Monsieur,' she said, 'I have no wish to deceive the law. These shoes are not mine, nor are the clothes.'

'Thank you, Madame, I wanted to hear you say it. It was perfectly obvious to me that they weren't your size. So whose are they? Does your younger brother, Monsieur – your brother-in-law, Madame – sometimes wear women's clothing?'

'That may occasionally happen,' said Duchamplan, embarrassed. 'I assume it's just a game, some harmless amusement, a carnival joke, the stuff of masked balls and——'

'How often?' asked Nicolas.

'Several times a week,' said the woman, with a kind of spite.

'Alas,' said Duchamplan, 'I fear my younger brother is perversity itself. He has become accustomed to dressing up like this for parties. I have no idea what he does at these parties . . . but I'm always terrified to see the state he's in when he returns.'

'Did your elder sister know about these practices?'

'She surprised Eudes some time ago. He made up some vague story about helping the Duc de La Vrillière to seduce some girls, the go-between being none other than our brother-in-law Missery, the minister's major-domo.'

'So your sister knew . . .'

For a moment, he envisaged a new scenario – Sister Louise of the Annunciation informs the Duchesse de La Vrillière, and the duchesse confronts the minister – but it did not get him very far.

'I ought to have both of you incarcerated until this affair has been settled,' said Nicolas. 'But I will trust in your good faith. You will remain confined to your home. Rest assured that you will be watched day and night by my men. Please withdraw.'

Once the couple had gone out, he picked up the bloodstained shirt and wrote something down in his little black notebook.

'Wouldn't those two be better off at the Châtelet?' asked Bourdeau.

'It's possible they're being watched by someone other than ourselves, and I don't want to raise the alarm. In any case, as I've discovered here, I'm not the only one to take precautions and leave by the back way!' He told Bourdeau about his departure from Rue Montmartre. 'Is the British embassy under surveillance?'

'Permanently, since the peace treaty. Of course, routine may have set in.'

'Lord Ashbury may try to find refuge there, so we need to tighten the surveillance. What have we found out so far about the growing of pineapples?'

'Rabouine is going through the list at the Châtelet and has flooded Paris and the suburbs with spies. He may have found what you're looking for by now.'

'I fear for your Sunday, Pierre. Your family will curse me.'

'They're used to it after a quarter of a century!'

They closed up the secret passage, barricaded it to prevent anyone coming in from outside, and placed seals on the front door. It did not take them long to get back to the Grand Châtelet, where Rabouine was waiting for them, looking very excited.

'I would guess your search went well,' said Nicolas, 'judging by that air of smugness.' He placed the bloodstained shirt on the table.

'Judge for yourself,' said Rabouine, waving a paper. 'Of all the residences on the list, only one attracted my attention, for two reasons.'

'Tell us what they were.'

'The first is that the person who lives there is in our records. He appears in Marin's daily reports, once intended for Monsieur de Sartine and now for Monsieur Lenoir, on the information gathered by our inspectors and spies. He comes into the category dealing with prostitution and licentious behaviour, and inhabits the borderline between vice and crime.'

'He's got us hooked!' said Bourdeau, sitting with his elbows on the table and his head on his folded hands.

'Anyway, to cut a long story short, it appears that the man in question is very well known in the world of vice. Why?'

'Yes, why?' said Nicolas impatiently. 'Come on, Rabouine, get to the point! We don't have much time, and you're keeping us waiting.'

'All right. He's the grand master of a libertine society known as the Order of Happiness. His followers vow to make each other happy. They're an androgynous group, who like men to become women, women to become men, and all points in between . . .'

'And where do they meet?'

'Sometimes at the grand master's mansion in Montparnasse, which is where he has his greenhouse of exotic plants. Sometimes in the quarries at Vaugirard, sometimes in other places we have yet to discover.'

'This is indeed most strange! And the second of your reasons?'

'This lover of young flesh, whose influence within the society seems to increase with every passing day, is none other than the Marquis de Chambonas, who married Mademoiselle de Lespinasse-Langeac, the illegitimate daughter of the Duc de La Vrillière and the Beautiful Aglaé.'

'Good Lord!' said Bourdeau.

'And that's not all,' Rabouine went on. 'The only motivation for the marriage was to shore up Chambonas's failing fortune. But when things didn't live up to his expectations, he unearthed a nasty secret he's been using to blackmail the minister: the Beautiful Aglaé is said to have once married a certain Comte Sabatini, who was wrongfully deported to the West Indies on the minister's orders.'

'Let's not waste any time,' said Nicolas. 'I want the Marquis de Chambonas's mansion to be put under surveillance immediately. What Rabouine has just told us matches the information we had from Restif, the things La Paulet hinted at to me, and what we found in Rue Christine. Bourdeau, take this shirt and go straight to the Saint-Florentin mansion. Find the minister's valet and spare no effort to discover if the shirt belongs to his master. Last but not least, and I don't care how we get it, I must have, as soon as possible, a detailed report on the Duc de La Vrillière's movements over the past week so that we can check his alibis.'

'There's no need, Monsieur Nicolas,' said Rabouine. 'I'm already on drinking terms with the minister's coachman, who likes a tipple whenever he has a moment to spare. With a little bit extra thrown in, solid this time rather than liquid – I'll put in my expenses claim as usual – I've managed to get the necessary information from him.'

'Rabouine, you will have your reward, plus a bonus.'

'There are always bonuses for immorality,' said Bourdeau wryly.

'It sometimes happens, Inspector,' said Nicolas, 'that men whom we believe to be without principles are strongly imbued with the religion of efficiency. We're listening, Rabouine.'

'Well, his magnificence the Duc de La Vrillière has not been sleeping at home for several months . . .'

'There's nothing new about that. There was the Beautiful Aglaé, and plenty of other loose women before her.'

'That's as may be,' continued Rabouine, 'but at night, he asks to be driven to different places, then dismisses his coachman and disappears. His servants are very intrigued and have tried to follow him without success. Anyway, what that means is that the minister has no alibi for any of the three murders we've been investigating.'

'My God!' cried Bourdeau in alarm. 'We know that these crimes are linked. Who knows the horrors that may have been committed before our attention was called to the Saint-Florentin mansion?'

'Which makes your mission all the more important, my dear Pierre,' said Nicolas. 'We must find out if this shirt is indeed the minister's.'


Nicolas remained alone in the duty office. He needed this interlude to see how things stood with the investigation. He took out his little black notebook. As he read through it, he noted particular points on a separate sheet, making a list which, he hoped, would lead him to discern a clear, logical path to the truth. He had reached a point where any advance in his understanding of the case could only be brought about by a stark, deliberate demonstration of authority. The more he reread his notes, the more he realised that the testimonies he had gathered at the time of Marguerite Pindron's murder had clouded his vision, confused his mind, and sent him off on false trails. Yes, he would have to go back to the beginning and drive the dubious witnesses into a corner. But he did not have time for persuasion. However distasteful he found the means of coercion available to the law, means that Sanson and his assistants could apply, he believed that the threat of torture should be enough in itself to convince the most stubborn. Only one thing held him back from resorting to it: being inclined to think that torture had the effect of making people confess even when they were innocent, he feared that its threat would do the same. Eventually, though, he made up his mind to play that trick, and he began reflecting on the best and most convincing way to put it into effect. He would have to choose the witnesses to be subjected to this test. It was useless to try it on all of them. After all, he could hardly put the Duchesse de La Vrillière in a torture chamber. He just had to pick the right targets. If a false picture had been built up about what had happened and when it happened, all it needed was one element to yield, and the whole thing would come crashing down. It seemed to him that Eugénie Gouet, the duchesse's head chambermaid, was the ideal element in this strategy. She would be more than a match for him. Next, a proper interrogation of Jacques Blain, the caretaker who had been in love with Marguerite, was sure to be of interest. He recalled something Bourdeau had said: why make a stew of three rabbits without adding blood to the sauce? Finally, a friendly conversation with young Jeannette Le Bas might well shed some light on the life of Marguerite Pindron. What Nicolas was hoping for from all this was to speed things up, to find the one thread which, pulled out of the warp and weft of the crime, would cause the whole thing to unravel.

He resolved to give himself a brief respite, unable for the moment to make a crucial decision. Wisdom dictated that he should wait for the results of the missions he had given his men. It was late afternoon by now, and he was starting to feel hungry. Leaving the old prison, he was caught up in the feverish activity of the surroundings. The smell emanating from an open-air pot of capons cooked in coarse salt tempted him, and he greedily devoured a bowlful of this stew. The grains of salt cracked beneath his teeth, and he closed his eyes and saw again the dazzling salt marsh at Guérande and himself as a little boy, licking his fingers as he collected marine crystals . . . He crossed the Seine on foot, the physical effort helping him to clear his mind of the clutter of contradictory thoughts and establish a clean slate on which he would then be able to map out a logical argument.

A longer walk took him beyond the boulevard, towards the Observatory. He knew there was an entrance here to the quarries which abounded in that area. It was late, and the porter was reluctant to guide another visitor, but Nicolas's position and the promise of a substantial reward soon overcame his reluctance. They plunged into a complex, shadowy labyrinth. It was easy to lose your way here, and the porter had to warn him frequently. The thing that Nicolas, who hated confinement, most dreaded was that their torches would go out, plunging them into darkness. He discovered to his astonishment a vast underground city, filled with weirdly shaped streets and crossroads and squares. Most of the galleries were of uneven height, and they were sometimes forced to stoop. There were stalactites in places, and the porter claimed, boastfully, that the river was just above their heads. Nicolas, who was well aware of the distance they had come, strongly doubted this.

For years, he had heard people talking about the danger these quarries posed for the city up above; it had been supported by them for many centuries, retrieving in the light of day what it borrowed from the earth. He noticed pillars half crushed beneath the weight bearing down on them and apparently on the verge of collapse,[4] and quarries on two levels where the pillars of the upper level were precariously balanced.

Engaging his guide in conversation, he learnt that some of the poorest families in the city took refuge in this place, especially in the dead of winter. Others used it as a hiding place, only coming out at night to gather provisions or commit crimes. These people included escaped convicts, deserters, and a whole collection of rogues and vagabonds, a true court of miracles. Lowering his voice, the porter said that there were also rumours of strange meetings held here, of groups indulging in reprobate practices. Nicolas tried to get him to say more, but to no avail.

This visit gave him an opportunity both to assess the dangers of this maze of galleries piled one on top of the other, and to get some idea of the uses that were made of it. The safety of Paris depended on the dimensions of this underground complex being duly noted by the King's engineers, a detailed plan being drawn up, structural weaknesses being identified, and stricter controls being put in place concerning the disquieting collection of individuals who haunted it. As far as his present investigation was concerned, the visit confirmed the plausibility of the rumours reported by Bourdeau about the very special use that some people made of the seclusion and intricacy of these hidden depths.

He found Monsieur de Noblecourt reading Montluc. Mouchette climbed on him and settled in her favourite place on his shoulders.

'I've just returned from the underworld,' he said simply.

'Monsieur de Sartine is right,' Noblecourt said with a smile, 'you create havoc. The whole of Rue Montmartre is talking about the High Mass this morning and the untimely appearance of the devil in the appetising form of a dazed and angry fatted ox. I think it deserves an inscription in marble, in gold letters, a fine lapidary formula we can ask Louis to translate for us, something like, *Here Nicolas Le Floch slew the minotaur, adding this exploit to his many others!*'

'You may well mock, I saw you leaping onto your pew like a young man! As for me, having already confronted the minotaur, I've now had to suffer the torments of the labyrinth and the terrors of confinement!'

He told Noblecourt of his descent into the quarries.

'They were always places,' said Noblecourt, 'conducive to strange practices, even satanic meetings. The Regent, the Duc d'Orléans, once tried to summon the devil there. It's beyond me how, in the century in which we live, people can still believe in such nonsense! It's been too long that people have been tearing each other to pieces, with the tongue and the pen, over the contents of a papal bull or a *billet de confession*, and that the *parlement* has been defying the authority of the monarch to the renewed cries of agitators foaming at the mouth over the tomb of an obscurantist deacon. Is this really the triumph of reason and philosophy? There is a balance to be struck. Look at the regent, a rational man apparently, a chemist, an engineer, a fine musician and a statesman. How could he become involved in such things? Now everyone's trying to go beyond the bounds of knowledge, striving to explore the treacherous regions of the garden of evil. I tell you this: we will see far worse things before the end of this century!'

He had raised his voice so much that Cyrus began howling lugubriously.

'You see, you've awakened the dog Cerberus!'

The evening continued with a light supper and a long discussion of the practice of tremolo in playing music, while from the servants' pantry there rose the delicious smell of quince jelly.

# XII

## CONFRONTATIONS

Assist me and stay by my side,
because I am about to attack them.
Montluc

*Monday 10 October 1774*

Sanson was operating while Nicolas watched attentively, sickened by this morning autopsy. Was it the sight of the executioner's clothes brushing against that mutilated face, or the feeling that he was getting close to the end of his investigation? He was restless with exhaustion and impatience.

'A man of about twenty-five,' announced Sanson. 'Well built. The face has been torn to pieces by a discharge of small shot. In my opinion, it's quite impossible for such a terrible wound to have been caused by the pistol you found beside the corpse.'

'As it happens,' said Nicolas, 'my examination of the inside of the cab did puzzle me: the shot had been scattered far too widely, and the windows had been broken. From which I conclude—'

'That it can't have been a suicide.'

'In which case, what weapon could have been used?'

'A hunting rifle seems a likely hypothesis, but I'm not happy with it. It would have had to be fired from quite a distance in order to produce such scattering.'

'So the mystery remains impenetrable.'

'Oh, no! There are weapons that could produce such a result, such as a blunderbuss.'

Nicolas began thinking aloud, while Sanson, who had broken off his work, looked on curiously. 'Now that's strange. When I was faced with that scene of carnage, two things struck me. I couldn't help thinking that someone had tried to arrange things in such a way as to deceive a superficial examination. It seemed to me that all the elements were too neatly in place, and all led to the same observation: the body was that of a man who had killed himself, and the weapon he had used lay at his feet. And yet . . . several details had already attracted my attention: the shot scattered around the interior, but also the body itself. My friend . . .'

The word moved Sanson, whose amiable face lit up.

'. . . could you examine the hands and feet of this corpse and tell me the results of your observations?'

Sanson proceeded with a meticulous investigation of the parts concerned, then looked up with a puzzled expression. 'I'm not sure what I'm looking for. The only thing I can say for certain is that, despite the rich garments he's wearing, this was a young man of lower class. A worker rather than a bourgeois. I would even say a peasant. The hands are callous, the nails black and soiled with earth, and scratched by thorns. The feet are wide and also possess particular characteristics. Frequently walking barefoot hardens the heels. Not very well cared for generally. Does that satisfy you?'

'It confirms my suspicions. And when we know what this corpse was supposed to represent, or rather what it had the task of making people believe, there is, I think you'll agree, good reason to wonder about the fairy tale they were trying to dish up! Added to which, apart from a letter obligingly telling us the identity of the corpse, we discovered nothing in the pockets of his coat, none of those trinkets that everyone carries with them. Nothing!'

'Not even a little black notebook?' said Sanson with a smile.

'Nothing at all. All of which means that this was an attempt to lead us astray. However, it appears to me so obvious – so obvious in its very falsity – that I've even started to wonder if we were meant to notice the attempt.'

There was a thought lurking at the back of his mind, a thought he did not want to formulate too hastily. He had not yet seen everything, and other elements might emerge to confirm the possibility. Perhaps . . . No, it was too soon. There was not much more to be learnt from this corpse. Everything pointed to the fact that it could not possibly be the younger Duchamplan, but was actually Vitry, the young gardener rescued from Bicêtre to become a coachman, engaged for God knows what dubious errands. It was he who, by pure coincidence, had driven Nicolas to Popincourt: the number of the cab proved that.

He thanked Sanson and prepared with him the interrogation he was planning of some of the servants from the Saint-Florentin mansion. The instructions he gave were specific: what they had to do was inspire fear merely by displaying the instruments of torture. He hoped that the terror this display would instil in witnesses who were little accustomed to the ways of the law would dissuade them from lying. His method consisted of paralysing the will to resist, but without, however, going as far as to exert direct pressure, which would take away any likelihood of honest answers.

At that moment, Bourdeau appeared, with a package in his hand. He greeted Sanson in a friendly manner.

'So, Pierre, anything to report?'

'I put all the servants at the minister's house through hell, and finally, having wooed the linen maid in the wash house, I obtained what we were looking for.'

He untied the package and took out two shirts, one bloodstained, both freshly ironed, both identical in style and size.

'That's very good,' said Nicolas. 'I hope the linen maid was comely.'

The three friends laughed, then Nicolas summarised the results of the autopsy for Bourdeau.

'You're losing me,' said the inspector.

'I'm not surprised,' said Nicolas. 'But let's look at it logically. Either we're wrong in our observations, and this body is that of Eudes Duchamplan. In that case, which is highly unlikely, for the reasons that I've stated, in whose interest was it to kill him? Or else the body we see here is that of the cab driver, Anselme Vitry, the gardener from Popincourt and Marguerite Pindron's former fiancé, and if we take into account a few doubtless deliberate blunders, it seems as though someone wanted us to assume, thanks to that bloodstained shirt, that the Duc de La Vrillière had been involved in another murder. Having been implicated in this latest one, that would confirm him as a suspect for the others.'

'How could anyone have foreseen that we would search the apartment in Rue Christine?' asked Bourdeau.

'It was an easy assumption to make! Whether we took the body at the pleasure gardens for Duchamplan or someone else, the note found on the body was bound to take us to Rue Christine. What they hadn't counted on was how quick we'd be. We arrived so early that we surprised Lord Ashbury.'

'And what if all this was the work of the minister? What a brilliant idea, to implicate himself in such a way as to give us good reasons to exonerate him! He may be in league with Eudes Duchamplan, having probably frequented the same places of ill repute, with his major-domo as the go-between. That would tally with what the elder brother told us.'

'Let's not go too far,' said Nicolas, 'but stick as closely as possible to the facts. We have a corpse which someone tried to pass off as that of a suicide. We find a bloodstained shirt in the lodgings of the supposed victim. Whom does it implicate? The Duc de La Vrillière.'

Nicolas was pacing up and down.

'It may be that we came in on the first part of something that had not been completely thought through,' he resumed. 'The linstock hasn't yet reached the fuse. Imagine this shirt linked with the corpse at the pleasure gardens; the staging increased the horror of the crime and pointed to the supposed perpetrator.'

'What are you planning to do now?'

'I've given instructions to our friend Sanson here.'

'I'm going to prepare everything in total earnest,' said Sanson, 'just as you asked.'

'Are you going down that route, Nicolas?' said Bourdeau, with a disapproving look on his face.

'I have to, but it'll only be a piece of play-acting.'

'You do realise that, in such cases, a confession is merely a way of avoiding pain.'

'I'm not necessarily after confessions, but information which has been concealed from the eyes of the law. I know I'm disregarding all the rules, since those I am summoning have not been accused.

It's just a question of flushing each one out from his position, using the elements of surprise and threat. Some of them, I fear, are concealing a great many secrets.'

'We need to arrest them, then,' said Bourdeau.

'You will summon them to follow you to the Châtelet without further ado for an interview with Commissioner Le Floch.'

Nicolas tore a sheet of paper from his black notebook, scribbled a few lines on it, and handed it to Bourdeau, who nodded and left without a word. Sanson remained in his lair, lighting his fires like Vulcan in his forge. Nicolas went back up to the duty office and again went through his notes, his lead pencil in his hand.

An hour later, Bourdeau reappeared, his face quite flushed.

'You seem upset,' said Nicolas.

'I've had to confront a female dragon, whom the social graces demand I call the Duchesse de La Vrillière. She fought tooth and nail to stop me from proceeding with the arrests. Like all women, the last card she played was a fit of the vapours. I took advantage of that to leave her in helping hands.'

'Good,' said Nicolas. 'She'll get over it. We're going to play several acts one after the other. Have these people taken into the corridor. We'll leave the door open, and talk about it so that they think they're in for a little interview designed to soften them up.'

Everything went as planned. Bourdeau returned and asked, 'What are your intentions, Commissioner?'

'Keep the witnesses ready to appear — I say witnesses, I ought to say suspects — in the torture chamber. I believe the torturer and his assistants are ready to get down to the job?'

'Indeed they are.'

'Then let's proceed with the preliminary session.'

'An extraordinary one?'

'Oh, no. Ordinary. I think that'll suffice.'

'Yes, of course. Five or six tin cauldrons. Tying the suspect to a plank and drowning him usually loosens his tongue.'

They both laughed.

'Anything else?'

'The boot, of course. We need to make sure the legs are held tight in the frames. Separate the kneecaps and ankles with two thick planks and put wedges between them. Wood for the women and iron for the man. And don't forget to hit hard with the mallet. I think we should take the number of wedges all the way up to the authorised figure of twelve. That's all. Take them down, I'll join you in a moment.'

Nicolas soon followed Bourdeau and joined the group of witnesses, who were sitting, surrounded by members of the watch, on a stone bench in the dark gallery leading to the torture chamber. Strange noises were coming from the chamber, a particularly frightening din for anyone who had just heard Nicolas's words. He decided to begin with Madame de La Vrillière's head chambermaid, Eugénie Gouet, hoping to confound her with this atmosphere of menace. But she entered with her head held high and no apparent emotion. She was no longer as fresh and white as she had been before; her complexion now was grey, with red blotches. She gave him a look of defiance. In the gothic chamber, the assistants bustled about to the orders of a man in a green coat.

Bourdeau was standing behind a lectern, pen in hand, ready to take down a verbatim record of the interrogation.

'You are here,' said Nicolas in a monotonous voice, 'as a witness and suspect of the murder committed at the Saint-Florentin mansion on 2 October 1774. The apparatus of justice you see around you should encourage you to answer my questions with complete honesty, the only response that will satisfy me as a magistrate and save you from the worst consequences.'

This speech did not seem to have any effect on the woman, but she was convulsively clenching her left fist, something Nicolas had already observed during her first interrogation and noted in his little black notebook.

'Master Sanson, ask your assistants to be silent.'

The assistants froze. Only the crackle of the coals in the brazier continued to awaken echoes in the depths of the chamber.

'Let's begin,' said Nicolas. 'Were you the mistress of Jean Missery, at least until he developed a passion for the victim?'

She did not reply, her eyes fixed on the floor.

'Am I to take your silence as assent?'

She raised her head. 'I prefer to tell you the truth. Yes, Jean had been my lover. He'd even promised to marry me.'

'That, in fact, is what the Duchesse de La Vrillière told a friend of hers, who passed the information on to me,' said Nicolas, lying with an impassiveness that astonished Bourdeau.

The chambermaid's reaction was one of despair, and she looked from right to left like an animal caught in a trap.

'You agree, then. We know also that this domestic Don Juan had some difficulty in satisfying his new young friend, and wasn't always in a state to—'

'He wasn't like that with me!' she said angrily.

'I believe you unreservedly. He wasn't like that with you. But let's imagine that someone gives the poor man some relaxing potion, something that would – not to mince words – make him impotent? Couldn't the sleeping draught used and abused by Madame de La Vrillière have the ability, much appreciated by a neglected and jealous lover, to calm and even extinguish the ardour this man feels for another?'

She said nothing.

'And if we imagine that the poor man, to overcome this new infirmity, starts using other more efficient additives, wouldn't it then be advisable to double the dose of the potion in order to stop him joining his young mistress in ecstasy? I order you to speak, or I shall immediately hand you over to the torturer, who will extract the truth as he sees fit, I promise you that. I accuse you of having known that Marguerite Pindron would be in the kitchen that evening. Who was she meeting?'

Again she moved her head from side to side. Suddenly there came the sound of hurried footsteps. The door of the torture chamber was flung open and Monsieur Lenoir appeared, red-faced and out of breath, his double chin held tightly in his cravat.

'Monsieur, I order you to cease this unjustified interrogation. It is contrary to all the rules established under my authority, which cannot be contravened. Free this unfortunate woman immediately, as well as the other witnesses currently awaiting your pleasure.'

Nicolas made a sign to Bourdeau, who conducted the Gouet woman, Sanson and the assistants out of the room.

'So, Commissioner,' said the Lieutenant General of Police

sternly, 'I find you engaged in an unauthorised interrogation, without having requested permission of the Criminal Lieutenant, without even – I hardly dare utter these words – without even informing me! Of course, Monsieur Testard du Lys has already had to suffer on account of your illicit procedures! How am I to describe such an attitude which violates all principles and is an insult to the majesty of the law? Well? Aren't you going to say anything?'

Nicolas felt annoyance rise within him like a desire for violence, but he restrained himself. Monsieur Lenoir's prompt arrival proved that not everyone here was his friend and that envy was still rife. Or else – although he found this hard to believe – that the Duchesse de La Vrillière had been quick to act. Or the duc . . . Not that it really mattered.

'Monseigneur,' he said, 'I am here on the orders of the minister, who expressly gave me the responsibility for this affair. When your untimely arrival interrupted the interrogation, I'm sure I was on the point of obtaining vital information that would have helped me to understand a case whose ramifications you are unaware of and in which the greatest haste is called for.'

'I can't believe your insolence! It's beyond me. What on earth are you saying? If I'm badly informed, whose fault is that?'

'It's the fault of those who attack the Crown and its servants. How much time have I had, would you say, to devote to an investigation which at present involves four corpses, including three young women, one almost a child, affairs of State, secret societies, the moral failings of men in high places and the interests of a powerful enemy? It is quite unwise to give instructions from a distance to a subordinate and then leave him alone to confront the difficulties. Since he has been entrusted with a mission, one should rely on him and not hamper him with other assignments which the constantly changing circumstances make it impossible to carry out.'

'Monsieur!'

But Nicolas was launched. 'An investigation in which I myself was the object of an attack which I narrowly escaped,' he went on. 'How else would you like me to describe such a sequence of events, and how, knowing nothing of the way things have developed, can you accuse me of violating laws which I have been serving for fourteen years under the authority of the late King and your predecessor, Monsieur de Sartine?'

'I beg you to lower your voice and forget the absent and the dead,' replied Lenoir curtly. 'You're letting your mind wander! How could you possibly think that, under an easy-going King and my authority, you would be justified in flouting the law and using means which are well known for providing confessions but no proof?'

'Why don't you ask me, instead of demanding but not listening? The only reason I set this solemn and terrifying apparatus in motion was precisely in order not to have to use it. I was hoping that merely displaying it would dissuade these false witnesses from lying. My intention was to dig deep into these frightened souls, to draw out the past and the future, the involuntary word, the barely concealed admission, the detail long held back. That said, Monsieur, allow me to tell you that your words hardly surprise me, coming from a man who, from the beginning, has shown me nothing but rejection and disdain, and made light of a devotion developed over long years.'

He knew, in saying this, that he was exaggerating, but that it was necessary to lance the wound. Otherwise, it would be impossible ever to establish trust between them, and he himself would lose his self-esteem.

'You are forgetting yourself, Monsieur,' said Lenoir, his broad face turning red.

'I describe things as I see them. If you wish to remove me from this case, do so. If you wish me to leave the police force, demand it. If you are determined to conceal the truth and leave this case unsolved, then continue to hamper the work of your investigators. To someone whose loyalty has been called into question, it really doesn't matter any more. I shall see His Majesty, who hoped that I would see this through to the end, and when he questions me on the progress of the case, I shall admit to him immediately that, on the orders of the Lieutenant General of Police, he can no longer count on his commissioner for special investigations. Exit Monsieur Le Floch. The Marquis de Ranreuil is off to hunt stags at Fontainebleau. I bid you farewell. Your humble servant!'

Nicolas was striding towards the door when Monsieur Lenoir ran to cut him off before he reached the gallery. 'Monsieur, why didn't you tell me all this earlier?'

Tense and inscrutable, Nicolas did not reply.

'I'm sorry if I gave you the impression that I did not trust you,' continued Lenoir. 'The cases in which you have been involved over the years were of such a nature as to give rise to an unreasonable feeling of suspicion in me. I fear I was mistaken, and that I have offended you so seriously that I feel angry at myself. But put yourself in my shoes. I was bewildered by the very small amount of information coming back to me, and angry when I learnt that you were using torture. I was deceived by false information. I am sorry about that. You are an honest man, for who else would dare to talk to me as you have done? With such arrogance . . . Did you ever attempt that with my predecessor?'

'As a matter of fact, I did,' said Nicolas, whose anger had immediately abated. 'I once presented my resignation to Monsieur de Sartine. It was at the beginning of my career, and he had seen fit to use me as a plaything in an intrigue of his. I told him a few home truths.'

'And how did he take it?'

'Lieutenants General of Police come and go, and are all pretty much the same. Like you, he made honourable amends, to which I responded as I respond to you: I am touched by your words and I am all yours. However, Monseigneur, we don't have much time. Sit by this brazier. One can catch one's death of cold in these underground chambers. Let me enlighten you.'

Nicolas spoke for a long time, in the dancing blue light of the coals. From time to time, Monsieur Lenoir would look up in surprise. He asked a few questions, reflected for a while, then stood up.

'Monsieur, I fear I may have spoilt your skilful performance. You can't catch birds twice in the same trap. This case may have repercussions we can barely begin to imagine. Did you know that Monsieur de Chambonas, to whom my attention has already been drawn, has some very highly placed friends? The Duc de Villars, the Duc de Bouillon, the Comte de Noailles and others of his kind are working on his behalf . . . Take care, the man has cutthroats at his disposal, who would be only too happy to silence anyone who talks too much. If your suppositions prove correct and you remain the target of the English enemy . . .' He paused for a moment. 'I am pleased that the misunderstanding between us has been dispelled. It was quite unjustified, except perhaps by my constant concern for the King's service. We must be grateful for this outburst, which has allowed us to put aside the false impressions under which we were both labouring. Rest assured that, from this point on, the Lieutenant General of Police grants you his full and total confidence and that he asks you to consider him as you considered Monsieur de Sartine.'

Nicolas smiled and bowed. 'I would be very ungrateful not to defer to your wishes, for that, Monseigneur, is how I always understood my place with you. My position is an unusual one, forged year after year by my presence beside the late King, by my birth, and by the very unusual cases in which I have been involved. The only thing to which I aspire is truly to become once again the instrument in your hands of the King's service, the only concern that drives me and gives me satisfaction.'

'What are you planning to do?'

'Continue with the surveillance, see what it brings us, and finally confound the guilty parties.'

'Do you think that the Duc de La Vrillière is implicated in this series of crimes?'

'I don't think so, Monseigneur. But I understand your legitimate anxiety regarding the minister. Nothing will be done by me to implicate a person so close to the throne; you would be duly informed and the decision would no doubt revert to the King. In such a case, it would be sensible to avoid any kind of public reckoning. That would be contrary to the dignity of the State, and other measures would have to be envisaged.'

'Commissioner, I am completely satisfied. You mentioned His Majesty . . .'

'The King has been kept informed of this affair and is hoping for the imminent success of the investigation. So is the Secretary of State for the Navy; the presence of an English spy and the attack upon myself which seemed at one point to have been targeting the minister, all these things—'

'Yes, yes, I understand, there's no need to go back over all that. Until we meet again, my dear Commissioner.'

Lenoir withdrew, his old affable self. Nicolas took a deep breath. It was as if a weight had been lifted from his chest. The great confrontation had taken place; it had been necessary, and it had been complete. Its intensity had thrown light into the dark corners of a hierarchical relationship which could only be exercised happily when trust was given and accepted. The rest had been nothing but empty promises. He could now hope that on that front at least, he would be protected and have freedom of movement. Nevertheless, the Lieutenant General's sudden appearance in the torture chamber remained fraught with consequences. Now, the slyest of witnesses – and the Gouet woman clearly belonged to that category – would clam up like oysters. He called Bourdeau. His deputy's eyes expressed both amusement and anxiety.

'Monsieur Lenoir just passed me, looking red in the face but surprisingly serene. What fly bit you and transformed you into that ranting and raving monster?'

'Please don't exaggerate,' replied Nicolas. 'We exchanged a few words. I only raised my voice a little.'

'Yes . . . like the trumpet on the Day of Judgement.'

'Nothing that went beyond the rules a subordinate of a certain rank sets himself with regard to a magistrate of a higher rank.'

'So what happened?'

'What I said was very well received, and I have reason to believe that it will facilitate our work. It's just a question of knowing when to appear sincere . . . You know how things are, Pierre. There is always a risk in confronting someone when you are of unequal weight: it's the earthenware pot against the iron pot. Nobody can escape it in the course of a life in which the mark of subordination is uncertainty. The fact remains that if, at that decisive moment, your moral strength abandons you, you will never regain it, nor will you ever again be in a position to convince others. We had reached that crossroads. From now on, the clouds are dispelled, except that it spoilt our little piece of play-acting.'

'The Gouet woman hastened to decamp, along with the caretaker,' said Bourdeau. 'I made no objection, not wishing to irritate Monsieur Lenoir more than was necessary. Only little Jeannette, who was shaking and sobbing, didn't dare move an inch.'

'Send her in. Who knows? Perhaps she can help us.'

A red crumpled face soon appeared. The girl was trembling and looking wildly about her. Nicolas took her gently by the arm and sat her down on a stool.

'So, Jeannette, you're not like the others, are you? You're a good girl, and we have no wish to harm you, you can rest assured of that. I just need you to clarify certain details, do you understand?'

She was breathing in convulsive little spasms. The sweat had plastered her curly hair to her forehead, and in a flash Nicolas saw the Fausses Reposes woods, and Aimée d'Arranet's face in the pouring rain. He shook himself, took out his handkerchief and blew her nose as if she were a child. This simple gesture appeared to relax her, and she gave a little half-smile.

'There we are, that's better. Now listen carefully to what I'm going to ask you. You don't know anything, you were asleep, you didn't see anyone, you didn't hear anything. That's fine, I believe you. But you were Marguerite's friend, and the other day, before you were taken ill, you were about to tell me something.'

She lowered her head, and again assumed a stubborn, distant air.

'Your friend was supposed to be meeting somebody that night. A young man, I assume. You were her confidante, did she tell you about him?'

She shook her head from side to side, blank-eyed. Nicolas clapped his hands and she stopped immediately, and went back to normal.

'Just calm down. Admit it: Marguerite told you she was meeting someone.'

She looked at him for a long time before making up her mind. 'Yes, she did, and she also told me she didn't like it but couldn't get out of it.'

'Good! Was it her young man? The one you call Aide?'

'No! It was the old man, the major-domo.' She was expressing herself more firmly now.

'Are you sure? Did you hear her arrange to meet him?'

'No, of course not. I saw the note. She was supposed to be in the kitchen that evening.'

'Did you read the note?'

'No, I can't read. But I saw it.'

'Can you describe the handwriting?'

'It was in big letters, that was all I could recognise. It was on an old piece of paper used for wrapping candles.'

'And did Marguerite keep this piece of paper?'

'She was so fed up with the whole thing that she tore it up into little pieces and threw it out of the window.'

'I'm grateful to you. Is there anything else you have to tell me?'

'No, Monsieur.'

'You can go. Would you like a carriage to take you back?'

'No, I'd be ashamed. I'll go down Rue Saint-Honoré.'

'As you wish. Don't tell anyone what we talked about, your safety depends on it. Please don't forget that.'

She left the room, glancing behind her in panic as if fearing that she would be recalled.

'I'm starting to think we're making progress.'

'A fine haul, indeed,' said Bourdeau. 'A young girl, and the Lieutenant General of Police. By the way, I didn't know you were now claiming your title of marquis.'

Nicolas smiled. 'It was intended *ad usum Delphini*, a little oratorical fig leaf. I think Monsieur Lenoir is sensitive to the prestige of rank. To return to our case, let's sum up. The corpse in the cab is almost certainly not Eudes Duchamplan. He didn't kill himself. We may assume it's the gardener, Vitry, the Pindron girl's former fiancé.'

'That's good to know, but doesn't get us very far.'

'I agree, but it does narrow our search. What about the Duc de

La Vrillière's mysterious midnight flits? Where does he go? And what about the surveillance of the Marquis de Chambonas's mansion? That's where we'll pick up the threads again. And where is the second young girl from Brussels?'

Bourdeau looked at him, puzzled.

'I fear I haven't mentioned that to you,' Nicolas went on, having noticed the inspector's expression. 'The clothes and appearance of the corpse on Île des Cygnes reminded me of something Monsieur Lenoir requested me to look into: the case of two young girls who fled Brussels for Paris. The victim is one of them, and I assume we can fear the worst for her sister. But there's still a chance we may save her, if she's fallen into the same hands. It's a question of time. From my conversation with Monsieur Lenoir, I gather that the Marquis de Chambonas is protected, which means we won't be able to take a close look at his mansion. It's likely that he's being cautious at the moment and that his Roman orgies are now taking place in more secluded spots.'

'I agree with you. So we're dependent on our spies, surveillance, and all the usual methods of a well-regulated police force.'

'We have to wait for something to start. Then we'll pursue the hydra, faithful Iolaos.'[1]

'The many-headed hydra.'

'Indeed. In the meantime, I'm going to pay the minister a visit. I want to set my mind at rest.'

'Is that wise?'

'I'm not risking anything. I'm sure he knows all about my suspicions. My questions at Versailles regarding his silver hand can have left him in no doubt about that. He's aware of what we know and what we suspect. Either he's guilty, and my words, which I hope will be blunt and to the point, can only lead to an extreme reaction, or he's innocent, in which case he must help us and allow us to establish that he has nothing to do with these murders.'

Nicolas left the Châtelet. He was breathing more easily now. Something that had been weighing on his mind since the death of Louis XV had vanished: a nagging sense of shame and grief which had led him to feel guilty of a sin he had not committed, hurt as he was to the depths of his being by a sense of betrayed loyalty and despised trust. The force that had driven his replies to Monsieur Lenoir derived from this legitimate resentment. It seemed that the Lieutenant General of Police had understood his suffering. The reaction to statements which he himself had known were excessive redeemed in his eyes a man who, until now, had been sparing in his respect. He hoped he was not wrong in his observation; what he wanted more than anything was to get back to the former situation of devotion and loyalty.

His steps led him to the banks of the river, and he decided to let his unconscious choices guide him. With a calm mind and a sharp eye, he contemplated the spectacle of his beloved city. On Quai de la Mégisserie, he thought of Naganda on seeing a group of crimps eyeing up some likely-looking young customers. Whores, gambling, alcohol and food would be the traps laid for them. The Micmac had almost been enlisted, and only the vigilance of the police had saved him. Where was he now, that distant friend? No doubt tirelessly pursuing the mission he had set himself:

continuing to serve the King of an ungrateful country. A little further on, an old woman was stoking an oven, enveloping passers-by in smoke. The smell that assailed his nostrils as he passed told him that, instead of using decent oil or lard to fry her doughnuts, she was using pork grease, which she probably stole from the drivers who used it on the wheels of their coaches. A stocky dark-haired, bow-legged workman was devouring one of these hot, sticky delicacies straight from the oven. Coming to the arcades of the Louvre, he had a look at the second-hand clothes market. A penniless crowd frequented this place, where old clothes suspended on string were buffeted in the wind like hanged and shrivelled bodies. The police sometimes dispersed the crowd, for it was quite common for the clothes of those who had died of consumption or pneumonia to be sold here instead of being burnt. The infected clothes passed from the bodies of the dead to those of the living, and the diseases were passed on with them.

Nicolas announced his name at the entrance to the Saint-Florentin mansion. On the grand staircase, he passed the Duchesse de La Vrillière, who responded to his greeting with a look of terror. She seemed to have been weeping and was now getting ready to go out. She was dressed in a large grey coat with a black lining, her head covered with a grey hood. He was still climbing the steps when he heard a murmur behind him. Turning, he saw that the duchesse had stopped, and was looking at him imploringly.

'Marquis . . .'

Another one! They all thought they could get round him by giving him his title, but hadn't he himself used it when dealing with Monsieur Lenoir?

'My cousin Madame de Maurepas holds you in high esteem,' the duchesse said. 'May I present you with a plea?'

'Madame, I am your servant.'

'Help the duc. He won't listen to me. In fact, he's never listened to me.'

'Madame, you can help him by helping me. I am convinced that you know more about this affair than you have been willing to tell me thus far.'

She was twisting one of the ribbons in her wig. 'I can't tell you anything. There was nothing else we could do . . .'

'What do you mean? Madame, I beseech you.'

'Save him, Monsieur.'

She turned abruptly and flew rather than walked to the front steps.

Here, thought Nicolas, was something that amply justified his decision to talk to the minister at all costs. The valet did not conceal his surprise when he appeared and began by refusing to inform his master, who had told him that he did not want to be disturbed. The commissioner firmly pushed the servant aside and went on. He reached the gallery, and then the study where this whole adventure had begun. He tapped at the door and, without waiting for a reply, entered resolutely. Monsieur de La Vrillière was sitting slumped in an armchair by the fireplace. He was in shirt and breeches, with his cravat untied, and wore over his shoulders a thick brightly coloured cloth, the ends of which he had pulled tight over his chest. He had taken off his wig, and his bald cranium gleamed in the firelight. It was a pitiful sight. He looked like a sick, crushed old man. Nicolas felt compassion for someone whose manner had always been more commanding.

'What is it?' said the duc. 'Why am I being disturbed, and who gave you permission?'

He had not recognised Nicolas.

The commissioner leaned towards him. 'This is urgent, Monseigneur. What I have to say to you cannot be postponed.'

'I'm tired.'

Nicolas dismissed the objection and gave a complete account of his investigation, omitting none of the details, not even those – and there were many of them – that incriminated the duc. He presented and commented on the various hypotheses, but the few questions he asked went unanswered. The only thing he omitted to mention, out of caution, was the practical measures he and his men had taken to discover the motivation behind this affair. He insisted on the fact that four people had paid with their lives for the sake of some obscure plot that everyone was striving to make even more obscure. In conclusion, he recalled the new King's desire to see light cast on the various aspects of this tragedy. Last but not least, he talked of the security of the State – this to a man who had long believed himself the embodiment of it – and underlined how disturbing it was that the secret representative of a foreign power should be involved in a criminal case in which so many illustrious names were implicated.

The minister seemed increasingly overwhelmed by all this, unable to stop his head collapsing on his chest. At last, though, he pulled himself together.

'Alas!' he sighed. 'I can't tell you anything, nor do I wish to. The late King loved you and put all his trust in you. If I were to tell anyone a secret, it would be you, having known and respected you for years. But you yourself, who have served me, how can you believe these vile slanderers and walk into the trap set by their bloodthirsty machinations? I don't claim to be a saint, but how could I have committed these terrible murders? There is nothing, I swear to you, to link me with these horrors. Will you believe me, Nicolas Le Floch, you whom the King considered the purest of his servants? Truly, truly . . .'

'Monseigneur, you only have to tell me one thing. Where were you at the times that these crimes were being committed? It's a simple question, and requires a simple answer from you.'

The minister looked straight at him, and Nicolas was surprised to see tears running down his face.

'I won't tell you, even if I have to pay the price for my silence a hundredfold! Monsieur de Chambonas . . . Nothing will oblige me to reveal what I wish to keep to myself.' He sighed again. 'It is the one and only part of myself which I hold dear, along with my loyalty to the late King . . . Please go now.'

Nicolas withdrew, lost in thought.


A sedan chair took him back to the Châtelet, where a long wait began. He once again brought his notes up to date, trying to omit none of the elements that had continued to pile up. There were so many of them that the sheer volume made it hard for him to see his way through. On the stroke of one, Old Marie silently and considerately let him share his lunch. This turned out to be an appetising stew of cow's udders, a dish of which the common people were fond due to its cheapness. This meal was washed down with a cheap wine, which, remarkably, was not too vinegary. Nicolas finally dozed off with his head between his arms on the table, the accumulated fatigue of an emotionally and physically draining week crashing down all at once on his shoulders.

At five o'clock, Bourdeau and Rabouine appeared and woke him from a strange dream. In it, an unknown man had been working an automaton, like those of Vaucanson, its right arm, equipped with a silver hand, cutting the throat of another doll whose face, he was horrified to discover, was the Queen's. He struggled and tried to intervene, but an unknown force held him still, as if paralysed.

'We have news,' announced Bourdeau, 'important news! And on all fronts!'

'It's about time,' said Nicolas, now completely awake. 'I was beginning to despair!'

'Well, you won't be disappointed. We've gleaned two pieces of information which, I believe, should give us something to keep us occupied for a while and help us make progress.'

'Don't keep me on tenterhooks. My wait and Old Marie's wine made me doze off, otherwise I would have been dying of impatience. I'm listening.'

'It's your head wound, it's healing up but it's also getting you heated. Right, listen to this. Rabouine here, who's quite a good-looking fellow beneath his gangling exterior, sometimes combines business with pleasure. Mademoiselle Josse, better known under her *nom de guerre* of La Roussillon, a vivacious brunette with a pretty face, has a soft spot for our spy. She's constantly teasing him and, if he consented, would make him her beau.'

Rabouine, whose face had turned red, lowered his head.

'In short,' continued Bourdeau, 'one thing leading to another, she tells him all her gossip. She's really a terrible gossip, and can never keep anything to herself. Anyway, she tells our man here that she's been feeling increasingly guilty about the kind of things that go on at parties organised by . . . can you guess who?'

'The Marquis de Chambonas?'

'No. A suitor whose description she gave to Rabouine. He can take over from here.'

'The description matches Anselme Vitry, but in the light of what you've discovered it's much more likely to be Eudes Duchamplan.'

'And why does this girl complain about such parties? They should be part of her usual activity.'

'She's a good girl, and she's had enough of the vile acts she's seen committed. In addition, one of her prostitute friends caught a terrible disease from these parties, the kind you don't catch in a convent or when you're celibate. She doesn't want to have anything more to do with that kind of debauchery. She was invited to another party this evening, and refused.'

'This is all well and good,' said Nicolas, 'but I need something more concrete if we're going to be able to do anything about it. Where, when, how?'

'I should say, Monsieur Nicolas,' said Rabouine, 'that her gossip isn't just idle chatter. She's let me in on a number of secrets in case anything unfortunate should happen to her. It was a kind of guarantee for her.'

'I understand. Carry on.'

'A cab is supposed to be coming to fetch her from the corner of Rue des Vieilles Tuileries and Passage du Manège at ten o'clock this evening. She doesn't know where the party will be held. The previous times, they took place in private houses or in underground quarries. She's also noticed that she wasn't necessarily invited on every occasion.'

'How is it that she has finally agreed this time?'

'I persuaded her.'

'In return for what?' asked Bourdeau.

'Our protection and support. She's been very sensible and has put together a little nest egg. As a native of Bordeaux, she wants to move back there and take up an honest profession.'

'Well,' said Nicolas pensively, 'that should be possible. Anything else that might be of use to us?'

'Yes! The guests at this party have to wear masks and show a card, the ace of hearts, half torn in the middle. Which means that one of our men could certainly get in.'

Nicolas took a piece of paper and started writing, speaking as he did so.

'Gather all our men together, including the spies. Inform the French Guards and the watch. We'll need men around the quarries near the Observatory and spies to track any unusual movement of carriages. I doubt that the surveillance will be easy. It's quite likely that these people don't use the official entrance, and I know that many private houses have special access via the cellars – that's our misfortune! Remember, Pierre, the cellar of the Lardin house in Rue des Blancs-Manteaux. Apart from that, we're going to need people at Montparnasse . . .'

'There's already permanent surveillance there,' said Bourdeau.

'We also need surveillance around the Saint-Florentin mansion. We really can't afford to lose sight of the minister if he goes out and abandons his carriage. I want to know the destination of these nocturnal adventures he stubbornly refuses to explain. Some spare carriages at the Châtelet, and a good mount for me. Not a nervous animal that stamps all the time, a quiet, good-natured horse. It's vital that I'm not noticed.'

'I hope you're not planning to go in person,' said Bourdeau anxiously.

'I certainly am.'

'That's madness! At least let me go with you.'

'Oh, no, my dear Pierre. You'll remain at the Châtelet and be the guiding light of the operation. Knowing you're here will be a comfort to me and a guarantee that everything will go according to plan.'

'So if I understand correctly, you want to follow La Roussillon and enter the location of the party in secret? You're too well known, you'll be recognised immediately. Think of the consequences . . .'

'That's not a convincing argument. I'll be wearing a mask, and I'll be armed. Someone find me an ace of hearts and a large black cape with a detachable collar. It'll all be show. I'll pretend to be a greybeard who's acting younger, with a blond wig, a cerused face and a lot of rouge.'

'All right. I still think you're being reckless, but I'll go now and start getting things ready. Where will you be stationed?'

'In Rue des Vieilles Tuileries, obviously, where La Roussillon has her rendezvous. Otherwise, we'd lose too much time, having someone come to inform me . . . So, a horse for me, and a second rider to follow me at a distance and take my mount when I reach the destination. A third rider in reserve ready to take messages or to lend a hand. He'll be the one who'll have the task of—'

'The second rider,' interrupted Bourdeau in a resolute tone, 'will be me, whether you like it or not.'

'Out of the question!'

'On the contrary, it's vital. Look at it logically. Think of the time it will take to inform me where you are, think of all the coming and going that would involve.'

Nicolas looked at the inspector. 'All right, I give in. It's true we'll need at least three-quarters of an hour to surround the scene of the operation. Well, as my father, who was at Fontenoy, used to say, it's up to us to support the King's house.'

He had continued writing while he was talking, crossing out a word from time to time, as if he were keeping the minutes of this conversation. He folded the paper without sealing it, handed it to Rabouine, and asked him to take it straight to the Lieutenant General of Police in Rue Neuve-Saint-Augustin.


The end of the day was spent preparing and going over the various scenarios which might occur. Monsieur Lenoir had hastened to reply to Nicolas, granting him a free hand and full powers to decide what to do depending on how the evening developed. The commissioner was pleased to see that the note concluded with an expression of concern that Nicolas should not lay himself too open to danger in this risky undertaking. By eight o'clock, all the arrangements were in place and Nicolas made an appearance, much to the astonishment of Bourdeau and Rabouine, as an old rake, stooped and made up like Richelieu, beneath a curly blood-red wig. He was brandishing a torn ace of hearts.

The next stage went as planned. He waited on his horse just inside a carriage entrance set somewhat back from the meeting place. The street was deserted and poorly lit, especially as street lighting was not allowed when the moon was full, and the moon tonight was veiled by clouds. Just before ten, a figure who could only be La Roussillon appeared. She might have been a soldier, pacing up and down as if on parade, her tall hat surmounted by a plume. She wore a mask, and her Polish-style dress emphasised the curve of her waist. A few minutes after ten, an ordinary cab appeared and came to a halt. La Roussillon approached it and negotiated for a few moments, then gathered her petticoats and hoisted herself inside. The vehicle set off at a jog trot. Nicolas waited for a moment and only gave his horse its head once the cab was almost at Rue du Cherche-Midi. Nicolas could hear, far behind him, Bourdeau and the third rider. What kind of apocalypse were they heading towards?

# XIII

## TRAPS

Be quiet! Can one say such things?
RIVAROL

The route took them along Rue du Four as far as Place Saint-André-des-Arts, then Rue de la Huchette and the Port aux Tuiles. The carriage crossed the Tournelles. Nicolas noted with a shudder that they had returned to one of the places that had already figured in the investigation. The cab slowed down and suddenly turned towards the river. It came to a halt not far from the bank. Nicolas saw La Roussillon extricate herself and walk towards the river, stepping hesitantly in the mud. The rising fog seemed to swallow her up. Where could she be going? There was a gap in the clouds for a moment, revealing a long barge, clearly a floating bathhouse. The establishment resembled two houses with an entrance in the middle, indicated by a lighted lantern. The girl vanished inside. Hidden behind a pile of wood, Nicolas struck a light and looked at his watch. It was after ten thirty. He heard Bourdeau, and soon saw him approaching on foot, his horse's bridle over his arm.

'Good, here's the place!' he whispered.

'Outside the walls, therefore outside police supervision . . .' said Nicolas.

'Let's apply our plan.'

'Go back to our courier, and tell him to head straight back to the Châtelet and give Rabouine the go-ahead. Action stations. In three-quarters of an hour, at exactly . . .' he again looked at his watch, – '. . . twenty past eleven, everything must be in place. Make sure the boats are silent once they get past Île Saint-Louis. There are still some moored at Quai d'Orléans. We must keep an eye open for trouble on the side facing the river. The trap needs to be closed completely. Now go, Pierre, then come back and join me here. I suspect the other guests will be arriving soon.'

Having checked that the coast was clear, Bourdeau withdrew. He soon returned and the anxious wait began, punctuated by the guests gradually arriving for the party. Nicolas could not conceal his impatience. He had stopped looking at his watch, fearing that striking a light might reveal their presence. Eventually, they saw Rabouine appear. The plan had been applied down to its smallest detail and some sixty men were now surrounding the barge. It was possible to go in but certainly not to come out. On the river, three boats were patrolling in the fog, and they would be able to approach the floating establishment if necessary. The moment had come for Nicolas to go in.

He adjusted his tricorn, feeling as he did so for the pocket pistol concealed in one of the wings of the hat. This gift from Inspector Bourdeau had got him out of more than one tight corner. He also checked that his sword was in place. He shook the inspector's hand, then Rabouine's, and walked with a firm step towards the landing stage. He crossed the gangway and was greeted at a kind of counter by a footman who, without saying a word, checked his torn ace of hearts. Still silent, the man pointed to his hat, cape and sword. He hesitated for a brief moment, but managed, as he took off his tricorn and unfastened his cape, to slip the pocket pistol into his coat. He was glad he had not chosen the Marquis de Ranreuil's sword, which was reserved for nobler expeditions. The entrance hall led to two symmetrical staircases which descended towards a much larger central room, from which he could hear the sounds of a party drifting up. He walked down and discovered a crowd of masked people, all drinking. The wooden walls of the room were hidden behind hangings of pink taffeta set off with silver braid. Candles gave a bright sheen to the guests' make-up. Nicolas was attracted to a little scene being played out in a corner, and went closer with some difficulty because of all the people already gathered around.

Two young people, a girl and a boy, were uttering a string of obscenities. Each phrase was echoed by double entendres and vulgar jokes from the audience, accompanied by gestures that revealed a deep corruption. Gradually, the atmosphere of the place was changing. Eyes gleamed behind the masks, words and gestures became more provocative. Couples were forming, and sometimes groups, who headed towards the bathing cabins. Nicolas thought he ought to do something to allay suspicion. He had spotted La Roussillon, recognising her from her plume and her arched back. She seemed nervous, could not stay in one place, and rejected all advances. With some difficulty, he went up to her and whispered in her ear that he had been sent by Rabouine and had to talk to her. To get away from prying eyes and ears, he proposed they take refuge in one of the cabins. That way, everyone would think they had got down to business. She immediately drew him into the central gangway, on either side of which were the cabins. After trying several doors and provoking cries of protest, which indicated to Nicolas that the rooms were not provided with locks, they managed to find a free one. In it was a copper bathtub, a bench, a pedestal table on which a bottle waited in a cooling pitcher, a toilet bowl and a chaise longue. He also noticed a curious contraption he had once seen in an actress's house. It was a kind of tin basin mounted on a wooden base, with a leather border, a sponge and two glasses of water. He remembered that it was known as a bidet – Semacgus, with his love of the risqué, had once called it an ornamental pond for the thighs.

No sooner had they entered than a valet dressed in blue twill, whose expression was anything but servile, brought them towels, bergamot-scented soap and two pairs of slippers. He came in and went out several times, pouring pitchers of hot water into the tub. This task over, he asked Nicolas, with a winning air, if the young lady and he wished to take advantage of his services. He did not conceal his disappointment at being dismissed with the usual tip.

'That's one of the stallions who cater for the vices of some and the impotence and exhaustion of the others,' explained La Roussillon.

'Rest assured, Mademoiselle,' said Nicolas, 'that we shall not forget your help. If we were to do so, Rabouine would certainly hasten to remind us. I'm not going to stay in this cabin. My aim, as I'm sure you realise, is to prevent the person who organises these parties from doing any more harm. He's holding a young girl whose sister has been murdered. We must find him. You're a good girl and I'm sure you're going to help me. Where do you think he is?'

'I'll do as you ask, Monsieur. But you must agree to protect me, as I'm running a great risk doing this. As you've observed, we're in the corridor on the left-hand side. On the right the bathrooms are reserved for the organiser's associates. I have every reason to believe that it's there they do mysterious things that are forbidden to anyone who hasn't been specifically invited.'

Nicolas closed his eyes, trying to come up with a feasible plan. 'We're going to pretend we're doing what they expect us to be doing . . .'

'With you, Monsieur,' she said, giving a little curtsey, 'it would have been a pleasure.'

He laughed. 'I like Rabouine too much to do that to him! We'll block the door with the bench in case they come to check the veracity of our lovemaking, then I'm going to go out of the window and try to get to the other side of the boat. How many rooms on each side?'

'Five or six. Not all of them have baths. Some of them are steam rooms.'

'I assume there's a handrail all round the deck?'

'It's very narrow, and the whole thing moves. The river's high because of the autumn rains.'

'All right. While I'm trying to get to the other end, make all the noises you need to, to convince anyone spying on us that we really are making love.'

She smiled; the prospect seemed to amuse her. He opened the window, and a damp draught blew in, making the candle flames flicker. The wooden frame was wet, and he almost slipped and fell. No sooner had La Roussillon closed the window than he heard muffled sounds of water and moans. He was sure she was someone who always tried to amuse her customers. He tried not to think about the black waves beating on the hull of the barge not far below him, and felt reassured at the thought of the boats moving around, ready, if necessary, to come to his rescue. He reached the middle of the barge. An unpleasant surprise was waiting for him there: an iron gate with spikes barred the way. Strips of cast iron, sharpened at the ends, protected the gate on both sides. Nicolas made such an effort trying to push it that he was suddenly bathed in sweat despite the cold of the night. Going back was tantamount to giving up the whole operation. Calling one of the boats floating invisibly on the river risked attracting the attention of those on the barge. In the course of his career, similar situations had often presented themselves, and he had always found a way out of the difficulty. His fertile mind was toying with various solutions, each more fanciful than the other when, having approached the gate, his coat got caught on one of the strips of iron. It was not easy to get free, but the incident made him think, and a light went on in his mind. He would take off his coat and use it as a kind of rope to get over the gate, avoiding all danger of contact with the strips and spikes. He immediately set about applying his idea. He took off his coat after emptying the contents of the pockets into a kind of broad gusset sewn into the inside of his breeches, which usually provided a safe hiding place for documents or rolls of *louis*. He managed to get everything into it, including his pocket pistol. For a moment, the thought crossed his mind that he could have used his unrolled cravat, but he feared that the fine muslin would not withstand either his weight or the sharpness of the metal.

He hooked the collar of his coat onto the top of the gate, raised himself up on tiptoe, as far as he could go, hoping that the stitching – the work of Master Vachon's apprentices – would stand the strain. He gave a sharp tug, and nothing tore. He now had to judge his jump. Any error would be fatal: he would fall back with all his weight and would inevitably impale himself on the cast iron. Stepping back, he retreated to the handrail, stretched the line of fabric, pressed hard with his right foot on the side of the boat and jumped. It all happened very quickly: a leap, a rustling sound, and a violent landing on the other side. He hit the side of the barge head first. The impact left him stunned. He staggered back, his feet sliding on the damp wood. He slipped and fell, but grabbed the handrail with both hands and finally managed to steady himself. He sat down with his legs dangling, out of breath. He felt a hot liquid spreading over his stomach. The dim lights on the barge did not provide enough illumination, but the pain that went through his body took his breath away and made him realise that he was injured. He put his hand on his stomach then raised it to his mouth: blood. One of the strips of metal had sliced through his shirt and cut him on the abdomen. It was a painful but superficial wound. He was glad he had kept his cravat. He wrapped it tightly around his stomach, using it as a bandage to stem the flow of blood. He waited for his breathing to settle and his heart to slow to its usual rhythm.

Now he had to get down to the serious work. Was the mysterious organiser of these parties behind one of these windows? He shuddered, thinking that he could just as easily be in a bathrooom situated on the shore side, facing the Port au Bois. Nevertheless, it seemed to him that, out of caution, the man was likely to have chosen the side facing the river, which was more hidden. He walked forward. His stomach hurt. The first room, a steam room, was empty. In the second, two couples in indecent positions were paying homage to Venus. With horror, Nicolas recognised one of the participants as one of the great names of France. The third was some kind of storeroom. Approaching the fourth, he heard muffled cries. He looked in through the window and saw a heavily made-up woman take a blackish substance from a little box and dissolve it in a glass of water. He was about to proceed to the fifth window when more distinct moans reached his ears. He could not see the part of the fourth room from which they seemed to come. He hesitated. Was this another of those scenes of which he had already had a taste, or was it . . . The woman was brandishing a riding crop and striking someone. The other person screamed now, and the scream was like a child's. There was an unusual amount of venom in the woman's actions. To set his mind at rest, Nicolas went and looked in the last room; it was empty. He retraced his steps. The woman was still half bent over her victim, viciously beating her. It was then that he noticed it: beneath the frills and flounces of the dress was a pair of men's riding boots. So the woman was a man, which threw a new light on things. He still had to decide what to do. Go back? He'd have to get over the gate again, which was risky. Hail the police boats? Although the men on the shore would stop the guests escaping, it would put paid to any idea of catching any of these people *in flagrante*. The culprits could well get lost in the panic following a police raid. Everything depended on him, as usual. It was he, the King's commissioner, who had to act appropriately. But how?

Could he force open the window and jump into the room? It might be possible to take a leap from the top of the handrail. He tried the window with his hand, in the unlikely event that it was not locked. It was. Manifesting his presence by knocking on the window might force the man to open up, but in doing so he would lose the advantage of surprise. The idea crossed his mind that he could shoot the unknown man through the window, but he rejected it immediately; he was too honourable to fire at a suspect without a specific reason. Nevertheless he had to rescue the young girl, who might well be one of the two fugitives from Brussels.

A variation of the previous option occurred to him. He would fire his pistol at the window handle to get inside the room. He would place himself to the left of the window for a better aim and to avoid hitting anyone in the room, then climb inside, his smoking pistol in his hand. He looked in one last time, and the sight of the tortures the victim was suffering convinced him to act without further delay.

He fired. The fragile frame shattered. He threw himself inside, fell on his shoulder and rolled on the ground, losing his pistol as he did so. Everything happened in a flash. He saw the girl tied to the bed, lying on her stomach, with bleeding stripes across her back. The creature had immediately turned and leapt for his sword, and was now walking towards Nicolas, who was still on the ground. He rolled on his side, still stunned by his fall, and grabbed a stool as a weapon. He made an initial parry. The sword thrusts came thick and fast, ever closer to his chest. But then the sword became stuck in the soft wood of the stool. Nicolas pressed so hard with the stool that the weapon first bent, then broke with a snap. The creature threw the broken sword at him, then came towards him with his hands out. He grabbed him by the neck and tried to strangle him. They struggled for a while, with neither man yielding, until, having gone round and round the restricted space of the cabin, they found themselves by the shattered window. The broken pane rattled each time their feet hit the floor. The man redoubled his efforts to strangle him. Nicolas felt his strength waning and his stomach wound opening and bleeding profusely. He tried to thrust his attacker off him. What was left of the window frame shattered and collapsed. Tightly bound together, the two men fell into the river.

Entering the black icy water was a ghastly moment for Nicolas, who hated darkness. He felt as though he were sinking into a tomb. The vice was tightening round his neck. He was swallowing the muddy water. He could not breathe. Red and yellow flames danced in front of his eyes. He felt himself yielding, and lost consciousness.

'He's moving! He's moving!'

A familiar voice was grunting somewhere in the distance. 'To lose consciousness twice in a few days! These Bretons do just what they like! I told him to be careful, but he didn't listen to me. He's always so foolhardy . . .'

'A man of strong character does not worry about threats,' said another voice, in measured tones. 'I was worried too, knowing his reputation.'

Nicolas could feel the heat of a blazing furnace somewhere nearby. There was whispering round him, but he could not understand a word that was being said.

'It's all thanks to my cordial! He's already had some.'

Suddenly, he opened his eyes and yelled, 'My notebook! Give me my little black notebook!'

'Well, now,' said the first voice, 'he hasn't lost his common sense. The first thing he thinks of is the one thing he needs.'

A familiar face bent over him: the friendly face of Bourdeau. 'Bless the inside pocket of your breeches,' he said. 'It didn't let the water in. The notebook is intact. Your sword and even your pistol have been recovered.'

Another face entered his field of vision.

'Monsieur, I am very pleased to see you out of danger. What would we do without you?'

He recognised Monsieur Lenoir, and was moved by his concern. 'Monseigneur, I'm—'

'Don't speak! You must stay calm and rest.'

'But I'm curious to know what happened after I thought I was drowning, strangled by that creature.'

'The inspector will tell you everything.'

'You fell in the river while struggling with your attacker,' said Bourdeau. 'The noise of your fall alerted one of our boats and you were both fished out with hooks. You lost consciousness. You were brought back to the Châtelet, undressed, dried, warmed up, and Old Marie did the rest.'

Nicolas made a gesture. 'What about . . . the other man?'

'Don't worry, he's under guard, chained up in his cell.'

'Well guarded?'

He remembered the livid face of an old soldier found hanged in his cell. Thanks to a lack of precautions . . .

'Very well guarded. I know what you're thinking about . . . Alarmed by the turn events had taken, I immediately launched our offensive. Our men surrounded the establishment, and the sister of a previous victim was found and taken to the Hôtel-Dieu to be tended and comforted. The poor girl had suffered incredible tortures. Unfortunately some of the guests—'

'Who shall remain nameless,' Monsieur Lenoir cut in.

'Some guests were able to withdraw without being bothered,' continued Bourdeau in an acrimonious tone. 'Including Lord Ashbury, who was also caught in the net.'

'He, too!'

'We couldn't keep him,' said Lenoir. 'An hour, no longer than that . . . The English ambassador appeared in Rue Neuve-Saint-Augustin as if by magic and ordered me to hand the fellow over, as a plenipotentiary enjoying the King's immunity. Ashbury gave us a look of total contempt and arrogance and said that although Commissioner Le Floch's life had been spared in England, he was still an enemy of the English King and needed to constantly beware.'

Nicolas sat up in a rage. He realised that he was in the Lieutenant General's study, lying wrapped in a blanket on the large Savonnerie rug by the hearth, in which a fire blazed.

'On the other hand,' continued Lenoir, 'trailing the Duc de La Vrillière has brought results. We now know where he goes at night. To a little apartment on the second floor of a house in Rue des Tournelles . . .'

'What? Rue des Tournelles!'

'Yes, opposite the monastery of the Minimes, almost on the corner of Rue Neuve-Saint-Gilles.'

'Quai des Tournelles, Rue des Tournelles. Why does that name keep cropping up? Do you remember that piece of paper we found in the younger Duchamplan's apartment? Could it be he knew the minister's secret? Which would mean Ashbury also knew it!'

'The house is being watched,' said Bourdeau. 'We'll let him come out without showing ourselves, and only then will we investigate the nature of these nocturnal visits.'

'I'm going there right now.'

'You're hardly in a fit state.'

Lenoir intervened, somewhat briskly. 'I do in fact think that it's the commissioner's place, and that, if his condition allows him, it would be preferable and more appropriate . . .'

Nicolas looked at Bourdeau's stubborn face. 'You can come with me, Pierre.'

Bourdeau relaxed. Nicolas understood his chief's concern. What would he discover in that apartment? The fewer witnesses there were, the better it would be for the honour of the King's councils. Not that the Lieutenant General mistrusted Bourdeau, but he knew that Nicolas was more accustomed to these State secrets, which he was always able to bury deep in his consciousness.


*Tuesday 11 October 1774*

He thanked Old Marie for his care, went back to the duty office to change, and then he and Bourdeau rushed to their carriage.

'How has Eudes Duchamplan been behaving himself?' asked Nicolas. 'I'm sure it was him on the barge. I hope he didn't have the effrontery to deny his identity?'

'He was very indignant, though he didn't conceal his name. I noted, once he had taken off his make-up, that he was bleeding, and we saw that he had a wound on the left side of his face. I found that interesting.'

'What do you deduce from that?'

'That it was a scar from a recently closed wound that had just been reopened, perhaps deliberately. I thought of your account of the attack on you at Versailles, when Semacgus's coachman struck the would-be assassin with his whip. That was on the left cheek, wasn't it?'

'Everything in fact tallies with what you're telling me. So it was he who shot at me . . . How did he take it?'

'I was careful not to let him know. Curiously, he claimed, of his own accord, that the wound was the result of his fight with you. He said he'd had no idea why you burst in like that, threatening him, and he'd taken fright.'

'What about the girl? Had he been whispering sweet nothings in her ear?'

'He claimed she was only there for the usual amusements common in that kind of party, and that he'd never met her before!'

'In other words, he's a gentle soul, who denies everything. He must be confident someone's going to come to his rescue.'

'As if those who ran off into the darkness with their hands over their faces, looking for their carriages, are going to intercede on his behalf! He has a curiously naive idea of the compassion of men in high places!'

'As soon as possible,' resumed Nicolas, 'we'll have to set up a hearing before Lenoir and the Criminal Lieutenant. There always comes a moment when Monsieur Testard du Lys needs to be, let's say, "accommodated". And I'll wager the Lieutenant General of Police won't spoil the party. I have an idea of how we can stage it for maximum effect. I'll have to talk to you about it.'

'This expedition worries me on account of your health . . .'

'I'm perfectly fine, don't worry. My head's a little empty, my stomach's like cardboard, but my curiosity's aroused! Old Marie's cordial would waken a dead man!'

'Rue des Tournelles begins at the Bastille, doesn't it?' said Bourdeau.

'Of course! And stretches almost as far as Place Royale, being joined to it by Rue du Pas-de-la-Merle.'

'Your knowledge of the city amazes me! The Bastille and Place Royale! Amusing, even significant. The two Tournelles are connected.'

'That remark is typical of you!'

'I wanted to thank you,' said Bourdeau. 'I wasn't fooled earlier. I know Monsieur Lenoir was trying to keep me away.'

'Quiet, now. There are times when it's best not to know too much.'

Bourdeau smiled and said nothing. Both men felt moved; this exchange had spoken volumes. They continued crossing the nocturnal city. They passed a few late walkers, a few whores standing beside bollards, some dubious-looking men who jumped into the shadows as the carriage passed, watch patrols and a priest carrying the holy sacraments to a dying man. They soon reached Rue des Tournelles.

'The duc,' said Bourdeau, 'abandoned his coach in Place Royale. After that, he looked around cautiously before hurrying to his destination.'

'Did he notice anything?'

'Nothing at all! We wouldn't be here otherwise. Our men stayed with him in relays of three, always one behind the minister, another preceding him, and the last one as relief. He couldn't have escaped.'

They positioned themselves in Rue Saint-Gilles, standing a little way back, but with a good view of a tall narrow house in Rue des Tournelles. On the second floor, a weak light could be seen in one window. Shadows were moving behind a curtain.

'He's still there,' whispered Bourdeau. 'And our spies too, I can see them.'

'You have good eyes!'

'They're the colour of walls,' said the inspector with a laugh.

Nicolas looked at his watch. It was nearly two. Bourdeau squeezed his arm. 'We've arrived just in time.'

A man wrapped in a black cloak, his tricorn pulled down over his eyes, was leaving the house. He hesitated a moment, peering right and left into the darkness, then took up a position under the lantern at the corner of the two streets. He glanced suspiciously at the stationary cab. The stillness of the driver, who was pretending to sleep, seemed to reassure him that the coast was clear. With hurried steps, he turned into Rue des Tournelles.

'There is no doubt he's going back to Place Royale,' said Bourdeau. 'His carriage must be coming to pick him up.'

'I assume we're going to make sure he returns to the fold?'

'That's the plan. For the moment, I don't think you have any other choice than to go in. In the meantime, I'll watch out for trouble outside the house. Let's not forget the English threats.'

The commissioner appreciated his deputy's sensitivity. It showed that, having implicitly understood Lenoir's anxiety, Bourdeau was determined to act accordingly and in such a way that his friend should not be constantly aware of it or, if he was aware of it, did not need to talk about it. More than anything, this kind of understanding revealed their complicity, a complicity which had been strengthened over the years by all the many trials they had been through together and had never once faltered.

Once he had entered the house, Nicolas had to strike a light to find his way. On the second floor, he knocked at the one door lacking a knocker. An anxious voice immediately asked, 'Is that you, Charles?'

'I am a commissioner of police.'

The door slowly opened. Lit by the candle she was carrying, a young blonde woman stood there, looking him up and down in alarm. She was bare-headed, and wore a lilac chenille undershirt.

'Oh, my God, something must have happened to Charles. I'm always telling him not to go out at night. Is that it, Monsieur? Don't try to hide it from me.'

He entered, and looked around at the apartment. It was small, but furnished in exquisite taste and far more luxurious than might have been expected from the exterior.

'Calm down, Madame. It's nothing serious, I assure you. I simply need some information about the man who has just left this building.'

'Why, what has he done? Why are you concerned with him?'

She could not have been much more than twenty, he estimated.

'His movements at such a late hour have attracted our attention.'

'The poor man! Such a good friend, so generous!'

'What does he do and what's his name?'

'Charles Gobelet. He's a bailiff at the Châtelet.'

Nicolas could not help smiling at the profession chosen by the Duc de La Vrillière. 'And may I ask what he is to you, Madame?'

She blushed, lowered her head, and murmured in a confidential tone, 'He's my friend and the father of my child.'

Taking him by the sleeve, she drew him into a small white room in the centre of which was a wicker cradle covered in muslin. She pulled aside the fabric and he saw a pretty infant, fast asleep. Without a sound, they went back to the other room.

'How did you meet him?'

'My name is Marie Meunier. I was born in Meaux. A year ago, I lost my mother, who had long been a widow. Having nothing to live on, I came to Paris to ask for charity. Someone must have noticed me, for, soon after my arrival, a very polite man brought me here, and then Charles arrived. He said he wanted to help me. I believed him. Thanks to him, I have found a home and sustenance.'

'And what of the child?'

She blushed again. 'Charles convinced me of the sincerity of his affection. I owed him everything. That's our child, and its father showers us with such care and love you yourself would be moved by it.'

'Madame, I am satisfied with these explanations. There will be no need to bother Monsieur Gobelet. Please don't mention my visit to him.'

'I shall do as you say, Monsieur. Charles's peace of mind matters to me more than anything. He seems so worried sometimes.'

'One last question. Why does he keep your house and his visits so secret?'

'Alas, Commissioner, it's because he has children from a first marriage! They wouldn't be very happy to find out—'

'I understand. Thank you for that explanation.'

She walked him to the door. 'Protect him, Monsieur. He takes so many precautions that sometimes I imagine he must feel threatened.'

He remembered the Duchesse de La Vrillière's last plea. All of the duc's women wanted to protect him.

'We'll be sure to,' he said.

Nicolas rejoined Bourdeau, who was waiting for him downstairs. They walked back to their carriage. After a long silence, which the inspector respected, he recounted his visit, but as if talking to himself.

'So that was it!' he said in conclusion. 'The pure side of an impure man.'

'Heavens!' said Bourdeau. 'Please stop "Noblecourting", and put it in plain words.'

'The minister has a secret family: a charming young lady, and a child about a year old. It's clearly a side of his existence he wants to preserve at all costs. Hence these nocturnal escapes and this desire to keep his double life a complete secret.'

'What a man!' exclaimed Bourdeau. 'Who would believe it to look at him? The Beautiful Aglaé, countless other women, responsibilities of State, and what else?'

'As for me,' replied Nicolas gravely, 'I have no idea where the truth of the man lies. In his licentiousness or in this garden of innocence preserved as it was before the Fall?'

'Anyone listening to you would think that the more like a devil a man is, the more he aspires to get back to the Garden of Eden.'

Nicolas laughed and grimaced at the same time. 'Don't make me laugh, it pulls on my wound. I'll only be able to smile for the next few days, although the circumstances hardly lend themselves to much smiling. I'm going to get a few hours' rest and then we'll meet again at dawn, at the Châtelet.'

'What are your instructions?'

'Send some men to Rue Christine to collect the contents of the younger Duchamplan's wardrobe and bring them to me. We'll also have to get the body of the unfortunate Vitry identified, or at least what's left of him. It won't be easy, but I don't have much doubt it's him. I'll go and see Lenoir and Testard du Lys. Not forgetting Sartine, if he's in Paris. I'll put together my case, and the day after tomorrow we'll summon the suspect.'

'Who for now is only charged with acts of debauchery on a minor.'

'Not forgetting kidnapping, which, if all goes well, will earn him the whip, the brand, the iron collar and life imprisonment in a house of detention.'

'That's true, although I fear we can expect a lot of argument and a lot of outside interference from those trying to thwart our procedure.'

'That's why I think it's vital that we expedite things as quickly as possible. Like you, I expect the worst.'

'What about Chambonas?'

'I fear he's untouchable. The Lieutenant General has had proof of his secret activities for a long time now. To implicate him would be the equivalent of untangling a thread that would lead us too close to the throne.'

'Will the time ever come when the law applies to everyone?'

'When the Bourdeaus are in power,' said Nicolas affectionately.

Nicolas gave his last instructions concerning the interrogation of the younger Duchamplan and, if need be, other protagonists in the case, as well as some special instructions which he had now had time to think about. He was a little angry with himself at not opening up more to Bourdeau, but he did not like to reveal a plan of campaign which depended to a large extent on his intuition – even though there was a degree of material evidence to corroborate it. It was a kind of superstition in him to keep quiet about his intentions. A detective was like an artist: he did not like to reveal too much all at once.

In Rue Montmartre, the whole household was asleep; only Mouchette was waiting for her master. She gave some questioning little cries and disapprovingly sniffed the smell of muddy water that he gave off. He decided to remedy this, unable to imagine slipping into his bed in such a filthy state. Hot water was cooling in the kettle on the stove. He undressed, and as he did so, weariness overcame him, and all his pains revived. Catherine, wakened by the noise, found him as naked as the day he was born, trying unsuccessfully to wash himself. She gave a cry when she saw the bloodstained bandage around the middle of his body. She took matters in hand. He was washed, soaped, combed, and rubbed down, and his bandage gently but firmly changed. After sipping a schnapps eggnog flavoured with cinnamon, he went upstairs, exhausted but already feeling his old self, and slipped into his bed for a few hours' rest.

The day was a long one. Nicolas, although feeling as tired as he had after his hurried return from England a few months earlier, nevertheless gave his utmost. He went to see Monsieur Lenoir, who approved his plan. Next, he had to confront the long pale face of the Criminal Lieutenant. Overtaken by events as usual,

Monsieur Testard du Lys at first balked at the commissioner's plans, denouncing practices which were alien to him. Nicolas had to remind him that he had never had reason in the past to complain about initiatives which might not have conformed to the routine way of doing things but which had always led to the confounding of the guilty and to the King's having an even higher opinion of a justice system of which the Criminal Lieutenant was the most eminent representative. Of course, Monsieur Testard du Lys did not have the wit to realise that these solved cases did not bring anyone any reflected glory, since they were all special investigations, mostly relating to the private justice of the monarch. Defeated, he washed his hands like a new Pilate and irritably dismissed Nicolas. As a final argument, the name of Sartine had been bandied about; he still filled the Criminal Lieutenant with fear.

The contents of the wardrobe in Rue Christine were carefully recorded and examined item by item. Nicolas also received Sanson. He next went to the Hôtel-Dieu, where he questioned the girl discovered in the bathing establishment. She confirmed everything they had assumed. She and her sister, starving, lost in Paris, had been picked up by Duchamplan who, under false pretences, had taken them to an unknown house, and then delivered them, in a number of different places, to the lust of his accomplices.

Nicolas then had himself driven to Quai des Tournelles, where the spies who were protecting him from a distance, on Bourdeau's orders, saw him indulging in some strange exercises, with his nose to the ground. A final meeting at the Châtelet reunited him with the inspector. It was followed by an inspection of the hall of the Basse-Geôle, which had been laid out for the following day's secret hearing. Finally, he signed a safe conduct for La Roussillon, whose help and cool head had been vital to the success of the operation.

Again, he went to bed quite late. Catherine had waited up for him, concocting one of her special dishes for him. It consisted of steaming cabbage cut into slices and those roots she stubbornly cultivated in the kitchen garden behind the house, much to the despair of Poitevin: those potatoes which people were starting to talk about at Court and in the city. She would roughly crush the two vegetables, making sure that the flesh of the cabbage remained somewhat crunchy. She would then throw the mixture into a cast-iron dish in which some diced smoked bacon had been cooked in salt, pepper, nutmeg, garlic and juniper berries. You had to make sure to keep turning it all over with a spoon, so that everything benefited from the heat, until it had turned a nice golden colour. This dish revealed to him how sweet the new root could be when treated in this way, set off as it was by the crunchiness of the cabbage and the softness of the bacon, the whole thing covered in a grated cheese crust during the baking. This robust snack, washed down with a bottle of Burgundy from Irancy, which Noblecourt always called the great King's wine, led him to a peaceful, restorative sleep.

# EPILOGUE

So you will perhaps have powerful objections to make to the principles
I have just established. Convey them to me and I will receive them
gratefully, because I am looking for the truth in very good faith.

LAMOIGNON DE MALESHERBES

*Wednesday 12 October 1774*

Everything had been meticulously prepared. In a hall close to the
Basse-Geôle, a kind of courtroom had been installed: a long table
and two armchairs with flaps, one for Nicolas and one for
Bourdeau, who would keep a record of the hearing. The various
items of evidence lay on the lid of a chest in the centre of the
room, in front of the defendant's seat. Opposite the long table,
two trestles supported a half-open coffin, revealing the bloodless,
livid face of the corpse found on Île des Cygnes. Two candlesticks
framed it. Always thoughtful, Old Marie had seen fit to install a
kind of brazier on which incense burnt. Torches fixed into rings
on the wall threw their dancing light over the scene.

The Lieutenant General of Police and the Criminal Lieutenant
entered in magistrates' gowns and sat down, after throwing
alarmed glances at the coffin. Nicolas walked towards them and
began to speak.

'Gentlemen, we are gathered here today in a hall of the Grand

Châtelet, in an extraordinary and secret commission, to try to bring to an end a case which has cost the lives of four people. I shall attempt to untie the threads of a mystery which inextricably combines the passions of human perversity and the deleterious actions of agents of a foreign power . . .'

'Allow me to express surprise,' exclaimed Monsieur Testard du Lys, 'at the unfortunate revival of such an outrageous procedure of common law! I had dared to hope that under a new reign, which has already led to certain changes, we might have avoided recourse to such regrettable arrangements.'

'It is by order of the King, on my instructions and with my support,' said Lenoir, 'that Commissioner Le Floch has been forced, given the circumstances, to adopt such unconventional measures.'

'But did he have to subject us to such an unfortunate confrontation?' muttered the Criminal Lieutenant, lifting a fine cambric handkerchief to his nostrils.

Nicolas pretended to ignore this exchange. 'Allow me, gentlemen,' he went on, 'to remind you of the circumstances under which I was assigned this investigation. The Duc de La Vrillière, Minister of the King's Household, summoned me, through the intermediary of Monsieur Lenoir, to his mansion near Place Louis XV, to inform me that Marguerite Pindron, the duchesse's chambermaid, had been discovered early that morning in the kitchens with her throat cut. Near her body, the major-domo, Jean Missery, had been found unconscious and wounded. My first observations turned up a number of clues. There was no weapon matching the victim's terrible wound. The major-domo's wound was of quite another nature. Everything led one to suppose that, after having murdered his young mistress, and struck with the horror of his action, he had tried to take his own life. The kitchen knife found near him appeared derisory in comparison with the victim's horrible wound. The cellar floor had been much trodden over. A trail of bloody footprints led me to the second floor and onto a balcony overlooking the gate of the mansion. Clearly someone had escaped by that route. In the kitchen, I found some silver thread and observed that Marguerite Pindron's slippers resembled, in their luxury, those worn at balls. The first testimonies revealed panic and a certain amount of confusion as to how exactly things had happened. Some said it was pitch dark when the bodies were discovered, others that the day had already risen. One thing that surprised me was that everyone was keen to tell me how bad their relations with the major-domo were. Some admitted that they had not been indifferent to Marguerite Pindron.'

'But this major-domo wasn't dead, was he?' the Criminal Lieutenant cut in. 'Did you question him?'

'He couldn't remember anything, only that he had fallen asleep. In addition, his wound was a light one, hardly a scratch, which didn't exactly explain the amount of blood there was around him.'

'How do you know,' said Lenoir, 'that this blood did not come from the body of the young woman?'

'The two pools of blood were quite distinct in nature. For the rest, I found, as is common in a great house, the usual conflicts among the domestic staff.'

'But surely this was a simple affair,' said Testard du Lys. 'You had a culprit, in the person of the major-domo. The nature of his wound was of little importance. Why go searching all over the city?'

'Alas, Monseigneur, the reality is much more complex, and a number of discoveries led me to rule out such a simple solution. Inspector Bourdeau was invited by Jacques Blain, the caretaker of the mansion, to try some rabbit stew.'

The Criminal Lieutenant sat up in his chair, very red in the face. 'Here again is one of these whims so frequent in Monsieur Le Floch's repertoire. What are you trying to prove now?'

'I'm simply trying to point out, Monseigneur, that you can't make a good stew without mixing some of the animal's blood in with the sauce, along with a trickle of vinegar.'

'What of it? I don't follow you at all.'

'What of it? That sauce didn't have any blood. Is it normal for someone to go and get three rabbits from their hutch in the middle of the night, kill them and cook them? This caretaker fellow seems not only to suffer from insomnia, but also to have a formidable appetite!'

'And what do you conclude from that?' asked Lenoir.

'Let me tell you a story. Poor Marguerite Pindron, about whom I made enquiries in Faubourg Saint-Antoine, left her family after breaking off her engagement with young Vitry, a gardener, and wandered the streets of Paris for a long time. I don't know how, but somehow she ended up as a chambermaid to the Duchesse de La Vrillière. Who introduced her into that noble house? Thanks to my investigation, I can state that it was Eudes Duchamplan, the brother-in-law of the major-domo, Jean Missery. The latter, a widower, believes it's his right to press his attentions on the female staff of the house. He falls madly in love with Marguerite. Why would he have wanted to kill her? Did he suspect the relationship between Marguerite and Eudes? Was he angered by the other male servants' interest in her? I don't believe any of that. Marguerite Pindron was killed by someone from outside the house. The autopsy performed on the victim allowed us to determine the nature of the murder weapon. A cast was made from the wound. Its shape was that of a hand, and was an attempt to implicate the Duc de La Vrillière who, after a hunting accident, was given an artificial silver hand by the late King.'

'Another tall tale!'

Nicolas ignored this interruption from the Criminal Lieutenant. 'The fact is,' he continued, 'Marguerite Pindron had to die. Many reasons can be adduced. She may have witnessed something she should not have seen and been blackmailing the person or persons involved, or she may have constituted a financial threat to the Duchamplan family if Jean Missery had taken her as his second wife. Eudes Duchamplan has, I believe, access to the Saint-Florentin mansion. He also has in his possession the Duc de La Vrillière's silver hand, no doubt stolen. That Sunday, he gets into the house. He's made an appointment with Marguerite, who is to be in the kitchens to meet her older suitor.'

'How do you know that?' asked the Criminal Lieutenant.

'The testimony of Jeanne Le Bas, known as Jeannette, another chambermaid, who saw the note in question, anonymous and written in large letters. Marguerite was sure it came from Jean Missery. She therefore makes her way to the kitchens. There, her throat is cut.'

'But if the intention was to implicate the Duc de La Vrillière,' objected Lenoir, 'why wasn't the murder weapon left at the scene?'

'It couldn't be left at the scene. If the duc is guilty, can one imagine him incriminating himself by leaving his silver hand in such a conspicuous position? What is done is much more subtle. If the murder weapon disappears, it is because it has to reappear. However, other clues have to be left which implicate the master of the house. So it is that I find a silver thread which can reasonably be supposed to have come from the minister's coat, being in conformity with the end of the period of mourning. But something else will complicate this fiendish plan: the actions of a jealous woman.'

'We seem to be in a novel by Crébillon!'

'The truth is always stranger than fiction, Monseigneur,' said Nicolas with a smile. 'Eugénie Gouet, the head chambermaid, used to be the major-domo's mistress, and seems to have nurtured the hope that she would one day marry him. The awareness that she is getting older and has been abandoned sharpens the resentment she feels towards her younger rival. The conversation between Marguerite and Jeannette about that evening's rendezvous is overheard by this angry woman. It gives her the means to take her revenge. Oh, we're not talking about a crime, but about a very wicked act. She takes the duchesse's sleeping draught – she will claim later that the bottle was broken – and drugs her former lover with it.'

'But how?' asked Lenoir. 'That's not so easy to do. There needs to be a pretext.'

'Which she finds, Monseigneur. Eugénie Gouet knows all about Missery. She knows that, although his desire is insatiable, he's sometimes unable to perform. Having pretended to remain his friend, she advises him on this matter and persuades him to take this potion in place of the usual aphrodisiacs that he uses – we found pastilles of cantharides in his room. As a result, he sinks into a deep sleep. Eugénie obviously wants to savour Marguerite's disappointment, or at least to scold her for being there at such an uncommon hour. As she gets to the kitchens through the service passage, she sees a man in a grey coat running away along the corridor to the staircase leading to the upper floors. Taken by surprise, she's convinced it was Monsieur de La Vrillière she saw. She carries on to the roasting room, hears no noise, lights a candle, and discovers Marguerite lying there with her throat cut.'

'Let's stop for a moment,' said Monsieur Lenoir. 'If this unknown killer was able to get into the house, why did he have to escape through the upper floors?'

Nicolas approached the long table and handed the two magistrates some documents. 'These are the plans, cross-sections and elevations of the Saint-Florentin mansion, as drawn up by its architect, Monsieur Chalgrin. You will observe on the plan of the ground floor that the staircase is the only exit for someone who's trying to leave the kitchens and can't take the service passage leading to the courtyard. To Eugénie Gouet, there's no doubt. She's been serving the Saint-Florentin family since she was very young, and is totally devoted to it. No one is either black or white, people are mixed. The best and the worst cohabit. What's going on in her mind? We can try to imagine. She believes she has to do everything she can to save her master – we can't rule out the possibility that she may once have been his mistress. She probably waits for a while, until she's sure the duc has managed to get out of the house, then runs to tell the Duchesse de La Vrillière. The duchesse immediately takes matters in hand. Something will have to be done. They confer. Eugénie Gouet admits her plot against Jean Missery. The fact that he's still unconscious constitutes their last hope. They decide to take him down into the kitchens. But the man is too heavy for the two women, and they're forced to tell some of the other servants. They give him a superficial cut and, to make it more convincing, they spread the blood of three freshly killed rabbits all around his body. The duc returns early in the morning; it's impossible to be sure of the exact time as the testimonies are so confused. He finds the house in a state of agitation, but no one dares tell him about the events of the night. The duchesse visits Jean Missery's sister-in-law, Sister Louise of the Annunciation, and opens her heart to her.'

'Didn't it take you a long time to rule out the possibility that the duc might be guilty?'

'With good reason! He claimed to have returned from Versailles. But we gradually discovered that he was in Paris and in fact, for the three murders that followed, it was quite impossible to verify his alibis. Questioned by me after I had noticed that he wore a wooden replica of his hand under his glove, he was unable to indicate to me where the original was, or if it had been stolen or lost.'

'And the supposed murderer?' asked the Criminal Lieutenant in a more affable tone. 'How did he escape? Had he remained in the house?'

'I just had to follow the bloody footprints which I mentioned at the beginning of my presentation. He escaped through the gate, from the first-floor balcony. It should be mentioned, incidentally, that this was a difficult thing to do, only possible for an agile young man, since it involved descending a stone column to reach a side gate.'

'One last point,' said Testard du Lys. 'Why did the major-domo only have a slight wound? If one wanted to pin the blame on him, killing him would have been more appropriate.'

'Monseigneur, think of the horror of that terrible night, of those two distraught women, who are trying to find a way to exonerate the duc. They make the decision together. They won't go any further than a small cut. They are not criminals.'

Monsieur Lenoir raised his hand. 'At the point we have reached in your account, Commissioner, the motives and consequences you describe seem plausible. The fact remains that this whole edifice rests on nothing but your discursive intelligence and your intuition, not to mention your imagination. Of course, there are many clues, and they seem to corroborate your theories, but we need evidence, some confirmation so obvious that it will convince us that the presumed killer, Eudes Duchamplan, not only committed the murder in the Saint-Florentin mansion but also the other three murders. For the next two, that of the prostitute whose body was found beside the river, and that of the young fugitive from Brussels, the killer's methods were identical. One may therefore presume that we are dealing with the same perpetrator. For the fourth, that of Anselme Vitry, a firearm was used. Commissioner, we are listening.'

'For the Marot girl, known as L'Étoile,' replied Nicolas, 'we have a piece of corroborating evidence. The owl . . .'

'What's an owl got to do with it?'

'The Criminal Lieutenant may be unaware,' said Lenoir, with a touch of irony, 'that this is the *nom de guerre* of one of our most distinguished journalists, Monsieur Restif de la Bretonne. His dissolute life sometimes allows him to show some welcome consideration towards the police.'

'Are you implying that you turn a blind eye to some of his aberrations?'

'Certainly, if that allows us to pursue criminals who disturb public order.'

'To cut a long story short,' Nicolas went on, 'the owl stole the slippers from this girl's feet, and they turned out to be identical to those found next to Margerite Pindron.'

'The fact that one pair of slippers resembles another pair of slippers,' said Testard du Lys impatiently, 'does not convince me.'

'See for yourself,' said Nicolas, pointing to the two pairs on the chest. 'I understand the Criminal Lieutenant's reticence. Fortunately, I have another piece of evidence.'

He walked towards the chest and unfolded a jade-green coat adorned with imitation gemstones.

'Look at this coat, gentlemen. It was seized, in the proper fashion, from the wardrobe of the younger Duchamplan. Note, beside this buttonhole, a series of imitation gemstones, bluish white in colour, of which one is missing.'

He took from his pocket a small piece of paper, folded in four, which he placed on the long table and unfolded.

'Here it is. It was found on the river bank, next to the body of the Marot girl.'

A long silence followed Nicolas's demonstration.

'Fortunately, heaven sometimes aids the law,' resumed Nicolas. 'It allows us to discover the silver thread deliberately abandoned by a killer and then helps us find a stone accidentally lost by the same killer. Heaven also favours the investigator, helped, admittedly, by the skill of doctors able to see what others cannot in the secret depths of the human body. Thanks to an examination of their entrails, it was discovered that both the Marot girl and the young girl found on Île des Cygnes had ingested, not long before their deaths, large quantities of the fruit of the pineapple, an exotic plant from the West Indies which a number of noble houses have been trying, with some difficulty, to acclimatise. I once saw some fine ones in the late King's hothouse at Trianon.'

'Apart from these loathsome details, you are not claiming, are you,' said Testard du Lys indignantly, his pale face growing longer at the thought of the prospects this opened up, 'that these victims frequented royal houses?'

'Certainly not! On the contrary, I carefully avoided sending my investigators there. Our search was confined to civil residences, not too distant from those places beside the river where the corpses were found. Imagine our surprise on discovering that this fruit was cultivated in the Montparnasse house of the Marquis de Chambonas, a person to whom our attention had been drawn by a brothel-keeper well connected with circles in which certain nocturnal parties are held. The bathing establishment where Duchamplan was arrested gave us some idea of the nature of these parties.'

'It should be pointed out,' Monsieur Lenoir said to the Criminal Lieutenant, 'that this person is well known to our inspectors for his extravagant behaviour. He is the grand master of a libertine society created by his father. He has many debts and a highly dubious reputation. He married one of the Duc de La Vrillière's illegitimate children, the daughter of the Marquise de Langeac, the

Beautiful Aglaé. It is said that the couple are very ill-matched and that the marquise is beaten repeatedly. Her husband, having seen in this marriage the possibility of both financial gain and social cachet, bears a grudge against the minister for his mother-in-law's fall from favour and the consequent dishonour of such a misalliance.'

'I understand what you're saying,' said Testard du Lys. 'But all this jumble of information makes me even more confused. What connection can there be between all these crimes?'

'Monseigneur,' replied Nicolas, 'I am firmly convinced that someone wanted to implicate Monsieur de La Vrillière in a series of murders. The first, that of Marguerite Pindron, met a number of needs. Drawn by her young lover into attending parties which revolted her with their criminal excesses, I imagine that she became a danger, in that she might either speak out or resort to blackmail. Add to that the advantage for a Duchamplan of getting rid of someone Jean Missery might be thinking of marrying, thus avoiding any squandering of the fortune from which the major-domo had benefited since his wife's death. Subsequently, since the first attempt seemed to have failed, there needed to be further opportunities to compromise the minister. I fear that the reality of the matter is that Eudes Duchamplan is a monster who used the plot in which he had become involved to satisfy his own perversions. I saw him, with my own eyes, torture a young girl, with a terrifying expression of morbid delight on his face. The madmen at Bicêtre look more human in their frenzy.'

'"I imagine, I think, I believe . . ."' The Criminal Lieutenant was hopping on his chair like a doll worked by a spring.

Nicolas bowed. 'I must now bring in a new element which

directly concerns the interests of the kingdom. This plot is not simply a family affair, the work of a madman, but the culmination of a conspiracy woven in secret by the representatives of a foreign power. Lord Ashbury, a member of the British secret service, whom I know well from having met him in London, was recognised by me in the lower gallery of the palace of Versailles. He fled when I approached. Our investigations led to us seeing him again at the Hôtel de Russie in Rue Christine, near the Duchamplan house. Sought by all the police forces of the kingdom, it is in that house that he goes to earth, doubtless convinced that it is the last place anyone would think of looking for him. When I search it, I discover a fragment of paper mentioning the Tournelles. Eventually, he is arrested in our raid on the bathing establishment in that very place.'

'Why should this plot have targeted the Duc de La Vrillière?' asked Lenoir, who had been taking notes as he listened to Nicolas's demonstration and had made him an imperceptible sign of caution when he had mentioned the Tournelles.

'We are at peace with England,' said the commissioner, 'but the English fear that we are actively supporting the growing unrest in their American colonies. They suspect us of wanting, in this way, to take our revenge for the treaty of Paris and the loss of New France. The reason Lord Ashbury, alias Francis Sefton, is in Paris is to take personal charge of setting up a plot whose aim is to weaken the kingdom. The Duc de La Vrillière is an ideal prey, because of his private conduct and also because of his family connection with the Comte de Maurepas. Compromising him would eventually bring about the fall of the government and a scandal which would tarnish the circles around the throne.'

'But surely, Nicolas,' said Lenoir, 'if that were the case it might also bring about the return of the Duc de Choiseul, who is well known to be hostile to their interests and concerned to wipe out the memory of past setbacks.'

'That's an eventuality they didn't take into account, because they're convinced that the King would never accept Choiseul's return, given his animosity – despite the Queen's insinuations – towards a man who gravely offended his father the Dauphin. They are counting on the confusion that would follow the success of their actions. So much for that objection. The English services have done their work well and know the lives of our great men in detail. Lord Ashbury makes contact with the Marquis de Chambonas, and doubtless teams up with the younger Duchamplan. Do you need proof of that? The day after I recognise Ashbury, someone tries to kill me at Versailles. The guilty party? The younger Duchamplan, whose left cheek still bears the trace of the whiplash inflicted by Dr Semacgus's coachman. Yes, truly, there is a foreign plot, concealed beneath the terrifying disguise of a web of private vengeance and corruption.'

'There remains the last murder,' said the Criminal Lieutenant, who seemed nonplussed by all this. 'How do you explain that?'

'It is without doubt the most difficult of these murderous acts to get to the bottom of. Duchamplan recruited young Anselme Vitry, the rejected fiancé of Marguerite Pindron, from among the venereal disease sufferers at Bicêtre, a hospital of which his brother is an administrator, and which he often visits out of an unhealthy fascination with states of madness. He hires him as a driver in his brother's cab company and uses him at every opportunity. Was it he who drove Duchamplan to the Saint-Florentin mansion on the night of the murder? Be that as it may, it was certainly he who, by an extraordinary coincidence, drove me to Popincourt where I was making enquiries about his fiancée. I was struck by the stains in the interior of the cab, which could only have been blood. The driver seemed to be hiding his face. That is understandable if it was indeed Vitry, who did not want to be recognised in an area where he had lived. The body found in the cab near the pleasure gardens was unquestionably his. The mud on the cab is identical to that on the bank near the Tournelles bathing establishment. What did Vitry's killer hope to achieve? You have to bear in mind, gentlemen, that he was counting on two possible scenarios. In one, the watch, or ourselves, would take the fake suicide at face value. Then Duchamplan, dead in the eyes of the world, could disappear without encountering any opposition. It is likely, in that case, that the shirt stolen from the Saint-Florentin mansion would have reappeared, implicating Monsieur de La Vrillière in another murder. The most extraordinary thing in this affair is that Duchamplan had also foreseen that we might not be convinced after all, and in that case, too, the shirt would have been used, with the same results. I sense a question coming from the Criminal Lieutenant. Why did Duchamplan kill Vitry? One could say out of pure cruelty and because he needed a young man's corpse. I fear – but here again I must imagine – that he simply wanted to get rid of an inconvenient witness, or else that he had no wish to describe Marguerite Pindron's hideous death to the poor boy, thereby provoking an angry reaction that might prove deadly. With that terrible observation, gentlemen, my demonstration is over. I am firmly of the belief that Duchamplan is not only an accomplice in a plot against the State, but is also guilty of four dreadful murders.'

A great silence fell over the hall. Old Marie entered to stoke the brazier and throw in more pieces of incense. For a long while, the two magistrates did not move, apparently lost in thought. At last, Monsieur Testard du Lys spoke up.

'Commissioner, I have listened to you with great interest. My interventions, untimely as they may have seemed to you, were only intended to gain a better grasp of the truth. But however much I have gone over your words and put your arguments side by side in an attempt to make sense of a story whose elements are scattered like the pieces of a playing card that has been cut up, I remain unconvinced by all this. I need to ask you two vital questions before I make a judgement. If Monsieur de La Vrillière, to whom everything points, is innocent, where are his alibis? And secondly, you have amassed observations, clues, assumptions, suppositions and a whole hotchpotch of details, as if trying to convince us by sheer volume. Give me one piece of evidence, regarding one of these murders, that proves that Eudes Duchamplan is guilty, and I will accept all the accusations you have made as true and legitimate.'

'Monsieur,' intervened Lenoir, 'before Commissioner Le Floch defers to your request, I'm going to answer your first question. You have my word, Monsieur, that the Duc de La Vrillière has unimpeachable alibis for the times when the four murders were committed. However, I am unable, on the orders of the King, to communicate them to you. I leave the floor to Monsieur Le Floch.'

'Bring in Eudes Duchamplan,' said Nicolas simply.

A young man in chains entered the hall, surrounded by men of the watch. He was wearing a shirt and maroon breeches. Nicolas was struck by his resemblance, in shape and height, to young Vitry. Only his long, thin hands did not belong to a gardener. On his left cheek was a gummed taffeta bandage. He threw the two magistrates a defiant look.

'I protest, gentlemen!' he cried. 'I am being held here against my will.' He indicated Nicolas with his chin. 'I have been a victim of this gentleman, who tried to drown me during a private party.'

'We shan't go into those details,' replied Lenoir curtly. 'You are accused of a conspiracy against the State and of the murders of Marguerite Pindron, the Marot girl, a young girl who had fled the Low Countries, and the gardener Anselme Vitry. In addition, you are charged with the kidnapping of minors and the attempted murder of a magistrate of the King. Commissioner Le Floch, please continue.'

The man looked Nicolas in the eye. The commissioner suddenly saw again Brière's snake-like gaze, the green eyes of Mauval and his brother. He shuddered and made an effort to pull himself together. Evil was still abroad in the land.

'Monsieur Duchamplan,' he said at last, 'it would be customary for me to list in detail all the accusations which have been brought against you. That would be tiring for us, and for you, so I am going to present to the magistrates just one piece of evidence concerning one of these murders. If this proof is conclusive, it will mean that not only are you guilty of this one, but also of all the others.'

Nicolas stood up and walked slowly towards Duchamplan. The dancing light of the torches projected his huge shadow onto the wall. He seized the young man by his shirt collar, lifted him from his seat and, with a great clanking of chains, dragged him towards the coffin. With a blow of his fist, he threw the lid down on the flagstoned floor and forced Duchamplan to lower his head so that it almost touched the head of the corpse.

'Look at your work, that mutilated face, those hollow eyes! Contemplate one of your victims and dare now to claim that you did not kill her!'

He let go of him, leaving him moaning beside the coffin, and walked quickly back to the long table.

'Gentlemen,' he continued, 'I ask you to look at that man. During the discovery of the victim on Île des Cygnes, I found in the young girl's undershirt, in the presence of Inspector Bourdeau, a human fragment. A nail which had got caught on the cloth and been torn off, taking a piece of skin with it. Here it is.' Nicolas took out his little black notebook and carefully unfolded a piece of silk paper containing a fragment of nail and dried skin.

'Eudes Duchamplan, approach.'

Bourdeau had to go and get him.

'Remove his chains.'

As if filled suddenly with an absurd hope, the man rose to his full height, once again as arrogant as ever; he had not even heard what Nicolas had said.

'Show us your hands,' said Lenoir.

'What reason would I have to show you my hands?'

'Don't argue.'

The two magistrates leaned forward. Duchamplan had rather long nails. But the nail on the middle finger of the right hand was broken, and there was a still visible cut on one of its edges. Nicolas approached, and grasped the hand firmly. The fragment in his possession exactly fitted the wound on the finger.

'What's the meaning of this?' stammered Duchamplan.

'The meaning, Monsieur,' said the Criminal Lieutenant, 'is that the evidence gathered by Commissioner Le Floch confirms the accusations made against you. Take him away.'

*December 1774*

'So, Nicolas,' said Noblecourt, carefully putting down the fine porcelain cup, 'the year has finished better than it started! What a terrible, unbelievable series of events!'

It was two months since Nicolas had confounded Duchamplan at the Grand Châtelet. He lifted his head with a sigh.

'Alas, they're not over yet. I've just learnt some surprising news.'

'Tell me.'

'Duchamplan, secretly tried by an ad hoc commission, has escaped the death penalty. The galleys for life, that's not much to pay.'

'I already knew that. Secrets are never well kept . . . I was told that your brilliant demonstration and the weight of the evidence presented didn't completely convince the learned assembly. What else did they need? It was only a pretext, I fear, to spare someone who knew too much about certain people.'

'What you don't yet know is that Duchamplan was discovered to have choked to death on the road to Toulon. His companions on the chain hadn't noticed a thing. The dust from the straw in the prison at Clamecy is believed to have asphyxiated him!'

'Was there an autopsy?'

'Of course not! He was immediately buried in a common grave.'

'Are we certain it was really him?'

'I dare to hope so. With Mauval and Camusot still at large, not to mention my English friends, that now makes a lot of people after me. I really need to be careful.'

'You've been through some difficult times: 1774 will remain for you the year of mourning and slander . . . both against you and against La Vrillière. Did the duc at least show his gratitude for having got him out of trouble?'

'I was hardly expecting him to do so. There's a kind of embarrassment between us now. I know too much about him. And he still doesn't know the main thing. He's still a minister, but it's been noticed at Court that the King is more distant towards him than before. The duchesse sent me a gracious message through Madame de Maurepas, who is still very besotted with "young Ranreuil".'

'Now you really are "new Court"! At the home of Philemon and Baucis . . . In a way, the wife of the gravedigger.'

Nicolas did not understand the allusion. 'The gravedigger?'

'Alas, my friend, close as I may be to the *parlement* and its little schemes, I've always supported the rights and prerogatives of the Crown against the encroachments and ravings of a body which has led us, among other things, to chase out the Jesuit fathers, with the consequences I once pointed out to you. Now, on 12 November, the well-chosen day of Saint-René . . .'

'The first name of the Comte de Maurepas.'

'Precisely! That day, the King presided over a bed of justice ratifying the recall of the *parlement* and sounding the death knell of the Maupeou reforms.'

'It's a mistake, when you really look at it.'

'A mistake, yes. A sin, certainly. It will remain vaguely in people's minds that the *parlement* is a power that cannot be broken since we are forced to reinstate it. The whole of Paris is repeating the comment of Chancellor Maupeou: "Thanks to me, the King won a trial which had gone on for a hundred and fifty years. If he wants to lose it again, he is the master!"'

'Now I understand what the English ambassador meant,' remarked Nicolas. 'Monsieur Lenoir, whose complete trust I now enjoy, asked me to translate for him an extract from a dispatch intercepted from Lord Stormont.'

'What did it say?'

'Basically, that the young King thought that his authority had been sufficiently established by this act of recalling the parliament. He concluded with this terrible phrase: "Clearly he will be disappointed by the end of his reign."'[1]

'May heaven grant that I do not see it! The late King would never have yielded, I'm sure of that.'

'To get back to our case,' said Nicolas, 'the young girl from Brussels has returned home, her mother having immediately come to fetch her. They left in tears, taking back the remains of their sister and daughter. You know the role that corpse played.'

'Yes, all that was well arranged. What about Chambonas?'

'The marquis seems to be recruiting again.'

'And those mysterious creatures whose strange appearance at Trianon you told me about?'

'They have been seen on two occasions, still dressed in those extraordinary garments. No one has yet been able to explain their presence. The last time, the alarm having been raised, the gardens of the Trianon were surrounded by guards and servants. It was nothing more nor less than a hunt, an attempt to lure the unknown women into a trap. Nothing! No one! In this particular case, my foresight has been called into question. The Queen has gently mocked me. What can I do?'

They were silent for a moment. A log collapsed in ashes in the fireplace.

'And how is your son?' asked Noblecourt.

'Oh, he's a Breton, which means he adapts well to difficult circumstances. He's been accepted and has avoided the roughest ragging, although I suspect he's received and distributed a few blows along the way.'

'He seems to have his father's powers of seduction.'

'And his grandfather's! In his last letter, he asked me to thank you again for the *friponnes* from Cotignac that you gave him. They contribute very pleasantly to the transition between day and night and make a welcome change from the dreary repetition of the college routine. Hard bread, stringy beef, beans in rancid oil, lentils with stones, rice mixed with weevils, sour vegetables and dessert noticeable by its absence. I quote him.'

'It seems,' said Noblecourt, barely containing his gaiety, 'nothing has changed in our schools, whether they are Jesuit or Oratory! Your son describes it very well. I predict he'll be a skilful wielder of the pen. His father knew how to tell a story, the son will know how to write. Like father like son, as our late lamented monarch liked to say. I was sometimes unfair towards him. Despite his many faults, he was a king!'

Darkness was falling. It was a moment of peace, a moment to daydream. Cyrus and Mouchette lay asleep on the floor near the chimney screen. Poitevin entered the room carrying two letters, which he handed to Nicolas. A porter had delivered the first, and the second had been handed in from a well-appointed coach.

Asking Noblecourt to excuse him, the commissioner began reading. The old magistrate, who had been dozing off, opened his eyes when he heard a sigh from Nicolas.

'Bad news?'

'Some bad, some good.'

'Then they cancel each other out.'

'One won't make up for the other.'

Silence fell again.

Nicolas, as if reluctantly, began speaking. 'I've had a letter from Antoinette, informing me that she's leaving Paris. She's sold the business in Rue du Bac and is moving to London to open a lace shop there. She left the city two days ago after paying a visit to Louis in Juilly . . .'

He stopped, a lump in his throat. So many images and memories had suddenly risen up from the past.

'She preferred not to see me. She entrusts Louis to me.'

With a grave air, Noblecourt sat up in his armchair. 'What happened to explain this unexpected gesture?'

'I think I know, and I alone am responsible. In October, when I was at Versailles for my investigation, I met La Satin in the lower gallery of the palace. She was there on business, selling trinkets from a stall a few days a week. Her presence there upset me, and I wasn't quite able to conceal my reaction. In addition, at that moment, I recognised Lord Ashbury and set off after him . . . An unfortunate combination of circumstances.'

'I understand what was at the bottom of your mind, Nicolas. It wasn't that her presence was inconvenient to you, am I right?'

'Of course not! I was thinking of Louis, the last of the Ranreuils. I don't know if my half-sister Isabelle is married, or if she will ever have any offspring . . . I suddenly imagined, somewhat frivolously I admit, Louis as a page to the King, or as a bodyguard, to which his name entitles him . . . And his mother selling things in the gallery.'

Noblecourt was thinking, his head nodding gently. 'My friend, without absolving you of your reaction, which you were unfortunate enough to reveal, I think you should consider the possibility that La Satin understood the situation perfectly. It would have been better for her to think before she acted and avoid placing you in such a delicate situation. The wrong having been done, she decided to sacrifice her love as a woman and a mother for the future of her son. Understanding you without a word being spoken, she has elevated herself to a kind of heroism, and you should be grateful to her. There's no point now in feeling remorse. The only thing she can expect of you is to respond to her silent appeal by guiding Louis towards a destiny worthy of the glorious name he will no doubt bear one day. She made the right decision. Remember she's still young, and so are you. Your life is still ahead of you, and she is entitled to a second chance. It can't have been easy for her to remain in your shadow, you to whom she owed both love and loyalty.'

'But what of Louis? What will he think? He'll be angry with me.'

'I'm certain La Satin didn't tell him about your encounter. The reasons she will have put forward won't set the son against the father. Louis is mature enough to have already understood that your relationship had ended. At his age, he needs you. Reassure him and reassure yourself. And what of the good news?'

'Oh, a trifle. Admiral d'Arranet has invited me to dinner in Versailles in three days.'

'That's very good. You're young, you should take advantage of such things. They say he has a lovely daughter.'

Noblecourt knew nothing, but always suspected everything. Nicolas sighed. Happiness was never unalloyed. You always had to pay for it, and dearly. This terrible, painful year was coming to an end. Time was slipping away like sand in an ever-open hand, and at the same time strengthening his soul. He closed his eyes and took a deep breath. The shores of his childhood reappeared, swept by wind and sea spray. He saw the horizon receding in the distance, and a new headland emerging. He was going to have to reach it before discovering the next one. The way appeared clear and free, but he knew now that he would have to allow for the opposing currents of life. Realising that fact nourished his anguish and his hope.

*La Marsa, la Bretesche, Glane, Ivry*
*August 2002–November 2003*

# NOTES

## CHAPTER I

1. See *The Nicolas Le Floch Affair*.
2. The author would like to thank Professor Daniel Teyssère of the University of Caen for these details about La Borde.
3. A kind of tunic worn over armour in the Middle Ages.
4. See *The Phantom of Rue Royale*.
5. Saint Greluchon was prayed to in cases of infertility.
6. Boileau, *Art Poétique*, chant III.
7. The hospice of the Grand-Cour des Quinze-Vingts was founded by Saint Louis in aid of a brotherhood of crusaders blinded by the Saracens. It stretched from the present-day Place du Théâtre-Français to a third of the way down the Cour du Carrousel. In 1779 it was transferred to Rue de Charenton.

## CHAPTER II

1. See *The Phantom of Rue Royale*.

## CHAPTER IV

1. Fagon (1638–1718), Louis XIV's doctor.
2. See *The Nicolas Le Floch Affair*.
3. François de Malherbe, 'Dure contrainte'.
4. Statue of Henri IV.
5. Place Louis-le-Grand is now Place Vendôme.
6. See *The Nicolas Le Floch Affair*.

## CHAPTER V

1. See *The Phantom of Rue Royale*.
2. Ramponneau was a famous innkeeper in La Courtille.
3. This debate is taken from contemporary archives, as quoted at length by the historian A. Franklin.

CHAPTER VI

1. See *The Châtelet Apprentice*.
2. These masks were destroyed in 1793 during the violation of the royal tombs.
3. Rousseau's *Émile*.
4. See *The Châtelet Apprentice*.
5. See *The Nicolas Le Floch Affair*.
6. Lord Ashbury: a character in *The Nicolas Le Floch Affair*.

CHAPTER VII

1. This subtle analysis is borrowed from Crébillon.
2. La Harpe (1739–1803) was a critic.
3. See *The Phantom of Rue Royale*.
4. In August 1901, two Englishwomen, Miss Moberly and Miss Jourdain, were transported to the eighteenth century while walking at Trianon and met people in period dress. This journey through time remains a mystery to this day. I thought it might be amusing to tell the story the other way round.
5. See *The Nicolas Le Floch Affair*.
6. The Maurepas had been exiled to Pontchartrain by Louis XV.
7. Madame de Noailles was a lady-in-waiting known as Madame l'Étiquette.
8. See *The Phantom of Rue Royale*.

CHAPTER VIII

1. See *The Châtelet Apprentice*.
2. The Menus-Plaisirs was the establishment that made sets and costumes for Court celebrations and ceremonies.

CHAPTER XI

1. Jean-Baptiste Massillon (1663–1742), French Catholic preacher.
2. This incident actually happened.
3. A reference to a revolving fireplace used by the Maréchal de Richelieu during an amorous adventure.
4. Many houses collapsed at the time.

CHAPTER XII

1. Iolaos was Hercules' companion in his struggle with the hydra.

EPILOGUE

1. A genuine quotation from Lord Stormont after the recall of the Parlement in 1774.

# ACKNOWLEDGEMENTS

First, I wish to express my gratitude to Isabelle Tujague for devoting such care, and so much of her free time, to preparing the final version of the text. I am also grateful to Monique Constant, Conservateur Général du Patrimoine, for her encouragement over a long period; to Maurice Roisse, for his tireless checking of my manuscripts; and to my publisher and his colleagues for their friendship and support.